Love Finds You
IN
Lahaina
HAWAII

Love Finds You
IN
Lahaina
HAWAII

BY BODIE THOENE

summerside
PRESS

Summerside Press™
Minneapolis 55438
www.summersidepress.com

Love Finds You in Lahaina, Hawaii
© 2010 by Bodie Thoene

ISBN 978-1-935416-78-4

All Scripture quotations, unless in the Hawaiian language, are from
The Holy Bible, King James Version (KJV). Scripture quotations in the
Hawaiian language are taken from Baibala Hemolele (New York: The
American Bible Society), 1868.

The town of Lahaina is a real place, and Crown Princess Kaiulani
Cleghorn was a real person. Though this story is based on actual events
in the princess's life, it is a work of fiction.

Cover and Interior Design by Müllerhaus Publishing Group
www.mullerhaus.net.

Back cover photos of Lahaina and interior photo of banyan tree taken by
Ed Zafian, www.flickr.com/photos/edzaf. Used by permission.

Author photo © 2010 by Robin Hanley, www.RobinHanley.com

*Summerside Press™ is an inspirational publisher offering fresh, irresistible
books to uplift the heart and engage the mind.*

Printed in USA.

Dedication

....

With love,
for Robin Lynn Hanley

Oaka oia i kona waha ma ka naauao;
A o ke aloha oia ke kanawai o kona alelo.
Nui na kaikamahine i hana pono,
A ua oi aku oe mamua o lakou a pau.

PROVERBS 31:26, 29

Aloha nui loa! Ke Akua Mana E!

Acknowledgments
....

Our grateful thanks to:

∾ Lydia K. Aholo

∾ Leslie Stewart, Schofield Barracks, Hawaii

∾ Luke Thoene (www.familyaudiolibrary.com),
for invaluable research

∾ B. J. Sams

Princess Kaiulani

Lahaina's famed banyan tree

FOR MOST OF OUR ADULT LIVES, BROCK AND I HAVE SPENT every spring writing and teaching in Hawaii. Lahaina Town, on the beautiful Valley Isle of Maui, is the Crossroads of the Pacific. Over the centuries Lahaina has seen whaling ships, royal palaces, Christian missionary efforts, and the clash of civilizations. It is the premiere spot in the world from which to launch humpback whale-watching expeditions and scuba-diving trips, which we enjoy sharing with our kids and grandkids.

But for our family, Lahaina is also a location rich with history and romance. The story of Princess Kaiulani and what might have been first stirred my imagination in 1976. Brock and I met an old Hawaiian woman with a binder of early photographs beneath the enormous banyan tree across from the Pioneer Inn. It was among those sepia photographs that I first saw the haunting face of the beautiful young princess. When I asked the old woman about Princess Kaiulani, she smiled and said, "There is a difference between Legend and the Truth. All is not as it seems in the history books. The true story of the Kingdom of Hawaii is a secret that has not yet been written." This is, in part, the story we heard that day.

Bodie Thoene

Prologue

....

Lahaina, Island of Maui, State of Hawaii
March 1, 1973

Sandi stared out the window of the Aloha Airlines 737 commuter jet as it grazed the West Maui Mountains and sugarcane fields on its final approach to Kahului Airport. As vivid colors swept beneath her, she gasped, feeling something like Wendy must have felt, flying with Peter Pan, swooping down on Neverland for the first time.

Tossing her auburn shoulder-length hair, she whispered, "First star on the right and straight on till morning."

Neat, silver-blue pineapple fields spread out like patches of metallic corduroy outlined by red volcanic roads. The island of Maui gleamed in the morning sun like a cosmic artist's giant canvas upon which the paint had not yet dried. Jade, emerald, and watery pistachio green shallows were bordered by white lace waves and an ocean comprising of a hundred unnamed shades of iridescent blue.

Raising her camera to snap a picture, Sandi knew a photo could never capture the experience.

"First time Maui?" asked an aged, bird-like Hawaiian woman in the seat beside her.

Sandi nodded, not taking her eyes away from the vision. "First time in Hawaii."

There was a long pause, followed by the incredulous question that had been asked a dozen times since the ticket counter in Los Angeles. "You come to Hawaii by yourself?" A longer pause, then, "*Aloha*. I'm Gramma Leda."

"A pleasure to meet you. Sandi Smith. Yes. On my own this trip."

Sandi's entire life was bound up in her answer. At twenty-one Sandi had been the wife of a ground soldier missing in action over Viet Nam. Word of John's fate and MIA status had reached her as she was packing to meet him in Honolulu for R&R.

For four-and-a-half long, lonely years, she had gone to bed never knowing if John was dead—or alive in a Viet Cong prison. Now, at twenty-five, Sandi had completed her undergrad degree in history at UCLA and was working on her master's in American history. There was no need to go into the personal stuff or to tell the old woman how much she had dreaded coming to Hawaii without John. She decided she would just "stick to the facts, ma'am."

Settling back as the seat-belt sign winked on, Sandi replied, "I'm part of the UCLA History Department's *Fifty States History Project*. For my master's degree. Fifty students are interviewing eyewitnesses to history across the fifty states. I drew Hawaii. Lahaina."

The old woman shook her head. "*Auwe!* You sure smart. Lucky, too." Looking at the ring on Sandi's left hand, Gramma Leda winked. "They don't let you bring your husband? Who knows? Maybe he come anyway, and love find you in Lahaina?"

"Maybe. Someday. But for now, I'm just looking for a great story."

"Lots of that around. Who you gonna talk to?"

"The oldest woman in Hawaii."

"That's Old Auntie Hannah. *Auwe*! Sure. Old Auntie Hannah, she live the history. Saw everything. Knew 'em all—all the old ones. Kings and queens. Before my time, for sure. I was born in 1901, after it was all done. The princess was Hannah's best friend, they say. Old Auntie Hannah'll talk story, all right. Hope you got lots of paper to write."

"Tape recorder too. Lots of batteries." Sandi smiled and sat back, focusing her mind on the task ahead. She was grateful for this confirmation that she was on the right track.

"Lucky you. Where you stay?"

"Pioneer Inn. You know it?"

"Everybody know Pioneer. On the harbor. Right across from the old banyan tree. Dey bring in the old whale ship this year for tourists." Gramma Leda held up a bony finger for emphasis. "I remember real whalers drinkin' in the bar. Pioneer the only hotel in Lahaina till a few years ago. Where Old Auntie Hannah lives now. Corner room so she can see everything. Dey change her sheets and bring her meals. Got two rockers on her *lanai*. Don't need nothin' else to see whales breachin'. That ol' lady got good eyes. Better'n me, and I'm twenty-five years younger, too."

The jet floated onto the tarmac. If all aged Hawaiians were as lively as Gramma Leda, Sandi was going to need more batteries for her recorder.

A mob of family members engulfed the old woman, covering her with kisses and *leis* as she descended from the jet and hobbled toward the gate. Dwarfed by a circle of love and plumeria blossoms, she waved a gnarled hand in *Aloha*.

The warm Maui air moved like a silk scarf against Sandi's cheek. The atmosphere was redolent with the scent of flowers. A quartet of snowy-haired women in matching blue *muumuus* strummed ukuleles and sang in Hawaiian as small, barefooted children danced the hula. Locals wearing a bouquet of bright-colored shirts displayed shell jewelry and souvenirs for sale on card tables. Sandi adjusted her sunglasses and pretended not to notice couples walking hand in hand to collect their luggage beneath the tin roof of the baggage claim area.

Behind her a child's voice called her name. *"Aloha!* Hey! Miss Sandi! Miss Sandi!"

Sandi turned to see a nut-brown boy of about seven or eight, dressed in shorts, a tattered red T-shirt, and flip-flops. He ran toward her waving a plumeria *lei,* ivory petals tipped with yellow.

Bright brown eyes smiled up at her. Sandi stooped, nose to nose with his beaming face.

"Gramma says you *malihini.* Come all the way from the mainland to talk story with Auntie Hannah."

"And what's your name?"

"Alex." He thumped his chest. "Gramma says she liked talking story with you on the plane, and you are very lonely. Gramma says nobody should come to our island without a kiss and a *lei.* She says you should have a proper *Aloha* when you come to Maui." He held up the garland, urging her to bow her head slightly so he could slip it around her neck. Kissing her cheek, the boy smiled broadly. *"Aloha nui loa."* He was not shy.

"So, Alex, cool. *Aloha* back at you. My first kiss and my first Hawaiian *lei."*

"I tell Gramma you are very pretty. Brown eyes and red hair together. Very pretty. So Gramma sent me after you."

"Thank you, Alex. You are quite the ladies' man." She laughed and stood erect, raising the blooms to inhale their scent. "And tell your gramma I hope to see her again. Tell her I said *Aloha* too. *Aloha.* From me."

He bowed slightly, then hopped away in the awkward shuffle of a boy trying to run too fast in flip-flops. Sandi gazed after him for a long moment. Alex vanished into his tribe at the end of the shed.

The *lei* was cool and fragrant against her skin. The gesture of kindness unexpectedly brought tears to Sandi's eyes. Was her loneliness so obvious to a stranger on a plane? She twisted the wedding ring on her finger.

Alone.

The hope in recent negotiations between the U.S. and the North Vietnamese for the release of POWs had sustained Sandi. Perhaps John's name would be among those yet to be released. The thought had come to her that if John was alive and released from prison, the first stop would be a hospital here in Hawaii. She would be ready if and when the news came.

For now, Sandi had work to keep her occupied. Minutes passed. Fellow passengers clustered around the conveyor belt as suitcases tumbled out from behind a screen.

Sandi's bag was the last to appear. She plucked her black American Tourister from the pile, remembering that she had been packing it when she first heard the news about John. She had not used it until now.

The Hertz Rent-a-Car counter was staffed by a young Oriental woman wearing a red hibiscus in her straight, black hair. The line of tourists was long. The clerk took her time with each new customer as if there was no one else. By the time Sandi reached the head of the queue, there was only one small, red Toyota Corolla hatchback remaining in the cheap standard class.

"SR5 Coup," the clerk recited in a singsong voice. "Four cylinder, 88 horsepower, five-speed manual transmission. No air conditioning, I'm afraid."

Sandi blinked at her in disbelief. Never mind the air conditioning. There was a bigger problem. "Five-speed manual transmission?"

"Automatics mostly available in Honolulu. Here on Maui, you know, mostly manual. A problem? There's a shuttle to Lahaina every hour. Don't really need a car in Lahaina."

"No. It's okay. I'm okay." Sandi swallowed hard at the thought of managing a clutch and a stick shift on unfamiliar roads in a strange town. She did not admit she had only attempted to drive a stick once in her life. John had loved shifting gears in his red-and-white '57 Corvette and roaring down the freeway like an Indy driver. Sandi had enjoyed the ride but never noticed how it was done. The biggest argument in their marriage had come the day John put her behind the wheel of his precious 'Vette and tried to teach her how to make the car go forward. The memory of grinding gears and grinding teeth still made her cold inside.

Sandi replied lamely as she signed the rental contract, "My husband was—is—a soldier. Drove—drives—a Corvette. Loves cars with clutches and stick things and stuff."

"Well, then. You two enjoy. A Toyota Corolla is no 'Vette. But 88 horsepower plenty enough for Maui. I'll need to see your husband's license if he is the primary driver."

"No. Just me."

"Ah. Deployed?"

"Yes. Just me for now."

"Well, then. *Aloha.*" The woman smiled sympathetically and slid the key across the counter. "Whales are really jumping at Olowalu Beach, I hear. You might want to pull over and watch for a while along the way."

"I've got to meet someone in Lahaina. Business."

"Okay. Another time. Drive safe. *Mahalo.*"

Mahalo? The Hawaiian word for "thank you" hung on Sandi's tongue. She tried it out. *"Mahal-lo."* She hesitated. "But which way to Lahaina?"

"Only one road to Lahaina. Go straight when you leave the airport and just keep on going. A little more than twenty miles. No traffic lights. No stops. Just drive along the coast. You can't miss it."

This was good news. Maybe she could put it in one gear and never have to shift again. "First star to the right and straight on till morning, huh?"

The clerk stared, then blinked. "You got it. That'll be Lahaina Town."

The hinges of the red Toyota squeaked when Sandi opened the hatch and tossed her bag in. The cloth interior, hot from the tropical sun, smelled like old socks in a gym locker.

Sandi studied the shift pattern on the gear knob and then ducked to examine the extra pedal next to the brake.

"Oh, Jesus, help," she prayed as she practiced before turning the key to start the engine. Fifteen minutes passed as she forced herself to remember the argument with John on the day of her lesson. John's angry words were burned in her memory.

"SANDI! Come on, Sandi, listen to me. Push in the clutch with your LEFT foot. The clutch. The clutch! Not the brake! Put it in gear. That's neutral! Look at the diagram on the shift knob. R is for REVERSE. Yes. Okay. Better. Leave the clutch IN! Come on. Come on! Now let out the clutch slowly while you push on the accelerator with your RIGHT foot. Wait. Wait. Wait! Don't POP the clutch. Let it out sloowly!"

Even now her cheeks burned as she remembered his frustration. For the first time since that day she was thankful that John's angry words were branded on her brain.

As John shouted at her across time and space, Sandi calmly followed his instructions. *"Clutch in. Gear shift in neutral. Turn the key. Engine on. Slide the stick into first. Let the clutch out slowly as you push on the accelerator."*

The engine raced and then, slowly, the hatchback rolled smoothly forward!

"Thank You, Jesus!" Sandi cried, creeping out of the lot and onto the highway. A Hawaiian in a beat-up pickup laid on his horn. Pushing on the gas did not make the car go faster.

"Pedal faster, *haole*!" the Hawaiian shouted out his window as he roared by.

"Aloha!" she shouted back. Her heart raced with the engine. What now?

Pulling to the far right shoulder, Sandi watched traffic zoom by. She studied the knob. There were numbers 1, 2, 3, and 4 in an H-pattern.

John began to shout in her memory again. *"Sandi! Come on. You can't stay in first gear. Listen to the engine wind out. Sandi! Sandi! First. Clutch in. Second gear. Clutch out. Hey! Hey! Come on! You're gonna blow up the engine!"*

She inhaled and replied aloud, "A rental Toyota is not your Corvette. But thank you, John."

Sandi began again. Clutch in. First gear. Clutch out. Gas. The Toyota roared and leapt onto the road. The engine screamed like a tiger as she shoved in the clutch and slipped the stick into second, then quickly repeated her actions for third gear. What about fourth? The Toyota seemed content, rolling along the two-lane road to Lahaina at 38 mph in third. She decided this was as fast as she would go. The red hatchback now behaved like a normal automobile. Sandi didn't want to push her luck.

But what about when she had to stop? Beads of sweat popped out on her forehead.

Never mind—she'd worry about stopping when she got to Lahaina.

Eyes on the narrow road, Sandi forged ahead, only dimly aware of breaking waves on her left and volcanic mountains rearing up on her right.

Were the giant humpback whales breaching off Olowalu Beach? Were double rainbows blooming above the West Maui Mountains? Sandi did not care. Fellow travelers pulled over from time to time to take in the beauty, but Sandi kept both hands on the wheel and a steady 38 mph. Half-speed ahead. She might have been last in line at Hertz, but she would beat them all to Lahaina. John would be proud of her. She had finally learned to drive a stick shift. Well, sort of.

After thirty-two minutes, the long-awaited green road sign appeared: LAHAINA TOWN—1 MILE.

* * * *

Dark clouds gathered above Lahaina, and a sudden tropical wind sprang up. Sandi turned off Prison Street onto Front Street. Tall palm trees bowed, and warm rain fell onto the tin roofs of the little whaling village. It was easy to see why the Toyota smelled like a musty locker room. Water dripped in through the half-open windows, staining the gray upholstery. Sandi downshifted into second gear and fumbled for the windshield wiper switch.

There was hardly any traffic through the narrow lanes of the village. On the boardwalks of Front Street locals moved through the downpour in an unhurried, unperturbed gait. A schoolkid riding his bike through the overflowing gutter wore a T-shirt declaring Maui's motto: NO RAIN, NO RAINBOWS.

It was easy to spot visitors from the mainland as they covered their heads with real estate brochures and hustled to take shelter. Sandi decided she would accept the rain like a local. She cranked down the driver's side window and stuck out her hand, palm up, to catch the drops.

The enormous banyan tree covered about an acre of land in front of the pale yellow courthouse on her left. The dark green, plantation-style Pioneer Inn was just across the street. The partially assembled whaling ship for tourists that Gramma Leda had mentioned was moored at the dock in front of the inn.

Sandi sighed with relief. "Thank You, Jesus." Never mind that the engine lugged when she forgot to downshift. She slowed and coasted into a parking space in front of the hotel. From behind the white rails of the *lanai* bordering the Pioneer seven locals—men and women from midthirties to elderly—sat and smoked, observing her arrival. Leaving the Toyota in second gear, she popped the clutch, killing the engine. Smiles and nods from the audience prompted her to give them an amused thumbs-up as she climbed from the car.

"*Aloha!*" called a silver-haired, leather-skinned Polynesian man in a faded yellow and red Hawaiian shirt. A Lucky Strike dangled from his lip. Broad, flat feet overlapped worn-down flip-flops. Everyone on the Pioneer's *lanai* wore rubber flip-flops. Sandi decided she would buy some and stash her mainland footgear.

"*Aloha!* This must be the place." Sandi grinned and dragged her bag from the hatch. "The car died."

"We'll put up a tombstone. Checking in?"

"Yep." Sandi pretended not to notice as the downpour increased. The Polynesian snuffed out his smoke and stepped into the rain shower to take the suitcase from her. "Here, miss. I'll take it."

"Thanks. Great storm." She raised her face.

"No rain, no rainbows. You don't act like no tourist." He flashed a half-toothed smile. "I'm Joe."

"Pleased to meet you, Joe. I'm Sandi Smith." She searched the second-story *lanai* for some sign of Auntie Hannah. Just like Gramma Leda had described, two empty rockers marked a spot on the upper corner of the building. Was Auntie Hannah behind the shuttered windows observing her arrival?

"*Auwe*, Sandi." He called to his companions, "She the one from the mainland. Come to talk story with Auntie Hannah."

"That's me."

"Old Auntie Hannah tellin' everyone about you comin' to talk to her. Learn history."

"I'm excited to meet her."

"She sleepin'. Always after lunch."

"I'll just check in. Change. Take a walk."

"Shu-ah. Sandi, huh? We didn't know from your name if you was a boy or girl."

"Definitely a girl."

"Pretty, too. And younger than we thought. Auntie Hannah show us your letter. UCLA History Department, the letter say. Sounds important. We think you would be smart and old. You smart and young and pretty, eh?"

"Not too old to enjoy Lahaina, anyway."

Approving laughter bubbled from Joe and the audience on the porch. A chorus of *Alohas* welcomed her.

Joe was chief bellhop, desk clerk, maintenance supervisor, and unofficial manager of the Pioneer Inn. The team that had greeted Sandi at the door was his family and staff.

There was a single pay phone in the lobby. No TV. No credit cards were accepted at the Pioneer. Cash payment for one week in advance and a quick signature on an old-fashioned register were all that was needed to secure Sandi's room. She was situated on the opposite end of the hotel from Auntie Hannah's apartment.

The Pioneer had changed little since the 1920s. It was open to the breeze and smelled of tropical flowers from the grounds below and lemon oil polish. A broad flight of stairs with teak wood banisters led up to the second floor. A long, high-ceilinged corridor was decorated with vintage prints of whaling scenes.

As the door swung back, Joe remarked over his shoulder, "You get your own bath. Auntie Hannah say you get the best room in the house. So you get Lokelani Rose Room. Bridal suite."

Sandi smiled and shook her head with delight. It was as though she had stepped back in time.

The room was trimmed like the cabin of a sailing ship. The floor was tight teak planking covered by a woven bamboo mat. Walls were paneled in teak beadboard. An enormous, antique, four-poster bed, topped with carved pineapples and a matching armoire, dominated the space. The dark wood grain of the headboard seemed almost three-dimensional and reflected the light as if it were illuminated from within.

Joe said proudly, "Koa wood. Lots of *kama'aina* kids begin in this place. Nobody carve beds like dis no more."

An exotic quilt, handworked in green stitching, with red roses on a white background, was a work of art.

"Look at this!" Sandi exclaimed, running her hand over the petals of the appliqué roses.

"Every room different. Lokelani Rose." Joe inclined his head toward the bedcover. "Auntie Hannah teach the young ones how to make 'em over at The Mission House."

There was a chair beside a small round table, also koa but inlaid with ivory. The table was crowned with a blue Oriental vase filled with an arrangement of red torch ginger. Sunlight glowed on the polished wood tabletop, a perfect place for her to work. The bathroom was good-sized with a 1920s vintage pedestal sink, a chain flush toilet with the water tank above, and a large, clawfoot tub with bright brass fixtures. Shuttered doors opened onto a balcony overlooking the sea, Lahaina Harbor, the courthouse, and the massive hundred-year-old banyan tree planted to commemorate the arrival of the missionaries.

Rain danced on the roof. Fresh water gushed from the rain gutter downspout like a mountain stream.

Joe set her suitcase on the stand, spread his arms, and beamed. "You like?"

"No words. I'm breathless. Just, well, I may never want to leave."

"Yeah. Dat's the idea. You take your time. I'll tell Auntie Hannah you're here when she wakes up. 'Bout an hour."

Sandi tipped him. *"Aloha* and—*Maha-lo.* Did I get it right?"

"Pretty good!" He laughed. *"Alooh-ha!"* He closed the door quietly behind him.

She did not look at the bed. Would not let her mind wander to John. Best room in the house. Bridal suite. She caught a glimpse of herself in the mirror.

Alone.

Sandi stood at the window and gazed out at the newly scrubbed world. Far across the channel she spotted the mysterious island of Lanai swathed in clouds and floating in a mist.

She popped open her suitcase and pulled out Hawaiian history books, lining them up, spine out, on the table. Research material was the most important thing she had packed. She had a list of questions and felt well prepared to interview the oldest woman in Hawaii. Sandi's professor had likened the eyewitness interviews in the *Fifty States History Project* to climbing into a time machine. Thorough research was the travel guide that would help Sandi recognize the historical landmarks and know which follow-up questions to ask Auntie Hannah.

As for packing personal belongings, Sandi had heeded the advice of her older sister, who had traveled to the Islands years earlier. *"Maui's a real undiscovered backwater. Lahaina isn't exactly the social center of the Pacific. You could live your entire life in your bathing suit. Travel light."*

Sandi had packed light for her journey. Her bathing suit and underwear had gone in first, followed by three pairs of Bermuda shorts, cotton blouses, two summer dresses, and a skirt. Her sister had told her about the freezing wind she had encountered visiting Haleakula Volcano. Just in case, Sandi had thrown in a jacket, her UCLA sweatshirt, socks, and one pair of 501 Levis. The thought of driving the Toyota all the way to the top of the mountain made it unlikely she would need the cold weather gear.

Sandi hung the *lei* over the bedpost and stripped off her damp travel clothes, draping them over the tub to dry. Pulling on her pale blue plaid shorts and blue cotton blouse, she ran a comb through her wet hair and stretched out on her stomach across the Lokelani Rose Bridal Suite quilt.

Alone.

Downstairs, in the Whaler's Bar, ukuleles strummed as mellow voices harmonized love songs of old Hawaii. Within minutes, the soft Lahaina wind and the drum of raindrops on the roof lulled her to sleep.

* * * *

A chorus of myna birds perched in the massive banyan tree chirped Sandi awake. A rapping on her door followed.

"Who is it?" Sandi sat up and noted the beaming late afternoon sun. The storm had passed.

A woman's musical voice replied, *"Aloha,* miss! Miss Sandi? Auntie Hannah see you now. Room 12."

"Mahalo!" Sandi called as footsteps retreated down the hall.

Tying back her hair, she donned skirt and sandals and her plumeria *lei.* Briefcase and tape recorder in hand, she checked herself in the mirror for first impressions. The serious eyes in the reflection affirmed: *"Official. Capable. Scholarly."* The *lei* indicated a readiness to immerse herself in the culture.

Trekking down the long corridor, she passed a couple coming out of their room. She tried on a smile and mouthed the word, *"Aloha."* The man glanced at the *lei* and then the briefcase and nodded a mainland hello. Perhaps Sandi's skin was too pale to look like a real local.

The countdown of room numbers ended at 12. Auntie Hannah's door was slightly ajar. Sandi hesitated a moment before she knocked on the doorframe. *"Aloha?* It's Sandi Smith."

Auntie Hannah answered with a gentle voice. Her words were surprisingly colored by a British-tinged accent reminiscent of a Greer Garson movie. *"Aloha.* Come in, and welcome, my dear. I have been expecting you."

Sandi nudged the door open, taking in the room. The layout was identical to that of the Lokelani Suite, but the furnishings and adornment were nothing like a hotel. Teak floors were covered by rich Oriental carpets. The carved koa canopy bed, neatly made up with an intricately patterned quilt, was positioned to face the open French doors overlooking the harbor. Against the wall behind the old woman, a delicate spinet piano was open. Three music stands were filled with sheet music and open hymnals, suggesting that musicians were frequent visitors. Nearby, a walnut phonograph and bookshelf was devoted entirely to old record albums, including a stack of Gilbert and Sullivan operettas.

The ceiling-high double armoire was carved with the royal crest of old Hawaii. The matching chest of drawers was topped by a crowd of faces gazing out from old photographs. Beadboard walls were hung thick with portraits and paintings of old Hawaii.

In the center of it all was Old Auntie Hannah, looking much like the blossom of a hibiscus in her red and yellow *muumuu*. She was erect and alert in one of two overstuffed red floral chairs flanking a Victorian reading table. The table was crowned with a Tiffany lamp with bronze peacocks for the base and a multi-colored shade of leaded-glass peacock feathers. Beneath the lamp was a thick Bible with faded pages detached from the spine. The cracked leather cover was open to the Psalms. Different colors of ink underlined passages. Handwritten notes and dates crowded the margins.

Auntie Hannah's silver hair, done up, was crowned with a woven wreath of flowers. Around her neck she wore a fresh tuberose *lei* that filled the room with a powerful, sweet aroma, something like gardenias. Deep brown eyes smiled at Sandi from a face lined with nearly a century of memories.

Auntie Hannah extended her arms, inviting Sandi into her embrace as though she were a family member. "*Alooha,* my dear girl." Auntie kissed her cheek.

"Aloha," Sandi replied, suddenly made shy by the great dignity in the mannerisms of the centenarian. "I have so been looking forward to meeting you."

"Sit. Sit." Auntie Hannah disarmed Sandi's uneasiness as she gestured to the empty chair. "Very pretty. Very pretty." She leaned forward and winked. "There was a wager among the staff as to whether you were a *kane* or *wahine*."

"Sandi with an *i. Wahine*."

"Of course. And your signature. Lovely handwriting. I won the bet, though I had not guessed you would be so young. It's a good thing we did not wager on the year of your birth." The old woman's glance grazed Sandi's wedding ring.

"I'm twenty-five. A bit older than the other researchers in the project."

"And I am nearly four times that, but I still feel surprisingly young. I dream the dreams of a young girl sometimes: see myself among childhood friends, running down to the water to catch a wave, or dancing with a beau on the Parker Ranch. A century passes quickly."

"Yes. Yes. That's what we—I—don't want to miss." Sandi felt a surge of excitement as she fumbled with the tape recorder. "Do you mind? I just have to set up."

Auntie Hannah observed her with quiet amusement. She did not speak again until Sandi pushed the record button. "Have you taken tea yet? West Coast time is much later. Are you hungry?"

Sandi's growling stomach replied for her. She had missed lunch. "I am a bit, thank you."

Auntie Hannah glanced out the window as if the time were written on the sky. "It is almost four o'clock. Joe's wife, Emma, has prepared a little something for your arrival. She will serve tea shortly."

As if on cue, Emma, a smiling, heavyset Hawaiian, knocked once, then entered pushing a tea trolley with plates heaping with sandwiches and pastries. *"Aloha,* Auntie! *Aloha,* Sandi!"

Auntie Hannah greeted Emma with a regal sweep of her hand. "And this is Emma. Emma, this is Sandi. Sandi with an *i*. A *wahine*, as you can see."

"Okay! You win, Auntie Hannah. Extra jar of *lilikoi* jam. I bring it for breakfast tomorrow." She patted Sandi's shoulder. "Don't make any bets with Auntie Hannah. You never win. She knows the future."

"I'm wise to her." Sandi relaxed. *"Mahalo."*

Emma addressed Auntie Hannah. "She's pretty good, eh? Already knows the lingo." Emma spread the feast. "Bet you're hungry. Come all the way from the mainland to talk story! Okay. Leave you girls to it!" She exited with a wink.

Auntie Hannah surveyed the meal and the delicate hand-painted teacups. "Sandwiches and scones." She lifted the lid of the teapot and inhaled. "I am particularly fond of jasmine white tea. Emma has discovered a source of tea buds from China's Fujian province. There is a Chinese fellow with a teashop on Prison Street. We don't know how he manages to import real Chinese tea, but it is the best I've tasted since I left England." She poured the tea with a flourish like a scene from *My Fair Lady.*

"England. Yes. Your accent. I was under the impression that you were born in the Islands."

"I was."

"But you spent some time abroad?"

"My education was in British schools. Eight years in Europe in the company of the Crown Princess Kaiulani."

"And when did you come home?"

Auntie Hannah sipped her tea thoughtfully and raised her eyes to meet Sandi's probing gaze. "Shall I tell the end of the story before the beginning?"

"Just conversation."

With a nod Auntie Hannah indicated a carved wooden correspondence chest on the top of the spinet. "I've written it all down. It's in the stationery box. Fetch it for me please, my dear."

Sandi retrieved the carved box and placed it in the old woman's hands.

Auntie Hannah opened the lid to reveal a stack of spiral-bound notebooks. "It's all here for you."

Sandi was breathless. "You wrote it down?"

"Based on diaries and letters. A summary. All there." She inclined her head toward the bed. "The original documents are prepared for you in boxes under the bed. When I knew you were coming, I wrote what I know and heard about events, friends, enemies—and what we felt. It is surprising how much of our lives revolved around love. And friendship. The kind of love that would make a friend lay down her life."

For the first time the façade of strength wavered. Auntie Hannah's eyes brimmed. "It was a long time ago. But I must not get ahead of myself." She reached for Sandi's left hand, grasping her wedding ring with thumb and forefinger. "But you know something of heartache I think, eh?"

"How can you know that?" Sandi asked quietly.

"Your eyes."

"My husband, John. A soldier in Viet Nam. No word. Missing four years. I am hoping…the Paris peace negotiations. Perhaps some word soon."

"*Auwe*, I will pray for you, and for John."

Sandi wondered if God would hear the prayers of an old woman when He had been so silent for so long. "Thank you. I mean, *mahalo*."

"And so you try to get on with your life, though your world is unsettled and shattered."

"Something like that. I'm here, picking up pieces. I ask questions about your life while I don't know the answers to my own."

"It is no accident that you have come so far to meet an old, old woman. Your steps are ordered by the Lord." Auntie Hannah passed the wooden box back to Sandi.

Sandi blinked at the priceless, handwritten document in her lap. "You compiled the research for me."

"History books are nothing. The writers of history know nothing of our hearts. Facts? They are details sifted from the truth, interpreted and recorded by conquerors." A pause. "My dear girl, you must start at the beginning. The story you long to know is a love story first of all. And the greatest love story I know began the day Princess Kaiulani was born." Auntie Hannah lifted her teacup and settled back in her chair.

Sandi caressed the box. "*Mahalo*."

Auntie Hannah smiled brightly and shrugged. "But you asked me about tea. Speaking of tea, an appreciation of great tea came later in our lives. Let's see, then. Yes. Yes." The old woman inhaled the rising steam. "This is the best cup of tea I've tasted since we left England. No one serves tea like the English. I have missed it." She savored a sip, then peered into her cup and raised her eyes to scan the pictures on the walls. With a sigh she recited the date. "My last really great cup of tea? That would have been 1897. But you see, the story begins some years before that."

Sandi opened the cover of the first notebook. The same handwriting that marked the pages of the Bible filled the lined pages....

PART ONE

Chapter One

....

Royal Kingdom of Hawaii, 1889

It was the rose hour, just before the dawn. Steamer trunks, not yet removed to the waiting ship docked at Honolulu Harbor, littered the bedchamber.

Princess Kaiulani's waking thought was that today they would sail far away from Hawaii and Ainahau, the only home she had ever known.

Hannah stood gazing out the window at the lush tropical grounds bordering the shoreline of Waikiki. She was not yet dressed. Tossing her straight black hair like a mane, she raised her eyebrows slightly in a challenge: "Race you!"

In what was perhaps their last act before the end of childhood, Kaiulani leapt from bed. In billowing white nightgowns and bare feet, the blossoming teenagers sprinted across the expansive lawn of the Cleghorn family estate. They clambered up the branches of the enormous banyan tree planted by Kaiulani's Scottish father to commemorate her birth.

Breathless and laughing, the duo clung to the limbs and shielded their eyes against the rising sun. The mess from last night's farewell *luau* had vanished, but the aroma of *lomi lomi* and *imu* pig lingered in the air.

"How can I be so hungry when I ate so much last night?" Hannah moaned.

"Do the English have *luaus*?"

"The *haoles* come to Hawaii when they want to eat good food."

Kaiulani considered the fragile health of her writer friend, Robert Louis Stevenson. "And to enjoy our warm weather. Like Mr. Stevenson."

"And the whales."

"The whales have almost all left Hawaiian waters now." Kaiulani searched the waters beyond the reef. "Every year I hate to see the humpbacks go."

"The *kohola* always come home again," Hannah replied. "You'll see. Next year."

"Next year." Neither girl was really discussing departing whales. Kaiulani and Hannah would be gone from home for a year. What if it were longer?

As if in a farewell salute to the princess and Hannah, a great humpback gave a full-on breach just beyond the reef. He splashed down in a geyser of white water. After a moment, the dark fan of the tail flukes flashed and then vanished in the direction of Diamond Head. The ancient volcanic cone crouched on the horizon like a brooding sphinx.

"Look, he is sounding," Kaiulani said. "The sun will be up before he surfaces to breathe. Today is the end of whales for us, I fear."

"One year only. Not too long to bear." Hannah squinted against the glare, seeming to hope for a second leap from the depths, but the sea remained calm, yielding no affirming sign from the great beast.

Would their exile only be a year? Kaiulani did not turn her gaze from the spot where the creature vanished. "I have never told anyone, Hannah. The secret. What Momma said to me."

Hannah's golden Tahitian skin was dappled by sunlight seeping through the banyan leaves. Though everyone had asked about the last words of Princess Kaiulani's mother, she had never spoken of it. The expression on Hannah's delicate features remained unchanged, as if learning Kaiulani's secret did not really matter.

Kaiulani continued, "Just before she died—"

Hannah raised her chin in protest. "Maybe you shouldn't tell me. Maybe she meant it to be just between you." Hannah did not want to pry into the sacred details of a dying woman's last words to her daughter. "Look, Kaiulani, the sun is rising like a gold *kahili*. A good sign for a royal princess."

"Everyone else has asked about Momma, and I never tell. Don't you want to know, Hannah?"

"Only if you want to tell."

Kaiulani inhaled deeply. "Momma sent everyone from the room. I sat beside her. She whispered to me, 'Kaiulani, soon I am going to die.' I raised my hand, begging her to say no more. Then she told me she had seen my future. Momma whispered to me, 'You will go far away for a long time. You will never marry. You will never be queen.'"

Hannah was silent for a time, as if to mull over the grim revelation. "People who are dying sometimes say strange things. So I hear."

"What if it was *your* mother? What if she said such things to *you*?"

Hannah scooted farther out on the limb. "I don't want to be a queen. I never knew my mother. She died the day I was born on my father's ship. We were halfway around the world from my mother's home and family in Tahiti. If my mother had last words for me, my father never told me. If they were unhappy words, I would not believe them true. Papa used to say we are created for joy. Like *kohola*."

"Whales are hunted and killed." Kaiulani frowned at the vision of the wealthy white landowners who dominated the commerce and politics of the Islands. Many among them sought to put an end to the Hawaiian monarchy.

"Life is too wonderful for unhappy thoughts or dark words," Hannah chided. "Now my papa is in heaven with my mother, and I am here with you. Like *kohola*, our souls are destined to return home."

Kaiulani reached for Hannah's hand. "We are like sisters, Hannah, you and I. Both of us daughters of a double race: half Scot and half Polynesian."

"Half earth and half sea."

"What will our fathers' white world be like, I wonder?"

"We look enough alike in the eyes of *haoles*. They won't be able to tell who is who."

"But more than that, we are true sisters of the heart." Kaiulani was sorry she had brought up last words spoken by the dying. She searched the sea for a whale spout. "I felt very alone after Mama died—for a long time. Even shut you out. I'm glad our fathers were such great friends. Glad you came to live here. How would I survive if you and Annie weren't coming to England with me? My heart is breaking."

Hannah's straight white teeth flashed as she smiled down at the peacocks strutting beneath the banyan. "No broken hearts, Kaiulani! Listen! I sailed around the world with my father when I was little. Even been to England once. The logbooks of Papa's ship tell the story. But I don't remember any of it. The only home my heart knows is here in Honolulu. Here at Ainahau with you and Papa Archie. This journey will be our first real adventure together. Your uncle, King Kalakaua, has decided. And your father, Papa Archie, agrees it is best for the education of the future queen of Hawaii."

"I would be happier here." But there were rumors that perhaps it was also best for Princess Kaiulani's safety for her to go abroad. Though the island kingdom appeared placid as the flat-calm sea, political turmoil roiled just beneath the surface.

The princess could not derail Hannah's optimism. "So, this is how it is, Kaiulani. You and I, we'll go to this British girls' school together and learn to be gentlewomen and maybe even fall in love. So much can happen in a year. So much can happen in one day! And then listen, Kaiulani! We'll come back home to Ainahau. To climb this banyan tree. Like the whales, we'll swim and leap and sing in the waves." Hannah released her grip and stood up, balancing on the slick limb high above the ground.

"Stop! You'll fall. Hannah! Stop!"

"I can't fall! Ha! I am daughter of a Scots sea captain! Into the rigging and let the trade winds howl! O Mighty God! *Ke Akua Mana E!*"

Kaiulani laughed. "You are always cheerful. It is irritating sometimes."

"Why?"

"Because life is so uncertain. Seems like you could recognize that once in a while."

"*Auwe!* What an adventure. Ask yourself." Hannah cupped her hands around her mouth and called loudly, "What is God going to do for Princess Victoria Kaiulani today?"

Kaiulani shouted her reply across the green lawns to the lapping waves: "I don't want to leave Ainahau to find out."

Hannah sighed with contentment and began the climb back to earth. "If we don't go to England, we'll never know what we would have missed."

* * * *

Though the SS *Umatilla* was scheduled to weigh anchor at noon, it was obvious from the moment Kaiulani's carriage emerged from the Ainahau estate they would be late reaching the docks. Though the last week had been crammed with round after round of formal good-byes and visits of state, sailing day was all about the common people. They turned out in force to witness their princess's departure. They would not be denied their right to send her off with much *Aloha*.

Just as it was no ordinary day, neither did Kaiulani and Hannah journey in any ordinary conveyance. The carriage of state that had belonged to Kaiulani's mother was pressed into service. The tall, dignified coach was freshly painted entirely bright red, from its high-backed leather seats to the spokes of the wheels. The only part of the carriage not scarlet was the oiled black cloth of the roof, and it was folded back out of sight on this brilliantly sunny occasion.

Despite the holiday air connected with the moment, Kaiulani could not help brooding. No more than five minutes into her journey she was already homesick for Ainahau, the banyan tree, and her pet peacocks.

Hannah dug her elbow into her friend's side. "It's an adventure, remember? What new thing will God show Kaiulani today?"

The matched team of coconut-husk-hued horses stepped out smartly, but Papa Archie stopped their progress as soon as he saw the crowds. Kaiulani and Hannah had taken their usual places on the rear-facing seat at the front of the coach, but Papa made them switch places with him and Kaiulani's half sister, Annie.

"This is all about you, my dear," he murmured in Kaiulani's ear. "These are your people and you are their princess. Please try not to disappoint them."

"See?" Hannah added. "Some of them are crying already. Smile for them. This isn't a funeral! Go on! Wave!"

Dutifully Kaiulani plucked a lace handkerchief from her sleeve and fluttered it at the onlookers.

Immediately an immense cheer broke out from thousands of throats. The word of her approach spread along the lanes with the speed of a breaker rushing ashore on Waikiki Beach. "She's coming! The princess is coming!"

Kaiulani forced herself to raise her chin, nodding and acknowledging the acclaim.

"Better," Hannah said approvingly. "I knew you could do it."

"Then you better wave too," Kaiulani scolded.

Voices from the crowd called:

"Aloha, *Princess!*"

"Come back to us soon!"

"We have great holes in our hearts when you go away!"

As the carriage finally pushed through the throngs and made the turn onto the approach to Honolulu Harbor, uniformed members of the Hawaiian Royal Guard were posted along the route. The soldiers made a show of flourishing "present arms" as the carriage passed.

It was like a continuous magic trick, unfolding over and over.

Kaiulani even forgot she was sad.

King David had ordered the Royal band to perform for the occasion, and they were already playing on the Oceanic Wharf. The sound of trumpets and drums could be heard from quite far away, and as the distance lessened, flutes and clarinets added their softer, more fluid notes to the air.

The only unpleasant note to the day happened when the carriage passed the two-story-high offices of the Reform Party headquarters. The railing of the second-floor veranda was lined with anti-royalist officials and office-seekers, including the pointed beard and pinched face of Lorrin Thurston.

Two years earlier Thurston had written a new Hawaiian constitution. It was he who led the movement to force King David to accept *The Bayonet Constitution*, severely limiting the powers of the monarchy.

"Don't look at him," Hannah said when she noticed Kaiulani's stare. "Just a sight of him makes babies cry, dogs howl, and curdles milk!"

Kaiulani laughed and the momentary chill she felt under Thurston's disapproving gaze passed as quickly as it came.

* * * *

The huge crowds on the Oceanic Wharf were jammed closely together in the greatest outpouring of emotion Kaiulani had ever witnessed—and it was directed at her! All the onlookers seemed to be waving and swaying in unison. Aloft they held plumeria and *pikake* and *maile leis,* until the scene resembled an immense flower garden in the grip of an earthquake.

On every side of the carriage well-wishers presented the princess with their floral tributes.

"Don't take any," Hannah cautioned. "If you accept even one, they'll *all* start tossing them at you. Might sink the ship!"

The SS *Umatilla* was a squat vessel, looking more like a seagoing warehouse than a sleek sailing craft. It had almost no rake to stem or stern. Kaiulani, who had grown up being comfortable in, on, and under the ocean, remarked to her friend that the steamship looked to be a slow sailor.

Formed around a single smokestack that jutted up amidships, *Umatilla*'s blockiness betrayed the fact she was a cargo ship first and a passenger carrier second. As if further proof were needed, cargo masts bloomed both fore and aft, and from each of these poles spouted a trio of freight booms. This trip to San Francisco would be a very different voyage from pleasure cruises around the Islands aboard King David's yacht.

Since it was impossible to speak and be heard, Kaiulani devoted herself to storing as many images of this moment as she could. The memories acquired today might have to support her heart through many months abroad. She felt almost desperate to gather everything possible of her homeland.

It was not just the throngs massed around the gangplank that made the air seem thick and heavy. Honolulu Harbor deserved its designation as the Crossroads of the Pacific with all the cargo being loaded and unloaded there, each with a distinct aroma. Outgoing mountains of sugar bales and mammoth heaps of crates of pineapple for export freighted every breath with an oppressive sweetness.

Kaiulani never regarded it this way, but she was also smelling the wealth of the Islands. Sugar made greedy men hungry to control Hawaii's destiny; some of them were willing to do anything to possess her.

Across the harbor the import wharf devoted to lumber offered the tang of redwood and cedar and the piercing, turpentine-odor of pine.

Over all the rest was the miasmic, gritty feel of coal dust. Day upon day and night after night, the steam engines of the sugar mills devoured every fragment of black fuel the clanking conveyor belts of the colliers could deliver.

Compounded with the salt-sea and the flowers, this combination of aromas could locate only one place on earth: *Hawaii Nei,* "Beloved Hawaii."

Kaiulani closed her eyes and drank it in. Even if she lost her sight on this journey, she would know home again at her first intake of breath.

When she opened her eyes again, Kaiulani was startled to see a thin, pale, moustached *haole* smiling quizzically at her. He extended his hand to assist her exit from the carriage.

"Mister Stevenson!" she exclaimed as she recognized the novelist.

"You didn't think I'd miss the opportunity to wish you *Aloha* and bon voyage, did you? Especially since you are journeying from your homeland to mine? I fear my country will not bestow as warm and delightful a welcome as this outpouring upon your departure."

"I treasure the suggestions you made about what I must visit in England," Kaiulani said. "And the kind things you wrote in my autograph book."

Stevenson's head bobbed agreeably. "Hawaii's temporary loss will be the old country's gain. Dear Island Rose, you will be a breath of tropical springtime to brighten Europe's chill."

"I'll miss you," Kaiulani said. "Be well! When I come back, we'll talk story for days and days. *Aloha.*"

"*Aloha nui loa,*" Stevenson returned.

Was that a twinge of sadness in his eyes?

"Come along." Hannah grasped Kaiulani's hand and linked arms with Annie. "We need to get aboard before the dock collapses!"

As if to emphasize the urgency, *Umatilla*'s steam whistle blasted a warning.

"Please, Papa," Kaiulani urged, "can we go up on top of the wheelhouse, where we can see everything?"

"Of course, child. Just don't fall overboard—or jump either!"

The fervor of the multitude was muted when Kaiulani disappeared up the gangplank, only to break out again when she reappeared on the highest spot above the steamship's bridge. The temporary break in the clamor was sufficient for the Royal band to again make itself heard. The strains of "Hawaii Ponoi," the Hawaiian national anthem written by King David himself, drifted up.

A moment later the crowd was singing to her as well: *"Hawaii's own true sons, be loyal to your chief!"*

As the plaintive notes ended, the steam whistle blared again. Nearby the wailing siren of the British warship HMS *Cormorant* added urgency to the departure.

As the stern line was cast off, *Umatilla* crawled up on her bow mooring. The human flower garden on the dock exploded with shouts, cheers, calls of *Aloha,* and a shower of *leis* cascading into the widening gap of water between ship and shore.

Kaiulani's right arm was sore from waving, so she switched to her left. As she did so, the angle of her view changed and she saw for the first time a young man on the deck below her. He was not looking back at Hawaii. He was staring insolently up at her. About seventeen or eighteen, broad-shouldered and narrow-hipped, with sandy-colored hair and wide-set blue eyes, he studied her with what seemed a disapproving gaze.

Elevating her nose and looking off toward the Punch Bowl crater, the princess nevertheless jerked her chin in his direction as she asked Hannah, "Who is that rude *haole*?"

"I don't know," Hannah replied. "But he's really handsome."

"Is he?" Kaiulani returned dismissively. "I didn't notice."

All too soon a cloud passed in front of the sun, dimming the verdant greens of Beloved Hawaii. The love-laden chants and the haunting melodies faded.

Long after Honolulu was swallowed up in the heart of the sea, Kaiulani continued to watch every craggy *pali* and gaping canyon of her homeland until these, too, almost faded from view.

Chapter Two
....

The engines pulsed beneath the feet of Kaiulani, Hannah, and Annie as they stood together at the stern of the ship. The V-shaped wake of the *Umatilla* pointed away from everything Kaiulani loved. The variegated turquoise of familiar waters darkened to the deep, purplish-indigo-blue of the open sea. Far distant now, the islands of home were concealed by clouds impaled upon jagged, volcanic peaks.

Kaiulani said to her half sister Annie, "I wonder if we will ever see our home again, or perish in some distant, unfamiliar country."

Annie, usually a simple and cheerful companion, was stricken. Her brows furrowed, and she began to sob. "*Auwe*, little sister, my very thoughts! The very thing I have feared most, and now you have spoken what I was thinking. Perhaps it is a prophecy. Perhaps we will never see *Hawaii Nei* again! I am suddenly unwell. I cannot bear it any longer." Annie covered her brown face and ran away to her cabin.

Hannah's mouth was tight with disapproval. She glared at Kaiulani. "That was kind of you."

Kaiulani feigned ignorance. "What? What did I do?"

"You know Annie, sweet Annie. You know she could hardly bear the thought of leaving home. She only agreed to come along to keep you company, to cheer you up. Now you will not be cheered unless you make her miserable."

Kaiulani shrugged. "I say only what is on my heart."

Hannah adjusted the broad brim of her sun hat. "As I must also: Kaiulani, I say we are standing at the wrong end of this vessel. As for myself, I must be facing future, not lamenting the past. You'll find me at the bow of the ship. " Hannah turned on her heel and left Kaiulani brooding above the churning screws and roiling water of the wake.

Stubborn tears stung Kaiulani's eyes. What had she done to upset Hannah? What right did Hannah have to judge the emotion Kaiulani felt in saying farewell to her people and her kingdom? Annie was right to weep, and Kaiulani was right to wonder if they would survive to return to the Islands.

Kailulani decided she would not speak to Hannah again unless she apologized. Perhaps she would jot her a note and—

Behind her, a male voice with a faint Scots accent interrupted her revere. "Historic moment, eh?"

Kaiulani turned to face the handsome young man she and Hannah had noticed earlier on deck. His expression was impudent, his lips curved in a slightly mocking smile. He was attractive and seemed to know it. He acted far too familiar with her. Did he not know she was a royal?

"Historic?" Kaiulani asked.

"I've seldom seen such adoring crowds," he replied, leaning against the stern rail beside her. He stuck out his hand. "I'm Andrew Adams. Traveling home to Scotland with my father."

"*Aloha.* I am—"

"You are Hannah Lilo Duncan."

"Am I?" Kaiulani smiled and did not look into his eyes. "You pretend to know an awful lot for someone I have never met."

"We must become acquainted. This ship is not so wide as an island."

"Why do you think there were such crowds on the wharf? Who had the people come to see?"

"The royal princess, eh?"

"Yes."

"I was also waiting for her to leave, so I might have a word with you."

"Who?"

He was cheerful as he reported what he had seen. "The princess seemed quite unhappy with you."

"The princess?"

"I passed her when she left you. Her expression was very regal and displeased."

"You mean"—Kaiulani turned to scan the deck for sign of Hannah— "she is…the princess is not…how did you know which of us three is Princess Kaiulani? How do you know she is the princess?"

"When we, that is, my father and I, spotted the three of you on the docks, my father told me. 'Kaiulani, the tall one,' he said."

"She's not much taller than I."

"No. That's true. Not too much taller. Younger, though. You are what? About sixteen? A year or two younger than me? And the princess? A year or two younger than you? But there is fire in her eyes. Quite striking, she is. We could see she has a regal, confident air about her. Conquer the world. She is not a person I would approach casually. Then there is Annie Cleghorn. Half sister to the princess. My father tells me Annie is also daughter of Archibald

Cleghorn, the Scottish father of the princess. What do you know about that? Why was Annie Cleghorn crying just now?"

"You ask a lot of questions." Kaiulani enjoyed the freedom in this deception.

"Curiosity. It is in my nature, so I am told."

"Curiosity killed the cat. So I am told." How long could she keep the truth of her identity from this young commoner? Perhaps Hannah would agree to play the game of who's who for a while.

"Cats are said to have nine lives."

"How many have you lost so far—sticking your nose into other people's business?"

"This may be my first demise."

"You are very young to start so early."

"I am of age. Celebrated my eighteenth birthday on the Island of Maui last week. We traveled with the king and Robert Louis Stevenson to the king's estate at Ulupalakua. There we celebrated my birthday. In such exalted company I had my first cigar and my first taste of spirits."

"Congratulations." So Andrew was a braggart as well as nosy. "Very fine company, indeed."

Andrew squared his shoulders, as if certain of impressing her. "Are you familiar with Mister Stevenson's novels?"

"Somewhat." Kaiulani resisted the temptation to retrieve her autograph book from her stateroom and open it to the page R. L. Stevenson had inscribed to her. Nor would she mention her long talks under the banyan tree at Ainahau just now. "Mister Stevenson is fond of Princess Kaiulani, they say."

"Yes. So he told me," the brash young man asserted.

"Mister Stevenson told *you*?"

"Yes. He spoke about her to King Kalakaua, and to my father and me, at length. Very fond. I have traveled half the world in the company of my father, who publishes Mister Stevenson's work. Father came to meet with him and collect the manuscript of his new novel. Now we're returning to Edinburgh. I've learned how little time there is on sea voyages to become acquainted with fellow sojourners. Therefore it is important to learn all you can up front." He flashed a grin. "Then you can move into further discovery. But I will be content to hear the details of questions raised by first impressions. So why did the half sister of Kaiulani flee?"

"Annie is very sensitive. Homesick already."

"Ah. Youthful emotion, rather than seasickness. Glad to hear it. I assumed a true Hawaiian would not get seasick. Look at you, for instance. Clear-eyed, wits about you, though a bit wistful. I assume you do not greatly regret leaving Honolulu."

"You cannot guess what I might be feeling. You go too far in your assumptions."

"The journey has only made me hungry to travel farther and learn more."

"I think I shall not tell you more. I'm offended by your arrogance."

"Me? Andrew Adams, arrogant?" He held up his hand in pledge of truth. "Curious, only."

"Yes? Then I'm offended by your curiosity. Yes, offended on behalf of Princess Kaiulani and her sister, Annie."

"How will I learn if you won't answer my questions? Are you some sort of relative too? I've heard there are lots of royal relatives roaming about."

"Not so many as there once were, I fear."

There followed a long pause, punctuated by the thrumming of the freighter's engines. He seemed to consider the significance of her answer. "Of course. Hard times for the descendants of the Hawaiian kings." He shook off the reverie. "And so to the point. Exactly to the point. I was wondering, since we are traveling the wide sea together, if you might condescend to a favor on my behalf."

"A favor?"

"Yes. You see, I would very much like to be introduced to the young royal princess. I would like to interview Princess Kaiulani. To write an article about her for *The Times*, perhaps. Her feelings about…well, everything. The monarchy. The future of Hawaii, from the perspective of a princess. The views of a royal heir. That sort of thing."

It was growing dark. Kaiulani smiled into Andrew's eager face. "An interview. I'll ask Her Highness. Perhaps she would consent. Well, we must dress for dinner. A pleasure to meet you. *Aloha*, Andrew."

"*Aloha*." He bowed slightly and thanked her as they parted company.

There was a spring in her step and a gleam in her eye as Kaiulani returned to her teak paneled stateroom. Two steamer trunks containing a carefully selected travel wardrobe had been unpacked for the voyage. On the dressing table lay the silver mirror, brush, and comb that had belonged to her mother. Beside them was Kaiulani's autograph book, covered with red Oriental silk. A bright peacock feather served as her bookmark. She opened the pages and found the distinct verse written by Robert Louis Stevenson: "Forth from her land to mine she goes…."

* * * *

1973

The first light of dawn crept over the West Maui Mountains. Across the Pailolo Channel, clouds seemed impaled on the peaks of the island of Molokai. Sandi looked up at the blue morning and pondered Auntie Hannah's description of Kaiulani's red autograph book.

Three file boxes of corroborating letters and yellowed news clippings were on the floor beside Sandi's makeshift desk. Was there documentation of the autograph book? Was the actual inscription of R. L. Stevenson among the material?

What would such a thing be filed under? *A* for autograph? *K* for Kaiulani? Or *S* for Stevenson?

Leaving the notebook open on the bed, Sandi clambered onto the floor and lifted the lid of the cardboard file labeled *A to K* and spread the contents on the bed.

A shaft of sunlight swept in from the open door of the *lanai* and illuminated a gleam of dark red silk inside the last *A* folder in the box: *Autograph Book.*

Could it be?

Sandi held her breath and carefully lifted the priceless object. It was wrapped in clear plastic. The tip of a peacock feather protruded from the pages of the book.

"I'll be!" Sandi stood and carefully placed the package on the bed. Mindful of the likely fragility of a book over eighty years old, she washed and dried her hands before removing the covering. Then, with a sense of awe, she carefully peeled away the protective wrapping, revealing the shining silk cover that encased the treasure.

"Where are you, Robert Louis Stevenson?" Sandi wondered aloud as her hands hovered above the volume.

Her brow furrowed as she thought of Stevenson and the young princess under the banyan tree as peacocks roamed about. Would Kaiulani have marked the great author's inscription with a peacock feather?

Sandi opened the page indicated by the colorful bookmark. She gasped with pleasure at the elaborate Victorian handwriting and the signature *R. L. Stevenson* at the bottom of the page.

As sunlight chased shadows across the sea, illuminating the highest peaks of the island of Lanai, Sandi read Stevenson's words aloud:

> *"Forth from her land to mine she goes,*
> *The island maid, the island rose,*
> *Light of heart and bright of face,*
> *The daughter of a double race.*
> *Her islands here in southern sun*
> *Shall mourn their Kaiulani gone,*
> *And I, in her dear banyan's shade,*
> *Look vainly for my little maid.*
> *But our Scots islands far away*
> *Shall glitter with unwonted day,*
> *And cast for once their tempest by*
> *To smile in Kaiulani's eye."*

Beneath the stanza followed a tender postscript in the poet's hand.

"Written in April to Kaiulani in the April of her age, and at Waikiki, within easy walk of Kaiulani's banyan. When she comes to my land and her father's and the rain beats upon the window (as I fear it will), let her look upon this page; it will be like a weed gathered and pressed at home; and she will remember her own islands, and the shadow of the mighty tree; and she will hear the peacocks screaming in the dusk and the wind blowing in the palms." [1]

Sandi let her weary eyes linger on the page as she imagined Kaiulani, far from home, must have done. Over three-quarters of a century had passed since Stevenson had written the poem to comfort the anxious heart of the Island Rose. How could either have known how much would happen to the Islands between the day of his writing and the end of their brief lives?

This record of pleasant days beneath the banyan tree and their parting on the docks of Honolulu suddenly became Sandi's memory. The princess and the poet were no longer characters in a history book, but living, breathing, grieving human beings.

Sandi held the peacock feather up to the window. Where a commoner would press a blossom between the pages of a book to remember a place, a day, a moment, the young princess had pressed the tail feather of one of her favorite pets.

"Beautiful." Sandi sighed.

A wave of exhaustion swept over her. She had pressed the first rose John had ever given her in her Bible, but the memory of that joy did not give her comfort. Instead, a sort of melancholy longing crushed her.

Was John alive somewhere? she wondered. Did he think of her? Week by week more news was coming to light about American POWs. The possibility that he was still alive kept her going. Yet it also kept her from loving again; from starting her life over.

Closing her eyes, she slept on top of the quilt. A soft rapping awakened her.

"*Aloha.* Miss Sandi?" a woman's voice called. "You have a phone call from the mainland. It is your mother. She says it's urgent."

Sandi rolled over and squinted at the alarm clock: 7:19 a.m. in Lahaina. It was 10:19 a.m. in California. "Coming! Please tell her, a minute...."

Barefoot, Sandi padded down the stairway to the pay phone in the lobby. The receiver hung by the cord. There was no phone booth, no privacy. Sandi was aware of early rising hotel guests eating continental breakfast as they pretended not to notice her.

She picked up the telephone. "Mom? Mom? Is everything all right?"

"Sandi?"

"Yes, Mom. Are you and Dad okay? Everything—"

Her mother's voice cracked with emotion. "Oh, darling." A pause. "I'm so sorry."

Something awful must have happened.

"What is it?"

"What time is it there?"

"Time?"

"Yes. Have you seen the morning news?"

"It's seven thirty. There's no TV."

"I wanted to tell you before you heard the news."

"Mom?" Sandi's heart pounded. "Is it Dad?"

"No. The State Department…it was on the news. You didn't see it? North Viet Nam. The negotiations. They have released a list of POWs."

"Oh, Mom! John? Is he, was he…?" Every fear played out in her mind.

"Honey, Sandi? I am so sorry. John is not on the list."

"Not-on-the-list." The room spun around. Sandi leaned heavily against the wall. "Oh, Mom."

"No news, darling. I know you were hoping. I am so sorry."

She managed a whisper. "Not on the list of the living. But not dead. I can still hope. We can keep hoping he's somewhere…."

"Honey, I know how disappointed you are. We were all hoping."

"Disappointed? Oh, no. No. I was so afraid he would be dead, Mom. I won't give up. Not until I have to. Every night I go to bed with the feeling that he's still alive…somewhere."

Sandi's mother was crying softly. Sandi's eyes were dry. It had been such a long time. She had cried all her tears long ago. At least she could go on hoping for a miracle. Miracles did happen, didn't they?

Sandi hung up the phone and stood for a long moment with her head bowed and her eyes closed. When she raised her face she was aware of curious stares suddenly turning away from her. Everyone in the hotel lobby had heard the conversation. There was no keeping the secret. Sandi Smith traveled to Lahaina alone for a reason. Her husband was not deployed, but MIA.

She managed a brave smile, squared her shoulders, then joined the breakfast buffet line among a dozen couples dressed for a romantic vacation in the tropical paradise.

Sandi carried her coffee, guava juice, pineapple, and sweet rolls up to her room on a tray. Placing her breakfast on the *lanai* table, she sank down on the deck chair as the terror of the phone call finally hit home.

Sun sparkled on the water beyond the harbor. A large catamaran was returning from a morning breakfast cruise. Laughing couples stood at the railing as the boat docked. Sandi's Kona coffee grew cold. Her breakfast remained untouched. She retreated into her room. Lifting the precious documents from the bed, she lay on her back and gazed up. The woven fan blades spun above her. Kaiulani's autograph book was beside her on the night table. The peacock feather stirred in the slight breeze of the ceiling fan. A memory of better times shimmered in Sandi's mind. Another morning in the hotel in Monterey. She had lain in John's arms, and they had ordered room service breakfast. And later, lunch. Then, dinner, without ever leaving the room. She had pressed the room service rose in her Bible.

So long ago.

Now, here was reality. John was not on the list of those who would be coming home.

"I will not cry. Will not."

But a single tear rolled down her cheek.

* * * *

1889

The throbbing engines drove *Umatilla* into the waves with a relentless drumbeat. Because of a quartering sea a corkscrew motion accompanied every lunge forward. The rolling spiral that began with the boat's left hip continued through its right shoulder. It was as if the steam ship were an immense horse, forging ahead on a right lead.

Less charitable patrons said she "wallowed."

The ship's salon, while not luxurious, was perfectly adequate to the needs of the passengers. The ship's cook had produced a fine ragout of chicken stewed in coconut milk, which all the male diners praised.

The female voyagers remained in their cabins, subsisting on clear broth. For Kaiulani and Hannah, it was a point of honor to resist moaning audibly. Annie felt no such requirement, so the two younger girls spoon-fed her soup and sympathy.

So the wood-paneled salon was occupied exclusively by males. Three of them, Archie Cleghorn, William Adams, and Captain Samuels, enjoyed a dram and a cigar each.

Andrew, while allowed to stay with his elders, was not permitted drink, but was allowed tobacco. "Do you think the ladies are well, sir?" he inquired of Papa Cleghorn.

Cleghorn squinted into the cloud of blue smoke hovering in the cabin. "Well enough, young man. Better off where they are, I think, than here."

The other smokers chuckled and nodded.

"Should we send for the ship's doctor?"

Captain Samuels intercepted the question. "The ship's doctor managed to smuggle a bottle of *okolehao* on board. He'll be a decent enough physician by tomorrow night, but tonight he is worse than no use." Then, redirecting the conversation away from the crew's shortcomings, the skipper addressed Cleghorn: "Is it true your daughter is of Hawaiian royalty? I ask, you see, because while I've been master of this ship for more than a year, this is my first voyage to the Hawaiian kingdom. *Umatilla* has spent the past fifteen months servicing San Francisco, Seattle, and Vancouver."

Cleghorn inspected the green, barely cured, native-leaf cigar. "Kaiulani is indeed in the direct line. My dear wife, departed, was sister to the king. Since King David Kalakaua is childless, his other sister, Princess Liliuokalani, is his heir. As she is also without child, my daughter is next in the line of succession."

"Then how does it happen you are taking her abroad," the captain inquired, "since she is so highly placed?"

Cleghorn and the senior Adams exchanged a glance. "I would not care to bore your other guests with familiar history," Cleghorn said carefully.

William Adams shook away the objection.

Young Andrew said, "Please, sir, continue. I'm interested to hear it as well."

Scratching his beard, Kaiulani's father agreed. "There is a strong anti-monarchist sentiment in the Islands. By-and-large the men of the Reform Party are American in origin. They are men of business. Sugar, mainly. They want to take the kingdom under America's wing, believing such a move will benefit them personally. If there were no royals, it would be much easier for these men to accomplish their purposes."

"Is it true they are descended from the missionaries who came to Hawaii in the 1820s?" Adams queried.

Cleghorn's brows furrowed. "Many are. I include Thurston, their leader. Some Hawaiians are bitter against the missionaries, but most are not. Native families hold in high regard the faith and the education and the medicine the missionary companies brought. Missionaries saved the Islands from the onslaught of unscrupulous whalers and the like. But nobility of grandparent does not always arrive intact at grandchildren."

"How so?" Andrew asked.

"Greed is a very corrupting influence." Addressing the captain, Cleghorn said, "It is an old saw, but a true one: 'The missionaries came to do good, and their grandchildren have done very well indeed.'"

There was an uncomfortable chuckle at this bitter witticism.

"To give them their due," Cleghorn continued, "the king presented the reformers a perfect opening. He spent too freely, built too lavishly. He revived Hawaiian customs and music. This became an excuse for the whites to trumpet about offense to their morals. The reformers held enough seats in the legislature to withhold funds from the king. They forced him into a compromise, giving them even more control."

Andrew spoke up: "You speak of *The Bayonet Constitution*? Or so I've heard it called."

Cleghorn concurred. "Just a couple years ago the king was forced to accept a document increasing the legislative power at the expense of the king's authority."

"But isn't a constitutional monarch more modern? More in keeping with the times than a savage despot?" Captain Samuels ventured.

"Savage?" Cleghorn ran a hand over his wavy brown hair, shot through with gray. "It is the hypocrisy, sir," he replied sternly. "While prattling about 'doing good for the people of Hawaii,' they are stealing it from under their very noses. The new constitution requires that a citizen must be a landowner to vote." He snorted. "Landowner! The old Hawaiians had no concept of land ownership! When someone gave them a piece of paper saying they now 'owned' the property under their feet, more often than not they traded it for ready cash. Or gambled it away in rigged games. Or drank it up in *okolehao*." Cleghorn grimaced and stubbed out the cigar in a red clay jar filled with sand. "So you see, now only landowners can vote. Land is concentrated in the hands of the men of commerce and their supporters."

"They are stealing the kingdom!" young Andrew asserted.

"But you, sir," William Adams asked Cleghorn, "aren't you the Collector of Customs? How does it happen you can be so near to the king and retain your position?"

Cleghorn gnawed his moustache. "I am a straight speaker, sir. All parties know this. I tell the king when I think he has done wrong. I do the same to Thurston when he oversteps his bounds. And I am father to Her Royal Highness, the Princess Victoria Kaiulani Cleghorn."

"Are you afraid for her safety?" Andrew said.

Papa Cleghorn studied the young man before replying. "Other princes of the blood royal now study abroad. Kaiulani's cousin is in England. It is time for my daughter to broaden her view of the world. She may be queen someday."

* * * *

Six days and nights were ahead aboard the lumbering *Umatilla*. Kaiulani, Hannah, and Annie considered how they might fill the hours of the crossing between Honolulu and San Francisco. The ship was not as wide as an island. The attentions of Andrew Adams could be neither ignored nor avoided. He was already confused about the identity of the princess.

The morning of the second day dawned clear and calm. Seasickness passed as the trio of girls got their sea legs quickly. Kaiulani and Hannah, with the help of Annie, planned their entertainment for the journey. Deceiving Andrew Adams as to the true identity of the real princess was their plot.

Kaiulani and Hannah stood before the stateroom mirror and examined their oval Polynesian faces side by side.

Kaiulani said, "He mentioned that the princess—he meant you—is taller than I."

Hannah drew herself up straight. "Almost imperceptible, I think."

"But we wear the same size dress."

From her bunk Annie leaned her face against her hand. "You do look somewhat alike, perhaps, to someone who does not know you. We can fool this young fellow and everyone on the ship forever if I call Hannah by Kaiulani's name. But Papa is the issue. Papa will give it away in an instant. He will call Kaiulani, *Kaiulani*, and our game will be undone."

Hannah grinned. "The trick is, we must never be around Papa Archie when he is with Andrew."

Kaiulani laughed and snapped her fingers. "That's it. Who will doubt when Annie, my own sister, calls for Hannah and I turn and answer?"

Hannah frowned. "It's a bit dishonest."

Kaiulani corrected her friend. "No. Think of it as if...no, this: it is like playing parts in a play. Like Shakespeare. *Twelfth Night.*"

"I don't know." Hannah shook her head. "How does it work?"

"I saw the play with Miss Gardinier. There are always characters pretending to be someone else. Servants playing the roles of their mistresses. That sort of thing. Very entertaining! And it all comes round right in the end, with everyone falling in love with exactly the right person."

Hannah struck a regal pose. "So, in this play, I am the servant pretending to be royal. Is that it?"

"As if I am playing the role of Viola, and you are playing the role of Rosalind in *As You Like It.*"

"I like it." Annie's broad brown face beamed with delight.

"Andrew wishes to interview the princess." Kaiulani laughed. "You will be me. And I will be you."

"And if we are found out?"

"Then it was all a silly parlor game. He'll have to take it like a good sport, or we will think him a cad."

Annie sat up on her bunk. "If it seems that he begins to tumble to the truth, then Your Highness can pretend to be seasick and excuse herself."

"Brilliant." Kaiulani licked her lips as if the plot were some delicious dessert to be savored.

Hannah brushed and plaited her thick black hair. "We should

have some sort of code word if Papa Archie approaches from behind while I am Princess Kaiulani conversing with Andrew."

"*Auwe.*" Annie screwed up her face and stared out the round porthole. "What?"

Kaiulani gazed at the light fixture on the ceiling as if the answer was written there. "Something discreet. A Hawaiian word that this arrogant *malihini* will never understand."

"Papa Archie will be *Pappio.*"

"A fish!" Hannah's smile flashed as she paraded elegantly around the room. "*Pappio.*" It was too wonderful. "Wait. Wait! More than one code word. If I am a princess, then you commoners should address me in some special way."

Kaiulani kissed her hand and bowed. As if on cue, Hannah sneezed. Both Kaiulani and Annie said in one voice, "*Kihe, a Mauliola!*"

Hannah interpreted the phrase in English. "Sneeze, and may you have a long life!" She raised her hands in triumph. "There. We have it! The perfect way to greet me. We must teach Andrew the Hawaiian way to address a royal princess in public."

Kaiulani bowed deeply once more and took the hand of her friend. "Princess Kaiulani, *Kihe, a Mauliola!*"

The three girls howled with delight at the endless possibilities.

At last Kaiulani wiped tears of glee from her cheeks and inhaled deeply. "Brilliant."

It was almost after the breakfast hour before Annie hurried from the cabin to fetch the morning meal back to her fellow conspirators. The trio shared scrambled eggs and bacon and biscuits smothered in gravy as they carefully drafted a master plan. The game was sure to leave handsome Mr. Andrew Adams humbled, confused, and gasping for air before they disembarked on the docks of San Francisco.

* * * *

The trio of young women planned their foray against Andrew Adams like the generals of an army plotting a battle plan. Annie, who played the part of herself, was in no danger of being discovered, and was, therefore, the advance scout. Wrapped in a shawl against the cold, she left the stateroom and strolled along the planked decks in search of the enemy.

Andrew Adams sat alone in a teak deck chair, protected from the breeze by the shelter of a ventilation funnel. He was reading a copy of Robert Louis Stevenson's recently published novel, *The Black Arrow*. Andrew glanced up briefly and tipped his hat at Annie, who smiled and nodded graciously.

"*Aloha*," she said, pausing. "I see you are reading Mr. Stevenson's book."

"A masterpiece." Andrew studied the front cover of the tome where an image depicting its title was emblazoned. In a distracted tone he replied, "I am, I will confess, unable to put it aside. Every page leads to the next, until I am entirely caught up in it."

"It is good you have so much in common with Princess Kaiulani. She is fond of Mister Stevenson's novels as well."

"*Fond* is too light a word for such an experience as this. He gave it to me personally. It is inscribed. My greatest treasure."

"You know him, then. He is a great friend of Princess Kaiulani. They spent many hours together at our home—discussing literature, and Scotland, and whatnot."

Andrew rose awkwardly from the low seat and bowed. Snagging the toe of his boot in the chair leg exaggerated the movement. "Pardon me," Andrew said, as much for his clumsiness as for his lack of decorum. "I have forgotten my manners. A great story will sometimes do that to one. And you are, forgive me, you are the sister…Annie?"

"Annie Cleghorn." She extended her hand with a limp wrist.

"Sister, uh, to the Princess Kaiulani?"

"That is correct. Half sister. Elder sister. My father is Archibald Cleghorn."

Andrew scratched his cheek nervously. "I spoke to your sister's friend, Hannah. Hannah…oh, well. She said she might be able to arrange an interview for me with the Princess. But I have not seen either Hannah or the princess, and we have been on our journey now two full days. Are they unwell?"

At that moment *Umatilla* saluted a freighter passing on the reverse course with a loud blast of her steam whistle, completing obliterating Annie's response.

"I'm sorry," Andrew ventured. "What did you say?"

Annie shook her head from side to side as she recollected her memorized script. "The seas, when in upheaval, can be very discommodious for the delicate stomachs of royal personages."

Andrew pressed his lips together as if concentrating on deciphering a foreign language. Annie's phrasing sounded like a line from a Gilbert and Sullivan operetta, but of course he was too polite to voice such a comparison. Then, too, the Pacific was nearly flat calm this morning, but how could one argue with such an elegant description of seasickness? "Of course. Please express my best wishes to the princess for a speedy recovery."

Annie hesitated and gazed intently at the volume in Andrew's hand. "The princess loves to read. A good book is so difficult to find on a sea voyage. Perhaps a good story would distract her from the illness."

He was trapped. Removing his thumb reluctantly from the place it marked near the end of the book, he held *The Black Arrow* chest high, title outward. "Might the princess like to read...this? My father is Mister Stevenson's publisher."

Annie's brows rose with satisfaction. "Perfect. Princess Kaiulani loves a great story." Her right hand was extended, broad palm open.

Andrew's expression was one of instant regret as he surrendered the half-read masterpiece. "She'll have to tell me how it turns out," he said as he passed over the volume.

Annie accepted the novel, folding it in a two-armed embrace as if challenging Andrew to try and renege on the offer. "Thank you. Mr. Adams, is it?"

"Andrew." He did not seem capable of tearing his eyes away from the book. "Please give the princess my regards."

"I have no doubt that with such a fine gift she will forget her troubles and come out soon to thank you herself. Will you wait here?"

With an expression betraying misery, Andrew nodded. "I have little else to do."

Annie bustled back to the stateroom. Closing the door, she exploded with laughter and collapsed on the bed. As Kaiulani and Hannah hovered above her, she told of her encounter.

"...and he was fairly irritated, I would say, that I interrupted his glorious read. On top of that, when he offered it to me, I don't think he expected me to take it!"

Kaiulani clasped the leather-bound edition. "Identical to mine, which is also inscribed by Mr. Stevenson. Poor Andrew must feel he has lost his most beloved possession."

Hannah grinned and rubbed her hands together. "Our hostage!"

Kaiulani kissed the book and passed it to Hannah. "I've read it. And Annie read it as a serial years ago."

Annie recalled, "Papa sent old Chang to the docks to meet the mail ship every week. Then he galloped like a Chinese *paniolo* to bring us each installment."

Kaiulani's dark eyes shone with mischief. "*The Black Arrow* seems to me a divinely appointed plot to match our plot. The hero, Dick Shelton, rescues a boy from grave danger, only to discover that the boy is, in truth, a beautiful woman in disguise."

Hannah exclaimed, *"As You Like It!"*

Annie echoed, "I like it fine!"

Kaiulani tapped the book cover. "Hannah. You will pretend that you, playing the role of Kaiulani, have already read the volume. And so you will tell Andrew Adams that you gave his book to Hannah, as a gift."

Hannah clapped her hands. "He'll have no way to get it back except to cozy up to you, even though he thinks you are a commoner."

Kaiulani planted a kiss on Annie's head. "Shakespeare would be proud of you, dear sister."

"Heaven was smiling." Annie crossed her ample arms in satisfaction.

Kaiulani thumbed through the pages. "I'll re-read a portion of *The Black Arrow* every day. It will give me some topic to speak with him about."

Annie added, "To thank him."

Kaiulani interjected, "I can feed him the plot of it, bit by bit. Keep him alive in this cage of boredom with morsels of Robert Louis Stevenson."

Hannah howled with delight. "And can you imagine any greater torture than a great novel given up at its very climax? Seeing the story read and enjoyed by someone else, without any hope of discovering the end of the story?"

"Torment." Kaiulani sighed with contentment. "Greater than the torment of unrequited love."

Annie urged them on. "Go quickly, Hannah. I told him the Princess Kaiulani would no doubt be strolling past and might stop to thank him."

"This is better than a Jane Austen novel!" Hannah wrapped herself in Kaiulani's coat. "The plot thickens."

Kaiulani stopped Hannah with her hand on the latch. "Here, Princess. By way of thanks, present him with my Louisa May Alcott novel as a substitute. *Little Women!*"

Chapter Three

· ·

The second wave of the attack on Andrew Adams was launched when Hannah emerged from the portal of the stateroom. Drawing herself erect, she strolled regally forward as she imagined a princess from a fairy tale might process.

The wind tugged at Hannah's shawl, uncovering her thick mane. Her hair burst into a wild tangle of curls.

Andrew leapt to his feet and almost stood at attention when she approached. His eyes were wide and apprehensive. He stepped forward too eagerly in order to properly address the teenage girl he believed was a royal princess.

"Your Highness? Kaiulani?" He bowed deeply, doffing his deer-stalker hunting cap. The earflaps, freed from their restraining cord, pulsed in the breeze.

"You know my name, do you?" Hannah asked. She struggled to restrain a giggle at the sudden image of a long-eared hound.

"I would know you anywhere."

Hannah suppressed her impulse to grin. "How do you do? And you are Andrew Adams?" She nodded only slightly, as if Andrew were a fly buzzing near her face that she wished to avoid. She extended her hand, palm downward.

"I am. Andrew...Adams. Just Andrew, Your Highness," the young man stammered as he took her hand.

"As you like it."

He pulled over a chair for her, but she did not sit. The two remained standing as the wind increased. "Are you well, Princess Kaiulani?"

Hannah decided that the best way to answer was with a question. "Well?"

"We heard you were quite ill from the wallowing of the ship."

Hannah gazed at him with what she hoped was dignity. It was, in fact, an icy stare conveying the sense she was profoundly offended.

Andrew squirmed. While Hannah stood inboard and sheltered, his cheeks were exposed to the spray blowing in from the sea. He wiped his cheeks and waited.

Hannah considered the proper way to reply to a query about the galloping nausea that had confined the girls to their cabin the first day out. The memorized reply about seasickness that they had rehearsed at length with Annie suddenly leapt to Hannah's mind and out of her mouth. "The seas, when in upheaval, can be very discommodious for the delicate stomachs of royal personages."

Andrew frowned and stared at her with a quizzical expression. "So I've heard. It must be true."

Hearing her own voice pronounce *discommodious* aloud, Hannah instantly regretted speaking. The word uttered in the open air sounded too much like *commode*. The vision of a toilet was vivid in her imagination. Had Andrew understood? She blushed. "I said, most DIScommodious." Saying it again did not help. The blush deepened.

"I am sorry for the inconvenience to Your Highness." Andrew seemed at a loss. He flicked drips of salt water from his brows before they could get into his eyes.

"Never mind. Never...mind." Hannah regrouped. "The air is most invigorating. I came out to thank you personally for your kind gift. Robert Louis Stevenson. Mister Stevenson is a friend of ours and a frequent visitor at our home."

Andrew seemed pleased and relieved. "I hope you enjoy *The Black Arrow*. It is the most—"

Hannah nodded. "A stunning adventure. I previously devoured *The Black Arrow*. Therefore, I have given the volume to my dear friend Hannah as a gift."

Andrew's smile froze on his face. "You gave? You gave *The Black Arrow*—to Hannah. Of course. Logical."

Hannah exuded good cheer. The wind from astern stretched twin banners of white steam and black smoke overhead. "To repay your kindness, I brought you a gift. It should keep you entertained during the many days of our passage." Hannah kept the title of the volume concealed beneath the fringe of the shawl.

"Very kind of you, Princess. I am certain I will enjoy it."

"I must ask: have you read the works of this American author? Alcott is the name."

Andrew cleared his throat and took a deep breath before he exhaled slowly. "No. No, I don't think...Alcott?"

"Alcott has written a tale taking place during the American Civil War."

Andrew perked up. "Civil war?" Perhaps it would take the place of the unfinished story of the English War of the Roses. "Ah. Yes. America. The war between the states."

"I enjoyed the novel very much. I learned an immense amount about the Civil War, as experienced on the home front."

"Sounds promising. The voyage is many days before us."

"Many hours to fill." Hannah smiled and stretched forth the thick volume. Sunlight glinted on the gilt lettering stamped on the cover: LITTLE WOMEN, BY LOUISA MAY ALCOTT.

Andrew swallowed hard. The color drained from his handsome face. He tilted his head from one side to the other as if by reading the title and the author's name from a slightly different angle he might change the words. No matter how he turned his head or squinted his eyes, the sentence remained unchanged.

"Little Women." Andrew gallantly attempted to appear appreciative. "Your Highness is...too kind."

Hannah set the hook. "A trifle. I enjoyed *Little Women* very, very much. One might even say it is among my favorite novels, except, of course, for Jane Austen's works, and, of course, the latest by Mister Stevenson. *The Black Arrow* was the most thrilling story I have yet read. But I would be most delighted to discuss *Little Women* from a male perspective; talk about an American novel with an English gentleman."

Andrew accepted the volume but quickly tucked it inside the breast of his frock coat as if it were contraband. "A pleasure. I had hoped we might become acquainted, possibly. I am most interested in discussing your opinions of the politics of the Hawaiian monarchy."

Hannah cut him off with a wave of her hand. "You are too forward, Mister Adams."

"Andrew. Please call me Andrew."

Hannah ignored the plea. Coolly, she responded, "Politics requires thought that is often unpleasant. We must meet more formally for such a discussion. Such an interview must be arranged through the proper channels. As I was saying, literature is a much more pleasant place to begin an informal dialogue."

"Of course, Princess. But literature will not be a topic the world wants to read about. They rather wait to hear what Princess Kaiulani thinks about the conflict in her own government and nation."

"Politics. Perhaps Hannah can arrange a convenient time for us to speak on official topics?"

"Hannah?"

"She is my companion. You met her. She serves as my social engagement secretary."

Wheels seemed to be turning in Andrew's mind. "Well, then, yes, if that is the protocol. I will speak with Hannah about an appointment with you to discuss politics."

"I'll send Hannah out shortly to speak with you. She has my appointment book."

And so the stage was set.

* * * *

Kaiulani pulled on Hannah's plain black coat and planted her delicate hands in a muff. "How do I look?" She glanced at her reflection in the oval mirror.

Annie scrutinized her. "Like a girl who should be named Hannah."

Hannah rubbed the tip of her nose. "It's cold out there, Kaiulani. Wind whipping the spray. He was already soaked when I finished with him."

Kaiulani tucked an errant curl beneath her cap. "I'll throw a little more cold water on him."

Hannah opened the copy of *The Black Arrow* and studied the inscription. "Tell him the princess is worried that the copy of *Little Women* might get damp. Tell him my social calendar is all filled up."

Kaiulani laughed over her shoulder as she slipped out. "We're being cruel to this poor fellow."

If there was a twinge of guilt in Kaiulani, it was soon enhanced when she saw Andrew huddled against the vent shaft for warmth. The long ears of his cap flapped in the breeze. He raised his eyes miserably and gave her a half-hearted wave with the volume of Miss Alcott's work.

"Ah, Hannah!" he said to Kaiulani. "I am glad to see it is you coming."

"Good day."

"Miserable day," he replied.

"Cold winds, like something from a Gilbert and Sullivan play."

He answered, "A Mikado day, eh?"

She quoted the well-known lyrics, "'To lay aloft in a howling breeze.'"

His full lips curved up on the left in a crooked smile. "You've seen it?"

"A touring company passed through Honolulu. I was seated with the princess in the royal box."

Andrew saluted like a sailor in the play. "I saw it at the Savoy in London. Bought the sheet music and memorized the lyrics."

Kaiulani raised her hand in a cheer. "'Hurrah for the homeward bound!'"

He sang, "'Hurrah for the homeward bound.'"

The two began to laugh as if the play, performed worlds apart, was a shared memory.

Andrew grew bolder. "I imagined your home in Honolulu was a backwater."

"Do you know you are arrogant and rude?" she asked with a smile.

"I am not. I am honest and outspoken."

Amused by his answer, Kaiulani considered him for a long moment. "And careless with your words. Do you not fear losing our good opinion of your character?"

He scoffed, "Me? Fear three little maids from school?"

"We three are much more than characters in a Gilbert and Sullivan play."

Andrew scrutinized her as if he were looking at a costumed actress. "I know one thing. Since *The Mikado* was performed, all of London society has gone wild for things Oriental. They will be mad for Royal Princess Kaiulani."

"We are far from the Orient."

"It is more a fascination with exotic beauty. Three beautiful young women. Dark eyes. Thick black tresses. Laughter like a mountain stream. And an appreciation of British theatre."

"You are surprised."

"I confess: I am. You are not at all what I expected."

"What do you hope to uncover?"

"Something more exotic."

Kaiulani turned away from his probing eyes. "The plumage of a peacock rather than a sparrow?"

"I am surprised that you, Hannah, companion of Kaiulani, seem more the peacock than the princess. What can you tell me about her?"

"Kaiulani was raised in captivity, though her soul longs to be free." Kaiulani felt color climb to her cheek as Andrew lifted her chin and searched her eyes for a long moment.

He murmured, "And what's behind the glorious golden face of an island maiden? What secret thoughts course through her?"

She stepped away from him. "This is what London society longs to know?"

He frowned and shoved his hands into his pockets. "Yes. But I must experience the truth of the natives of the South Seas before I write about them."

"You intend to enlighten London about the gentle people of *Hawaii Nei*. Why?"

"It would establish my career."

"So nothing noble in your desire to discover the heart of nobility?" Kaiulani moved out of his reach.

"Hannah, I confess, after seeing you the first time beside the princess, it is not the royal family that most fascinates me. I can't know the heart of Kaiulani, but perhaps you, Hannah...I am—forgive me—I find myself drawn to you."

Andrew's stammering confession warmed Kaiulani. She did not dare look at him. What had begun as a prank seemed suddenly dangerous. "My heart and the heart of Kaiulani are one. We care only about fulfilling our destiny for the Kingdom of Hawaii. Love has no place. We are all *kapu*—forbidden. You stand on dangerous ground. Kaiulani would not be pleased."

"I think I can handle myself quite well in the presence of a barbarian princess."

The tender moment passed. The wind stung Kaiulani's cheeks.

"Barbarian?" Kaiulani was not offended, but neither was she impressed by Andrew's high opinion of himself.

"So she is. A barbarian on her mother's side. A few generations removed from human sacrifice."

Kaiulani raised her chin and glared at him. "I was tempted to pity you, but you deserve what comes your way. We'll see how well you fare when we match wits."

"The three little maids from school." He smirked. "I'm not intimidated."

"You should be. We are all three half-barbarians, as you say. All *hapa-haole*. And half Scots, at that! A fierce and bloody people, the Highlanders."

"I am entirely Scot. And I fear not what fate a barbarian princess may devise for me." He bowed deeply. The wind howled, snapping his deerstalker cap from his head. It tumbled across the deck. "I am, perhaps, too outspoken. But I like you very much, Hannah."

"Sure you do." She closed her eyes briefly and drew on her memory of *The Mikado*. "It was Ko-Ko who was condemned to death for flirting."

He snatched his hat from the deck and shoved it into his pocket. "He escaped death by his charms. But say, I'm not so charming that I don't need your help getting a word with your friend, the princess. An interview, Hannah."

"It can be arranged." Her voice was clipped.

"Have I offended?"

"Yes."

"Unintentional."

"Nonetheless."

"But you will help me, Hannah?"

Kaiulani's lips curved slightly. "I am your only hope if you wish to speak with the Princess Kaiulani face to face."

"So all along, you are the gatekeeper, it seems. You hold the key to access to Her Highness."

"So it seems. Andrew, you must justify your request to me. Why do you care? Or do you care at all?"

"There is turmoil in the Islands, and I long to write about it before the Hawaiian monarchy vanishes with the wind."

Andrew Adams had stepped too far over the line. Kaiulani flared. "You know so much about our Islands and the life of the royal princess. Some say she is the hope of the future."

"It depends on whose future." His grin faltered. He seemed to understand that he had gone too far.

"Why bother to ask her questions if you think you already know the answers? Why should I help you?" Without waiting for his reply, Kaiulani stormed away, back to her stateroom.

* * * *

Viewed through the porthole of the darkened stateroom, a canopy of stars arched over the vast Pacific. To Kaiulani's forbears, the night sky had been a roadmap from Tahiti to the islands of Hawaii.

As Hannah and Annie slept, Kaiulani searched the heavens and replayed her conversation with Andrew. His accusation stung her. Child of a double race, could she be ashamed of her mother's people?

Barbarian princess? What was it you told me, Mama? What? I am a child of the King who made all things. I am His....

Kaiulani whispered the verses of Psalm 19 her mother had taught her as a toddler. Mother and daughter had sat beneath the dark night sky and recited:

> *"The heavens declare the glory of God;*
> *and the firmament sheweth his handywork.*
> *Day unto day uttereth speech,*
> *And night unto night sheweth knowledge.*
> *There is no speech nor language,*
> *Where their voice is not heard."* [2]

Had the ancient Hawaiians understood the voice of the Lord when they looked into the arch of the heavens above their island home?

> *"Their line is gone out through all the earth,*
> *And their words to the end of the world."* [3]

Kaiulani knew the hearts of her mother's race had heard the voice in the heavens before they knew God's name. Her legendary grandmother had torn down the idols and embraced the gospel eagerly when the first missionaries came to the Islands.

Only two generations later the grandchildren of those same missionaries had set aside God's love. The whites despised the descendants of the Christian converts as "barbarians." For sugar and for gold the *haoles* sacrificed the very people with whom their fathers had shared God's love.

Kaiulani said aloud, *"Ke Akua Mana E!* You are great, Lord. Though the children of Your servants would steal our kingdom, Your kingdom will come."

Perhaps there was more to be ashamed of in the heritage of her white father. Who were the true barbarians?

How quickly the children of the missionaries had betrayed the faith of their fathers. And in so doing, they had betrayed the Christian people who first looked to them for truth.

The careless accusation of Andrew Adams had only illuminated a sad reality Kaiulani knew in her heart: *Child of a double race...and yet, I am a true child of the God who made the stars.*

Chapter Four
....

Convincing Andrew to participate in the last night celebration took a relay of Hawaiians. Annie was first to broach the subject, just after breakfast on the last full day of sailing: "You know, Captain Samuels says we will arrive off Golden Gate in the middle of the night, tonight. He says the pilot boat won't come out until tomorrow morning to lead us into harbor."

Andrew looked up from the copy of *Little Women* he held. As ardently as he professed to be enjoying Miss Alcott's work, Annie noted with amusement that his thumb had not advanced from the mark it last held. "Ah, yes?"

"So we must have a last night *luau*. It is a tradition, Captain Samuels says."

"That sounds—interesting."

"Of course, there must be entertainment."

"Naturally."

"At first we thought Hannah would play her ukulele and sing."

"Charming."

"But then we thought, we can do much better than that. We are enough to actually put on a show. Even the princess might condescend to join us."

Andrew's face glowed with sudden interest. Clearly the notion of a royal princess performing for his benefit was much to be preferred over spending his last night afloat reading *Little Women*.

"Excellent idea," Andrew said.

Annie had been well coached. She knew not to push too hard. "I must go," she said, leaving Andrew to his thoughts.

Kaiulani was next to appear. As "Hannah," it was perfectly proper for her to sit in a deck chair beside Andrew. She did not speak but peered intently at a flock of seabirds diving on a school of baitfish.

Andrew glanced at her. He tried valiantly to re-devote his attention to Meg, Jo, Beth, and Amy, but failed miserably. "Annie—Miss Cleghorn—tells me you are planning a last night entertainment?"

Kaiulani shook her head sadly. "It was a wonderful idea. Gilbert and Sullivan. But the princess has decided against it."

"Oh? Did she give a reason?"

"Of course the princess cannot perform any physical labor. Such a thing is not to be thought of; it is *kapu* in our culture. And what a shame! We have practiced the music of Mister Gilbert and Mister Sullivan. Annie plays piano very well too."

"I still don't see—"

"Moving the piano, rearranging the salon, setting the stage. Annie and I cannot do all that by ourselves." Her face was a mask of disappointment, though Andrew failed to see how she studied him out of the corner of one eye.

"But there's me!" he declared. "I can help."

"Would you?" Kaiulani said. "We don't want to impose."

"Nonsense, Hannah! Tell the princess I'd be happy to oblige."

Kaiulani smiled. "I'll tell her so at once." She departed briskly.

Out at sea a pack of ravening dolphins prodded the school of sardines into a boiling, frightened mass that kept pace with the lumbering freighter. Andrew stared at the spectacle, but it seemed only an instant before he was confronted by three Hawaiian females.

Jumping to his feet, Andrew bowed to the princess—Hannah.

In a regal tone Hannah inquired, "Is it true you have agreed to help us stage our production?"

"Of course," Andrew agreed. "Anything to assist Your Highness."

"You understand that I must be able to rely on you completely. We cannot tell Papa Archie and the others about our plan and then fail to deliver." Hannah drew herself up proudly. "The word of a princess is a sacred trust."

"You may count on me completely, Highness," Andrew declared. "For anything."

Hannah regarded him coolly. "I believe you are a man of your word, sir. Annie," she added, "go tell the captain that there will be a performance from *The Mikado* tonight."

Annie's smile was as wide as a dolphin's as she hurried away.

Hannah called after her: "And tell the captain that Mister Andrew Adams has agreed to perform the role of Nanki-Poo."

Andrew was so stricken, his face so frozen, that he failed to see a dolphin leap out of *Umatilla*'s bow wave, a struggling mackerel clasped firmly in its grinning jaws.

* * * *

Kaiulani, Hannah, and Annie were costumed in their best long gowns, combined with floral print *muumuus*, all drawn out of the depths of their trunks. The effect, if not strictly accurate, was oddly suitable for a musical set in Japan.

The trunks themselves had been retrieved from the hold of the ship on the back of Nanki-Poo—Andrew Adams. He had also spent the afternoon dragging the piano and the salon furniture into position.

But Andrew's main concern was not trunks, chairs, or musical instruments.

Nor was he more than dimly aware of his own costuming. Somehow the girls had managed to stitch together a suit of motley for him. He wore a white-and-black checkerboard tunic with a cone-shaped, pointed hat of matching fabric.

Andrew had requested a mask, but this suggestion had been denied on the grounds it would muffle his singing.

Throughout the day Kaiulani had presented him just enough encouragement to keep him from pretending a sudden attack of tuberculosis. She reminded him he was the only male voice they had; that Nanki-Poo was the hero of the tale; that the role had been sung to great acclaim from London to New York to Honolulu.

Now the fatal hour had arrived. Despite Andrew's prayer for a severe storm that would prevent the planned festivity, the fog-shrouded ocean was flat calm. At sunset Andrew thought briefly of jumping overboard and swimming ashore but discarded it after seeing Captain Samuels point out a passing white shark as big as a longboat.

Annie at the piano, Kaiulani gestured encouragement from the sidelines. With Hannah staring at him coolly, Andrew nodded and the accompaniment began. In a clear but uncertain tenor he sang:

> "A wand'ring minstrel I
> A thing of shreds and patches,
> Of ballads, songs and snatches,

And dreamy lullaby!
And dreamy lullaby!"

Seeing his father eyeing him curiously as if viewing a complete stranger, Andrew hastily redirected his attention elsewhere.

"Are you in sentimental mood?
I'll sigh with you,
Oh, sorrow, sorrow!
On maiden's coldness do you brood?
I'll do so too—"

Hannah stared at him. Her expression registered more the disapproval of an Eskimo queen than the encouraging warmth of a tropical princess. Swallowing hard, Andrew lost his place and bobbled the next line. Annie let the melody die, then brought him back to attention with a crashing chord.

"To lay aloft in a howling breeze
May tickle a landsman's taste,
But the happiest hour a sailor sees
Is when he's down
At an inland town,
With his Nancy on his knees, yeo ho!
And his arm around her waist!" [4]

A burst of laughter greeted these lyrics. The off-watch sailors had been invited to attend the performance and heartily approved from where they crowded around the open hatches and outside the portholes.

William Adams looked scandalized.

The only relief, and it was very slight, was that both Archie Cleghorn and Captain Samuels seemed merely mildly amused. Andrew had been afraid that the one graybeard would demand, and the other agree, that Andrew should be fed to the trailing white shark!

Andrew's agony subsided with the end of his number. There was polite applause from the Hawaiians, raucous support from the crew.

Because the evening was not a performance of the play but merely a selection of its musical numbers, the order of the songs had been chosen by Hannah and Kaiulani for purposes of their own.

In a beautiful, sweet harmony the girls delivered:

> *"Braid the raven hair*
> *Weave the supple tress*
> *Deck the maiden fair*
> *In her loveliness*
> *Art and nature, thus allied,*
> *Go to make a pretty bride."* [5]

Hannah and Kaiulani matched the lyrics with a set of hula movements illustrating each step of the bride's preparation.

They looked so sweet, so demure, so harmless. How could Andrew have believed that anything they did was born of cruelty? Reaching this conclusion gave him little comfort. His worst nightmare still lay ahead.

The evening's entertainment continued through more musical offerings from the girls, leaving Andrew plenty of time for his tension to build still further.

And then he was up again.

"The flowers that bloom in the spring,
Tra la,
Breathe promise of merry sunshine—
As we merrily dance and we sing,
Tra la,
We welcome the hope that they bring,
Tra la…Tra la…Tra la." [6]

There could have been twenty or forty choruses of Tra-la-la, but it didn't matter. Andrew could not be more humiliated than he already was. His father looked mortified. More than one pair of sailors had exchanged gestures signifying some doubt as to Andrew's masculinity.

Sinking into a chair on the sidelines, Andrew believed his disgrace could not be more complete. He was scarcely paying attention when Kaiulani announced that the following number would be the last: "Three Little Maids from School Are We."

"Three little maids from school are we,
Pert as a schoolgirl well can be
Filled to the brim with girlish glee
Three little maids from school!"

The rendition continued to the delighted approbation of the audience. The fragment of Andrew's brain still able to focus was mildly surprised at the roles. Why wasn't the princess singing the lead?

> *"One little maid is a bride, Yum-Yum*
> *Two little maids in attendance come*
> *Three little maids is the total sum.*
> *Three little maids from school!"* [7]

The performance concluded to thunderous clapping and the stomping of feet that set the deck planks ringing.

While Andrew would have preferred to slink away, he was called up by Captain Samuels and made to stand beside the three Hawaiian maids from school. "Our delighted thanks," the skipper said, "to Andrew Adams. He possesses...unexpected talents."

Then before Andrew could jump overboard in hope of meeting the shark, the captain continued, "We also are grateful to Annie and to Hannah. Beautifully rendered. Well done. But I must offer our greatest appreciation—"

Andrew was confused. Why was Samuels urging Hannah to step forward?

Samuels continued, "Our deepest indebtedness goes to the Princess Victoria Kaiulani, for suggesting and organizing tonight's festivities."

Only now was the cup of Andrew's humiliation complete. Not only had he made a fool of himself, but he had been duped for days into treating Hannah as a royal princess and speaking very familiarly to one he supposed was a servant.

It might have eased Andrew's pain if he had perceived a small frown on Kaiulani's features or the slight look of regret in her eyes.

But he was sunk too far in his own misery to notice.

* * * *

1973

Sandi sipped iced tea and tapped her foot. The rocking chairs on the *lanai* of Auntie Hannah's room creaked as the old woman croaked musical numbers from *The Mikado*'s second act. Her recollection of the lyrics was perfect. It was as if she had performed the operetta yesterday.

> *"Sit with downcast eye—*
> *Let it brim with dew—*
> *Try if you can cry—*
> *We will do so too."* [8]

Sandi, an audience of one, applauded enthusiastically.

Auntie Hannah bowed and waved her hand as if she saw the faces of the sailors grinning before her. *"Mahalo. Mahalo!* Oh, we three were indeed three little maids from school—Kaiulani, Annie, and Hannah. All flown away now, but me." She tossed a crumb of banana nut bread onto the planks. A brown myna bird swooped down from the banyan and snatched the morsel. He blinked at her, as if expecting more. "That's all. That's all for now, Nanki-Poo."

The aged woman laughed as Sandi shook her head in admiration at the deception. "It was so elaborate. So clever."

Auntie Hannah drew herself up. "We were a bit cruel to poor Andrew, I confess. By the end of the voyage he had fallen in love with the Royal Princess of the Kingdom of Hawaii, whom he had believed was just a commoner named Hannah. Our entertainment broke his heart. Loving Kaiulani was an impossibility for him. But certainly Princess Kaiulani was also falling in love with Andrew."

"Hard to tell she loved him by the way she treated him."

"Kaiulani had no experience of love. Andrew was the first awakening of desire. I am certain she did not realize how cruel our charade was to him." A flicker of sorrow passed through Auntie Hannah's eyes. "*Auwe.* We were schoolgirls. How could we know of such things? How could we know how deep love would grow? How painful the story would become in the end?"

Auntie Hannah closed her eyes and seemed to doze a moment. Or was she replaying some long distant memory? A smile danced on her lips as she gently spoke the name of Kaiulani's beloved: "Andrew. What did we do to your heart?"

* * * *

1889

The royal entourage disembarked from the *Umatilla* with little fanfare. Unlike the great crowds at the wharf in Honolulu, Americans seemed disinterested in Kaiulani's arrival. One reporter from *The Examiner* was at the bottom of the gangplank to greet the princess as she stepped onto American soil. He was from the society page of the newspaper and no doubt was unaware of the political turmoil taking place in the Islands.

Kaiulani, in the shadow of her father, stopped only briefly to speak to the man. Andrew Adams pushed past without greeting. His eyes were downcast, and his sullen face betrayed anger at being bested by three little maids from school.

The barbarian princess stared coolly after her adversary as Andrew and his father hailed a horse-drawn cab. She hoped this was the last she would see of the brash young man.

The Occidental Hotel, located on Montgomery between Sutter and Bush, was the finest establishment in the city. Four stories, of Italianate styling, the Occidental was the *ne plus ultra* of Victorian fashion. Days passed with visits to family and friends, parties, and high teas. Young Andrew Adams and his father were nowhere to be seen. Perhaps, Kaiulani thought, father and son had gone directly to the train and were already on their way to the East Coast.

However, on the morning of Kaiulani's departure from San Francisco, Andrew once again briefly appeared in the gun sights of the female war party. Kaiulani's heart leapt when she saw him enter through the revolving door and dash across the plush red and gold gilt lobby.

Hannah nudged her in the ribs. "Our victim still lives."

Annie stared openly. "And he inhabits the Occidental."

Hannah scowled. "He's not a gentleman. Look how he avoids us."

Kaiulani's eyebrows raised slightly at Andrew's handsome but downcast appearance. "He's vanquished. What care we?"

At that moment Andrew caught sight of the triumphant trio. He quickly looked away. Anger clouded his face. Chin up, full lips slightly clamped together, he did not tip his hat in greeting.

"Did he notice us?" Annie, ever charitable, asked.

Hannah remarked, *"Auwe.* He noticed us all right."

Kaiulani gazed after Andrew as he hurried toward the broad staircase and took the steps two at a time. "He runs like a rabbit, in hopes we did not see him."

Annie bobbed her head. "Good riddance."

Hannah's eyes narrowed. "Barbarians indeed."

Kaiulani concurred. "No doubt when the flush of his shame finally dims, he will only repent that he gave away his copy of *The Black Arrow.*"

Hannah reached into her valise and produced it. "An excellent novel. Finished last night. All's well that ends well. Right conquers might."

"We should not let him believe Hawaiians are thieves as well as barbarians." Kaiulani took the volume from Hannah and penned a note on hotel stationery, which she tucked beneath the front cover. "Now that the truth of our identities has been revealed, we must not part from Nanki-Poo, leaving him in suspense about who won the war of wits." Kaiulani gave the book to the bellman. "When we have departed, will you please see to it this book is delivered swiftly into the hands of Mr. Andrew Adams and no other?"

Chapter Five
....

The weather in Oakland was dismal. A thick, damp blanket of fog shrouded all of San Francisco Bay. The crossing by ferryboat had been punctuated by the mournful wailing of foghorns. Though Kaiulani was back on land once more at the East Bay rail station, the impenetrable mist remained.

Nothing about the miserable day lifted Kaiulani's spirits. This clinging moisture was like nothing she had ever experienced back home. Despite a heavier coat than she had ever worn, the dank cold penetrated her very bones, even to her heart.

Leaving *Hawaii Nei* had been difficult but could have been tolerated as a temporary adventure. Kauilani had so far pretended this journey was just a brief shared experience—a memory to be revisited with Hannah amid much laughter on banyan tree evenings.

The impatient chuffing of the black beast of a Southern Pacific locomotive engine insisted otherwise. Though this was the first railroad Kaiulani had ever ridden—and three thousand miles of track lay ahead—there was no excitement in the day.

Today she would bid farewell to her father.

Papa Archie was turning back here. He would be returning to the sunshine and rainbows of Ainahau even as Kaiulani, Hannah, and Annie approached New York.

"*Auwe,*" Annie said, wiping a film of moisture from the window with her sleeve and straining to study the bustling platforms of the

Southern Pacific terminus. "So big! Great brutes, these engines. Is it true they go a hundred miles an hour? However do they stop?"

Annie's words, while sounding frightened, conveyed the delicious excitement of pretended danger.

For Kaiulani, the train was likewise a beast, but one determined to carry her away from where she wanted to be. Even if the engine were a fire-breathing dragon, no knight would appear to rescue her.

"Two minutes," called the stentorian voice of the conductor in the passageway outside the private compartment after he'd knocked on the door. A moment later he repeated the announcement outside the compartment occupied by Kaiulani's chaperone, Mrs. Walker, and her two young children. "Train Eleven. Departing for Salt Lake City and points east in two minutes. Two minutes."

Papa Archie, looking older than Kaiulani had ever seen him, squared his shoulders and straightened the front of his frock coat. Until that moment Kaiulani had not realized this parting was also painful for her father.

"Girls," he said, his gaze embracing Annie and Hannah but coming to linger on Kaiulani, "the time has come for farewell. I expect you to write me often and tell me everything. I shall do the same. And we will not be apart for so very long. You'll see. The time will pass quickly. Of course, if anything exciting happens, I will cable you the news. This modern age has shrunk the world to the size of a marble."

His words were brave, but his tone was strained and his throat husky.

"Kaiulani," he said, "you are young, and I have no wish to burden your youth. Only remember this: you are a princess of Hawaii.

You are going to a land where they have a long tradition of royalty; see that you act the part. Never think for a moment that what you say and do will not be known in Honolulu. Those who wish you well, and those *others* will be watching. Have fun; add to the sum of your experience. But never forget: *you* are the Princess Victoria Kaiulani."

Had Papa deliberately stressed the word *you* in that sentence? Did he know about the deception they had practiced on Andrew Adams?

Papa leaned close to whisper in Kaiulani's ear and remove all doubt: "William Adams is a well-known and respected publisher and journalist. It may be fun to fool a newspaperman's son, but don't make a habit of it. They have devious ways of striking back."

"No, Papa. I understand," Kaiulani murmured.

"Hannah," Papa Archie added, "I rely on you and Annie to keep Kaiulani reminded of her position."

Hannah, around whose eyes had lurked a giggle, dropped her face. "Of course, Papa Archie."

"Now, hugs all around."

From the great, wide ocean and the bustling metropolis of San Francisco, now Kaiulani's world did shrink indeed. Though spacious and richly appointed, the private compartment was scarcely large enough to contain all the tears that flowed.

"All aboard!" echoed the length of the train station, stabbing Kaiulani with greater grief than she had known since her mother had died.

Slowly, great drive wheels slipped on the wet rails, then gained purchase and tugged inexorably forward. Train Eleven, bearing the

Princess Victoria Kaiulani and her retinue, began its transcontinental journey and the second leg of the trip that would carry Kaiulani halfway around the world, to England.

Kaiulani's father remained on the platform. His fluttering handkerchief stayed visible for the briefest of moments before being swallowed up by the fog.

* * * *

1973

It was late—a hot Lahaina night. At the open-air restaurant at the Pioneer Inn a grizzled Front Street musician strummed a battered guitar and belted out a last Jim Croce song before the bar closed down. Sandi perched on the wide stone wall of the breakwater. Waves splashed gently against the black lava rocks on the beach. Snatches of lyrics rose and fell with the rhythm of the waves.

> *"...such a long time ago,*
> *I was walking...*
> *...tired of dreaming alone,*
> *Like all the lonely people I had known."*

Beyond the lights of Lahaina the stars filled a moonless sky and reflected in the calm sea. A gleam shone from the deck of a returning dinner cruise boat packed with tourists. At the end of the breakwater a couple kissed like a slow dance.

"We spent the whole night talking.
You said you'd like to see the sunrise.
But in the gold of morning,
There was nothing that I had not seen in your eyes." [9]

Sandi searched the early spring sky and imagined John looking up at the same stars. The guitar strummed, and in the next breath she imagined John looking down at her from the stars.

The music stopped. The mic buzzed a moment before the singer switched it off. He was almost alone in the bar.

Sandi watched him as he emptied his tip jar. No future in Front Street singing. No future singing someone else's songs. He packed up his instrument and downed the last of a flat beer before leaving the platform that served as his stage.

And the lights switched off. It was mostly dark except for the stars. Lahaina was suddenly almost quiet.

Sandi tossed a stone into the lapping waves and looked up into indigo night. She whispered her complaint: "Oh, God. I'm trying. I really am. Happy, yes, for all the other families. I am, God. But what about my life? If only his name had been on the list."

Suddenly from behind her and above she heard music and a sweet soprano voice singing.

"Sorry her lot who loves too well,
Heavy the heart that hopes but vainly..."

Sandi turned and followed the source of the music to Auntie Hannah's open window. She stood beside the wall, arms limp at her sides, and searched the darkness. Had the old woman been watching? Had she seen Sandi sitting alone?

> *"Sad are the sighs that own the spell*
> *Uttered by eyes that speak too plainly;*
> *Sorry her lot who loves too well..."*

The scratching of the old woman's phonograph record could not conceal the message.

> *"Heavy the heart that hopes but vainly,*
> *Heavy the sorrow that bows the head*
> *When love is alive and hope is dead!*
> *When love is alive and hope is dead!"*

A white shadow emerged from the French doors as Auntie Hannah stepped onto her *lanai*. Hobbling to the railing, Auntie Hannah raised her hand, acknowledging Sandi. Sandi returned the gesture, palm up, imploring the aged woman not to go. Auntie Hannah nodded slowly, then sat in her rocking chair.

> *"Sad is the hour when sets the sun*
> *Dark is the night to earth's poor daughters,*
> *When to the ark the wearied one*
> *Flies from the empty waste of waters.*
> *Sad is the hour when sets the sun..."*

The two women, young and old, lives separated by time and continents and history, listened together, their hearts in the music.

> *"Dark is the night to earth's poor daughters.*
> *Heavy the sorrow that bows the head*
> *When love is alive and hope is dead!*
> *When love is alive and hope is dead!"* [10]

PART TWO

Chapter Six

....

Victorian England, 1889

It was fortunate Kaiulani made her first visit to the home of her guardian, Theo Davies, in high English summer. Located north of Liverpool, the Merseyside area called Southport was a cheerful, bustling beach resort when seen in July. The breeze off the Irish Sea had no bite. The sky was blue like the water—not a vivid blue-green, like off Lahaina Roads, but a sensible, deep English blue. Crowds of pleasure-seekers came from all over England to enjoy summer holiday at Southport.

Kaiulani stepped off the train at the Southport rail station almost into the arms of a broad-shouldered, well-dressed young man. "Here," he insisted, "let me take that for you." Tipping his straw boater, he reached for her portmanteau.

Hannah appeared on the platform one step behind Kaiulani. "A moment, sir," she said frostily. Then in a none-too-subtle aside she remarked, "Don't give it to him. No uniform. He could be a thief."

"What? Me, a thief?" the handsome stranger bumbled. "There's some mistake."

"There certainly has been," Hannah retorted. "Yours. And unless you leave immediately, I shall summon a policeman."

The heads of nearby travelers swiveled to witness the disturbance.

The young man's face colored up to the line of his dark, wavy hair. He backed up abruptly, hands widespread to protest his innocence.

The phalanx of three Hawaiian maidens confronted him in a wall of suspicion.

"My father, you see, he's detained. He sent me...oh, dash it all, I'm Clive Davies."

Suddenly all was explained. Clive was Theo's son. He was also home from school for a summer holiday. A few years older than Kaiulani, Clive was to be their guide to the summer entertainments of Southport.

In further nonverbal defense of his blamelessness Clive gestured toward a trio of porters swarming around the baggage car and then pointed to a waiting carriage. "Please, forgive me! Father will banish me to outer darkness if I've offended you, Your Highness."

Kaiulani was ready to let him off easily. "My apologies as well for the misunderstanding." She handed him her satchel. "But since we're going to be friends, you must call me Kaiulani. Or Victoria, if you prefer. Mister Davies, this is my friend, Hannah, and my sister, Annie."

"Charmed," Clive said, never taking his eyes off Kaiulani's face. "Victoria, I say, like the queen. Shall we?"

Clive was the essence of politeness as he handed each of the three women up into the carriage, but his grip on Kaiulani's elbow lingered a moment longer than was strictly necessary.

"Southport is smashing in summer," Clive commented. "Swimming, boating, tennis. I say, do you ride?"

"I'm already missing it," Kaiulani admitted.

"Wonderful! I mean, we have stables. Riding in the park just in back of our place is splendid."

Kaiulani noticed Clive directed all his questions to her alone so she suggested, "Hannah rides as well. Annie doesn't care for it, but she is an excellent tennis player."

"*Auwe*," Annie commented when the carriage turned off Park Crescent and up the Davies' drive. "This house is almost as big as King David's new palace."

The home's three wings hung above the green lawns like a three-story-high tapestry woven of red brick and black timbers. "Welcome to Sundown," Clive said.

"It's beautiful," Kaiulani replied.

"Not a bad old pile at that," Clive said. "Looks like a Tudor fantasy, but I assure you, it's modern throughout. Father had it all refitted a few years ago. Gaslights and coal heat, eh?"

Kaiulani recognized the ruddy-faced, stocky, middle-aged man who appeared from the front door. "My dear princess," Theo Davies said, "welcome to my home. Your home in England. Welcome to Sundown."

Kaiulani, Hannah, and Annie were escorted to the floor of the west wing reserved exclusively for them. The view from the girls' bedrooms disclosed a rose garden, tennis courts, the stables, and beyond these, the genteel tangle of Hesketh Park.

When they had changed out of their traveling clothes, the trio entered the parlor above the *porte cochere,* where tea was laid on for them and Theo Davies waited.

"Sundown is remarkable, sir. Did you select the name yourself?" Annie asked.

Theo nodded agreeably. "They say the sun never sets on the British Empire. Well, my empire is not so broad or so grand, but since the sun rose on my business in Hawaii it seems right to honor this end of the arc as well."

Theophilus Davies had built an empire out of sugar. He did not grow the cane. He did not refine the sugar. Davies did not own the shipping company that freighted the precious white crystals. Nevertheless, in back of all these different businesses was Theo Davies, putting all the partners together and making it all run smoothly.

If London was the face of British culture and fashion, surely Liverpool was its shoulders. The great harbor on the Irish Sea handled cargo from as far away as China—tea, to be sweetened by Hawaiian sugar.

So it was natural for Theo Davies to locate his home there.

"Will Clive be joining us for tea?" Hannah asked.

"Don't think so," Theo observed. "He said something about wanting to check on the stables. Thought you might like to go riding later, Princess."

* * * *

Clive asked Kaiulani to join him at the stables at three in the afternoon. She rounded the corner of the barn as the bells of a nearby church finished striking the hour, but Clive was not in sight. "Mister Davies?" she called. "Clive?"

Had she mistaken the time?

An elderly groom, stooped of back, emerged from the stable, pitchfork in hand, and tugged his cap respectfully. He was evidently hard of hearing, too, for he shouted, "Won't be but a moment, miss! Master Davies asks, would you please wait? He'll be along directly."

Clive, in riding britches and tall boots, was less than a moment appearing. He led a magnificent chestnut hunter, who pranced as he emerged into the sunshine.

Kaiulani was struck by the lean, muscled flanks of the animal and by how his glossy, dark coat was identical in hue to Clive's hair.

"Hello, Highness," Clive said in greeting. "Isn't he marvelous? Got him from my friend Winston. Thank you, Suggins," Clive added. "If you'll hold Blenheim for me." He passed the lead rope to the groom and went back into the barn, while holding up an index finger in plea for another instant's grace.

Kaiulani waited expectantly.

When Clive returned, she was disappointed but hoped her expression remained unchanged. He was clearly so pleased with himself the princess did not want to hurt his feelings.

Clive was followed by a bay mare, fully two hands shorter than the chestnut. She was pretty enough but evidently elderly. She walked docilely, like an overgrown, faithful dog. And she was outfitted with a sidesaddle.

"Esmeralda," Clive said proudly, naming the mare. "Princess? Will you permit me to assist you?"

He seemed so puppyish in his eagerness that Kaiulani consented. Hands on her waist, Clive lifted her into the sidesaddle, looking aside politely as Kaiulani adjusted her skirt and limbs.

Clive controlled the hunter with some difficulty. When he received the reins from Suggins, the chestnut pranced two complete circles around the mare before Clive got his mount in hand.

A bridle path opened directly out the back of the grounds of Sundown. It twisted through a heap of gorse and gnarled trees until it emerged in Hesketh Park. In the center of the greensward was an hourglass-shaped lake for boating. Around the perimeter the dirt path was broad and smooth. The soft yellow soil was so deep that Esmeralda made furrows as she dragged her hooves with each plodding step.

Blenheim was clearly frustrated, tossing his head in evident unhappiness at being hindered from running.

They circled the lake at the slowest of paces, Clive chatting happily about how he hoped Kaiulani would enjoy Southport. He asked questions about what school subjects the princess enjoyed, what she had seen of England so far, and what she hoped to see.

It was pleasant enough, but ponderous.

"Could we go a bit faster?" Kaiulani asked. "Your horse seems to want it."

Clive looked dubious. "My father made me promise not to endanger you in any way. He made me swear to not be reckless."

Kaiulani was offended but determined not to be cross. "I am an experienced rider. Perhaps just to trot a little?"

Without waiting for Clive to make up his mind, Kaiulani flicked the reins across Esmeralda's withers. The mare responded with a stumbling trot but soon settled into an easy lope.

Kaiulani gave Clive credit for not shouting "wait" or "stop." He simply allowed Blenheim to close the gap, which the chestnut did with ease.

At the north end of the circuit another path branched off from the main route, ascending a slight incline into a tunnel formed of overhanging plane trees. "Where does this lead?" Kauilani called after she had already turned onto it.

"The heath," Clive responded. "And beyond that, wilderness all the way to the Yorkshire Dales."

Despite Kaiulani's urging, the little mare could not, or would not, pick up the pace any further. Shafts of bright sunlight picked their way through gaps and crevices in the leafy bower, suffusing the inside of the cavern with a lime-hued aura. The warm, moist air trapped beneath the canopy smelled green in a way that made sense to Kaiulani, even if she could not have explained it. Memories of long rides across the Parker Ranch on the Big Island of Hawaii came to her mind. Sudden squalls and races through the rain with old friends made her momentarily homesick for her friends at home.

Now, half a world away, beneath the dappled canopy flies buzzed in unhurried circles. Clive looked at her with dewy-eyed admiration, making her uncomfortable.

The brightly lit hole at the far end of the passage grew larger as they approached it, then exited at last onto the flank of a gently sloping verdant hillside.

Blenheim pranced expectantly. "This is where I let him out," Clive explained. "Do you mind?"

"Not at all," Kaiulani agreed, knowing he was showing off.

At the barest touch of Clive's heels the chestnut darted forward, as if shot from a bow. Clive let the animal stretch out into a thundering stride that made the horse's muscles ripple beneath his coat. A quarter-mile up the path, the knoll was bisected by a meandering rock wall.

Kaiulani watched as Blenheim dug in his heels when Clive brought him to a halt before the barricade and spun him about. Horse and rider returned almost as quickly as they had gone. The chestnut was not the least winded, was not lathered at all.

"I'm afraid that was rude of me," Clive admitted. "Bit of showing off, eh?"

"I will forgive you," Kaiulani offered, "if—"

Clive walked, all unsuspecting, into her trap. "Anything! Name it."

"Let me ride Blenheim."

"My father will kill—"

"Your father need not know," Kaiulani returned, "unless you decide to tell him. I certainly won't. Now you must decide. I've told you the cost of my pardon. Will you pay it or not?"

With resignation Clive agreed. "Give me a moment to change the saddles."

"Absolutely not!" Kaiulani protested.

Clive said no more but looked all around for the spies he seemed certain would carry the tale to his father.

Once seated astride the chestnut Kaiulani did not give Clive the opportunity to change his mind. Leaning over the horse's neck, she urged him on, and that was all the encouragement needed.

It was exhilarating! She was home on the back of a horse. Wind whipping her hair back from her face, Kaiulani felt the most alive she had been since leaving Hawaii.

Back on the sandy beaches below Ainahau, Kaiulani had ridden as fast as this, bareback. She could have mentioned it to Clive, but these *haole* males were all so certain they knew everything! It seemed better to prove him wrong with actions rather than argument.

As they approached the rock wall, Kaiulani neither slowed nor turned. She had already planned the fitting climax to this object lesson.

Far behind her she heard Clive calling urgently, "Princess! Princess! The wall! Stop!"

Satisfied Blenheim was as confident as she, Kaiulani set herself for the jump. At precisely the right moment she cued the animal, and they flew over the barricade, landing without breaking stride.

She decided Clive had been punished enough. Kaiulani reined up and turned back down the slope.

Clive, perhaps certain she would fall and break her neck, was whipping the mare into a bone-jarring trot to reach the barrier as fast as he could. "Wait there," he demanded. "Don't try to do that coming down again. Too dangerous."

Not wanting to make him into an enemy, Kaiulani complied.

Letting the mare crop the grass of the heath, Clive clambered over the wall. "You are experienced."

"Every day at home," Kaiulani said, "since I was three."

Clive managed to look embarrassed and impressed at the same moment. "Perhaps we can find something a bit more spirited than Esmeralda," he admitted. "But please, let me take over from here. Landing a jump properly on a downhill is a bit tricky."

Kaiulani agreed, sliding down and surrendering the reins.

Retreating a suitable distance to get up speed, Clive set Blenheim at the wall, lifted off properly, landed awkwardly, and fell off on his back on a thick tussock of coarse grass.

"Mister Davies! Clive!" Kaiulani shouted, climbing over the wall and hurrying to his side. What had she done? Had she killed her host's son?

He was lying on his back with his eyes closed, moaning softly.

"Clive? Are you…? Is anything broken?" She bent over him, stricken with remorse. "Can you speak? Should I go for help?"

His eyes opened when their noses were mere inches apart. Reaching upward, he grabbed her shoulders and pulled her down, kissing her soundly.

"There," he said, releasing her after her startled gasp. "I had to prove I wasn't the only one with daring."

Kaiulani gasped and then slapped him. Leaping to her feet, she bounded to Blenheim and was in the saddle in a flash.

Clive's shout made her laugh as she tapped the great beast into a gallop and fled across the hills.

* * * *

Blenheim was walked and brushed and in his stall by the time Clive and Esmeralda plodded into the stables.

Kaiulani, still in her riding clothes, had already finished a tour of the stalls. With Theo as her guide, she had examined a dozen hunters.

"You are an experienced horsewoman. Of course you may have your choice of mounts." Clive's father scowled as Clive dismounted and handed the reins of the mare to Suggins the groom.

"I can see I was foolish to worry." Clive ran his fingers through his tousled hair. "You made it back home in short order."

"And high spirits." Kaiulani stroked Blenheim's nose. "Thank you, Clive, for allowing me the pleasure of riding such a fine horse, while you rode the sweet old girl back. I have not had so much fun since I left home."

"You fancy Blenheim?" Theo asked.

"I do." She ran her hands down the gelding's shoulder onto his leg and picked up his hoof. "It is a rare thing to find a horse with such spirit, yet with such fine ground manners."

Clive shifted his weight uneasily. He stood back from Kaiulani and his father. Briefly his hand went to his cheek, as if he still felt the sting of her slap.

Kaiulani continued, "Spirit in a handsome animal is danger-ous unless it is controlled." She cast an accusing look at Clive. "If I learned anything on the Parker Ranch, it was that I will never mount a horse that cannot be trusted. Good horse sense and manners. I think Blenheim has all the best qualities."

Theo seemed content with her analysis. "Well then, it seems you have won his heart."

"And he has won mine."

"It is settled. For as long as you are here, Blenheim is yours."

Kaiulani produced a lump of sugar and fed it to the gelding. "Isn't he Clive's horse?"

"He belonged to no one till now," Theo remarked. "I did not think him well broke enough for cross country."

"Nor did I," Clive replied. "I misjudged your experience, Princess."

"You certainly did." Kaiulani gave him a warning glance. "I can handle myself very well. A match for any man on a hunt."

"I shall keep that in mind in the future," Clive promised.

The matter of Kaiulani's horse settled, Theo left Clive to escort Kaiulani back to the house. The couple walked slowly, silent most of the way back.

At last Clive burst out, "Dash it all! I don't know what got into me."

"You left no doubt what got into you."

"I beg your forgiveness."

"My forgiveness is conditional. Your father is my father away from home. You are, therefore, my brother."

"From the first moment I laid eyes on you—"

"I won't tell our father, unless it happens again."

He held his hand up in oath. "I am abject. I am disconsolate."

"If you are to be my brother, then you must behave like a brother."

He snatched his cap from his head. It was clear that this was not what he wanted to hear. "You are so dashed beautiful. Not like the plain, garden-variety girls I know on this side of the world."

"I am half Scots." Kaiulani lifted her chin. "And half Hawaiian. I am entirely woman. I will thank you to remember that both halves of my heritage, and my gender, deserve respect."

"I meant no disrespect."

They reached the wide patio of the house. Kaiulani presented a tight-lipped, matronly smile into Clive's miserable gaze. "You'll have to prove yourself to me now, I'm afraid. Ground manners."

"Yes. Back there. At the fence. I—I just looked up and saw your face and seemed to be dreaming. That's the truth."

"I will remember from now on to let sleeping dogs lie." At that she strode through the French doors and up the broad stairway to her rooms.

Chapter Seven

. . . .

The air was littered with steamboat whistles, the happy chatter of children, the plaintive screeching of gulls, and the soft susurration of the waves. The pleasure pier at Southport was famous. When constructed decades earlier, it was one of the first of its kind in the world. At over four thousand feet in length, jutting into the summer swells and winter fogs of Liverpool Bay, it was still among the longest. The approach to the pier was marked by the gleaming glass dome of the pavilion, modeled after London's Crystal Palace.

It was beautiful, impressing even a trio of Hawaiians for whom coral reefs and waving palms did not seem exotic.

To the quartet of Annie, Hannah, Kaiulani, and Clive was added a fifth member. Joining them on this outing was Clive's friend from school: Winston Leonard Spencer Churchill. When the school term recommenced, Churchill was leaving Harrow School to attend the Royal Military Academy, Sandhurst.

At just six inches over five feet in height, Churchill did not have the impressive physique Clive possessed, but he did have something of a presence. Kaiulani was well aware that Annie, two inches taller than Churchill, admired the deliberate bravado with which he overcame his natural shyness. Kaiulani also knew that Annie wished to mother him, in the best tradition of Hawaiian matriarchy.

"Shall we go all the way to the end?" Clive addressed his question to Kaiulani. Southport's Sunday promenade was famous as a place to see and be seen. The men in suits; the women dressed in hats, long skirts, tailored shirtwaists, and carrying parasols; the afternoon stroll was the Merseyside equivalent of parading up the Strand in London.

The dusky island maidens attracted more than their share of attention.

"Everyone is looking at us," Annie said.

"Everyone is looking at *you*," Clive confided to Kaiulani. "But I'm the one walking beside you."

Churchill, hands on hips, elbows akimbo, expounded to Annie on the history of the pier as they walked. "A thousand feet longer now than when first built," he said. Jabbing with his thumb, he indicated the small-scale steam locomotive that hauled passengers and baggage the half mile from the steamer landing to the shore. "No pier-train in those days."

While Churchill discoursed on engineering, Kaiulani reveled in the sparkling light on the wind-ruffled waves and in the sea gulls using the breeze to remain almost stationary above the dock.

Clive's attention never strayed from the princess.

"Boring you, am I?" Churchill inquired after delivering another cargo of facts.

"Not at all," Annie assured him. "Go on."

Having insisted on buying toffee apples for the group, Clive was clearly now at a loss. Kaiulani carried her parasol in one hand and the candy treat in the other. She had no hand free for him to hold, which she could tell he desperately longed to do.

A brass band paraded past. Their uniforms were a trifle snug around some midsections, and the gold embroidery of their cuffs a tad frayed, but they played bravely and with gusto.

When the quintet and the musicians arrived abreast of each other the band was concluding "Hunters' Chorus" from *The Lily of Killarney*.

To Kaiulani's amazement, upon the next downbeat they launched into "Hawaii Ponoi." The music was clearly unfamiliar to the performers, and the tempo awkward, but it was mysteriously affecting to hear the Hawaiian national anthem played so far from home.

Kaiulani felt a tear hang in the corner of her eye.

"How…," Hannah wondered aloud.

"I asked them to play in honor of the princess," Clive explained.

"Thank you," Kaiulani murmured.

Churchill's lower lip protruded, but whether in criticism of the poor quality of the performance, or because he was impressed with his friend's romantic qualities, he did not say.

The rendition concluded, the musicians gave Kaiulani three cheers and a huzzah. The rest of the holidaymakers applauded with some bewilderment, before movement on the pier resumed.

Kaiulani responded with a brilliant smile that embraced the crowd but warmed Clive's heart most of all. Then the princess solved Clive's dilemma for him. "Would you please carry my apple for me? I think I'll save it for later."

And she allowed Clive to take her hand.

When they reached the terminus of the pier, Churchill stared into the west, as if seeing his destiny written on the waves. "The Irish

Sea," he declaimed portentously in a dramatic fashion only partially spoiled by his lisp. "They say all great English leaders come to grief if they attempt to deal with the Irish problem."

"Then the answer's simple," Annie said. "Don't try. Let the Irish alone. Let them solve their own island's problems, without interference."

"All island nations agree on that!" Hannah asserted forcefully.

"Hear! Hear!" Clive said.

At the terminus of the pier a mother with four red-headed stairstep children was trying to keep them all in order. The two oldest and the youngest agreed to be herded along, but one, a precocious six-year-old boy, refused to be corralled.

Over the protests of his mother he clambered atop the railing and began walking along the rim between earth and sea.

"Harold! Get down," his mother scolded. "Come here this instant."

Harold ignored the command.

"Clive," Kaiulani said, sensing danger, "do something."

"Harold," the mother continued, "I shall tell your father, and he will take the birch to you! Now come here."

"Mustn't scare him," Clive replied, sidling sideways to intercept the child's progress along the wooden railing.

Harold glanced up at Clive's approach, then made the mistake of gazing down at a white-foamed breaker rolling past beneath him. The semblance of movement and the slight sway of the pier made the boy overcorrect his imbalance.

He toppled head first, shrieking, into the water.

"Help!" his mother cried. "Won't somebody help?"

Churchill was first to respond. Shedding shoes and coat, he leapt atop the rail and dove into the sea. When his head popped up, he looked about for the child, just as the next wave tossed him forcefully against a piling.

Kaiulani did not hesitate. Stripping off to her camisole and bloomers, she plunged over like a diving pelican.

As Churchill clung to a wooden crossbeam, Kaiulani yelled, "Where's the boy?"

He could not have disappeared so fast! Kaiulani was terrified he had already been swept away. The long shore current moved past the end of the pair like a millrace.

"Where!" she demanded again.

Gesturing frantically, Clive pointed to her right, where a chubby white hand slapped the water before slipping beneath it. "There!"

Diving under the next roller and coming up from below, Kaiulani seized the boy in one arm and began towing him toward a platform beneath the pier.

Clive located a ladder and climbed down. "Here," he shouted, "hand him to me."

Moments later, while Harold was restored to his mother, Kaiulani stood dripping in Clive's jacket. She gestured helplessly at the destruction of her hair and stockings. "Destroyed," she said.

"Not at all," Clive refuted. "Like Venus rising from the sea."

Churchill was dripping equal parts of water and embarrassment. "I don't swim that well," he admitted.

Annie gave him a ferocious Hawaiian hug. "Then that makes you the bravest of all."

* * * *

1973

The sun rose behind The Mission House. The shade of fragrant plumeria trees provided a nice place to cool off in the hot Lahaina morning. The day was well on its way to the forecasted 84 degrees, and the humidity felt as thick as a fog.

While Sandi waited for Auntie Hannah to arrive, she gazed back toward Front Street and read the museum's modest sky-blue sign, quietly apprising the public of the building's history:

MISSIONARY HOME OF
THE REV. DWIGHT BALDWIN, 1834
MUSEUM OPEN DAILY, 10 A.M.

By special arrangement for Auntie Hannah, they were scheduled to go through the place much earlier than that; it was just now seven o'clock. Any later, Hannah had said, would be too hot for her old bones.

Sandi flipped to a new page on her spiral pad, dated it, and copied the information on the sign. She would have brought the tape recorder but thought it might be intrusive if she kept shoving it in Hannah's face to make sure it caught everything. Instead, Sandi would scribble the shorthand she'd invented for the classes of one of her professors— the one who lectured as if practicing speed-reading out loud.

A creak sounded behind her, and she turned to see a young man about her age standing half inside the building. He held the hunter green door open and locked its spring open. He didn't notice Sandi and disappeared inside again.

Must be the caretaker, she thought, and turned back toward the street. Auntie Hannah was walking toward her. She looked every bit the lady-in-waiting, Sandi mused. Everything about the way Hannah carried herself spoke of modest refinement and dignity.

Auntie Hannah wore an ankle-length floral print dress, printed with deep purples, blues, and greens. Her reed-thin cane was topped with a silver handle, and in spite of a real dependence on it for walking any distance, she was able to make it seem like a fashion accessory, like the silver brooch she wore near her collar. Her white hair was bound up but flowing nonetheless. Several loose curls that must have taken her hours to arrange fell around her shoulders and covered her neck.

"You're beautiful, Auntie Hannah," Sandi gushed. "If I'd have known this was a formal occasion—"

"Tosh, my dear," Hannah interrupted. "You are the very model of perfection yourself. Dressed splendidly for such a day. I think you're quite at home on our little island, don't you?"

Sandi looked down at her wrinkled sundress, one of only two she had with her, and couldn't help but wonder how many of these field trips Auntie Hannah would ask her to take.

They ascended the front steps together and were met by the man Sandi had seen earlier—and a view of him she had not seen. He was wearing a patch over his left eye, and his left hand was missing at the wrist. In its place was a chrome pincer that looked to Sandi like two silver coat hangers. She tried her best to look only at his right eye as Hannah made the introduction.

"This is my great-grandson, Archibald David La'amea Kalakaua. Archibald, I present to you Missus Sandi Smith."

He reached out his right hand to take Sandi's but didn't shake it. Instead he gave a slight bow as though he might kiss her fingers. Sandi was relieved when he didn't.

She smiled and said, "That's quite a name. I'm afraid mine's pretty boring by comparison."

"Archie," he said. "Everybody just calls me Archie."

"Well, it's a pleasure to meet you, Archie. I've been having the most wonderful conversations with your great-grandmother. What do you call your great-grandmother, by the way?" She raised her pad and pen, poised to scribble whatever he said phonetically, then ask for a proper spelling later.

"I call her...are you ready?" He paused, then spoke slowly, "I call her 'great-grandmother.'"

"Archibald!" Auntie Hannah feigned shock. "I'm sorry, dear, he's such a card. Everyone just calls me Auntie Hannah—even my own children these days. Now, Archie, you behave!"

"Yes, Archie," said Sandi, "you have delighted us long enough."

"Ouch!" Archie replied. "*Pride and Prejudice?*"

Taking Auntie Hannah's arm in hers, Sandi swept past him saying, "Most people call it sarcasm. Considering your delightful use of it, I'd have thought you knew."

Archie clutched his chest as if he was mortally wounded, but a broad smile betrayed his enjoyment at the exchange. Auntie Hannah patted Sandi's hand, saying, "Well done, my dear. Now, Archie, will you be so kind as to give us our nickel's worth?"

"My pleasure." Archie launched into his memorized introduction of the old buildings. "My name is Archie Kalakaua. I am the *volunteer*," he stressed the word, "docent here at the Baldwin Home Historical

Site, more commonly known as The Mission House. The house was built by the Reverend Ephraim Spaulding in 1834. The construction is mostly hand-hewn lumber and cut coral stone, roughly two feet thick in the walls. That kind of construction is like primitive air conditioning. You can feel how much cooler it is inside the home compared to outside."

Auntie Hannah added, "It was always the coolest place in Lahaina, so everyone came. If these walls could talk…"

Archie bowed slightly. "In place of the walls, I'll do my best. The Reverend Doctor Dwight Baldwin took it over in 1836 when Spaulding returned to the United States. In 1840 the Baldwins added a bedroom and study, followed by the entire second floor, completed in 1849.

"The Islands were in desperate need of a doctor at that exact moment. Whalers brought such lovely gifts as whooping cough, measles, dysentery, and influenza. Some even blame the introduction of mosquitoes on them, perhaps as larvae in fresh water kegs dumped out here when they could replenish their supply."

As he spoke, Sandi couldn't help enjoying the look of his face. The deep tan was contrasted with pale lines in wrinkles that only revealed themselves when he wasn't smiling. *Which must not be often,* she thought. His good hand was big and muscled, calloused from some work other than "volunteer docent."

"…and remained in their family until just six years ago, when they donated it to the Lahaina Restoration Foundation. The house was completely gutted and restored to what you see here, more closely resembling what it looked like in the eighteen hundreds. Now, if you'd like to head upstairs…"

Hannah led the way. Sandi followed, keeping watch to catch her if the elderly woman stumbled.

Auntie Hannah peered up the narrow stairs. "You two go ahead. I'll wait here." Ignoring a velvet rope across the arms of an ancient upholstered chair, Hannah unsnapped the barrier and took a seat.

Sandi climbed to the top with Andrew following close behind.

"Hello?" someone called from the front door when they were near the top of the stairs. Archie turned back to deal with the sound of many feet arriving on the planks of the *lanai*.

"Uh, sorry, we're not actually open yet," Sandi heard Archie say.

Sandi heard the voices of children then: "Wow! Look at that! He's got a hook! And a patch!" The parents were trying to hush them, but Archie seemed to enjoy the attention.

"Arrrgh, maties!" he growled, "I lost this hand in my piratin' days to a wee little shark, while divin' for sunken gold. As I reached through a hole in the bow of a sunken—"

One of the kids, an older voice than the rest, interrupted with skepticism. "You were a pirate?"

"Aye, laddie. Sailin' the Spanish Main. Me and my first mate, Fluffy, were the—"

Sandi had to stifle a laugh.

"How'd you get to Hawaii?" asked the younger one.

"After Fluffy glued on me hook, I took a nice long catnap. While I slept, someone called Teddy dug a trench through Panama and me ship floated through. When I awoke, I was docked in Lahaina, and Fluffy had run off with me eye!"

"Ewwww!" the kids squealed in unison and laughed, the sound fading as they ran away in the yard.

The parents thanked Archie for interacting with their children.

"No problem," he said, returning to his normal voice. "If you come back at ten, I can take you through then."

When Archie returned upstairs, Sandi caught a hint of sadness in his features and realized this entertainment was simply a well-rehearsed means of dealing with children's fear and revulsion at his disfigurement. But when he caught her eye, the moment was gone, replaced with his perfect smile.

"Now, where were we? Oh yes, the furniture was...."

Sandi hoped she might find another time to ask about the real cause of his loss but knew that time wasn't now. She turned her attention back to her notes, focusing on the details of the ancient home's restoration.

Archie paused and said quietly, "If these walls could talk." And then, "It means a lot to her, your interest."

Sandi tilted her head slightly and dimly glimpsed her own reflection next to Archie in the antique mirror over the dresser. "She is such a special lady."

His eye color was blue green, like the sea beyond the reef. *A handsome man*, Sandi thought.

"I'm grateful to you," he said, "for coming all this way to talk story. Her life—incredible, you know. The way it was back then. What really happened. Important stuff, and no one has taken the time before now." He put his hand to his brow in salute. "*Mahalo*, as we say."

"She insisted I must visit The Mission House on Front Street."

Archie smiled wistfully and glanced out the window. "A sentimental journey. She and my great-grandfather were married right here. Downstairs. Sometimes she sits here and, by the look in her eyes, I think she can almost see him as he was."

"Your great-grandfather? She hasn't told me—"

"She likes everything to be orderly. With her, it's got to be first things first. You may have noticed."

"Where does Lahaina fit in?"

"She would say, 'I can't tell you the end before the beginning.' It's her story, you know." Archie motioned toward the dark, burled-walnut baby cradle. "So, back to furniture. Made locally, mostly. Koa wood, but a few small pieces are English and were shipped around the Horn."

* * * *

Victorian England

For the occasion of Kaiulani's birthday celebration, she and Annie and Hannah were back at Sundown. Clive returned from school. The number of celebrants neared a hundred as the party included Liverpool dignitaries, the Davies' Southport neighbors, and the families of Theo's business associates.

Sundown was so ablaze with lights it appeared to be completely misnamed. From the gas lamps lining the drive to the flaming torches in the garden, every corner of the estate shone like a lantern.

There had already been dancing in the main salon and strolls in the rose garden. The butler had just summoned the guests to a midnight supper when Theo Davies approached Kaiulani and touched her elbow.

"A messenger with a present for you, my dear," he said. "The train from London was delayed, but he had explicit orders to be here on your birthday, and he's arrived with just five minutes to spare. I'm sorry to take you from your guests but think we should honor his integrity, don't you?"

What could this mean? For a fleeting moment, Kaiulani's heart raced. She imagined Papa Archie arriving from home as a surprise, but quickly put that thought away as impossible.

Theo escorted her to the entry to the library, asking if he could remain, as he had something to share with her after the present.

The little man waiting beside the floor-to-ceiling oak shelves was not anyone Kaiulani recognized. He blinked watery eyes at her from behind round spectacles and tapped a gold pocket watch against the palm of his other hand. On the table in front of him was a package done up in heavy brown paper and wrapped with twine.

The slightly built courier bobbed his head agreeably as Kaiulani entered. "Ah, Your Highness. I promised to make this delivery without fail. Now I can give him a good report. I know it will please him."

"I'm sorry, Mister...Mister...?"

"Bain. James Bain," the diminutive man supplied.

"And to whom was this promise given?"

Bain's smile made his face crinkle from the corners of his mouth to the recesses of his eyes. Even his ears lifted with delight. "I think I should let the parcel speak for itself," he said, pushing the package across the table.

It was addressed:

HRH Kaiulani
Sundown
Hesketh Park
Liverpool

Theo stepped forward and snipped the twine with his scrimshaw-handled pocketknife before moving back to let Kaiulani unfold the wrapping.

A heap of books and the aromatic fragrance of new leather tumbled out. Clothed in matching green bindings were copies of *Treasure Island, Kidnapped, The New Arabian Nights,* and *The Merry Men*—all by Robert Louis Stevenson.

Beneath the title, each cover was embossed with gold foil:

HRH Kaiulani
From
R.L.S.

"Oh!" Kaiulani exclaimed, clapping her hands. "He remembered. I only mentioned once the titles I did not own, and here they are! But how—"

"A mystery easily explained, Your Highness," Bain asserted. "I have the honor to be Mister Stevenson's favored bookseller in London. He enlists me when he has a special binding request, as in this instance. In his letter of last April Mister Stevenson was very explicit as to his directions, which is why I came in person."

As she opened the cover of *Treasure Island,* Kaiulani's thoughts flew back across the intervening months. April! Her dear author friend had planned this moment before Kaiulani had even left Hawaii! In that instant she prayed for him, prayed that anticipating this surprise had given him as much pleasure as she had received from it.

Bain presented her with a letter with the distinct handwriting of Stevenson. "I thought perhaps Mr. Stevenson's letter of instruction to me might also give you pleasure."

Kaiulani opened the envelope and scanned the page.

April 1889—Honolulu

Dear Mr. Bain,

This is most important to me. I wish to get Treasure Island, Kidnapped, The Arabian Nights (1ˢᵗ series), and The Merry Men (illustrated) and have them bound for me as you know how and no man better, and to have on the binding of each of these, these words:

HRH Kaiulani
From
R.L.S.

elegantly imprinted. The little lady in question is the Princess of Hawaii—a pretty and engaging Royal Princess. As soon as you get the books bound, they are to be delivered to Her Royal Highness for her birthday, 16, October, c/o Mr. Theo Davies Esq. Sundown, Hesketh Park, Liverpool.

Pray give this trivial affair (to which I attach so much importance) your kind attention...

R. L. Stevenson

Kaiulani's eyes brimmed as she folded the letter and pressed it to her heart. "Thank you, sir. As we would say at home, *Mahalo.*"

Bain produced a business card from a waistcoat pocket and handed it to Kaiulani with a flourish. "Number One, Haymarket," he said proudly. "Perhaps you'd care to visit when your travel takes you to the capital."

"Thank you, sir," she replied. "You're very kind. More than kind. Won't you please stay to supper?"

"I mustn't impose," Bain protested.

"Not at all, not at all!" Theo replied. "Delighted to have you. I believe you saw the dining room on your way here? Splendid. We'll be along directly."

Kaiulani turned each volume over in her hands, stroking the fine leather and admiring the painstaking workmanship. When she lifted her eyes, she saw Theo Davies regarding her strangely. Was that a hint of sadness in his expression?

"Kaiulani," he said, "I very much hate to introduce any unpleasant note into your celebration."

"What is it? Not Papa? Is he well?"

Theo made placating gestures with his hands. "Nothing like that, I promise. Nothing personal. This is news of a—more of an affair of state. Let me explain." Theo produced a folded sheaf of paper from an envelope. "This came by the same carriage that brought Mister

Bain. I've received advance notice by cable from my New York office of a story that has just appeared in *The New York Times*. It concerns you, my dear. Once *The Times* of London gets wind of it, they will certainly seek a statement from you. I didn't want you to be unprepared. Journalists can be such *vipers* in the way they strike."

"Please tell me the news," Kaiulani said calmly.

"The American Secretary of State is calling for a Pan-American Union. An alliance of North and South American nations to lower trade barriers and provide for common defense."

Kaiulani strained to see the connection. "But what has this to do with me?"

Theo was grim as he replied. "As part of his speech, the secretary mentions Hawaii. He says specifically that Hawaii has much more in common with—" And here Theo read from the file: "'More in common with the vigorous, young democracies than with tired, outmoded, and corrupt monarchies.'" Theo paused to let the princess digest the implications.

"He is aligning himself with the Reform Party and against the king," she said.

"He is signaling that President Benjamin Harrison will back the rebels if Thurston leads a revolt against your uncle," Theo concluded bluntly.

"I know so little about affairs of state. I wish I were better informed, better educated. What must I do? What should I say?"

"If any newspaperman dares confront you tonight, you must say only that you will have a prepared statement to issue tomorrow. That will give us time to frame a proper response. I'm very sorry, but I could not let you be taken unawares."

"Thank you," Kaiulani said. "Please don't delay supper further. Offer some excuse for me. I'll be along soon. I just need to think."

Theo nodded and silently left.

Kaiulani sat in a chair beside the library table, deep in thought. She retrieved the copy of *Kidnapped* and turned it over in her hands beneath the green globe of the oil lamp. So it was true. The United States would swallow up Hawaii and spit out King David like a papaya seed. Could this force be resisted? Should she appeal to those in America who seemed friendly to the monarchy? Or should she appeal to Queen Victoria—one royal family desiring aid from another?

The library door creaked open, and Clive entered. "I'm sorry," he said. "I came looking for you. When Father spoke, I—I'm afraid I overheard it all."

Kaiulani nodded. Soon everyone would know. Most would not care what happened to a tiny island kingdom half a world away.

"But I would care. I *do* care," Clive said fervently.

Kaiulani didn't realize she had voiced her thoughts aloud.

Kneeling beside her, Clive took both her hands in his. "Please, I offer you my services. More than that, I offer you myself. I want to be your protector. I'll stand beside you. Fight beside you. Die for you, if need be."

The princess shook her head. Retrieving one hand from his grasp she laid it on his cheek. "Dear Clive, I cannot agree, cannot lead you on. I cannot be to you what you want me to be. Please understand. As Kaiulani Cleghorn, I care for you very much."

Clive brightened measurably at those words and his breath quickened, but Kaiulani saw him deflate just as suddenly with her next words.

"But as Her Royal Highness Victoria Kaiulani," she said, "my life is not my own. I may be asked, for the good of *Hawaii Nei,* to make a marriage of state. Something to save the kingdom. Something to save my people. I cannot promise you anything, or even let you hope."

Chapter Eight

. . . .

The crisp autumn stirred Blenheim's blood as Kaiulani led him from the barn. Head up, he pranced on the cobbles of the yard and snorted in the frosty morning air.

A western saddle, shipped from Hawaii by King Kalakaua for Kaiulani's birthday, was heavy on the big hunter's back. Still her weight, combined with that of the rig, did not amount to that of a man. Dressed in a riding skirt and tall boots, Kaiulani mounted and sat astride Blenheim as if ready for a cattle drive on the Parker Ranch.

Clive hurried from the house and called to her, "Kaiulani! Wait! I'll come with you."

She waved and mouthed the words, "NO, THANKS!" Then, as Clive watched with his hands hanging limply at his sides, she gave Blenheim his head and never looked back.

Kaiulani never felt as happy or free as she did on the back of the hunter. The cold tore at her face, stinging her cheeks. Her hair tumbled down her back, a tangle of curls in the bitter breeze.

As if the horse had some memory of her pleasure as his rider, he tore toward the rock wall and jumped it with ease. This time Kaiulani did not pull up or give any sign that she was finished. Blenheim galloped cross-country, leaping over hedges and fences for another mile. At last Kaiulani cued him into a gentle lope and reined him to a stop beneath the copse of leafless plane trees.

Blenheim's steamy breath matched hers. She leaned forward and stroked his muscled neck. *"Mahalo.* Good boy," she crooned. "I'll take you home to *Hawaii Nei* one day. We'll see if you have cow sense as well as speed."

Relaxed in the saddle, Kaiulani surveyed hedgerow pastures bisected by muddy lanes and stone walls. In the distance lay Hesketh Park and the great mansion of Sundown.

Kaiulani spoke quietly. Blenheim's ears turned at the sound of her voice. "I could be happy here for the rest of my life if, every day, I could fly across the countryside on your back." She patted him, then held her gloved hand to her nose and inhaled the tangy scent of his lather. "Who am I fooling?" She laughed. "What sort of English gentlewoman loves the smell of a horse? But I do. I confess to you, dear Blenheim, I do love the aroma of a horse barn too."

With a cluck of her tongue she urged him forward. With perfect precision she opened the gate and passed through to the lane. Drained now of excess energy, Blenheim headed home at a slow walk. The miles they had traversed in minutes took an hour or more on returning. The horse was cool and calm when, at last, Kaiulani rode into the yard and dismounted. Suggins tugged his cap and took his reins. "Never see this big fella so happy as when you ride him out, Miss Kaiulani."

Theo Davies was waiting for her when she returned, contented, to the house. Hannah and Annie were playing chess before the great roaring fire. They looked up only briefly, then returned to their game.

Theo called Kaiulani into his study. "Good ride?" He motioned for her to sit in the burgundy wingback chair before his desk.

"He is the best horse—most honest—I've ever ridden."

"He's yours. You've won his heart as no other."

"You think he'd be happy in Hawaii?"

Theo did not answer but slid a handwritten document across the blotter to her. "Touching on the matter we discussed last night, I have written out a statement for you in case you are asked about the events concerning the Hawaiian monarchy and the United States."

Kaiulani removed her gloves and scanned the paper. "Yes. Yes, of course. We are a sovereign nation. No other government may dictate our laws or, well, I don't really understand it all."

"No need. Read it. Commit the text to memory. If you are asked, this contains everything you should say in reply." Theo passed a silver tray with a letter on it. "From your uncle, the king. It came in the morning post."

"Oh! From Papa Moi! Only a day late for my birthday."

Theo's mouth turned up at the corners, but his eyes did not smile. "Perhaps the king has some instruction for you—for your statements to the press."

She broke the red wax seal, pulled out the letter, and scanned it quickly. "Asking me about school and such. Very cheerful. I'll have to write him." And then her smile faltered as a written warning, inscribed in the Hawaiian language, leapt off the page. Kaiulani recognized the Scripture in Psalm 55:12: "*No ka mea, aole he enemi, ka i hoino mai ia'u; Ina pela hiki no...*"

Kiulani lowered the letter without telling Theo about her uncle's terrifying words. "...and that's all."

"What is it, Kaiulani?" Theo's gaze bored into her. "Is everything all right?"

"Nothing at all." She laid the letter down face up on the desk, certain that Theo could not read her native language. He glanced at it. She touched her forehead, feigning a headache. "I–I've been in the cold air all morning and suddenly my head—"

Picking up the correspondence, she excused herself and hurried up the stairs to her room. On the settee in her bedroom, she again scanned her uncle's letter. The warning of the psalm continued with a personal note in Hawaiian. The king's message sent a chill through her: *"You must be on guard against certain enemies I do not feel free to name in writing...."*

* * * *

1973

"You're watching *TV Two, Eyewitness News at Ten,* with B.J. Sams and Bob Basso. Les Keiter, Sports."

Sandi stood at the Pioneer Inn's bar, a nearly untouched Joe's Special on the counter before her, sweating with condensation. The drink was a secret recipe, but at first taste, Sandi figured a principle ingredient must be Old Spice aftershave. She wasn't much of a drinker anyway, but the newsbreak appearing in intermittent rolls on the ancient black-and-white television above the bar made her forget about it completely.

The bar wasn't too busy, but against the waves crashing against the breakwater, the volume wasn't very high. Sandi had to strain to hear the newsman's voice: "Taken yesterday afternoon, these pictures come to you courtesy of the press pool assembled at Clark Air

Base, Luzon, the Philippines. There you can see the first of four jets carrying American prisoners of war, released just a few days ago from prisons in North Viet Nam."

The picture changed then to a podium in front of an airplane as an officer in full dress naval uniform walked up and began to speak. A line of text displayed under his face read: *Captain Jeremiah A. Denton, Navy, first American Released*. His voice was thick with emotion. "We are honored to have the opportunity to serve our country under difficult circumstances. We are profoundly grateful to our Commander in Chief and to our nation this day. God bless America."

The newscaster appeared on screen again. "Captain Denton has been in captivity for nearly eight years after his aircraft was shot down into the Ma River in July of sixty-five."

Next off the plane was Lieutenant Commander Everett Alvarez, Junior, the first American pilot shot down over Viet Nam, held in captivity for eight and a half years.

"Doctors at the base hospital said the men all appeared in 'reasonable condition,' though each was very excited about his first dinner on friendly ground. A dietician preparing the food said the most popular items were steak, eggs, and ice cream."

Tears welled in Sandi's eyes. The news was so good for so many people tonight, and she really was happy for them. It just wasn't good news for her.

Someone approached the bar at her left elbow, but she didn't want to show her tears, so she refused to turn. A moment later a man's voice, soft and gentle, spoke, and Sandi recognized it as that of Archie Kalakaua.

"It's great to see these guys free, isn't it?" he asked.

She nodded but kept her eyes fixed on the wavering images on the screen.

"I was lucky," he continued. "I just lost my hand and one eye. These guys lost years of their lives."

Sandi reached for a stack of cocktail napkins and grabbed a few to dab her eyes.

"Tears of joy?" Archie asked.

"Auntie Hannah didn't tell you about me—my situation?" Sandi asked.

Archie laughed. "Did she tell you about me before we met? Auntie Hannah's no gossip. You tell her something in secret, that's the way it stays. How about you tell me?"

At the renewed mention of the POWs, Sandi did feel a need to talk to someone about it all...about John. Especially to someone who had been there himself.

"My husband, John, was fourth infantry. In March of sixty-nine, his company was ambushed. Someplace called Kontum?" She paused as though he might agree he'd heard of the place but continued when she realized how silly the notion was—like a tourist asking, "So you're from California? Do you know so-and-so?"

"Anyway, they were relocating villagers away from combat zones. Their trucks hit mines along the road, and they were fired on from a hill across the river. They fought them off quickly, but my husband was wounded. They called for a helicopter evacuation for him and a few others.

"Turns out the VC hadn't been run off after all; they were just hoping to lure in more targets. When the helicopters came in, a new attack came from right next to them—the jungle on their side of the river. Both helicopters were shot down with rockets, and the scene was overrun by foot soldiers. By then, John was one of the few left alive. They dragged him off into the jungle."

Archie was stunned. "H–how do you know all this? I mean, who survived to—"

"A friend of his from his platoon was pinned under a truck after the second attack. They must've thought he was dead, or they'd have taken him too, but in any event, he saw it all. They swept through, killed the villagers—children too. Shot anyone who tried to run, bayoneted those too injured to be of use to them. A few, like John, are still out there somewhere."

"I'm so sorry, Sandi," Archie said genuinely, patting her shoulder.

But Sandi didn't want to hear condolences, not yet. As long as John didn't turn up on any list, dead or alive, there was reason to hope. She ignored Archie's words as though he hadn't said anything. "Missing in action, but not an official POW. But that's the way it is in South Viet Nam, I guess. My dad has a friend in the State Department who says that the camps in South Viet Nam are a lot less organized. There's some speculation that the North may not even know how many more prisoners they have down there.

"Anyway, look at me, going on like I know what I'm talking about. What about you, Archie? You've been there. You know what it's really like. Whenever John wrote, I always got the feeling he was trying to shield me from how bad it was. How did you get your injuries?"

It was Archie's turn to stare at the television, then, as if contemplating how much he should share. *Or maybe he's remembering,* Sandi thought.

After a long pause he said, "Ah, well. Nothing as dramatic as all that. Wrong place, wrong time is all. Happened to a lot of us."

As he stared up at the fuzzy picture rolling the newscast credits, Sandi scrutinized the right side of his face. From this angle, he certainly was handsome, and she wondered if he intentionally approached people on their left to keep his good side toward them.

In the awkward silence that followed, Sandi thought of the huge number of severely wounded Americans who were home or would be soon—over a hundred thousand so far. How she would rather have John back even missing one hand and one eye, than not at all.

She took a big swig of the now-watery drink and patted Archie on his shoulder, as he'd done for her. "Thanks for listening," she said. "I think I'll hit the hay."

Archie nodded without looking toward her, but she saw him turn to watch her leave the room.

* * * *

Victorian England, December 1890

The train from Great Harrowden School for Girls to London was old and drafty. The Midland Railroad professed to operate more frequent services by having fewer cars to each train. In practice, MR's penny-pinching ways meant poor maintenance and frequent breakdowns.

Annie slept against Kaiulani's shoulder as the misty countryside rolled by. Hannah, nursing a sniffle, read Jane Austen's novel *Emma* to pass the time. The journey was interrupted by whistle stops at every small village along the way from Northamptonshire.

As the train track curved away ahead of them, Kaiulani saw the engine's once-cherished paint scheme of Brunswick green and gold covered in soot and streaked with oil. The carriages, once stylish in chocolate and cream, were now a uniform muddy gray.

The railroad's coat-of-arms was displayed on a chipped, faded plaque hanging over the door. Most of the heraldic emblems were obscured, but the wyvern surmounting the crest was still evident, a cone of flames erupting from the dragon's mouth.

Kaiulani, grateful for the warmth of her sister against her, adjusted the wool scarf around her throat. Whatever heating properties the railroad's mascot possessed did not translate into wintertime comfort for the passengers.

Hannah lowered the book and peered at Kaiulani. "Christmas. Think of the beach in Ainahau right now."

Kaiulani did not smile. "Surfing. Warm sky. Warm water. Warm sand."

"Whales and *luaus.*"

"Parties beneath the banyan tree." Kaiulani closed her eyes and sighed with the memory. "Warm."

"As we three exiles travel the world, the only place we wish to be is half a world away from us." Hannah stared over Kaiulani's shoulder as the door to the train car opened and closed, and a blast of cold wind whipped past. "Don't look now," Hannah warned as she quickly buried her face in the novel.

"What?" Kaiulani turned to look and instantly regretted her curiosity.

Sauntering up the swaying aisle was Andrew Adams, recognizable, though swathed in layers of clothing with his bowler hat shoved down low over his ears. He was followed by a similarly dressed, though heftier young man of red cheeks, pink ears, and shining nose.

The university students wore matching school ties of broad navy stripes set apart by narrow crimson lines.

"Did he see you?" Hannah did not look up.

"Afraid so." Kaiulani managed a feeble smile at their archenemy.

Suddenly Andrew's smirking face intruded on their space. "Well, well, my three little maids from school."

Hannah sniffed. The smell of whiskey was on his breath. "And good day to you too, Andrew. Ever the gentleman, we see."

"What is the native greeting?" He was slightly drunk. He snapped his gloved fingers. "*Aloha.* George, meet Her Highness, the Royal Princess Kaiulani, and companions."

George swayed into a sideways bow and belched softly. His eyes were slightly unfocused.

"*Aloha,*" Kaiulani replied, not meeting Andrew's eyes. She stared at his necktie instead.

"Her Royal Highness, Princess Kaiulani, riding coach along with the common folk." Andrew took a silver flask from his pocket and unscrewed the lid. "A little something to keep off the chill?" He pretended to offer a swig to the scowling girls. With a shrug, he took a deep swallow and smacked his lips, then passed the container to George, who took a long pull. "London for Christmas break? I hear the great princess Kaiulani now answers to her English cognomen. Victoria is it? Vicky?"

Hannah raised the book higher in an attempt to ignore him.

Kaiulani lifted her chin and stared out the window at a line of winter-blasted elms. "At school I am Vicky. But among my close friends from home I remain Kaiulani."

Andrew slurred as the whiskey took hold. "School—or a savage island? That's the choice? Well, let me be the first in the greater civilized world to greet you, Vicky." He gave the end of his tie a flick. "London, King's College, salutes you."

The blue-uniformed conductor passing by gave Andrew a disapproving look. "Rugby. Next station stop is Rugby. Rugby, your next stop."

Kaiulani exhaled loudly. "You're looking well, Andrew. How is Mister Adams, your father?"

"And how is the king, your uncle? Sober yet?" Andrew laughed coarsely. Facing George, he lifted his eyebrows in an attempt to convey the subtle sarcasm of his remark. Andrew failed when his friend merely stood blinking and repeating, *"Alo-ah? Alo-hah?"*

Kaiulani pressed her lips together in an attempt to remain civil. "The Kingdom of *Hawaii Nei* still lives."

Andrew straightened, then rocked a bit with the motion of the train. "Mister Stevenson's letters have been filled with sad news—so sad—government chaos in Hawaii. It seems your uncle, the king, is losing his fight to maintain control...of his drinking."

Hannah snapped, "Like anyone else we know? It's Christmas, you blaggard. Can you not wish us well and be on your way?"

Andrew studied the feather in Kaiulani's hat. "How does one say Merry Christmas in your native tongue?"

Without opening her eyes, Annie replied, *"Mele Kalikimaka."*

Andrew pretended to write it down on his glove. "Can you spell that?"

Kaiulani answered Hannah quietly, "He's drunk. Pay him no mind. To argue with a drunkard is to argue with a howling dog. He has put a thief in his mouth to steal away his brains."

Andrew looked from one girl to the next. "Eh? What was that?"

Kaiulani smiled grimly. "I pray Mister Stevenson's health is improved. Now, Mister Adams, we bid you *adieu*."

He snorted. "*Adieu*? French. Not *Aloha*? *Aloha*. Love. Isn't that the meaning? Charming. Charming."

Hannah would not be deterred. "Perhaps this barbarian *haole* will repent and take the pledge and foreswear drink."

Andrew lifted his hat and let it drop on his head. "Take the pledge?" He made the sign of the cross. "Perhaps when the king of Hawaii takes the pledge. And with that, I bid you *Aloha*! Come, George." Andrew staggered down the length of the aisle, grasping for support at every alternate seat back.

George, to his credit, lifted his hat as a final polite gesture upon exiting. The proper effect was lost when the wind snatched it from his hand and sent it swirling into the Midlands countryside.

Chapter Nine

. . . .

Christmas in London!

Kaiulani studied the swirling snowflakes glimpsed through the window of their fourth-floor suite. She looked up from the book of Christina Rossetti's verse open on her lap. The poet's words were meant to evoke the birth of Jesus in Judea. The description of this time of year could have been drawn from the English countryside:

In the bleak midwinter, frosty wind made moan,
earth stood hard as iron, water like a stone;
snow had fallen, snow on snow, snow on snow,
in the bleak midwinter, long ago.[11]

It was so much easier to enjoy the poetry while seated in the warm, comfortable drawing room of the Savoy! A coal fire blazed cheerfully on the hearth. Beside the princess, on a round ebony-and-mother-of-pearl-inlaid table, was a pot of tea, next to a three-tiered silver tray of cakes. Annie stood staring out at the snow-shrouded Thames, cup of Darjeeling in hand. Hannah nursed her cold in a barrel-backed armchair drawn close to the fire, reading Bram Stoker's new novel, *The Snake's Pass*. Stoker's work told of the romance of a pair of tormented lovers—one Irish and the other British.

The Savoy had only opened six months earlier. It was not only the newest hotel in London but by far the most fashionable, the most marveled over by European society.

Their holiday stay was a gift from Kaiulani's English foster-father, Theo Davies.

This London interlude was also a family reunion of sorts. Kaiulani's cousin, Prince David Kawanakoa Piikoi, called Koa, was staying in London for the season.

Kaiulani heard Koa speak in glowing terms about the design of the hotel: the modernity of its elevators; the elegant design of its cupola-topped towers; the practical efficiency of its glazed brickwork that resisted staining by London's soot.

Kaiulani agreed with Koa's assessment of the Savoy's wonders but felt he had missed the most important. The elaborate bathroom in the girls' suite was fitted out with marble fixtures and featured hot and cold running water.

The Savoy was also the first hotel anywhere to be completely lit with electric lights. The clerk who escorted Kaiulani's party to their rooms had insisted on snapping on the switches in every chamber, while patiently explaining that it was not dangerous. "Every bit as safe as gaslights," he said.

Five minutes following that tour, the porter who delivered their luggage carried out an identical performance.

After he left, Hannah remarked to Kaiulani, "You don't have the heart to spoil their fun, do you?"

Some years earlier Kaiulani had herself thrown the switch that ignited Honolulu's first electric illumination.

Kaiulani shrugged and smiled wryly. "They expect barbarians

such as we are to be impressed with their magic fire. Why disappoint them?"

Brushing a couple of gingerbread crumbs from the bodice of her crimson, high-waisted afternoon dress, Kaiulani savored the recollection. She straightened her lace-trimmed sleeves and retrieved her volume.

Our God, heaven cannot hold him, nor earth sustain;
heaven and earth shall flee away when he comes to reign.
In the bleak midwinter a stable-place sufficed
the Lord God Almighty, Jesus Christ.[12]

There was a tap at the door. Turning from the window to answer it, Annie admitted Prince Koa and his friend, Clive Davies, Theo's son.

Koa had grown into a fine-looking man in his twenties. From being a broad-faced youngster, he was now an elegant figure sporting a neatly trimmed handlebar moustache.

"Ladies," he said as he entered with his arms full of parcels, "I have gifts."

Though rumors had circulated around *Hawaii Nei* for years that Koa and Kaiulani were the perfect royal match, his gaze immediately sought Hannah's. That was as it should be, Kaiulani reflected. Koa would always be her good and true friend and cousin, but she could not imagine being in love with him.

Clive, on the other hand, had matured into a handsome man. He had a broad forehead, a strong jaw, and wavy chestnut hair. The breadth of his shoulders and the narrowness of his trim waist were both set off by the belted Norfolk jacket he wore.

Koa might look dapper, but in Kaiulani's opinion, he was a poor stick next to Clive.

"*Aloha,* Clive," Kaiulani said.

"Princess," he replied. "Miss Hannah. Miss Annie."

Koa distributed a wrapped package to each of the young women, then accepted a pastry from the tray. He took a bite, getting powdered sugar in his moustache.

"Shall we open these now?" Annie asked.

Koa shook his head. "Big present first. Clive, you may do the honors."

How very English Koa's English sounds, Kaiulani thought. *I wonder if I will have a British accent one day.*

From an inside jacket pocket Clive produced an envelope, which he delivered to Kaiulani with a flourish. "Theatre tickets," he explained. "My father thinks of everything. May I have the privilege of being your escort for the evening, Princess?"

Hannah gestured at the snow falling heavier than ever. "Tonight?"

"Not to worry," Clive reassured her. "*The Gondoliers.* Next door at the Savoy Theatre. For all of us."

Annie poured Clive a cup of tea and drew another chair up next to Hannah's, all the time chattering happily about how excited she was to see the new Gilbert and Sullivan production.

Standing next to Kaiulani, Koa murmured, "May I speak with you for a moment, privately?"

While Annie, Hannah, and Clive compared notes on reviews of the new operetta—how brilliant it was, how certain to run for months and months—Koa and Kaiulani withdrew to the opposite corner of the drawing room.

"I have had a…how shall I put this? A cryptic letter from our uncle, His Majesty."

Kaiulani nodded slowly, her liquid brown eyes drinking in the worry imprinted on Koa's features. "As have I," she admitted. "I have not shared it with anyone—not even Hannah. I'm grateful to have you to talk to about it."

Koa raised his eyebrows. "Does his note to you speak of 'being on guard against unnamed enemies'?"

"Exactly the same. But what does he mean? If Papa Moi means Thurston and the reformers, why send a warning to us in England?"

"My question as well. I wrote him, asking him to clarify. How can we be on guard if we don't know whom to guard against? Not that I am afraid for myself," Koa asserted, "but you, Princess. You are—you stand nearer the throne than I. We must see that you are kept safe."

Kaiulani felt the corners of her mouth crinkle. Koa was being so serious. "Surely you don't think someone will storm the walls at Great Harrowden and carry me away captive?"

"No," Koa admitted. "But the king—and you—may have enemies in England as well as at home. What if the reason he gave no names was for fear someone you trusted would find the letter and read it?"

Suddenly Kaiulani had a horrifying thought: "He cannot mean members of the British government?"

Koa replied, "Your guardian, Theo Davies, is well connected to the British government and commerce between England and home. He would have heard whispers."

Her gaze shot across the room to Clive. "Theo Davies has been so kind to us. And you know Clive well. Like father, like son, I think. My father trusts Theo. You trust Clive."

"Like a brother," Koa concurred. "What's more, Clive is deeply in love with you, Kaiulani."

The princess was both shocked and pleased. She blinked at Koa. "Clive? In love with me?"

Koa laughed. "Wait! I wasn't supposed to say that. Please don't mention it—especially not to Hannah or Annie! Clive would be mortified."

"So the Davies hope to continue to be the protectors of the future monarchy of Hawaii," Kaiulani teased.

"Close protectors, perhaps." Koa offered a rueful, lopsided grin that made his moustache appear comical. "I am certain Clive Davies would like to be even more than a protector to the future queen of Hawaii." Then, resuming his older-brother-to-younger-sister attitude he suggested, "Just be careful, Kaiulani. Be guarded in whom you trust with your secret thoughts. Our uncle, the king, is concerned for our safety. Your father would want you to remember that, even here, the things of *Hawaii Nei* still touch us."

Noticing how Clive devoured her with his eyes, Kaiulani admitted to herself what a pleasant warmth his attention sent through her. She reflected that young Clive had long been the subject of his father's pride and conversation when Theo visited her father in Honolulu. Had the elder Davies had Kaiulani in mind as a possible match for Clive even then?

* * * *

Top hats and elegant evening dresses thronged through the entrance of the Savoy Theatre to attend the latest Gilbert and Sullivan operetta. The plush red lobby was crowded with members of London society shedding exotic fur wraps, top coats, and cashmere scarves at the coat check. Bottles of champagne and trays of caviar seemed to float above the theatregoers en route to the wealthy and privileged.

Swept along by the elegant current, Kaiulani and her friends climbed a flight of stairs to a corridor of doors that opened to private boxes. She clung tightly to Clive's arm. Annie and Hannah each held Koa's arm. The scent of bay rum and French perfumes filled the air like aroma of *pikake* blooms on a summer night at home.

Heads turned to stare openly as Kaiulani passed. Women whispered to one another from behind silk fans. Kaiulani heard her name as the crowds caught wind of her presence. "Princess Victoria Kaiulani."

Hannah leaned forward and whispered, "Don't look now. Our old friend Nanki-Poo is staring at you."

Kaiulani raised her eyes to see Andrew Adams in the midst of the crush. He was gazing appreciatively at her. Bowing slightly, he gave an almost imperceptible nod of approval at her royal blue velvet evening gown. She looked away quickly, as if she had not seen him.

His voice, and the curious questions of his female companion, followed her. "Second in line to the throne of the Sandwich Islands..."

"A lovely creature."

"That's her cousin Koa. Attending school at Cambridge, I think."

The woman's words seemed loud and harsh. "Barbaric culture."

Andrew, perhaps contrite after his last meeting with the princess, replied, "R. L. Stevenson writes that they are lovely, gentle folk. Christians, for the most part."

The woman scoffed, "Don't forget what they did to Captain Cook...and other victims."

"A different island than Princess Kaiulani's home."

The woman said too loudly, "They say the king, her uncle, is addicted to drink, and the monarchy may fall due to his excesses."

With effort, Kaiulani managed to avoid eye contact with Andrew. Color climbed to her face as others overheard Andrew's conversation with his woman friend.

Beside Andrew a second male voice chimed in, "Pretty thing, this princess. Who's with her? Is that Theo Davies' son? Clive? You and Clive were both at Eton, weren't you?"

"Eton. Yes," Andrew answered, "Clive's father is her guardian in Britain. He has an importing business in the South Seas."

Overhearing the mention of his name, Clive searched the crowd for the source. Spotting Andrew, he smiled and waved, then leaned close to Kaiulani's ear. "An old schoolmate of mine. Come on, then. He's seen me. You'll have to be introduced. He's coming our way."

"We know this fellow and—" Hannah started to protest but fell mute when Andrew stood before them.

Suddenly Kaiulani was face-to-face with Andrew. He was sober, at least. In the company of two other couples, Andrew allowed Clive to make introductions as though he had never met Kaiulani.

Clive seemed to know all the members of Andrew's party. He took charge of the introductions: "Her Royal Highness, Princess Victoria Kaiulani of Hawaii. Her cousin Koa and…"

Kailuani heard little after that. She felt Andrew's eyes fixed on her with some new appreciation.

Hannah spoke up indignantly. "We sailed from home on the same ship with Andrew."

Andrew replied, "Indeed, we did. We shared reading material as well. *Little Women*. Purely American novel. Surprisingly engaging."

Annie's normally cheerful tone was cool and reserved. "Imagine. Mister Adams had never heard of the American novelist, Louisa May Alcott."

Andrew managed a strained laugh. "It was quite good, actually."

His companion lowered her chin with a mocking smile. "Who would think any good novels could come out of America?"

Hannah's eyes narrowed, and Kaiulani heard her mutter, "Americans are barbarians too, are they?"

Andrew addressed Kaiulani. "We meet again. I am not sure exactly how to address you. Princess? Ah, well. It is good to see you."

Kaiulani replied regally, "Searching out new Gilbert and Sullivan roles to play, Andrew?"

Andrew ignored Kaiulani's swipe and addressed Clive. "So you're in town for the holidays?"

Clive observed the strained conversation between Andrew and Kaiulani. "I'll be staying here at the Savoy with Koa for a few days, then escorting the ladies home to Sundown. Koa and I are showing the ladies London. And you?"

Andrew answered, "Staying with Father till mid-January, then back to bachelor's quarters and school. Let's try to catch up before you leave, shall we? Roast beef at Simpson's? Tomorrow noon?"

"Agreed." Clive clapped Andrew on the shoulder. "Good to see you, old man. And all the lovely ladies as well. Cheers."

"Cheers."

Kaiulani's group took their places in the box opposite the vacant royal box reserved for members of Queen Victoria's family. The royal crest adorning the perch left no question about the lineage of the intended occupants.

Kaiulani raised her tortoiseshell opera glasses to search the shadowed royal box for some face related to her namesake. "It's empty." Kaiulani was disappointed. She had hoped to see Queen Victoria.

Clive leaned close to Kaiulani and whispered, "I heard that Prince Albert may be here tonight."

She acknowledged Clive's comment with a nod, even as she scanned the audience for another familiar face. Where was Andrew?

Excited voices blended in an unintelligible roar punctuated by the laughter that rose and fell above the crowd.

Kaiulani laid down the glasses and studied the programme. When she looked up again, Andrew and his companions were seated in the box beside the royal enclosure. His gaze was fixed on her, as though he had been waiting for her to look at him, expecting her to stare. Leaning his arm against the parapet, Andrew smiled and saluted her. He mouthed the words, Aloha, *Princess.*

She gasped and lowered the binoculars.

The house lights dimmed and the opening song of *The Gondoliers* began. Clive reached for Kaiulani's hand. She let him intertwine his fingers with hers.

Gingerly, she lifted the opera glasses once again and pretended to study the singers on the stage. Then she once more turned her view toward Andrew.

His face, clear and amused, came into focus. He smiled and winked at her, then with his open hand he tapped his heart, as if to say: *I'm smitten with you.*

Kaiulani fumbled and nearly dropped the glasses. The programme fluttered onto the floor. She vowed she would not look at him again.

> *"By a law of maiden's making,*
> *Accents of a heart that's aching,*
> *Even though that heart be breaking,*
> *Should by maiden be unsaid:*
> *Though they love with love exceeding,*
> *They must seem to be unheeding—*
> *Go ye then and do their pleading,*
> *Roses white and roses red!"* [13]

* * * *

As the applause died and the houselights came up, Clive leaned toward Kaiulani. "Let the others go on without us. A minute please, Kaiulani."

She lowered her eyes as their companions exited the box, laughing. "Clive, we'll lose them in the crowd."

He held tightly to her hand, compelling her to remain in her seat. "Not possible," he returned. "Supper at Simpson's. Just around the corner. Let them go. I have something I have to say."

"Please. Not now."

"When?" He studied her with intensity while Kaiulani sought to escape his scrutiny by letting her gaze rove over the emptying stalls.

"I don't know. Clive?" In that instant she raised her eyes and glanced across the theatre. Andrew Adams cast a last look her way before he vanished in the shadows.

Clive followed her glance, sighed, and sat back sullenly. "How well do you know Andrew?"

"I told you. We made the crossing together." The orchestra in the pit offered its final, crashing chord and received a smattering of applause from the handful of theatregoers who remained. "Why do you ask?"

Clive's face clouded. Almost to himself he muttered, "Maybe too well. Or, not well enough. Clearly."

"What do you mean?" She felt herself stiffen with resentment.

"I know him well. He's a bounder, Andrew is."

"I know enough. Arrogant and opinionated."

The conductor addressed the concertmaster, giving notes about corrections to the score.

Clive inhaled deeply, suddenly relieved. "Good. Good. I was afraid you were—"

"What? Afraid I was what?"

"In love with him."

"Why would you say such a thing?"

"The way you looked at him. And he had his eye on you most of the performance." Clive still held her hand in both of his, like a brother counseling his younger sister.

"Why would you care if I was…interested?"

Members of the orchestra were chatting amongst themselves amid the clatter of instruments being disassembled and the scrape of chairs pushing back from music stands.

Clive lifted her chin and searched her face. His expression was gentler now, less forceful. "Because I care about you. I don't want to see you hurt. You are dear to me. I think about you every day, you see."

The theatre was mostly empty. Kaiulani pretended to watch the remaining musicians in the orchestra pit as they packed up their instruments. The timpanist called loudly for a pint at the Coalhole Pub, to which the double bass responded: "Two!"

"You needn't worry about me, Clive."

"As any brother would worry about his...*sister*."

A swirl of tobacco smoke drifted into the box, having prowled up the stairs and through the crack under the door.

She smiled, grateful he had chosen such a platonic word to describe his feelings for her. "I've never had a big brother. Koa is the closest."

As if on cue, the door to the box sprang open and Koa's face peered into the compartment. "Hello! What are you two doing in here? They're going to close down the theatre." He gestured toward the vacant auditorium with the black cheroot in his hand. "Lock the doors, and we'll be trapped. Come on! Come on!"

"We were just catching up." Grateful for the interruption, Kaiulani stood and hurried out into the corridor. Locking arms with Hannah and Annie, she positioned herself securely between the two. Clive and Koa followed along to the restaurant.

* * * *

The Hawaiian party returned arm-in-arm from their night at the theatre. Their laughter and voices filled the hotel corridor with song.

> "Oh, 'tis a glorious thing, I ween,
> To be a regular Royal Queen!...

She'll drive about in a carriage and pair,
With the King on her left-hand side,
And a milk-white horse,
As a matter of course,
Whenever she wants to ride!
With beautiful silver shoes to wear
Upon her dainty feet;
With endless stocks
Of beautiful frocks
And as much as she wants to eat!" [14]

The evening came to a close with Clive and Koa sent off to their rooms. The three young women dressed for bed, then sat for hours before the glowing coal fire in the parlor of their suite.

A nearly empty box of candy was on Kaiulani's lap. She popped a chocolate caramel into her mouth. "'And as much as she wants to eat!'" she said and grinned.

Barefoot and clad in a long white cotton nightgown, Annie drew her legs up on the sofa. "Clive looked at no one but you, Kaiulani."

Hannah leaned her cheek upon her hand and studied the assortment of sweets. "But you were looking somewhere else. Someone else? Across the theatre."

Kaiulani attempted to dodge the subject. "And Koa's eyes were filled with you, Hannah."

Hannah laughed. "Koa always looks at every pretty girl. I happened to be the female closest to him tonight."

Annie said absently to Hannah, "Clive was holding Kaiulani's hand. I wondered if she noticed."

Kaiulani defended herself: "Clive is like a brother. Like Koa is. Brothers. That's all. True love is—"

"Belgian chocolate. Cream centers," Hannah opined.

Annie agreed. "Compared to plain brown bread."

Kaiulani laughed and took a dainty bite. "Exactly. Clive and Koa are brown bread to me."

"And Andrew Adams?' Hannah peered closely into her eyes. "The truth."

Kaiulani pawed through empty paper wrappers, holding up a final round bonbon. "Possibly the only chocolate-covered cherry in the box!"

"Or poison." Hannah raised her finger in warning.

Annie instructed, "Woman shall not live on chocolate alone."

"Who says?" Hannah bit a dark raspberry cream in half and savored the flavor. "Poor, poor Clive. Someone should let him in on the secret. Kaiulani's love for Clive is only brown bread. Alas."

Annie yawned and stood. The clock chimed twelve. Time for bed. "Kaiulani, why set your cap for a cad like Andrew Adams? When you have the cream of British manhood, and a Hawaiian prince, both at your feet? I am your sister, so I can tell you the truth." Annie tapped her temple and rolled her eyes to finish the point. A quick kiss on Kaiulani's cheek. "*Aloha nui loa.* Sweet dreams. I think I know who and what you will dream about tonight. And I don't think it will be brown bread."

Chapter Ten
....

1973

Sandi rose early and had a light breakfast of fresh pineapple and some unique fruit juice Joe was anxious and proud to have her try. He called it *pog*, and Sandi loved it. It was sweet and citrusy and buttery feeling on her tongue.

"Wonderful!" she raved. "What's in it?"

"Secret recipe." Joe smiled.

He seemed to be full of those.

"Well, I have to say I like this much better than your other secret recipe. How did you come up with it?"

The hurt look on Joe's face told Sandi she'd said something wrong. "Not my recipe," he said brusquely, dropping her check and walking away toward the kitchen.

For the next half hour, Sandi combed the narrow beach just south of the harbor for stones and shells. "Hey, *haole*!" somebody called from the breakwater, "Madame Pele don' like it when people steal sand from da islands."

More like the Madam Agricultural Inspector, she thought. Looking up and around, Sandi didn't see the person who gave her the advice, so she just called back, "Thanks, I'll keep it in mind."

With two pockets full of clean, dry stones, she retrieved the collection of Princess Kaiulani's papers from her room. It was too beautiful a day to work inside, so she sat at a red-topped picnic table under the banyan tree across from the hotel. After wiping the table down with a hotel hand towel, she began laying out the precious documents in piles that would help her make some sense of it all, each topped with a few stones as paperweights.

Should I do it chronologically, she wondered, *or maybe according to who she was writing to?* There was merit in both methods. If she read them strictly in order, she could get a good timeline of Kaiulani's travels from start to finish. She recognized short missives from Clive Davies and a stack of notes from Andrew Adams. But if she didn't read each collection of correspondence as a single conversation, she might miss or forget some point between letters.

To complicate matters, she had only the responses made to each of the letters sent from the Princess. Anything Kaiulani had mentioned in letters she wrote could only be inferred from what the recipient wrote back to her. *That and anything Auntie Hannah can fill in,* she thought.

The tabletop was full, and there were still more papers in the box. Sandi sighed and looked up from the stacks. She wondered how she could ever condense this into a single report. The *Fifty States History Project* was a noble idea to preserve personal recollections of amazing, eventful periods in time. But the lives of Auntie Hannah, Princess Kaiulani, and the people they knew could fill volumes—multiple series of volumes! How could she condense it into a hundred-page report?

As she thought it over, Sandi marveled at the tree providing the canopy of shade above her. When she first saw it and heard it was a single tree, she was dubious. But sure enough, sitting beneath it, she could trace all of the stalks back to a single giant trunk in the middle of the space. Over the decades since it was planted, vines had dropped from branches, taken root in the soil, and became their own sturdy trunks, supporting those branches as they reached farther and farther away from the center.

And the story of every human being who ever lived is a sprawling banyan tree. How can you capture it all?

"You read too much, *haole*!" A voice from behind her startled her out of the daydream.

"Archibald David La'amea Kalakaua," Sandi said, carefully pronouncing each Hawaiian syllable. "Was that you warning me about the wrath of Madame Pele?"

Archie walked around the table and touched his hand to his forehead, before sitting on the opposite bench. "At your service, miss. Always happy to help a *haole* stay curse-free." He rested his truncated left forearm on one of the stacks and Sandi couldn't help glancing at it. Without seeming offended, Archie asked, "I'm sorry, does it bother you?"

Sandi was taken aback. "No, of course not!" She reached her hand across the table and patted his forearm. "It's just that, whenever I see one of you guys who gave so much—"

"Ah, stop," Archie interrupted, leaning away. "I don't need your—"

"No, Archie, sympathy is much different from 'thank you.'"

He was stunned. It was a minute before he spoke again. "Well, thank *you*. You're right. We're either spit at or told how wrong it was for us to be sent there. But that's the first time I've heard a 'thanks' for what we did."

She smiled. "Well, it helps that I'm a military brat and that my husband believes in—" She paused, unsure whether she should use the past tense instead. *Not because he's dead!* screamed a voice inside her head, *but because the war is over.*

"Well, look," Archie said, sensing her hurt, "it's early yet. Auntie Hannah says you work too hard, and you need to see some *kohola*—the whales. I hear they're jumping big off Oneloa."

"Oh, good suggestion," Sandi said. "But I can't justify whale watching as a research expense."

"What expense?" Archie said proudly. "I got a nice sailboat I take tourists out on for cash. Thanks to a thankful U.S. government, I own her free and clear. Wind's free too." He was already getting up from the table as if the discussion was over. "And you know Auntie Hannah won't like it if you don't take her advice. Next group's going at ten. Be there at ten-till and bring a swimsuit. I got lots of snorkel gear on board. You can work off that *haole* tan!"

She thanked him and watched as he started across the park toward the marina. He jumped a low-hanging branch of the banyan tree like an energetic schoolboy, trotting away on the other side.

Sandi began collecting the documents from their little stacks, refiling them as best she could. *It will be a nice break,* she thought. *How long has it been since I've done anything but work and school—and worry? Besides, I may never get to come to Hawaii again!*

* * * *

Victorian England

Kaiulani's calendar was filled. Holiday invitations to London social events arrived each day with the morning post. This evening's soiree had been scheduled with the British Missionary Auxiliary at St. Mark's

Church, on North Audley Street. The main speaker was a preacher with the unlikely name of "Gipsy" Smith. Though Princess Kaiulani's attendance was minor on the bill, her appearance had been scheduled and advertised for weeks. She dreaded the encounter with five thousand devoted missionary supporters. Hannah had helped her prepare and practice a short speech to thank the attendees for their support of missionaries. All in all, Kaiulani was certain it would be a very dull event. Worse than that, she discovered she had not brought a dress appropriate to wear to the somber occasion. Her holiday wardrobe was a flower garden of velvets and silks.

"Black," Annie pronounced while scowling into the closet. "Of course you must wear black. Modest and demure. Anything else and it will be reported in the news that you have no sense of what is appropriate."

And so a shopping trip planned for Christmas gifts turned into a hunt for a gown Kaiulani hoped she would wear only once.

The expedition to Harrods Department store had begun with small expectations. First the trio of Hawaiians purchased a deadly dull dress, suitable for the missionary convention. Then, dividing up the cash, they set out in different directions to purchase gifts for one another and the Davies family.

After a morning wandering through every department of the famous department store, the round table in the hotel suite was stacked high with wrapped Christmas packages.

Kaiulani had intended to purchase only small gifts for the Christmas holiday. A pair of fur-lined gloves for her foster father, Theo Davies, had somehow become a wool overcoat. A single Sherlock Holmes novel for Clive had multiplied into a thirty-volume, green, leather-bound set of the works of Alexander Dumas. A bedroom clock for Mrs. Davies had become a bronze Junghans mantel clock with the cast figure of an elephant holding a gold-gilt eight-day timepiece in his trunk. Koa's gift was a new carved meerschaum pipe. Kaiulani bought Annie and Hannah matching peacock brooches.

Annie, exhausted by the excursion, dozed on the sofa.

Hannah towered over Annie's prone body. "She's dreaming of a peaceful Christmas day beneath the banyan tree."

Hands on her hips, Kaiulani considered the heap of gifts. "How will we get these to the Davies' house at Sundown?"

Hannah eyed the heavy, red-wrapped box containing Clive's novels. "You're crazy."

Kaiulani snapped, "After everything the Davies have done for us? They are our family in England."

Hannah sprawled on the wingback chair and poured herself a cup of tea. "After tonight you should donate the black dress to a funeral parlor. Everything else we bought looks like the dowry for the Queen of Sheba."

"Papa left it to me to represent the Kingdom of Hawaii and—"

"Such a gift. Thirty books. Clive will think you've fallen in love with him."

Kaiulani was indignant. "Clive?"

"What else would he think?"

"Papa sent money for Christmas shopping and—"

"And Clive is certainly in love with you."

"No more of that. Brown bread is brown bread."

"When does anyone buy brown bread thirty novels bound in green leather with gold gilt pages?"

"Papa's letter said I should purchase appropriate gifts. I represent Hawaiian monarchy. Pocket handkerchiefs would hardly impress anyone."

Hannah lifted a piece of chocolate cake to her lips. "The Davies would have been just as happy with a tea chest and a platter of dried fruit."

"I am not a kitchen maid."

"We've spent almost all of Papa Archie's allowance."

Kaiulani silenced Hannah with an angry glance. "We'll have to pack the gifts in a steamer trunk for the trip to Sundown."

"And where will we pack our clothes?"

"Or maybe two trunks."

A knock on the door interrupted their discussion. Hannah washed down her cake with a swig of tea. "I'll get it."

While Kaiulani laid out the black dress, Hannah threw open the door. A bellman bowed deeply. "A package for Your Highness." He passed a gift-wrapped, book-sized package to Hannah.

"No message. Who from?"

The man answered, "A young gentleman in the lobby asked me to bring this up and put it in the hands of Princess Victoria Kaiulani and no one else. I presume you are—?"

"Well, then, thank you." Hannah winked at Kaiulani over her shoulder. She tipped the fellow a shilling, then brought the package to Kaiulani. "You heard it. For Kaiulani and no other."

Kaiulani shook the package. "If it feels like a book and is the size of a book…" She tore away the wrapping, revealing the familiar cover.

With one voice she and Hannah cried, *"Little Women!"*

Then the two exchanged a look. Hannah said quietly, "So."

"Andrew." Kaiulani's heart beat faster. Her knees felt weak. An envelope protruded from the pages of the book.

Hannah pulled it out and opened it, scanning the masculine handwriting on the sheet of linen stationery.

"What does he say?"

A sly smile played on Hannah's lips. "You should sit down, Kaiulani."

Kaiulani sank to the chair.

Hannah read aloud.

"Princess Victoria Kaiulani,

Herewith, and with gratitude, I return to you my favorite novel: Little Women. *How could I have gone my entire life and never read this masterpiece?*

It could only be fate that we met again last night. I have had little sleep since my shameful behavior toward you on the train. I beg your forgiveness. I would do so on bended knee if only I might see you again face-to-face.

A mutual friend of ours has come into town and told me a most impressive story about a beautiful young woman who saved his life last summer. By way of his thanks and my apology, we have managed with great difficulty through the perseverance of my good friend, W. S. Churchill, to acquire box seats for the gala Christmas performance of As You Like It, *starring Miss Lillie Langtry as Rosalind. Drury Lane Theatre. Tonight. If you and your dear chaperone would accompany me and Winston to the performance, after theatre supper will follow at Rules Restaurant. If you, Kaiulani, will stoop to join*

me, I will bend my knee to a royal princess and pledge my
eternal faithfulness. I shall be waiting with my faithful friend
at my side in the lobby of the Savoy Hotel at seven o'clock.

> *Your faithful servant,*
> *Andrew Adams"*

Kaiulani's cheeks were crimson. "Winston! And Lillie Langtry! The Jersey Lily!"

"Not tonight," Hannah scolded. "Annie can go with Winston— now there's brown bread for you—but Andrew will have to find another date. You have a previous engagement."

"Oh, Hannah!" Kaiulani moaned. "I thought I'd never see Andrew again!"

"Why do you want to?"

"He knows our dear little Winston. Good friends. That says something redeeming about Andrew, doesn't it?"

"More about the character of Winston. That he would befriend such a rounder."

"I must go."

Hannah scanned the letter again. "You won't."

"I knew when I saw him last night…"

"You have a date with a couple thousand churchgoers."

Kaiulani covered her face with both hands and confessed, "Listen, Hannah. I dreamed about Andrew last night. We were beneath the banyan tree at Ainahau. I heard the peacocks call. I turned, and he was gone. I felt the most terrible panic. I looked and looked for him."

"And now this." Hannah placed the letter on top of Clive's package. "Poor Clive. Pocket handkerchiefs would have been kinder."

"What?"

Hannah pursed her lips. "The convention has been expecting to meet the Royal Princess for weeks. Kaiulani, you can't."

Kaiulani glanced at the plain black dress and then at the closet filled with evening dresses. "Hannah?"

"No."

"We've gotten away with it before."

"I can't. Kaiulani, they are expecting—are excited to see and hear the Royal Princess of Hawaii."

"You know my speech as well as I. Hannah, please!"

Hannah shook her head in resignation. "They're sending a committee to fetch Her Royal Highness at six o'clock."

"Who will know the difference?" Triumphant, Kaiulani selected a burgundy velvet gown and held it up before the mirror.

"This time Andrew will know the difference."

* * * *

Kaiulani and Hannah managed to keep the truth from Annie for several hours.

Annie knew only that Winston had somehow managed to get tickets to the Langtry performance and that Annie was invited. She bustled happily around the suite. "Imagine! Seeing dear Winston again."

It was almost six when Hannah donned the black missionary-suitable dress, while Kaiulani emerged dressed for the theatre in an elegant evening gown.

"What's this? What's this? Kaiulani? You can't go looking like that. Hannah, you're wearing Kaiulani's dress."

Hannah passed Andrew's letter to Annie to read and retreated into the dressing room.

While Annie studied the missive, the dark evening sky above London erupted in a downpour. Rain sluiced down the windows of the hotel suite as lightning flashed, reflecting in the River Thames. The peals of thunder bounced against the building like the solid clap of cannon shot.

"Umbrellas. Perfect. Umbrellas will complete the disguise," Hannah said cheerfully. "Everyone will be carrying umbrellas."

Hannah and Kaiulani stood side-by-side before the floor-length mirror and studied their reflections.

Hannah seemed very small in Kaiulani's severe black dress. Kaiulani was clothed in the blue velvet gown Hannah had worn to see *The Gondoliers*. She adjusted the bodice with a critical eye. Andrew would be unable to keep his eyes off her. Totally as it should be.

Hannah remarked, "You and me: the Princess and the Pauper. Pretty good." She adjusted her chin to the appropriate "royal" angle. "But really, Kaiulani. After tonight, you are so very much in my debt." She plucked at the puffy shoulder of the black monstrosity. "Don't think I won't collect, either."

Kaiulani tilted her head and mimicked Hannah's smile. "We should write a novel about us."

Annie, arms crossed, appeared at the door. She scowled at them and waved the letter. "That story has been already told. Mark Twain."

Kaiulani blinked innocently at her elder sister. "Blast. I thought we had a future in literature. After all, Andrew's father is a publisher." She picked up a black opera cape from the back of a chair and twirled it round herself like a matador preparing to face a bull.

Hannah did a two-step and took a bow. "We'll add a new twist to an old plot."

Annie's dark brown eyes glinted with resentment. "*Twisted* is the correct word! Papa sent me to England to look after you, Victoria Kaiulani. To see you perform your duties. Now look."

Kaiulani defended herself. Putting her hands on Annie's shoulders, she said, "But you'll be with Winston. And I with Andrew. So look after me, Annie. You remain the most perfectly proper chaperone. You are filling your responsibility. Besides, Hannah is the one who is going into harm's way."

"What do you mean?" Annie replied suspiciously.

"You know how treacherous those missionaries can be," Kaiulani said, winking at Hannah.

Annie stamped her foot. "But you—Kaiulani? How can you? Princess Kaiulani is supposed to be at St. Mark's," Annie insisted, "and I should be with her. How could I have imagined going to the theatre when we should be at the church together?" Annie's attention was drawn to the window by another flash of lightning. It illuminated the pulpit-shaped alcoves on Blackfriars Bridge. Annie blinked at the sight as if she saw judgment written there.

Kaiulani extended her hands, palms up, weighing the choices. "On one hand, theatre tickets to Lillie Langtry. On the other hand, a missionary convention at a church in Mayfair. A tough choice, Annie."

Hannah put her arm companionably around Annie's neck. "What harm? Who will know? I can manage. Go on, you two."

Annie shrugged off Hannah's touch. "But Kaiulani is my responsibility," she insisted, though less forcefully than before.

Hannah consoled, "A chance for you and Kaiulani to see Lillie Langtry in her last performance before she sails to America. Annie, you cannot deny such an adventure is heavensent. If I wasn't needed to stand in for Kaiulani among the missionaries, I would love to see the Jersey Lily."

Annie's resistance began to crumble. "If Andrew Adams was not so devil-may-care, I might agree. But he's so—"

"Handsome," Hannah finished. "Handsome."

"He knows it too." Annie pouted.

Kaiulani kissed Annie lightly on the cheek. "Come on, Annie. The missionary committee will be here any minute to escort the princess to the hall. All you have to do is this: you answer the door and present HRH Hannah to them. Hannah goes off to the convention and gives my little speech, and they will never know the difference."

Annie had no further opportunity to protest. The expected knock sounded at the door of the suite.

Kaiulani whispered, "As Holmes said to Watson, 'The game is afoot.'" Petticoats rustled as she retreated to the dark bedroom.

Annie froze. "What do I do?"

Hannah grinned. "Answer the door and introduce me."

Annie hesitated only a moment before she opened the door. There was no turning back now. Hannah stepped forward as the women in the hall curtsied deeply.

Annie swallowed hard. "This…this…may I introduce Her Royal Highness, Princess Victoria Kaiulani of the Kingdom of Hawaii?"

Kaiulani remained in the dark bedroom, listening to the excited voices of the four women who had come to escort the barbarian princess to the convention.

"You are so lovely, my dear."

"Your father is from Scotland?"

"Your Royal Highness! We have anticipated this moment for months."

"We have read in *The Times* that R. L. Stevenson is quite taken with you. He says you are the future of the Hawaiian monarchy."

Hannah, gracious and royal in bearing, thanked them all, then gave a backwards smile over her shoulder toward the half-open door where Kaiulani listened. "A pleasure to meet you," she said. "I've so been looking forward to this evening."

Chapter Eleven

....

Rules Restaurant, near Covent Garden, had been in continuous operation for over ninety years when Kaiulani, Annie, Andrew, and Winston visited there for an après-theatre meal. The dining room was a cramped narrow hall, sandwiched between the kitchen and the front windows looking out on Maiden Lane.

"They say Charles Dickens walked by here, smelling the roast beef and Yorkie pudding, when he was a starving boy. He earned just six shillings a week putting labels on boot-blacking bottles," Winston noted.

"Starving street urchin," Andrew said, removing his top coat, tossing his gloves into his top hat, and handing both to the attendant. "Like me. Famished."

Winston was in the dark blue dress uniform of a Gentleman Cadet of Sandhurst. To Kaiulani he looked both slimmer and more fit than when they had met at Sundown.

Andrew spoke over Winston's head to Kaiulani. "So poor Hannah is playing the role of the princess again tonight."

Kaiulani replied, "If I could have been two places at once…"

Andrew remarked, "Quite a phenomenon, this gypsy fellow. All the riffraff of London flock to hear him preach. I'm going tomorrow night to write a story about him. See if I can find the appeal."

Annie countered, "The appeal is the same as it was two thousand years ago. The kingdom of heaven."

Andrew laughed. "Heaven? Not for the likes of me. St. Peter would see me coming and slam the gates of heaven, I'm afraid."

Kaiulani studied Andrew over the top of the menu. "You're a difficult case, but there must be room even for you, Andrew. I'll ask Hannah's expert opinion tonight."

Rules was decorated with cartoons and satirical drawings of the most famous personages of the last hundred years. There were caricatures of literary figures, stage performers, and politicians. The quartet of young people was seated under a matched pair of drawings depicting Henry Irving as Hamlet and Ellen Terry as Ophelia. Irving's long face, aquiline nose, and bushy eyebrows lent themselves to exaggeration. The artist who depicted Miss Terry's sweet, troubled expression clearly had been more sympathetic.

"But why bother with drawings when we can gaze on the genuine article?" Andrew queried. "See?"

In the far, rear corner of the restaurant Irving and Terry were deep in conversation over their coffee.

"Partners in running the Lyceum Theatre," Andrew said, displaying a newsman's conceit at having insider knowledge.

"What did you think of Miss Langtry's performance?" Winston asked Kaiulani.

"I felt she lacked enthusiasm," Kaiulani remarked. "As though her thoughts were elsewhere."

"Too right!" Andrew said. "Probably on the prince. They used to have their assignations in the private room just above where we're sitting. But His Royal Highness, Bertie the Bounder, threw her over."

"That doesn't seem like a proper way to refer to the Prince of Wales," Kaiulani challenged.

Andrew shrugged. "Everyone calls him that, eh, Winston?"

Winston grimaced. "My cousin, Bertie the Bounder, who will someday be the seventh king named Edward, would have trouble denying it. But we were speaking of Miss Langtry."

"Were we?" Andrew challenged. "I thought we were speaking of juicy gossip."

"Miss Langtry has business interests in this country and in America," Winston said. "Besides being a performer, she owns ranches and raises race horses. She travels and keeps up on the news from both countries—something you are no doubt mindful of, Princess."

Kaiulani studied Winston's level gaze. He seemed to be offering her the chance to speak about politics and her concerns for her homeland. She admitted, "I know that certain parties in the United States have designs on my country. Is this a topic the gentlemen cadets discuss?"

Andrew chuckled. "Not likely! Between drilling and saluting and cadging the next bit of coin to pay their gambling debts, no time for world affairs. Here, waiter," he said. "Bring us a decanter of claret and the quail egg tart to start. We're perishing."

Andrew had not asked the others for their preference, but no one argued with his choices either.

Winston corrected, "We spend a great deal of time reading history and discussing world events. The price of rice connects to unrest in India; riots in Bombay; that sort of thing. Since a graduate's first posting may take him anywhere from the Sudan to China, he'd best be up on politics."

Winston directed his attention to Kaiulani and added, "We know America is interested in Hawaii for more than just sugar. America has reached the continental limit of her 'manifest destiny.' The U.S. is now looking beyond her shores. To do so she will need a permanent re-fueling station and naval base in the mid-Pacific."

Kaiulani agreed. "And Hawaii is halfway between the western U.S. and the Orient."

How much more assured and self-confident Winston was, she thought. Sandhurst agreed with him.

"Here's the wine," Andrew said. "French."

Kaiulani and Annie declined, while Andrew let his goblet be filled to the brim. It was clear that a discussion of politics was not what Andrew had intended tonight.

Yet Kaiulani thirsted for some insight into the concerns of her home. "The British Empire stretches around the world. If there was an alliance with England, how would England treat Hawaii differently than would America?"

Winston took a sip of his claret and set the glass down again. "In the future England must become allies with other nations—a close brother-hood of nations—perhaps a commonwealth of member states."

Kaiulani probed, "And if you were prime minister, this is how you would propose to treat *Hawaii Nei*? As a member of a British Commonwealth?"

Andrew mocked, "Can you imagine Winston as prime minister? He speaks his mind too freely—is too obstinate. Politics is all about compromise."

"Ignore him," Kaiulani urged Winston. "Please go on."

"Yes, do," Annie seconded.

"Ah, here's the tart," Andrew announced. The quail egg confection was a bubbling hot quiche of roasted quail eggs in cheese and rich sauce. Annie served out the appetizer.

Kaiulani noticed that Winston's portion was larger than the others received.

Winston, at a warning look from Andrew, wrapped up his remarks by saying, "From what I have read, Britain wants to partner with the Hawaiian kingdom, Princess, but not to dominate your government or destroy the monarchy. Along with that partnership would come the protection of the royal navy."

Andrew draped his arm around the back of Kaiulani's chair. "The princess already knows where to look for British protection."

Andrew was so forward, Kaiulani thought. Handsome and shallow. Why did she allow him to take such liberties?

"But enough of my barracks-room debate," Winston said.

Andrew snorted in his wine glass, then refilled it.

The roast beef trolley arrived. Carving the joint with a practiced hand, the waiter also served out Yorkshire pudding, brown gravy, and roasted potatoes. Andrew contemplated the meal with satisfaction.

"Tell me about your schooling," Winston asked, redirecting the conversation. "How do you like Harrowden?"

"The teachers are excellent," Kaiulani said, "but I despair of ever learning French. Art and music are wonderful, but there is no political discussion at all. I've learned more tonight in conversation with you than in an entire term at Harrowden."

"You're right to concentrate on languages," Winston encouraged. "I doubt that a girl's education at Harrowden is enough to prepare you for what your future holds."

"I would like to meet Queen Victoria," Kaiulani confided. "She was about my age when she came to the British throne. I want to know what she felt, and how she coped."

Annie nodded vigorously.

"I'm sure Queen Victoria will receive you," Winston said. "What would you ask her?"

Andrew tucked into the roast beef with more scraping of his knife and fork than strictly necessary.

"How to govern wisely," Kaiulani said frankly, "in case I am queen one day. Did she always know how, or did she have to ask for wisdom, like Solomon?"

"Kaiulani," Winston returned, "I'm certain the queen prays for wisdom every day. But she also surrounds herself with wise counselors, and she reads, constantly. Learning needlepoint and the proper way to serve tea is not the education you require."

"You're right, of course," Kaiulani agreed. "I must understand both policy and politics."

Winston saluted her with an upraised glass. "Perhaps you should be studying politics and military tactics at Sandhurst."

"And you, Winston, attend Harrowden Girls School," Andrew returned. "Then you might have a prayer of getting a girl to pay attention to you."

Andrew never saw the scowl Annie aimed at him, or he might have flinched, Kaiulani thought.

Winston leveled his gaze at Andrew. "We already know the princess can ride well enough to lead a cavalry charge. And her sharp wit is a two-edged sword that can pierce an English boor through the heart."

* * * *

1973

The theatre program featuring Lillie Langtry lay open on Sandi's lap. The black-and-white photo of Miss Langtry showed the imperious, unsmiling actress in Shakespearean costume.

Sandi scanned the list of performers and imagined Kaiulani, her sister, Winston Churchill, and Andrew as they must have been eighty years ago. A ticket stub and a single rose were pressed between the pages of the bill.

Auntie Hannah laid her head back against the cushion of her rocker and sighed with contentment. Did she hear some long ago melody Sandi could not hear? "It was a fine night," the old woman mused. "A night of awakening."

"For Kaiulani?"

The old woman smiled as though surprised to look up and see Sandi in the room.

"Oh. My dear girl, I almost forgot you were here. For Kaiulani. Ah, yes. That conversation with the young man, Winston. It was an awakening."

Sandi thumbed through the program. "And Andrew?"

Auntie Hannah wagged her head. "Poor Andrew. In those days, more interested in a pretty girl and a quail egg tart than the fate of a kingdom. By the time Andrew tried to kiss Kaiulani good night, she was finished with him. A cad. A bounder, Kaiulani told Annie. Andrew was too shallow and foolish, she said. He had no care for what would come upon the world. Her world. This world. *Hawaii Nei.* As the evening came to an end, Kaiulani was more and more impressed with Mister Churchill's wisdom. She made up her mind that if she would one day be a queen, she would invite Winston to be a part of her cabinet. She declared she would never marry. Like the first Queen Elizabeth, she would dedicate herself to her people and her nation. And poor Andrew Adams would be consigned to the dust bin of her memories."

Sandi studied her notes. "Yet Andrew Adams appears again in Kaiulani's life. Here in Hawaii. When she came back. A tragic figure. Sitting beside her tomb."

Auntie Hannah was silent for a moment at the memory. "My dear, you must not leap ahead. How will you understand the end of the story if you do not learn the details as they unfolded?"

A myna bird scolded from the rail of the *lanai*. Sandi double-checked her references. "Andrew Adams. It wasn't over between them."

Auntie Hannah wagged her finger. "The course of true love never runs smooth, they say. Hmm, a true saying. Love never carries our hearts where we think it ought. Do you agree?"

Sandi nodded as she thought of the dreams she had shared with John. Who could imagine that at age twenty-five she would live a lifetime without him? "So. Everything changed."

"Yes. Yes. When we least expect it. Miracles. Awakenings. That was the night everything changed. After dinner, Kaiulani and Annie returned to the hotel. It all seemed so ordinary, but in those few hours of separation, heaven and earth—every expectation of the future—our lives and eternity were altered."

* * * *

Victorian England

It was very late when Andrew and Winston returned the ladies to the Savoy. The good-byes in the lobby were brief. In the shadow of the closed coat-check room, Andrew stooped to kiss Kaiulani. She turned away abruptly, not attempting to conceal her contempt for him.

Winston had to run to catch the last train in order to get back to Sandhurst before he violated the term of his leave.

Kaiulani and Annie arrived at their rooms in two very different moods. The princess was deep in thought, pondering what she had learned from Winston. She vowed to approach her studies with a new commitment: she would gain all the attributes of a queen. Against this vow, Andrew Adams was a distraction.

Annie also arrived at their suite, thinking of their evening's companions. In her mind was a portrait of how well she could care for Winston and make him happy. What she had gained from the evening was a vision of an alliance between Great Britain and Hawaii. Naturally the coalition would require the presence in Honolulu of a dashing young officer named Winston Churchill.

Neither young woman was prepared for the change they would find in the third member of their trio.

Hannah was in her long white nightgown. Her bare feet were curled beneath her as she sat in the chair nearest the fire.

A Bible was open on her lap.

"Thank you for being me tonight," Kaiulani said. "Our evening was wonderful."

Hannah looked up but kept her finger in the Scripture passage. "You should have been there, Kaiulani."

Kaiulani was confused. Hannah's words were scolding, but her expression was radiant. "Why? What happened? Did someone recognize you? As not me, I mean?"

Hannah shook her head, and Kaiulani sighed with relief.

"No," Hannah said, "your talk was very well received. You thanked them for their commitment to sending missionaries. You reminded them that your kingdom is Christian because of those who carried the gospel to Hawaii. Then you quoted Saint Paul: 'How shall they believe in him of whom they have not heard? And how shall they hear without a preacher?'[15] They appreciated your words."

Kaiulani pulled a chair close to Hannah and kicked off her dress shoes. "Then, what?"

"Oh, Kaiulani, you missed hearing the preacher! Rodney Smith— Gipsy, they call him! Such a kind man. Such a gentle spirit. But he speaks with such *mana*, such power! And he was talking to you!"

Leaning forward, Kaiulani took both of Hannah's hands in hers. "What do you mean? What did he say?"

Withdrawing from her friend's grasp, Hannah lifted the Bible and angled it toward the light coming from the electric lamp on the mantle. "Listen," she said.

"The LORD appeared to Solomon in a dream by night: and God said, Ask what I shall give thee....

O LORD my God, thou hast made thy servant king instead of David my father; and I am but a little child: I know not how to go out or come in.

Give therefore thy servant an understanding heart to
judge thy people, that I may discern between good and bad:
for who is able to judge this thy so great a people?" [16]

Hannah raised her eyes from the text. Tilting her head to the
side she asked, "Do you know what the Lord replied?"

"Tell me."

"Listen!"

"The speech pleased the LORD, that Solomon had asked this thing.
And God said unto him, Because thou hast asked this thing,
and hast not asked for thyself long life; neither hast asked riches
for thyself, nor hast asked the life of thine enemies; but hast
asked for thyself understanding to discern judgment;
Behold, I have done according to thy words: lo, I have given
thee a wise and an understanding heart; so that there was none
like thee before thee, neither after thee shall any arise like unto
thee.
And I have also given thee that which thou hast not asked,
both riches, and honour: so that there shall not be any among
the kings like unto thee all thy days." [17]

"Do you see?" Hannah persisted. "God loves it when we ask for
understanding, for wisdom. That's a prayer He loves to answer. And
Mister Smith's words weren't just for kings and queens, Kaiulani!
They spoke to my heart, too."

Kaiulani considered the peaceful countenance of her friend.
Something was different. "You enjoyed the evening, then."

"*Enjoy.* A small word for such a night. More than that. I shall never be the same. But hear me, Kaiulani: Gipsy Smith prepared this sermon for your ears. For your sake He gave this message, and I am meant to bring it to you."

With a sense of wonder Kaiulani searched Hannah's clear eyes. "At the same moment I was learning; thinking about things for the first time—things I had not imagined. I have never understood the battle for my people and my nation. About why the grandsons of American missionaries, only two generations later, wish to destroy the monarchy and steal our kingdom. But I am certain that this is a battle for the souls of our people."

"Then God had a purpose for us to go our separate ways tonight. While you were learning about the kingdoms of men, I was hearing another greater truth about the kingdom of heaven. My heart is so light! I could fly away into the clouds." Hannah gripped Kaiulani's hands. "He is preaching again tomorrow night. Kaiulani! Annie! We three must go together. Such hope! You must hear him."

Chapter Twelve

....

The Royal Aquarium, located in Westminster just north of Westminster Abbey, had seen better days. Constructed to provide family amusement in the heart of London, "the tank" had degenerated over time. Now it featured card parlors and billiard tables and cigar smoke and dubious theatrical offerings.

But the auditorium at the Aquarium's west end seated thirteen hundred people. It was available for rent by the week…cheap.

It was the ideal location for a revival meeting.

Annie, Hannah, and Kaiulani were dressed simply, so as not to attract attention. Nor was their olive-tan skin unusual. Among the throng heading toward the hall were East Indians and others whose families still lived in distant, tropical islands.

The expectant onlookers included men and women in evening dress and laborers in stiff-fabric trousers. They were young and old, families and lone soldiers in uniform.

Kaiulani, Hannah, and Annie found seats on the aisle two-thirds of the way back on the main floor of the auditorium. The seats all around and in the galleries quickly filled, until the theatre's capacity was reached. Thereafter latecomers stood on the stairs and leaned in at the doors.

Kaiulani waited for the program to begin by studying the man seated on the platform. Swarthy-skinned, with brown hair and drooping brown moustache, Gipsy Smith projected a calm, agreeable demeanor. There was nothing egotistical or superior in the way he looked about with interest, smiling continuously. He nodded in time to the hymns being played on the grand organ in the gallery. The spotlights illuminating the stage glistened on his high, broad forehead.

The princess expected Smith to receive a formal introduction. Surely some noted educator or a famous church leader would call the meeting to order and recite the orator's credentials.

As the organ finished the last notes of a song and held the first chord of another, Gipsy Smith stood, walked to the very edge of the platform, and began to sing.

> *"I can hear my Savior calling,*
> *I can hear my Savior calling,*
> *I can hear my Savior calling,*
> *'Take thy cross and follow, follow me.'"* [18]

Smith's pleasant tenor voice rolled across the crowd. By the time he had completed three verses of the hymn, the audience was completely silent and attentive; much more so than if someone famous had introduced him.

As the last notes of *"I'll go with Him, with Him, all the way"* flew up to the rafters and then died away, Kaiulani was riveted in place to hear Smith speak.

"My text for tonight is First John, chapter four, verse seven," the preacher said. "'Beloved, let us love one another: for love is of God; and every one that loveth is born of God, and knoweth God.'"

"There it is," Smith said. "That's all the gospel in a nutshell. Do you realize that if all of you went out of here tonight able to say,

'I know God loves me,' and if tomorrow you said to everyone you meet, 'God loves you, and so do I—'" Smith paused to let the tension build. "If you did those two things, in a week I'd be out of a job?"

The hall reverberated with appreciative laughter.

"Now you may think that I just told a joke to 'warm you up.' You hear music hall performers do that all the time, don't you? But you'd be wrong! I am completely in earnest! If you committed to say those two phrases to everyone you encounter, within a week this nation would experience the greatest spiritual revival in history. And from this nation to all the world!"

Kaiulani glanced at Hannah. Her friend was listening intently.

"But what if you can't honestly say that you know God loves you? What if you think He can't love you? What then?"

Smith stopped and looked around the auditorium. His gaze was not penetrating or challenging. Instead, his expression carried the certainty that he already knew every fear, every worry, every struggle, in every heart, because he had experienced them himself.

"I was born a gypsy," he admitted. "No fixed abode. Not welcomed in any town. Name a crime, and I could be convicted of it before ever setting foot in a place. Once, when I was young, I went into a church meeting. As I walked into the gathering, I overheard someone say, 'Oh, it's only a gypsy boy. What's he doing here?'

"Can you imagine? Friend, have you been rejected by men? Do you feel unwanted? Let me tell you about a 'friend that sticketh closer than a brother.' [19] His name is Jesus!"

That was the moment Kaiulani spotted someone she recognized. Across the hall from her, heading near the stage with intense determination—and joy beaming from ear-to-ear—was Andrew

Adams. His notebook was in one hand, a pencil in the other. It was clear, however, that he was no longer there as a journalist. The message had captured his heart.

Annie was also moved. She took a handkerchief out of her sleeve. She was alternately twisting it and using it to dab her eyes. Leaning close to Kaiulani, she whispered, *"Auwe.* I have forgotten what it means. Forgotten. If only the *haole* sons of the missionaries in Honolulu who despise our people could hear. This is the message their grandparents came to Hawaii to tell us! The sons of the missionaries…so lost!"

"'But God shows his love for us in that while we were still sinners, Christ died for us,'" Smith quoted from Romans, chapter 5. Lifting his chin so that his voice carried to the topmost gallery, Smith posed this question: "Do you love anyone enough to die for them? Perhaps you do. But God says here's how much He loves you: while you are still a sinner, God's enemy, without you changing one thing about your life—without even fixing the things you know need to be mended—right now, tonight, God loves you enough that He sent His only Son to die for you!"

Kaiulani felt as though Smith were speaking directly to her. What had been missing in her spirit? Was this it? To know that God loved her, just as she was—an imperfect individual?

"Let me tell you a story about the way God loves you," Smith continued. "When I was a boy, I found an egg that had been kicked out of a nest but was not broken. I took it home and when the old speckled hen was up off the straw, I snuck it into her clutch. Now she sat on that extra egg, and soon enough, it hatched. Do you know, it was a wild bird! A partridge! But that mother hen loved that chick and cared for it and nurtured it and protected it with exactly the same measure she gave her own."

Once more Smith looked around the auditorium. His smile beamed at Kaiulani. He was unhurried. He made Kaiulani feel that if he had to remain all night long to make a connection with each and every person present, he was willing to do so.

Now Andrew stood beneath the pulpit. His countenance was changed. His eyes shone as he looked up at the preacher. Andrew, like a wild bird, had been gathered in. Kaiulani knew she was witnessing a miracle.

"That's the way God loves you," Smith said, looking directly at Andrew. "You feel like you've been kicked out of the nest, with nowhere to turn and no one to care for you or about you. But I stand before you tonight and promise you: God loves you…and so do I!

"Sisters and brothers," Smith proclaimed, "here's the Good News: you can be a new creation in Christ Jesus, now, tonight, and none of us—not one!—will think you're crazy! What do you say? Will you come up here and let me pray with you? Will you give your heart to Jesus, tonight? Come up here while we're singing. If you're here with friends, they'll wait for you. After all, God's been waiting for you for your whole life."

The hearts of hundreds hung on every word. When Kaiulani saw tears streaming down Andrew's cheek, she put her gloved hand to her cheek. It came away moist.

Once more Gipsy Smith began to sing:

> "*The dying thief rejoiced to see*
> *That fountain in his day;*
> *And there may I, though vile as he,*
> *Wash all my sins away.*" [20]

Kaiulani, Hannah, and Annie sang with him, their sweet soprano voices mingling with the multitude. Kaiulani saw Andrew Adams lift his hands and drop to his knees, as the preacher put his hand on his head.

"Do you want to go forward? I'll go with you," Hannah offered, linking her arms with Kaiulani and Annie. "Come on! I went last night! We three will go to the altar together."

Kaiulani felt a tug at her heart. A life-changing power had been unleashed tonight—an eternal love bigger and more powerful than she had ever felt.

"Yes!" Kaiulani cried. "I'll go!" The sisters joined the human current moving forward down the aisle to the front.

The preacher proclaimed, "From the throne of God to your heart! From your heart to England! From England to all the world!"

* * * *

The throng of people on the eastbound platform at the Westminster tube station had almost all come from hearing Gipsy Smith. Kaiulani and her companions were among those waiting for the train. When they had emerged from the service there were so many people waving for cabs that the Hawaiians merely allowed themselves to be swept along toward the Underground.

The mood of the crowd was jubilant, elated. Total strangers parted from each other, shouting, "God loves you, and so do I!"

Kaiulani tried to remember when she had seen such a mingling of joy and tears. She failed to produce a memory to compare with this night. Hannah talked excitedly of how what she had experienced the night before had been confirmed on this evening. She bubbled with enthusiasm to hear that Kaiulani felt the same way.

Annie cried softly into her handkerchief, bobbing her head when Kaiulani asked if she were all right. "You know," Annie said, "I felt as though he were speaking to me…just to me!"

The princess agreed she felt the same way.

Clouds of steam rose from the densely packed mob of umbrellas and soaked woolen overcoats. No one seemed to mind, nor did they complain when the first train to arrive was instantly filled to capacity and departed with twice that number still remaining on the platform.

Kaiulani, Hannah, and Annie advanced to the edge of the platform.

"There may be no seats on the train," Hannah observed.

"Doesn't matter," Kaiulani said. "It's just one stop to Charing Cross and our hotel."

The rattle of an arriving train could be heard far off down the tunnel. Instinctively Kaiulani turned toward the sound, though she could not see through the forest of tall hats.

What she did see was Andrew Adams' beaming countenance. Looking back into her eyes from down the length of the platform, she saw more than just his familiar features. She saw a changed soul. Andrew was radiant. There was no trace of the familiar cynicism that usually constricted his brow; no mocking sarcasm lurking in his smile.

He waved both arms—a broad gesture that brought wider smiles to those around him.

Kaiulani felt a rush of air as the approaching train pushed air ahead of it toward the platform. Then she felt a pressure in her ears, almost like diving down on the reefs of home.

Andrew was still waving. Then he was also pointing. His motions seemed to have an edge of urgency.

Someone in the crowd pushed Kaiulani hard from behind. She staggered sideways, clutching at Hannah, then toppled off the pavement, standing directly in the path of the on-rushing train.

There was no time to cry out, yet for a moment Kaiulani saw horror imprinted on the faces of the onlookers. She thought of her mother's favorite psalm: "He shall give His angels charge concerning thee...."

The train whistle screamed a warning, a shriek dwarfed by the anguished cry pouring from hundreds of human throats.

Then Annie's strong hands reached under Kaiulani's arms and dragged her up just as the engine thundered into the station.

Something sent Kaiulani's left shoe flying. Was it possible the heel had been struck by the train? Was that how close it had been?

Andrew came flying along the platform, shouting, "Out of the way! Get out of my way!" Pausing only an instant to confirm that Kaiulani was unharmed, he resumed sprinting up the stairs. Now he bellowed, "Stop him! Stop that man!"

While the throng in the station ebbed and flowed and the train departed, a breathless Kaiulani and panting Annie huddled with Hannah against the white-tiled wall of the tunnel.

Andrew returned. "He got away," he reported. "Don't know if he went outside or crossed to the westbound line. Sorry."

"But surely," Hannah remarked, "it was an accident."

"That's not what I saw," Andrew said. "Not at all."

* * * *

The inspector from Scotland Yard took copious notes as Andrew paced back and forth in Kaiulani's hotel suite and the trio of women looked on. Andrew said again, "I tell you, I clearly saw the chap staring at the princess with a cold, determined look in his eye."

The inspector's lower lip protruded, conveying his doubt. "Amongst all the crowd, you spotted this one fellow with a peculiar expression?"

Andrew defended, "He was the only person not smiling. There was dark intent in his expression as he made his way towards the princess."

The inspector addressed Kaiulani, "What say you, uh, Princess?"

"I only felt myself being pushed. I saw nothing but the train and then I felt the arms of my sister reaching out to pull me up at the last instant."

The inspector pressed her. "Then an accident, would you say? Is there anyone who would like you dead? Pardon my bluntness."

Annie, who had not let go of Kaiulani's hand, stammered, "Who could believe such a thing? Who would ever want to hurt my sister?"

The inspector snapped his notebook closed. With lips pressed together, he shrugged and shook his head at Andrew. "Sorry, Mister Andrews. There you have it. You seem to be the only one who believes the princess is in danger."

Resigned, Andrew nodded and retrieved his hat. He addressed Kaiulani. "I can't convince you of what I am certain. I'll write your guardian, Mister Davies, and your father in Honolulu. You should have a Pinkerton agent with you whenever you go out."

Kaiulani, exhausted by the ordeal, smiled feebly at Andrew. "I do thank you for your concern. I can't see how a Pinkerton would fit into my simple lifestyle. I should be safe enough at school. I don't want you to worry, Andrew. Please, until we meet again, don't give me another thought."

He was silent for a long moment. Staring at his shoes, he replied, "I fear I won't see you again...for a long time, Kaiulani. And I can't help but worry. You are truly, like Mister Mark Twain, an innocent abroad if you think the long arm of the enemies of the Hawaiian monarchy cannot reach you on these shores." He turned to leave with the policeman.

Kaiulani called after him. "Andrew? Please. Pray for me."

He paused with his hand on the doorknob. "I discovered tonight that my...care for you...suddenly makes me want to pray. I must first learn how."

Chapter Thirteen

....

1973

Archie's boat, *Royal Flush*, carried them slightly northwest out of Lahaina Harbor, pushed by a steady wind from the south. Sandi watched in amazement as he piloted the forty-two-foot vessel without any help. Occasionally he would slip ties around two spokes of the ship's wheel and leave the cockpit to tighten or loosen some rope. She'd never sailed before, so Sandi had no idea what he was doing, but considering he was able to do it by himself, she was impressed.

She had always imagined sailing was a hobby for at least two people working together: one to hold the wheel and bark orders, another to carry them out. And if someone went sailing by himself, she thought, certainly two hands would be a minimum. But Archie was confident and each move he made on the boat deliberate and precise. He must have noticed her admiring gaze, for he said, "She's a sweet little boat. Makes sailing easy. Almost as good as another hand."

Sandi suddenly laughed out loud as the meaning of the sailboat's name came to her. A royal flush was the highest winning hand in poker.

The other four people onboard, a married couple and their two teenage daughters, didn't seem to fully appreciate Archie's accomplishment. They leaned against the low side of the cabin roof, snapping pictures of the receding coastline and drinking little plastic cups full of more *poq,* poured from milk-container-like waxed paper cartons. Sandi smiled at the thought. Not such a secret recipe after all…poor Joe.

The view of the island really was astounding. High green ridges descended from unseen mist-covered peaks, divided by fingers of rich red soil reaching back from the sea. But Sandi found herself watching and enjoying the way Archie's mechanical arm worked. When she first arrived at the boat, she noticed that the grip on the end of the artificial limb had been changed. In place of the pincer were two rubber-lined, stainless steel half-circles that overlapped when closed. When he noticed her stare, he explained that he had a few different kinds of attachments for the arm—all with a different purpose. The one he wore on the boat was heavy duty, shaped specifically to grip rope.

It worked through a simple mechanical action, connected to a harness he wore around his shoulders. As he raised his arm from the shoulder, a cable pulled the grip open. When he lowered his arm, the grip closed by the strength of rubber bands strapped around its base. The reach of his left arm was much shorter than the right, and seemed to take considerable effort to manipulate, but he was still able to pull a line, hand over hand, almost as quickly as she'd ever seen it done.

They sailed far enough into the channel to see the eastern tip of the Island of Molokai. Archie warned everyone to hold on tight, loosened the sails, and with the last bit of forward momentum, spun the boat's wheel in a hard turn, back in the direction they'd come. Catching the question on Sandi's face, he said, "Don't go anywhere" and disappeared into the cabin.

"Funny," she mumbled as the sails flapped noisily in the breeze and the boat bobbed in the choppy water.

When he returned, Archie was carrying a large canvas bag. "Watch this." He smiled. "Now you're really gonna see something."

He hefted the bag to the bow, unzipped it, and attached a rope to something inside. Returning to the cockpit, he turned a crank, and Sandi watched as a canvas tube slowly uncoiled from the bag like a charmed cobra from its woven basket. Higher and higher it crept, ascending toward the top of the mast. Archie returned to the mast and worked at untwisting the tube, then attached another rope at its base. Finally, satisfied that all was correct, he pulled on a smaller, thinner cord that gathered the canvas skyward like a rolled-up sock, revealing a new sail inside.

As the wind caught its folds, it billowed outward, a dazzling spread of bright blue cloth that looked like a triangle of sky tethered to the boat. It whipped and cracked, as if trying to break free and fly home.

When Archie hopped back down into the cockpit, he excused himself around behind Sandi and turned a crank that tightened the bottom edge of the sail, pulling it toward the boat and forcing it to hold the wind that came at it. The boat slowly began heeling toward the north again, even before Archie loosed the wheel and gave it permission to do so. He trimmed the main sails again and everything snapped taut.

Sandi was on the low side as the boat headed northeast with the wind pushing directly into all three sails, the newest spread out in front of them like a hot air balloon. Though speed was hard to gauge over the monotonous waves, Sandi could tell they were traveling much faster than they had been.

"You might want to move up here," Archie said, patting the cockpit seat next to his wheel.

Looking back from the perch, she could see why: the railing where she had sat was now running close to the water as the wind pushed the boat hard over in its path.

"Fantastic!" she said, staring at the sail again. "What do you call that?"

Archie looked at her and smiled appreciatively. "Beautiful."

She felt color climb to her cheek. How long had it been since a man had held her with his glance? "I—I mean, what you just did… the…"

"I know what you meant." He turned away and explained in a businesslike way, "The sail's a spinnaker. Lots of boats have those. But that canvas cover is a new invention by a buddy of mine, Etienne. Guy's gonna be rich. See, a spinnaker's hard to set without getting it twisted in the middle. Like me. Some thought comes into my head and catches the wind…out it comes, all tangled up. Sorry."

She replied, "You only said one word."

"True. But maybe I shouldn't let the wind fill that sail."

"All this sailor talk, Archie. Right over my head."

He shrugged. "It's been awhile since I tried to talk to a female. I guess I've forgotten how."

"Beautiful was a good start."

"You are, you know."

"Well done, you. Brilliant follow-up line."

"Not bad for a one-handed sailor, eh?"

She paused, hearing some deep wound in his tone. "Who was she?"

"A girl I knew since we were kids. She's married now. Mainland. Has a baby. Life goes on, I guess."

A pang of guilt stabbed Sandi. What was she doing? Flirting with a man when John was still out there somewhere? "For some of us, life is on hold. It has to be. I can't—"

Archie seemed to recognize the unhappiness in her eyes. "Yes. I'm sorry. I didn't mean…" He glanced at her wedding ring, then quickly pointed to the spinnaker. His tone became that of the official tour guide. "That sock keeps the sail contained, out of the wind, until you're sure you've got it rigged right. When you're ready to take it down, you do the same thing in reverse, and it goes right back in the bag like a neat coil of rope."

"Uh-huh," she said, not really listening to his words.

Archie leaned against the pitch of the deck, steering confidently with his muscled right arm.

"Fantastic," Sandi said again but quickly looked away.

"Well," Archie said, "there's really not a whole lot else happening here until we get to the bay. You find a comfortable place to sit, and we'll be there before you know it."

She climbed up to the high side of the boat, past the tourist family holding tightly to the boat's safety railing. *One hand for myself and one for the boat,* she thought, *just like Archie said.* She moved as far forward as she could go and sat, letting her bare feet dangle off the side.

The teenage girls hadn't realized they were allowed to do that and quickly followed her example. The spray from the bow washed over their feet from time to time, cold and tickly. Sandi lay back with her arms spread along the line of the cabin roof, her face upturned full into the overhead sun.

She marveled at how the light washed right through her closed eyelids, filling her vision with a warm pink color. As the irregular, circular rhythms of the boat's movement coaxed the stress from her shoulders, she drifted in a state between waking and sleeping and wondered: *What is it I always see? Something when I close my eyes. And now it's just gone, washed out by this beautiful—*

Her eyes snapped open, and her stomach churned. She felt sick but knew it wasn't from the waves. The image she always saw when she closed her eyes was John's face. She wanted to always see that. She didn't want to forget him, not ever, not even for a second. He was still out there, and she felt unfaithful for having even the slightest good time without him.

She glanced back toward the wheel…and Archie. He smiled at her, and she tried to manage a smile back. *Oh, Lord, what am I doing here?* she prayed. They weren't even halfway through with the trip, and she already wished it were over.

"Whale!" shouted the other man on board. "Uh, one, no, two o'clock."

Archie had already instructed his passengers in the proper way to target whales, by using a clock face as a reference. "'Over there,'" he'd said jokingly, "is not a good description, especially when not everyone can see where you're pointing." He tapped his eye patch and everyone had laughed. Then he had shared a little rhyme with them. "Twelve is the bow, six is the stern. If you don't know the rest, it's about time you learn."

With a series of three quick movements, Archie loosed the sails, and the boat coasted to a quick stop in the choppy water. The giant beast was no more than twenty-five yards off the bow, between the boat and the land. Sandi stared in wonder as its back arched out of the water and it breathed quickly with a loud gust of air that vaporized water droplets into a fine mist. A moment later its white-streaked tail emerged, rising almost to vertical as the leviathan angled toward the depths again.

"Whoa!" said everyone but Archie, almost in unison, as though watching a fireworks display.

Sandi wondered why Archie hadn't joined in the chorus. She looked back toward the wheel and saw him shading his eyes with his right hand and scanning the water farther back along the boat, toward their "four o'clock." He was all business now.

"See another one, Captain?" the tourist father asked.

"Mm, maybe," Archie said. "There was a slick...do you know what that is? A slick is a little flat spot of water that gets left behind when a whale dives, like the one when this first guy went down—" He interrupted himself, pointing. "Five o'clock."

The whole row of tourists, including Sandi, had to stand to see where he pointed. Off the starboard side, back in the direction they'd come from, was the distinctive ridge of the back of a smaller whale. Everyone strained to hear over the lapping water and rippling sails. A second later, its breath came, smaller and higher pitched than the first one. It sounded to Sandi like the hiss of a steam iron as it heated.

"That's the calf," Archie said. "The mother has just had him this season. They'll stay, and she'll nurse him in the Islands until April or May, then they'll make the long trip back to Alaska."

"Wow! Alaska?" asked one of the girls. "They have to swim all that way?"

With absolute seriousness, Archie replied, "There are very few flights."

Sandi guffawed so abruptly she was able to pretend it was a cough.

After the family had snapped a few pictures of the mother and calf whales' leisurely dives and ascents, Archie got the boat underway again. Sandi settled back into her seat, determined to at least remember what she saw today, if for no other reason than to share it with John when he came home.

* * * *

Victorian England

Kaiulani took Winston's suggestion seriously that a future monarch must understand and speak fluently the languages of the great powers. She threw herself into her studies with renewed determination.

Madame Dominque Brun sat just like her four students on one of the five over-stuffed chairs around the room. Each girl had a small writing tablet on her lap, while Madame held a green, clothbound book.

"Nouns with two different plurals and meanings," she pronounced carefully. "Write for me each, *en francais, s'il vous plaît*, after I give you first, the singular. *L'aïeul*, the grandfather."

There was a clattering of chalk sticks on the boards as each pupil raced to complete the assignment.

Hannah finished first, turning her tablet toward Madame Brun. Kaiulani glanced up, frustrated that her friend took to the French language so much faster than she.

"*Bon,*" praised Madame Brun. "But do not forget—" She reached out and tapped additional punctuation in each of the words.

It was a reminder for Kaiulani to check her marking as well. She finished next and turned her work to Madame Brun.

"*Oui,*" the teacher agreed, as the other two girls finished. "The correct responses are '*les aïeuls*' and '*les aïeux*'—the grandfathers and the ancestors. A small, but important distinction, *non*?"

Each girl grabbed a fold of her own skirt and hurried to wipe her slate clean, eager to meet the next quiz from Madame.

I must remember to write Papa about that, reflected Kaiulani. That's how it is at Great Harrowden Hall. *The matrons are so kind and so trusting that the girls wish to please them as they would their own mothers.*

But as enchanted as she was with her school and with England generally, Kaiulani intensely disliked the weather. Every gauzy window at Harrowden Hall framed a perpetually gray sky. As she inclined her head to get a better view of the chapel's spires, the wavy glass undulated as though coursed with rain.

How Kaiulani missed the Islands' thick heat tempered by balmy breezes. She was grateful for the new experiences, the sights and sounds of cultures so very different from her own. *But the weather,* she thought, *surely that is what drove the poor English to exploration in the first place.*

Aside from pointing the way for the first missionaries to bring the Word of the Lord to the Islands, for which Kaiulani was truly grateful, she sometimes wished Captain Cook had just stayed home. *Then home is where I'd be too.*

"Mademoiselle?" called Madame, interrupting Kaiulani's reverie. Annie and the other two girls tittered. "Mademoiselle Kaiulani?

I think you are already contemplating the next word, non? *Le ciel.* The sky."

Les cieux, wrote Kaiulani, the heavens. Then, *les ciels,* skies in pictures.

"*Tres bon,*" said Madame Brun as Kaiulani beat Hannah to finish first and reversed the board for Madame's inspection.

Hannah feigned astonishment and Kaiulani smiled coyly.

A sharp rap sounded at the door, and Madame Brun rose to open it. Headmistress Bartlett peered in and spoke quietly to the teacher.

"*Mais oui,* Madame Bartlett," Madame Brun replied and turned, crooking a finger at Kaiulani. "Princess, Headmistress Bartlett asks to speak with you."

Kaiulani left her slate and chalk in her seat, dusting her hands on her skirt as she walked into the hallway. She pulled the door closed behind her. There she realized they were not alone. Her guardian, Theo Davies, was waiting also. To Kaiulani, he looked older some-how—ashen and troubled.

Immediately Kaiulani was alarmed. Whatever had caused Mr. Davies to make an unexpected journey from Sundown to the school was not good. "What is it?" she asked. "Mister Davies? Whatever is the matter?"

He stepped forward to greet her, kissing her on each cheek, as was their custom. "Kaiulani, I'm afraid I have some terrible news."

She clutched her hands to her bosom but said nothing. Head-mistress Bartlett stepped to her side and placed an arm around her shoulders.

"It's the king, your uncle," Davies continued. "I regret to inform you he has died, while on a trip to San Francisco. Just yesterday. Word came by telegram."

Kaiulani felt herself grow lightheaded. Steeling herself, she did not faint but swayed slightly in place. Headmistress Bartlett passed her a handkerchief in case she cried. *But I will not,* thought Kaiulani. *Not in front of anyone, anyway.*

She drew herself up, saying, "Of course. I knew he was ill. He had been for some…some time. Our Lord has called him home, and his suffering is over. It…I was caught off-guard."

Davies was shaking his head. "Kaiulani, he is your uncle. Your Papa Moi. It is not shameful to cry."

"Thank you, Mister Davies," she said. "And so I shall, when there is no one but God to see me. For what should a lost soul think if he saw me weep at this news, but that I think my Papa Moi is not with God; when rather, the truth of my tears will be much more selfish. I will cry for me."

Kaiulani nearly wept anyway when Davies hugged her and praised her bravery. "This changes everything at home, you know?" he asked. "The king's sister, Liliuokalani, will become queen, and that means you are next in line to the throne. I think it might be best if you and Hannah and Annie come away from school to Sundown for awhile. If you are called home, we should be ready to sail at a moment's notice."

"Of course," the princess agreed. "It will take us a few minutes to pack our things."

Headmistress Bartlett interjected, "The maid and the porter will take care of everything, dear. I will direct them myself. Don't trouble yourself about it at all. I am so sorry for your loss, and I want you to know how much you will be missed here. Come back soon, won't you?"

Madame Bartlett called Hannah and Annie from class then, and Davies explained what was happening to her as they made their way down the stairs and through the foyer to his waiting carriage.

Before climbing in, Kaiulani looked back longingly at the white stone buildings, then away to the chapel, shrouded by leafless trees. Somehow she knew she'd never return. *Just like Papa Moi,* she thought, *mes aieux en cieux.*

As she bade them all farewell in her mind, she also began composing a letter home to her aunt, the new queen:

Dear Auntie,

I have only just heard the sad news from San Francisco. I cannot tell my feelings just at present, but Auntie, you can think how I feel. I little thought when I said good-bye to my dear uncle nearly two years ago that it would be the last time I should see his dear face.

Please give my love to Mama Moi and tell her I can fully sympathize with her. I cannot write anymore, but Auntie, you are the only one left of my dear mother's family, so I can ask you to do that little thing for me.

I must close with love and kisses,

I remain,

Your loving niece,

Kaiulani

The carriage trounced over rutted roads in the seemingly endless fields of the Midlands countryside. "I'll have a letter home for the post," said Kaiulani.

"Of course," Davies replied. "Strange to say, but because of the telegraph line to America, we know of your uncle's passing well before anyone in Hawaii. It will be several days before the kingdom knows it has lost him."

* * * *

An unseen sun above thick gray clouds dragged a blanket of cold across the countryside on its way toward setting. A long gallop on the back of Blenheim did not lift the cloud over Kaiulani's heart. She walked the barren rose garden of Sundown Estate alone. Though she had promised herself a good cry over Papa Moi's death, she'd had no time by herself, and the opportunity never came. With the best of intentions, the associates and friends of Mister Davies came calling, one after another, offering condolences for Kaiulani's loss. The grief she longed to pour out to God remained bound inside her and she in it.

After a few days passed, the callers became less frequent, and at last she found some little space where she could be alone and pray. Even now she knew her sister and Hannah were likely watching her from their rooms, and she was quite sure that Mister Davies was, as he finished his afternoon tea in the parlor overlooking the garden.

She paused in a row of bloomless bushes, the last yet to be pruned back for the winter by Sundown groundskeepers. Absently, she pulled a thorny, browning cane toward herself as if inspecting some invisible flower with still-sweet aroma. But there was none. Nothing but dead and cold, she thought. No life here, no life.

She sank to her knees, pressing her palms into the fabric of her dress. The fine gravel path was cold and damp and began soaking her thick skirts. "*Makua Ke Akua,*" she cried. "I do not know Your mind, and I do not mean to question Your plan. But, *Iesu,* You know my grief. The pain You suffered for my sake is far beyond any I shall ever endure, yet my heart is broken as much as it ever shall be. How will the pieces ever hold Your hope again?"

A grinding step told Kaiulani she was no longer alone in the garden. She hurried to wipe her eyes on her coarse sleeves and patted her locks made curly by the mist, making sure everything was in its place before rising to her feet again.

"Princess?" a tentative voice called. It was Clive Davies. "Kaiulani? I saw you fall. I came to see…are you all right?"

Kaiulani was frustrated and shook when she said, still sniffing, "Isn't there anywhere a woman can be alone?"

Clive stretched out his hand to her, but she turned from him. He cast his eyes toward the ground. "Why do you insist on solitude? For what reason? I—" He corrected himself. "We love you and care for you and only wish to help you through this difficult—"

"It's not as though I'm running away, Clive," she said. "I only wish to be alone to grieve for my uncle and pray in private. There are things I must ask our Lord. Things I must say."

"Princess." Clive took a step closer. The musk he wore was the only scent in the brittle air. "Can't you say them to me also? Then I can pray with you."

"You think yourself a better confidant than God, Clive?" Kaiulani snapped, then instantly regretted it. "And now do you see? Not only am I cursed with such sorrow, now I must feel guilty when I refuse to show it." She was weeping, and Clive stretched out his hand once again, placing it gingerly on her shoulder.

Gently, he turned her toward him and offered his handkerchief, saying, "My father told me what you said—about not showing your grief. May I say: No one who sees you cry will think you've lost your faith in God. Rather, they'll see God in you when you show your faith in the midst of grief. Don't be afraid to admit how dark are the trials of man, but remember to speak also of the Light for which we live in spite of everything."

"Faithful Clive." She embraced him. "You bring the answer I was praying for. Bless you, brother."

Clive held her to his chest and laid his cheek on her head. *"Nohea,"* he whispered.

Kaiulani shrugged away from his arms and stepped backward. "What did you say?"

"Did I say it correctly?" he asked her, then repeated himself haltingly, "No-Hay-Uh? 'Lovely,' isn't it?"

"I know what it means, Clive. Why did you say it?"

"I have been practicing, Kaiulani. I thought if I could tell you how I feel about you in your own language, then—"

"Then what, Clive? In the middle of my mourning you would profess more romantic fancies?"

"Kaiulani, I love you. I've loved you since I first saw you. Things are dangerous for you, I know. I heard of Kalakaua's warning. Surely there are those who would not mourn if all the Hawaiian Royals were dead?"

"That was private correspondence!" she stormed. "I shared it with your father in complete confidence. How is it you come to know of it?"

"Kaiulani, please. Koa told me of it. I think he's worried for your safety also. Will you not even consider that you need someone to protect you?"

Sarcastically she asked, "Why? Do you know of someone who could?"

"I meant me, of course, Kaiulani."

"I know you did, Clive. And I don't agree. I'll never agree. I don't love you as a woman must love a husband.... I won't. I will not, not ever."

"You ought to think about what you're saying, Vicky." Clive's use of her informal British name was a jarring slap. "It's possible you may lose your kingdom...and all public favor as well. Who will take care of you if they call you an ignorant savage in a colonial backwater territory?" Clive cringed the moment he said the words. "I meant, 'When other people think—'" He tried to correct himself.

Kaiulani's eyes narrowed as a righteous anger filled her breast. The cold around them seemed to dissipate as she lifted her chin and squared her shoulders. "Now I know the truth of how you see me, Mister Davies. Well, know this: it is far preferable to be an ignorant backwater savage who knows, at least, the love of God, than to be the mere son of a rich man. Your father's greatness does not make you so, and I'm quite sure that a devil can quote the Good Book as well as any Christian, when it suits his purpose. So leave me be, Clive. I've wanted a friend, not a husband, but it's now clear that you will make neither."

"Kaiulani," he protested, "I didn't mean—"

Without another word, Kaiulani extended her left arm with a snap and pointed for Clive to leave the gardens.

"Please," he tried again, but she spun on her heel and marched away toward the stables.

* * * *

Dressed in the black of mourning for the king, Kaiulani, Hannah, and Annie rode in the closed carriage to the telegraph office on Front Street. Annie, her eyes red from a night of weeping, stared out at the bleak midwinter landscape. "To think that Southport here in faraway England has a street named Front Street just like our own little Lahaina Town. Do you think a homesick British whaler longing for his Southport named the streets of Lahaina? Do you think it could be, Kaiulani? That those sailors missed England as much as we miss Hawaii?"

Kaiulani nodded and squeezed her eyes tight against the sting of tears. She could not imagine any longing for home stronger than what she felt right now. "What I would give to grieve with our own people. To walk down Front Street in Lahaina."

Hannah turned her head toward the busy Southport sidewalk. "Mister Davies says the news of the king's death will not reach Hawaii until the ship arrives with his body. It is as if we know the future. No one in Honolulu knows he is dead. And look: people here come and go, never knowing or caring that in a few days the heart of Hawaii will be broken!" She wiped her eyes and shook her head slowly from side to side.

Kaiulani laid her head on Hannah's shoulder. "He is done with dying. In heaven now. I will fix my heart on the homecoming." The thoughts of all three young women were fixed on home. Never had the weight of exile seemed so heavy.

Kaiulani whispered hoarsely, "I would not have ever left if I had known. Never to see Papa Moi again. To think he's gone. With my mother in heaven. Now the only ones left of my mother's family are me and my aunt Liliuokalani. She will be queen, and I...I am next in line to the throne. I want only to return home. To run across the lawn of Ainahau and climb the banyan with you."

Fear of the future raced through her mind, yet the fear remained unspoken.

Hannah squeezed Kaiulani's fingertips. "The king, your uncle, sent you to England for a reason. You know it now as surely as we know. It isn't safe for a royal to be in Hawaii; for the last of the *Alii* to be too close to those who wish to destroy our Constitution and steal our nation. It isn't safe for you, Kaiulani. You understand what I am saying."

The sinister thought none had dared express seemed an almost physical oppression. Had King Kalakaua been murdered in San Francisco?

The carriage pulled up in front of the telegraph office. Suggins opened the door and set the step for them to descend.

Kaiulani arranged for a funeral wreath to accompany Papa Moi's casket from San Francisco to Honolulu. The princess filled out the order and paid the enormous sum for the trans-Atlantic telegram.

"And do you have a message to put on the wreath, miss?" the bespectacled clerk asked.

Kaiulani's pen hovered above the slip of paper. *Aloha me ka pau-make,* she wrote. *My love is with the one who is done with dying.*

* * * *

1973

It was the dead of night. All of Lahaina was asleep. Metal rigging rang against masts in the harbor like the sound of wind chimes.

On her bed, Sandi closed her eyes and pictured John with his guitar on the front porch.

Across from the Pioneer, beneath the banyan tree, someone played a guitar in a familiar melody. Sandi smiled and remembered John's face as snatches of the Beatles' "Blackbird" song drifted on the sweet night air.

1968. The Beatles' *White Album* was released. John had practiced the chords for hours until he could pluck the notes in exact duplication of McCartney's style. Happy. Hopeful. John had signed his last letter to her from Nam: *Remember the Blackbird, singing in the dead of night.*

On the day word came that John was missing in action the tune had come on the radio. She had run to the bedroom and thrown open his guitar case. Touching the strings, she remembered his fingers moving across the frets; almost felt him strumming her skin. Gazing at his guitar, the first discordant note of five years of uncertainty had sounded: "Broken wings...broken wings..." She would not start her life again until she knew, one way or the other, if John was alive. She could not sing; she could not fly; she could not rise. Sandi banished the hopeful song of the "Blackbird," switching off the radio whenever McCartney began his plucky tune. Five long years waiting for her husband to return had driven the familiar lyrics from her memory.

Why did she want to sing tonight?

She tried to sing along, "...broken wings...learn to fly."

How did it go? She couldn't remember, so she hummed the tune instead. The voices beneath the banyan faded into distant laughter, then moved on to melancholy folk songs. Sandi stood on the *lanai* and tried to remember what life had been like before John disappeared and everything in her shut down.

The stars shone over the channel. She could see the mast of the *Royal Flush* among other boats in the harbor. Was Archie sleeping? "I am waiting, Lord. Waiting to arise. Lord? I am so broken. Broken wings. Will I ever fly again?"

The ache of loneliness, the longing to be held and caressed and loved, became a physical pain. Startled by the awakening of long dormant desire, she turned away, climbed into bed, and prayed for merciful rest.

PART THREE

Chapter Fourteen

....

Victorian England

The lawns of Sundown seemed packed to capacity when Princess Kaiulani descended the stairs with Hannah and Annie trailing like ladies in waiting. Arranged by the Davies, the afternoon reception was called to commemorate the coronation of Hawaii's new queen and the official announcement of Princess Kaiulani's new position. Though Hawaii was a world away, the monarchy of Great Britain embodied kindred spirits with Queen Liliuokalani and with Kaiulani, the new heir apparent. The tea was only open to those of a certain class of society. A string quartet played Mozart beside the fountain. The hum of pleasant conversation drifted across the grounds.

Koa, second in line for the throne after Kaiulani, was elegantly dressed in a morning coat. The delicate china cup seemed strangely out of place in his square Polynesian hands. Laughing among a crowd of attendees, he paused midsentence when Kaiulani emerged from the house onto the patio.

"Ah yes," he said, striking his fist against his chest as a sign of his adoration. "She is the Hope of Hawaii."

All eyes turned to her. She wore a yellow gown, the royal color reserved only for Hawaiian *Alii*. The silk was stitched with delicate flowers resembling the gardens of Ainahau. Dark hair was coiled at the nape of her neck. She searched the crowd for familiar faces and spotted Andrew's back. He and his father were deep in conversation with Theo.

Andrew raised his head as though he sensed her presence. Polite whispers rippled across the gathering. Kaiulani bowed slightly. *"Aloha."* She passed through the partygoers. "Thank you for coming."

She was instantly surrounded by a guard of honor made up of young men from Clive's college.

A fresh-faced boy of about thirteen crowded in between his school chums. "Princess! I was born in Hawaii," he chirped in a voice halfway to manhood.

She snapped open her fan and said, "Why then, you belong to me."

The male laughter seemed to turn Andrew's head. His eyes caught hers in the midst of the herd, and he stood, motionless, taking her in.

She hoped there would be a quiet place where they could talk. There was so much she wanted to tell him.

* * * *

The guests thinned as the sun set and cool sea air swept inland. Kaiulani's head began to throb. She quietly retreated into Theo's library to escape the noise of her admirers.

She sat in the burgundy leather wingback chair and closed her eyes. If only she was home now, she thought. If only the party celebrating her official acknowledgment as heir to the Hawaiian throne could have been held beneath the banyan tree at Ainahau.

She had never felt so far from home and those she loved. "I don't belong here, do I?" she asked God quietly.

Andrew's familiar voice answered, "Everyone is asking for you."

She inhaled deeply and turned to see him in the doorway. He held a rectangular gift beneath his arm. The paper was yellow, like her dress.

Almost shyly he said, "For you."

"I was hoping I could talk to you alone."

"I saw this in a bookshop window on Haymarket."

"So many people. All talking at once."

"...and I said to myself, Kaiulani's eyes. Could be her portrait. Her soul." He extended the package to her. "Before I leave, a parting gift in honor of the Princess."

She held his gift. *"Alii* yellow."

"I have been studying your world for quite some time."

"Mahalo," she whispered, pulling the red ribbon and folding back the tissue paper. "Kind...Andrew." She gasped as the portrait of a beautiful young woman, Bible in her hand, gazed up at her from the cherrywood frame.

"It's called *The Soul's Awakening.*" Andrew ducked his head, clearly pleased by her response. "By Sant. The PRB painters. I heard you were learning to paint."

"Beautiful." She sighed.

"You. Your soul. I mean, what I saw that night. You know."

"I'll hang it in my bedroom, so I can see it last thing when I go to sleep and first thing when I wake up. And I'll think of you." She stretched out her hand. "Will you come again soon?"

He shook his head. A curious smile fixed on his face. "I'm leaving."

"Leaving?"

"Going away."

She felt strangely unhappy. "Why? Where? Andrew? What are you talking about?"

He cleared his throat. "Spent the last months studying for the ministry. I'm by no means ready, but Reverend Smith—Gipsy—he's helped me make contact with the mission school on Maui."

She gasped. Tears filled her eyes. "Maui? You? You're going home?"

"Lahaina. So much need. Your people. I thought, if there was anything I could do to help."

She covered her eyes with her hand. "Oh, Andrew! If only I could come too!"

He answered quietly, moving a step closer to her. "Your steps are ordered by the Lord, Kaiulani. He knew you before you were born and made you who you are. For such a time as this, I think. A strong voice for your people."

"I have no voice at all."

"You will."

She reached out to him, clasping his wrist and holding her cheek against his arm as he knelt beside her. "Take me with you, Andrew! Let me pack my bags and go away with you. Back to *Hawaii Nei*. Not as a princess, but just to live among my own people. Oh, Andrew!"

He traced the line of her jaw with his finger. "There is too much ahead for you to run away. Too much. They call you Hawaii's Hope, you know."

Silent tears fell onto the glass of the picture. "My soul is awake, Andrew. I pray and ask the Lord what He wants from me. But I am just a girl."

"The Lord says to you, Kaiulani, what is it? Jeremiah chapter one, I think. 'Before I formed thee in the belly I knew thee; and before thou camest forth out of the womb I sanctified thee.... Say not, I am a child: for thou shalt go to all that I shall send thee, and whatsoever I command thee thou shalt speak.... Behold, I have put my words in thy mouth. See, I have this day set thee over the nations and over the kingdoms, to root out, and to pull down, and to destroy, and to throw down, to build, and to plant.'" [21]

"When are you going?"

"Three days."

"Will you write me?"

"Every week."

"I have no one at home who tells me the truth about what is happening."

He kissed her hand and then her cheek. His mouth moved close to hers. "I will. My lips will speak love to your people. My eyes will see them for your eyes. My ears will hear their words. But my heart? My heart will be here with you."

"You are mine. *Aloha nui loa.*"

He kissed her gently. His warm mouth lingered over hers. A moment longer he waited. And then he rose and left her alone without a word.

＊ ＊ ＊ ＊

It was the season of good-byes.

Annie's trunk was packed for her trip home to Hawaii. The steamship *Teutonic* was at berth in Liverpool. At the summons of the new queen of Hawaii, Annie Cleghorn was retracing the route by which they had come from Hawaii. Clive, on his way to work in his father's Hawaiian branch, would accompany her to Honolulu. From New York they would cross the continent by rail and sail home from San Francisco. Annie planned to arrive in Honolulu in time for the official coronation celebration of Queen Liliuokalani. Already letters from home left the ominous impression that the new queen's opponents gave the monarchy little reason to celebrate.

Prince Koa had already sailed home from Portsmith and was prepared to take up whatever government post Queen Liliuokalani chose for him in Honolulu.

Of the Hawaiian royal party, only Kaiulani and her beloved friend Hannah were to remain behind in England.

Annie opened the armoire, displaying her English wardrobe to Hannah and Kaiulani. "I'll have no need of winter clothes in Honolulu. Try them on. If you can alter them, well, then. If not, give them to charity."

Kaiulani and Hannah sat on the bed and gazed forlornly at the plain dresses as though visualizing their world without Annie. Kaiulani also pictured her sister at home in the banyan tree and running along white sand beaches.

Arms crossed, Annie studied the interior of the steamer trunk and voiced Kaiulani's thoughts: "My coat for the crossing. Four blouses. Two traveling skirts. A gown for the coronation and, in a month, I'll be at Ainahau wearing a *muumuu*."

Memories of home, peacocks, and her horse, Fairy, filled Kaiulani's mind. She covered her face as silent tears began to stream down her cheeks. Hannah rubbed her back and shook her head from side-to-side.

Unspoken questions remained unanswered. Why had Kaiulani not been called home? Wouldn't the presence of Kaiulani have given some comfort to her aunt as she faced the opposition? Kaiulani and Liliuokalani were the only remaining family members in the royal line of Kaiulani's mother.

Annie was unaware of her half sister's tears as she cheerfully packed small souvenirs of Great Britain into the drawers of her luggage for friends and family. "And from Kaiulani, a new burled walnut pipe for Papa Archie—"

Kaiulani finally spoke. "And bring him my love, Annie. Tell him. Tell him my heart is breaking!"

Annie's face blanched as she turned around and rushed to comfort Kaiulani. The trio of women had been inseparable since they had left the Islands. The thought that one of them was being recalled from exile while two remained was almost unbearable.

Annie pulled Kaiulani against her. "Oh, Kaiulani! Sweet little sister! How can I go now? I've been so thoughtless! Thoughtless! Thinking only of myself."

"Why can't I come too?" Kaiulani sobbed. "Why do they leave me here?"

Hannah and Annie exchanged knowing looks. Though Kaiulani did not have a Pinkerton guard, she had not returned to school, nor would she. Letters between Archie Cleghorn and Theo Davies included dire warnings about Kaiulani's safety. She no longer rode Blenheim alone or left the grounds unless Theo or Clive was along.

Annie soothed, "When things in the government are settled. Then Papa will bring you home. You'll see. When it's safe again, you'll be called home."

There was little comfort in Annie's prediction. Kaiulani longed to be caressed by the warm trade winds of Ainahau. Her face held the memory of Hawaiian dawns as she turned toward the cold sun rising above England.

"I am a prisoner here." Kaiulani leaned heavily against Annie. "They're kind, all of them. But Annie, tell Papa...tell him I would rather die at home than remain in exile."

Annie brushed Kaiulani's tears with her thumb and held them to her lips. "I taste the salt of our warm seas in your tears." Annie sighed. "I will tell Papa. I'll do what I can."

"You'll write me. Lots."

"For the outbound steamer. Once a week."

"No one tells me anything. Please, Annie. You must tell me all the news."

"I will."

"The truth. Not watered down."

Annie kissed her forehead. "I promise." Taking Hannah's hand, she placed it in Kaiulani's open palm. "Now Hannah will care for you. Swear it, Hannah."

Hannah replied solemnly, "I swear before the Lord. My life for yours, Kaiulani."

The trio huddled together until the thump of footsteps sounded on the stair.

Clive, dressed for the journey to the wharf, appeared at the door. "It's time, Annie." His faced seemed strained with the prospect of leaving Kaiulani. "Could you spare me a minute?" he asked Kaiulani. "Alone?"

Hannah and Annie left the room. Kaiulani squared her shoulders. Head held high, she drew herself erect. "Clive."

"I hate to go."

"You must. Prepare yourself to manage your father's business."

He towered over her. Taking her hand he laid it on his heart. "I know you don't love me. But I believe you could, if you let yourself."

"Clive. You are so...I cherish your—"

He interrupted. "Stop with that word *cherish*. I will save my heart only for you. I expect to take over Father's interests in Honolulu within a very short time."

"Then I'll see you at home. Ainahau. When I am allowed to return."

He pulled her to her feet and held her close against him. She tried to push him away. He held her tight around her waist. "Clive, stop!"

Lifting her chin, he searched her eyes. "Kaiulani, I—I love you." He kissed her fiercely.

Still she resisted. "Clive, I can never love—"

"You will love me!" He kissed her again. Warmth coursed through her. Breathless, she pressed her cheek against the coarse tweed fabric of his jacket. He stroked her hair. "That's all I wanted to know."

"No promises," she said. "My heart belongs to *Hawaii Nei*."

"You need me."

"I don't," she insisted. "I can't."

"You will." His lips moved against her ear. "One last kiss, Kaiulani. I take you with me."

"And then, *Aloha*."

"*Aloha nui loa*."

* * * *

1973

The *Royal Flush* was anchored between two finger-like peninsulas of bare lava rock, each a few hundred yards away. Above a narrow white strip of sand, just beyond where vegetation took hold, the neatly groomed pineapple fields of the Honolua Plantation stretched away to the base of the West Maui Mountains.

Sandi stood in the bow, gazing down the anchor chain through thirty-five feet of opal blue water to the smooth bottom below. The boat rocked gently in the shelter of the cove as the father and his daughters kicked away from the stern wearing masks, snorkels, and fins, borrowed from Archie's supply. The mother seemed to have some fear of fish and repeatedly asked Archie for reassurances.

"And how big was that one?" she questioned.

"Well, that wasn't even near here," Archie said.

"But how big?"

"You asked me whether I've seen any sharks around the island. Of course I have, but I'm at this reef all the time, and I have never seen one here."

"Still, how big?"

Archie shrugged and shook his head. "I don't know. Four, maybe four and a half feet?"

The woman inhaled through gritted teeth.

Archie was getting frustrated. "Missus Compton, the sharks we have in Hawaii are more afraid of you than you are of them.

You won't ever see one, because they don't want anything to do with you, I promise."

"I know, I know," she agreed. "Tom says the same thing. But he's editing this book right now about a shark. He reads me parts and—"

"Your daughters don't seem too afraid. How about you try it for ten minutes? I'll stand up here and watch for anything suspicious."

Finally the woman did as he suggested, though she insisted her family rejoin her at the swim ladder before she jumped in.

Sandi laughed when Archie exaggerated wiping his brow as though he'd just tilled a field by mule-power. "This tourist trade is hard work!" he said. "How about you, Sandi? Would you like to be debated into a swim?"

She smiled at his choice of words. "I'd rather not. I'll do it the old-fashioned way."

Archie cocked his head in question. It reminded Sandi of the RCA-logo Dog.

She explained, "I mean, I've decided to go for a swim."

As she shed her sundress, revealing the modest one-piece swim-suit she wore underneath, Archie looked away quickly, as though she were undressing completely, and stammered, "Um, well, you know what they say—"

A splash interrupted him as Sandi dove from the boat while his back was turned.

"—about an argument waiting to happen." Archie shrugged and began detaching his artificial limb.

But Sandi called from beside the boat, "Archie! Aren't you swim-ming too?"

Holding his left arm behind his back, he peered over the side and shook his head. "I usually stay topside, in case anyone needs to be picked up."

"Oh, come on," Sandi argued, swiveling her head toward where the family of tourists was crawling out of the surf onto the warm sand. "They won't need you unless one of those rare Hawaiian land-sharks shows up." She imitated the woman's nervous question: "How big did you say that one was again?"

He laughed and went to fetch a couple more sets of swimgear for them, hanging each piece by its straps from his left forearm. Walking back to where Sandi dangled from one of the boat's inflatable bumpers, he dropped her mask and snorkel, then one flipper, then the other, making sure she was able to don each before handing her the next.

As he sat down beside the pile of elastic straps, plastic, and steel that made up his artificial arm, he sighed heavily and shook his head. Slowly, almost unwillingly, he raised his right hand to remove the patch that covered where his left eye had been, tucking it in the cuff of the prosthetic. He stuck the oval swim mask to his face, using the suction of its seal, then pulled the clingy rubber strap slowly over his curly brown hair.

Only then did he make his way to the cockpit and ease into the water. With some well-practiced contortions, he slipped on each fin and swam around to Sandi.

"Whoa," she said when he appeared. "You scared me. I was expecting you to come cannon-balling off the deck like I did."

"That'll get you an *A* for effort, but only a *C* for style."

As they bit down on their snorkels and kicked for the nearest outcropping of coral, Sandi watched the bottom rising to meet them.

Archie didn't use his arms while they swam, carrying them straight at his sides instead. Swimming just a few feet behind, she could stare openly at his left, noting that it was amputated just above the wrist. She could also tell how uncomfortable the prosthesis must be. There were deep red indentations in his skin from each of its seams and straps, running from his shoulder to the missing hand.

She was reflecting again on his resilience when Archie stopped abruptly and spun toward her, treading water. Spitting his snorkel from his mouth, he asked excitedly, "Can you hold your breath well?"

She didn't know what "well" meant, figuring she could probably do a minute underwater if she had to. She shrugged.

"Well, try," Archie said, inverting himself in the water and kicking for the bottom.

She followed his example, and they touched the sand about ten feet down. Archie looked toward her and raised one finger to his lips, then cupped his hand to his right ear to suggest the word: *listen.*

She cocked her head then and, just when she thought it was some silly joke and her lungs began to burn, she heard it. A deep guttural impact, like an intermittent humming, sounded three times, followed by what sounded to Sandi like a tuba, sliding from the lowest note it could make to the highest. This also repeated a few times. Sandi stared intently into Archie's mask, trying to convey the question she had.

Finally her lungs couldn't bear it, and she kicked hurriedly to the surface, gasping for air. "What was that?" she panted when Archie appeared a second later.

"Whale song!" He was panting too. "That's coming from probably miles out in the channel, but that's how they communicate with each other."

"It's beautiful," Sandi said. "Stunning. I could feel it in my chest."

Archie nodded. "There are some really cool projects going on in the Islands right now. The same people who fought to ban hunting them a few years ago are working on microphones that can record them underwater. Really neat stuff."

They recreated the descent four more times before both were too winded to do it anymore. Swimming back to the boat along Archie's right side, Sandi mostly watched the ocean bottom slide along beneath, but occasionally she shot a glance toward him, marveling at the world in which he lived and his obvious pleasure in sharing it with others.

She heard herself say, "Beautiful."

"Yes. Gotta tell the truth," Archie agreed, swinging onto the swim step. "She really is."

Chapter Fifteen

....

Royal Kingdom of Hawaii

Crumpling up a sheet of paper, Andrew Adams tossed it over his shoulder. It landed amid a heap of six other false starts. This literary effort had to get past the first paragraph if it was ever to be a story for the *Paradise of the Pacific* magazine.

The Master's Reading Room where Andrew had his desk was adjacent to The Mission House on Front Street. Since coming to the Islands, Andrew had filled a variety of roles for the American Board of Commissioners for Foreign Missions under which he served. In addition to maintaining the lending library, Andrew taught English to Hawaiian children and served as a scribe for illiterate sailors. Lahaina was also home to a school where ABCFM missionaries bound for the Orient came for language studies. Andrew's duties included overseeing their housing and organizing tutors for them.

All of which paid him very little. Andrew supplemented his allowance by contributing articles to Hawaiian papers and periodicals.

Just now he was working on a piece about the *paniolos*—Hawaiian cowboys—of the Parker Ranch. Leaning back in his chair, Andrew laid aside his pen to ease his aching neck muscles and stare out at the hedge of hibiscus blossoms. Despite the fact the calendar indicated January, the west Maui temperature was a balmy 75 degrees. There was a faint tang of sulfur in the air, wafted on the Kona wind from the volcanoes of the Big Island a hundred miles away.

A stack of back issues of *Paradise* was on the corner of the desk. As Andrew's boot nudged the table leg, the heap slid sideways, dumping across the floor.

Starting a new article was always the hardest part of his writing, and today's attempt seemed more difficult than usual. Andrew was restless—an effect of the Kona wind, or perhaps his longing for Kaiulani. His unfinished weekly letter was on the blotter. Filled with news from the Islands, it lacked the truth of what was in Andrew's heart. How could he tell Kaiulani that visions of her in his arms inhabited his every waking hour? The distance between Lahaina and London was more than half a world away. Her destiny as queen was too far beyond his reach. Andrew could never tell her how much he loved her.

He stood, yawned, and stretched. Maybe he should walk down to the harbor. Even if he found no additional inspiration there, he might at least throw off the crushing drowsiness.

Harlan Boyd, publisher of the *Paradise* and also of a newspaper called the *Lahaina Intelligencer,* loomed in the doorway. "Adams," he snapped, "you working on that *paniolo* piece?"

When had Andrew promised to have it ready? Could it really already be two weeks overdue?

"Just doing a little polishing," Andrew returned. "On your desk tomorrow."

"Never mind," Boyd said. "Got a newspaper assignment for you. Already cleared it with your ABC boss. There's something brewing in Honolulu. Want you to go sniff it out; write it up."

"Brewing?"

"My Honolulu correspondent has an abscessed tooth, worse luck. But his last dispatch said Lorrin Thurston had figured out a way to depose the queen. Said it was going to happen soon. Need you to look into it."

"Depose the queen? End the monarchy? With what—an armed uprising?"

"That's what you're going to find out. Here's five dollars' advance. Get going. You just have time to make the inter-island steamer."

* * * *

Though rushed in his leave-taking, Andrew had plenty of time during the crossing from Maui to Oahu to ponder what lay ahead. Every point he reviewed involved memories of Kaiulani. What would happen to her if the queen were really deposed?

Such a move would mean the end of the monarchy, and then Kaiulani would never be queen. What would the princess have to come home to, if she were not the heir? if there were no throne for her to inherit?

Would she ever come back to Hawaii at all, or would she stay abroad? It was not an idle thought. Andrew could not imagine Kaiulani's willing submission to being ruled by a thieving gang of shop clerks and sugar planters.

Ever since Queen Liliuokalani came to the throne, there had been rumors that Thurston and the Reformers were plotting something. The stories were mostly discounted, since everyone knew gossip was one of Hawaii's besetting sins.

There was one reason it might be different—worse—this time. The queen had often spoken of a new constitution, but her ideas about what would be changed had never been articulated till now.

If what Andrew had heard was true, Liliuokalani wanted to remove the property ownership requirement for voter eligibility. That change would give power to more landless native Hawaiians.

The other purported amendment probably stung the reformers even more. The queen wanted only Hawaiian citizens to be able to vote. The present constitution allowed resident aliens, which term included most of the Americans, the right to vote.

Taking the vote away from them would cause an all-out battle, and preparations for battle seemed to be going forward in the Honolulu Harbor.

Just offshore lay the U.S. man-of-war *Boston*. As Andrew watched, the gun crews carried out drill after drill, though no shots were fired. Parties of marines drawn up along the rails were armed with rifles.

Andrew could not believe Americans would forcibly invade the Hawaiian capital. What was going on here?

It was easier to obtain the answer than he expected.

Once on shore Andrew noticed a file of *haoles* traveling in a ragged column like pretend soldiers. They were unarmed but had the clenched-jawed look of men on a desperate mission.

A lone Hawaiian policeman fled at the men's approach.

Andrew joined the tail of the procession. "What's the trouble?"

"Who are you?" responded a man with twin brown streaks in his otherwise blond beard.

"Adams," Andrew replied tersely. "Reporter for the *Intelligencer*."

"Say, that's all right, then," the militiaman replied. "Just make sure you spell my name proper. Herrold, Alvin. H-E-R—"

"No talking in ranks, Herrold," boomed the captain of the troop, dropping back beside Andrew.

Herrold spat tobacco juice and clamped his mouth shut.

Andrew addressed the officer, who identified himself as Captain Colburn. "Can you tell me what's happening?"

"The Committee of Safety called out the militia," Colburn retorted. "Might be rioting if the queen publishes the new constitution. Gotta protect Americans and American businesses."

"So where are you going?"

"The armory on Beretania Street," was the reply.

* * * *

Once inside the Beretania Street Armory, Andrew slipped away from the militiamen and took a position in a shadowed alcove at the side of the hall. Among the merchants who were leaders in the Reform Party, there were many who knew Andrew supported the monarchy. Given the angry rhetoric, this was not the time to be denounced as an opponent.

Lorrin Thurston, the spitting image of his missionary grandfather, strode to a podium and raised his hands for silence. But Andrew knew Thurston's resemblance to his grandfather was only skin-deep. The man's heart was hard. He worshipped the twin gods of power and money. "The time has come," he said with a dramatic pause, "to liberate these islands from a corrupt and dissolute family of despots."

Shouts of "Hear! Hear!" rang over the arched ceiling of the chamber.

"Thanks to our good friends Misters Peterson and Parker," Thurston continued, "we have received timely and vital warning of the queen's treachery."

Andrew leaned forward. This was not only extraordinary exaggeration but outright hypocrisy as well. The two men being hailed as heroes were Queen Liliuokalani's foreign minister and attorney-general—traitors to their oath and their sovereign.

"They inform me that the queen intends to announce her wicked document tomorrow. My friends," Thurston said, spreading his arms to embrace the crowd. "My friends, this must not be allowed to happen. The queen is guilty of breaking her oath to uphold the constitution."

Andrew's head was spinning with the twisted logic. The queen, by proposing to change the constitution, was guilty of treason. But this gang of greedy, power-hungry men planned to use force against a lawfully elected sovereign because they disapproved of her ideas?

"And now," Thurston resumed, "we welcome another friend of right-thinking people: U.S. minister to Hawaii, the honorable John L. Stevens."

Andrew was now well and truly alarmed. Stevens, the bent, white-bearded curmudgeon, despised the Hawaiian royalty to the point of being rude to the queen. Had he convinced America to join in this coup?

Stevens bowed stiffly to acknowledge the cheers of the crowd, but it was Thurston who continued speaking. "Tomorrow, early, I and a delegation will go to the palace. We will denounce the queen as a traitor. We will tell her she must abdicate. We will tell her she has no choice, and that resistance will mean needless bloodshed."

The first stirrings of unrest circled the hall. "How many guards has she got?" someone called. "What if they arrest you and open fire on us?"

Thurston thrust out his chest and hooked his thumbs in his lapels. "The queen's force amounts to less than two hundred men. I see that number in this room right now. And Minister Stevens will certify that in order to protect American lives and property, the captain of the USS *Boston* must land an armed party of marines, which he has already agreed to do."

The level of cheering reached a new level of pandemonium. "Out with the old, in with the new!" they chanted. "Hawaii shall belong to America!"

"Away with bloated, drunken, heathen monarchs!"

"Now is the time to strike!"

A wave of dread swept through Andrew as he thought of Kaiulani. There was nothing the enemies of the monarchy would not do to gain power. The words of Psalm 94 flashed through his mind: *"They crush your people, O Lord…and they say, 'The Lord does not see'…does he who formed the eye not see?"*

When the militiamen began to march around the hall like at a political convention, Andrew thought it was time to leave. He had sidled along the wall as far as a side door when he glimpsed a familiar face near the platform.

Clive Davies gestured eagerly for Thurston's attention and received a tight-lipped smile and a curt bob of the head in reply.

What was Clive up to, speaking with Kaiulani's enemy?

Andrew melted back into the gloom to see what would happen next.

* * * *

The crowd inside the armory was a long time dispersing. For men who might be going into bloody battle, they acted remarkably cheerful and even giddy with excitement. Were it not for the fact that Thurston would not allow them to drink alcohol inside the armory, the celebration would have lasted still longer, Andrew thought.

Even after the militia departed in search of liquid refreshment, the leadership of the Committee of Safety conferred amongst themselves. Assignments were handed out: who was to carry the ultimatum to the queen, who was to direct the movements of the marines if their assistance should be needed, and who would climb to the top of the church steeple to direct the artillery fire from the ship.

Artillery fire? Against the native Hawaiians? Andrew was aghast. He remained in the shadows, listening.

Finally only Thurston and Clive Davies remained.

"Yes, Clive," Thurston inquired. "What is it? Very busy right now."

"Have you thought," Clive ventured, "about how the native population will react after tomorrow? I mean, what if there was a way to diffuse their anger at losing their queen?"

"Go on," Thurston said. "I'm listening. You have such a plan?"

"I have power in…in a certain quarter," Clive suggested, tugging a lock of his dark hair. "I believe—no, I know, I can guarantee—that the Princess Victoria Kaiulani would be welcomed home by her people."

"What's your point?" Thurston demanded.

"Put Kaiulani on the throne in place of the old queen," Clive explained in a rush. "Tell the people they can keep their precious monarchy—only you and the committee will run the government."

Only with great difficulty did Andrew restrain himself from leaping on Clive right then. He forced himself to remain still and listen, remembering that Thurston had hundreds of by now drunken militiamen within earshot.

"With yourself as prince consort, I suppose?" Thurston observed drily.

"I'm only thinking of the good of Hawaii," Clive said archly.

Thurston appeared to ponder the suggestion, then shook his head. "No, it's too late for that now. The monarchy must go. The kingdom must go. Hawaii must and shall become part of America, and before that can happen, we must do away with kings and queens."

Thurston exited the Armory then, leaving Clive to mutter to himself: "Either way, she'll have to marry me. She has no other choice."

"Not if I can help it," Andrew argued, stepping out of the darkness. "You utter scoundrel. The princess would never have gone along with your scheme, and she will certainly never marry a traitor like you."

Lunging forward with a shout, Clive swung his fist at Andrew's face.

Andrew slipped under the blow. A short, hammering right hand caught Clive in the ribs, making him double over. Then Andrew's left swung upward, striking Clive on the point of the chin.

Though heavier and slightly taller than his opponent, Clive flew backwards, hitting the back of his head on the wall. He slid downward, his arms out flung.

Andrew stood above his fallen foe. "I may not be able to stop what's happening here. But I can, and I will, stop you."

Chapter Sixteen

....

The streets rang with the chaos of an unleashed mob. Thurston's vigilantes smelled blood, and their eagerness to get on with the coup increased moment by moment.

Andrew slipped into the grounds of the palace by a rear gate. Members of the Hawaiian Royal Guard milled about the grounds. Summoned from their homes on short notice, and used to performing only ceremonial duties, half of them were unarmed and most were barefoot.

Andrew managed to get one of the officers to take him to the queen's chamberlain. Once in the presence of that austere, silver-haired, amber-skinned man, Andrew explained his mission. "You don't know me," he said. "But you know my father and our connection to the father of the princess. The queen needs to be warned about what's happening."

Queen Liliuokalani sat surrounded by six Hawaiian women, each as old as she. Four guards were posted about the chamber, one by each royal feathered standard or *kehili*.

"Majesty," Andrew began, "Mister Thurston—"

"I am already aware there is a plot underway," the queen responded. "Mister Thurston is coming to see me at noon. I will not be moved by his threats. He will not dare to offer violence to my person."

"Majesty," Andrew said slowly, "with respect, he has a large party of armed men, and the Americans may land a party of marines."

"I cannot believe the United States would be involved in the illegal takeover of a friendly nation," the queen returned.

"I hope you're correct," Andrew said, then added what he had seen of Minister Stevens at the rally in the armory.

Liliuokalani's face twisted in a grimace. "That man," she said scornfully, "is no friend of mine or of Hawaii. But even he is not foolish enough to start a war."

Andrew tried one last time to move the queen to action. "Then at least let all of your troops be armed. If you make a show of force, it may make the rebels hesitate."

"It is good," the queen agreed. "I will send a trusted officer to return with a load of weapons from the armory."

"Not the Beretania Street Armory," Andrew cautioned. "It is in the hands of the rebels."

* * * *

1973

The ancient gramophone in the corner of Auntie Hannah's room hummed softly, spinning the disc of a symphonic piece toward its crescendo. The rich red mahogany wood of the machine's cabinet had more scratches and grooves than the records it played, but its sculpted brass horn was brightly polished and still projected the sounds with a mournful clarity.

Sandi sat on the linen locker at the foot of the bed, listening as Auntie Hannah hummed along softly as though she were one of the instruments. Her tired, breathy voice had the same thin quality as the music, and when Sandi closed her eyes, it was difficult to distinguish between them.

"Do you like it, my dear?" the old woman asked, noticing Sandi's pensiveness.

"It's beautiful, Auntie Hannah. What is it?"

"Beecham, a great conductor. He preferred to perform the work of lesser-known composers. But when he applied himself to the greats, it was wonderful. This is his orchestra performing Beethoven's Seventh— very rare—a short arrangement of the second movement, so it could fit on the record."

"Beautiful," Sandi said again. Too soon the music was over. The horn hissed and crackled as the stylus slid over the paper label in the center of the disc. As Sandi walked to switch it off, her eyes swept over the framed photos adorning Auntie Hannah's dresser.

When the machine was silent, she returned to examine the pictures more closely. They stood like soldiers, ranked four deep, spanning a history of photographic technology from ancient, fading tintypes to a few modern, square Polaroids. It was one of those that caught Sandi's eye.

In it, Archie Kalakaua wore a jersey and football pads as he knelt on one knee in the grass, resting a fist on a helmet by his side. His number, 44, was emblazoned in yellow across his chest, and his attempt at a menacing stare made Sandi smile.

"Archie was a football player?" she asked.

"Oh my, yes." Hannah looked up from a letter. "In 1966 Archie was on a full scholarship at USC. He was so young and so fast, his teammates told him to change his number to 45. They called him 'The Colt.' He was drafted into the army before he played a game."

Hearing a note of sadness creep into her voice, Sandi couldn't help but ask, "What happened, Auntie Hannah? How was he injured?"

"Oh, well, he doesn't tell me much. He always says he was just in the wrong place at the wrong time. Why don't you ask him, dear?"

"I have. He said the same thing to me, but I have this terrible feeling he's simply trying to protect me. The way John always did in his letters. I don't need protecting. I want to know."

Auntie Hannah pursed her lips and considered Sandi's words. "I understand you, child. I have experienced that many times myself as a younger woman."

Sandi smiled and shook her head. Still holding the snapshot, she settled on the bed at Hannah's feet.

Auntie Hannah sighed. "When Archie was first transported to the hospital at Pearl, I made one trip to see him there. He was so surprised and happy to see a friendly face. But he decided that he should not tell it. Perhaps he never will."

Sandi gazed at the smiling face of the young football hero. The smile was the same. But the deepest wound was living a life alone. She understood that kind of hurt.

"But you should know," Auntie Hannah said firmly. "You should know what he deals with every day. If he seems distant, or ever upset…it's enough to say his friend was killed. The circumstance of his own survival is miraculous, at the least."

Auntie Hannah took the picture from Sandi and looked at it lovingly. "This is what he'd rather remember. Moments like this, and who he used to be. He's rebuilding his life slowly. Some of our boys may never be able to do that after what they've seen.

But Archie's strong. He's a fighter—like his great-grandfather." She paused, smiling then. "Fetch me another picture, dear?"

Sandi rose and Auntie Hannah directed her to a silver frame holding a black-and-white photo. But for his clothes and a mustache, the man pictured there looked just like Archie. Sandi whistled at the similarity.

"That's him," Hannah said. "A wonderful, loving man. And our Archie is just the same. A gentleman, if ever one lived. You'll see, dear. God has given him such a spirit. He may never be the same. How could you ever be the same? But someday he'll be as good as new." The old woman cocked her head as if she heard some faraway voice calling her.

Sandi cradled the old photograph in her hands. "Where was this taken?"

"Ulupalakua. Up country. We took the children back to show them where it really happened—the truth of it. No one knew. No one. Life was so uncertain then." She paused. "I knew I loved him, but he didn't give me a clear sign he cared in that way. I felt…warm, you know…when he was near. I was certain that he would protect us with his own life. That's who he was." She hummed at some vision of a long ago time and place. "And Archie's heart is so much like his— so much. You will see for yourself, my dear."

* * * *

Royal Kingdom of Hawaii

Queen Liliuokalani's loyal and trusted retainer—the one dispatched with Andrew to fetch a wagonload of arms—seemed as dim and tired-looking as the swaybacked, potbellied gray horse pulling the ancient cart. Keiwe was the only soldier who could be spared from the force protecting the palace, the guard captain told Andrew. After all, Keiwe was so bowlegged he couldn't march, and he didn't know how to load a gun anyway.

Nor did the captain offer to spare any of his men to guard the return trip from the arms storage. "But no one will suspect you, anyway," the captain assured Andrew. "Keiwe, he hauls the night soil from the barracks. This is his wagon."

Andrew did not like the look of the Honolulu streets. Women and children were nowhere to be seen, while the number of *haoles* carrying ax handles, pistols, and some rifles increased dramatically a few blocks from the palace. They loitered on street corners and gathered on *lanai*s, as if only awaiting the order to take action.

As Andrew and Keiwe neared the arms storage on Kiong Street, they discovered they were already too late. The rebels had broken into the armory and were even now stealing crates of rifles for their own forces.

"Back to the palace," Andrew urged. "Nothing we can do here."

"Wait," Keiwe urged. "My cousin, Leialoha, coming. Policeman." Down the street toward the rebels bustled a blue-uniformed Hawaiian patrolman. His uniform jacket, buttoned up to his chin, looked snug enough to be painful, but there was no doubt he intended to intercede against the pack of insurgents.

What could one lone officer do against this mob? Twenty rebels had already broken open a case of weapons and were brandishing them. Six more containers were stacked in place of the barrels on a beer wagon.

Leialoha seized the bridle of the beer wagon. "Get down," Andrew heard him order the driver. "No steal queen's guns."

"Turn loose, you heathen," the driver shouted, slashing at the policeman with a buggy whip.

The policeman grabbed the whip on the second blow and wrestled it out of the rebel's hands.

"Get down," he said again. "You under arrest."

To Andrew's horror the driver drew a pistol from his belt. "I warned you," he said as he pulled the trigger.

The Colt exploded with a roar and wounded the Hawaiian in the shoulder.

With that single shot, the battle of Honolulu was on.

When Keiwe rumbled forward to drag his injured cousin to safety, the militiaman Andrew recognized as Alvin Herrold drew a bead on him with a rifle.

Andrew leapt on the rebel's back. The rifle fired skyward, missing its target. Andrew and Herrold rolled over and over, struggling to possess the weapon.

As he lost the dispute for the stock of the gun, Andrew gave up his attempt to hold it and closed his fingers around Herrold's throat.

Eyes bulging, Herrold relinquished the rifle and slapped the ground to signify his surrender, just before a gun butt struck Andrew in the back of the head....

* * * *

When Andrew came to, he was propped against a wall in an alley. Who had pulled him out of harm's way, he never knew.

A squad of U.S. marines tramping up the street spotted him, and their lieutenant ordered a medical orderly to bandage his skull. "Lucky you got a hard head," the attendant said. "Nothing busted."

"What's happened?" Andrew asked groggily.

The orderly shrugged. "Nothing much. Few busted noggins, like yours. Gunshot wound or two. Captain sent us ashore first thing, and we got order restored double quick."

"I meant, what about the queen?"

The attendant eyed Andrew curiously. "You mean that cannibal chieftess? Say, you ain't one of them, are you?"

Andrew denied it, then said, "Can I go now?"

"Sure, only get off the street before dark. There's a curfew on. Orders to shoot looters and curfew breakers. 'Course that means Hawaiians, right? Just be careful."

Andrew headed toward the palace but was drawn to a large crowd assembled in front of the Hawaiian government office building. Lorrin Thurston climbed the steps and addressed the crowd. There were no Hawaiian soldiers or policemen anywhere in sight. Raising his hands for silence, Thurston announced: "The former monarch, Liliuokalani, has agreed to step aside."

When the cheering that greeted these words subsided, Thurston continued, "She recognizes that resistance would be futile. To prevent further bloodshed, she has ordered her guards to stack their weapons and go home."

More cheering.

Andrew's head throbbed.

"We, the members of the Committee of Safety, have formed a provisional government, effective immediately. Tomorrow we will send representatives to Washington, petitioning the United States to recognize us as the duly constituted, lawful authority. We will not permit anything, or anyone, to interfere with this spontaneous movement to preserve our precious freedoms."

In those words Andrew heard both irony and danger: freedom was what had been stolen today.

And now that the queen was a virtual prisoner, Kaiulani was squarely a target of Thurston's threat.

At a slight movement of Thurston's hand a bugler began to play, and Thurston turned his head toward the roof of the building. Drawn by his gaze, the onlookers stared upward as well.

As the trumpet sounded, the Hawaiian flag was hauled down from the pole, and the Stars and Stripes took its place.

Chapter Seventeen

....

Arrests of loyal cabinet ministers continued throughout the afternoon and evening of the monarchy's downfall. Many of Thurston's rebels used the turmoil as an excuse to settle old scores. Hawaiians who had refused to sell property to *haoles* were denounced as "dangerous to the Provisional Government." Such a recommendation, unsupported by any witnesses, was enough to get a man detained.

In Lahaina the old prison was called *Hale Paahao,* the "Stuck in Irons House." Andrew didn't know what Honolulu's jail was called, but he didn't want to learn its name by close acquaintance. He had not seen Clive Davies again since the conflict in the armory, but Andrew was certain Clive had condemned him to Thurston.

Even though the cocoon of bandages hiding his features was a good disguise, the sooner Andrew got away from Honolulu and back to Lahaina, the better. In the meantime, Andrew would not jeopardize any of his friends and family by going to their homes. Instead he took a flea-bitten room in dingy sailors' quarters by the harbor.

Andrew awoke in the blackness of night with his head hurting worse than ever. There was such a drumbeat in his brain that made it seem as if the rickety bedframe was shaking.

A dog began to howl. Soon there was a regular chorus of wailing canines and neighing horses.

Andrew's eyes snapped open, despite the pain. The room really was shaking. The wall over Andrew's head leaned toward him as if to whisper a secret. A cloudy, chipped mirror, the chamber's only deco-ration, plummeted to the floor and shattered.

Earthquake!

Tremors on these volcanic islands were common, and Andrew had felt many before. But this was a bad one.

The rumble from deep within the earth increased in both volume and intensity. The bass groaning of the island met a harmony of top-pling chimneys and plunging masonry, all set off against a melodic line of terrified shouting and drunken oaths.

Fires sprang up as collapsing flues spread live coals across wooden floors. Sparks, swirling in the breeze like malevolent fireflies, ignited thatched roofs.

Bracing himself in the doorway of the room, Andrew waited for the shaking to stop. It did so after what seemed like an hour but in reality was less than a minute.

Moans and cries for help punctuated the unnatural stillness; then the incessant clamor of fire alarm bells succeeded all other noises.

* * * *

Victorian England

The gas lamp flickered above Kaiulani's bed. Wind swept inland from the Irish Sea and howled around the corners of Sundown.

Kaiulani felt a shaking and heard a great rumble from deep beneath the earth. The keening wail of a Hawaiian woman was in the wind.

Kaiulani opened her eyes. She could dimly see an old Hawaiian woman, dressed in rags. She stood beside the portrait of the young woman in *The Soul's Awakening* hanging on the wall opposite Kaiulani's bed.

Was she dreaming?

Kaiulani spoke without moving her lips. *"Aloha,* old one. Why do you weep?"

"Ua paopao mai no lakou. They crush your people. *I kou poo kanaka.* They afflict your heritage."

Kaiulani sat up. The air was suffused with the scent of tuberose blossoms. The woman's face became clear before her. "Grandmother? Am I dreaming?"

Kaiulani heard the old woman's words as a psalm of mourning: "Though you sleep, my dear, your soul is awake. Listen to the cries of your people! *Pane mai no lakou me ka olelo iho i na mea howa.* They pour out their arrogant words! Kaiulani, even the ground of *Hawaii Nei* groans for the betrayal. The sons of the righteous have turned against the Lord!"

Again the earth rumbled and shook beneath Kaiulani. She stood on the warm shore of her home and saw the waters roiling. "Who? Who has done this to my people?"

"Kaena wale ka poe hana hewa a pau. All the evildoers boast!"

Kaiulani saw Lorrin Thurston looming beneath her banyan tree with an ax. Clive Davies stood beside him. Andrew, Bible open in his hand, stood between the tree and the upraised ax.

Andrew shouted, "He who planted the ear, does he not hear?"

Thurston laughed and replied, "I am not my father's father."

The old woman standing in the water cried, "They have taken our land. We have no place left to stand, O Lord. *Alu mai la lakou i ka uhane o ka poe pono.* They band together against the life of the Righteous. *A hoohewa lakou i ke koko hala ole.* They condemn the innocent to death!"

Kaiulani shouted, the sound of her own voice calling her to awaken. "Is Queen Liliuokalani alive?"

"The queen lives now as a captive. *Olelo no hoi lakou, Aole e ike mai o Iehova.* They say the Lord does not see what they do. Kaiulani, you must speak for your people. For those who have no voice!"

The bed shook violently. "Kaiulani! Kaiulani!" Hannah's worried voice pierced the fog of her dream. "Wake up, please! You're having a nightmare. Please!"

Slowly Kaiulani's vision began to fade. "What? Where am I?" Her eyes focused on the beautiful portrait of her *Soul's Awakening.*

"Sundown." Hannah held her tightly. "Oh, Kaiulani, are you all right? Please! Talk to me."

Kaiulani's heart was beating rapidly. "Hannah, something terrible has happened!"

"No. Just a dream. A nightmare."

Kaiulani resisted Hannah's logic. There was something about the old woman's warning. The words she had used to speak were familiar. "Hannah, the Bible—fetch my Bible."

"What is it?" Hannah gave her the worn, well-thumbed Bible from the night table.

"The dream. I saw Andrew and Clive and Thurston beneath my banyan tree. And in the water—no ground left to stand on—an old woman. She was our people. She spoke to me in Hawaiian. Her words were..." Kaiulani flipped the pages of her Bible open to Psalms. Kaiulani gasped as she read the words of Psalm 94. "Look, Hannah. Look. This is everything she told me. Here!" Kaiulani passed the book to Hannah, who read slowly.

"They break in pieces thy people, O LORD, and afflict thine heritage. Yet they say, the LORD shall not see." [22]

Hannah's face clouded with concern. "It was probably...only a dream, Kaiulani. Please don't worry. Try to sleep."

Kaiulani held onto Hannah tighter. "I am afraid of what I don't know and what I can't see, Hannah. I am so very far away from home."

"Then we will stay awake all night and pray, you and I. We will stay awake and pray."

* * * *

Republic of Hawaii

Andrew spent the rest of the night dragging wounded sailors out of burning buildings. The U.S. marines, already on hand to police the streets, took up new duties as rescuers and firefighters.

Political turmoil was momentarily forgotten in the aftermath of the natural disaster. No one was checking papers for fugitives as Andrew slipped aboard the inter-island steamer for his return to Maui.

As Andrew's ship churned out of harbor, he had a panoramic view of the destruction. Native construction, mostly of timber, had swayed and pitched but remained standing. It was the more elaborate constructions of brick and masonry, like the government administration building, that cracked and shifted off their foundations. Rubble formed of decorative cornices lay in the streets. Crumbled stone facades littered the steps of grand, pretentious structures.

Atop the government house, the flagpole bearing the American flag was bent at an awkward, embarrassing angle. The drooping banner was the last thing Andrew's eye followed as the steamer slipped out into the channel and away.

Chapter Eighteen

....

Hannah sat at the bedroom's writing table. A textbook, a grammar, a dictionary, and a copybook were all open in front of her. "I dislike German," she said, flipping pages and comparing instructions. "I despise it. I hate it. *Ich hasse es sehr viel.*"

"But you're so much better at it than me," Kaiulani observed. The princess was propped up against the headboard of the bed. "Too bad you can't study it for both of us. If you did, then I would volunteer to do both assignments in English literature."

Hannah made a sour face. "No, thank you. That's no bargain."

Though it was only midafternoon, the winter day was so dreary all the gas lamps were turned up full. An entire bucketful of coal blazed on the hearth, yet the room was still drafty and gloomy.

The clouds that had rolled in the day before had promised snow but delivered freezing rain instead. The smoke from the thousands of Liverpool chimneys seemed to have all collected on Sundown's roof. The icicles hanging from the eaves were the color of charcoal. They portrayed glistening black fangs, as if Kaiulani had been swallowed by a beast and was even now in its maw.

Kaiulani was grateful the post had brought something to counteract the grim day. Open on her lap was the fall edition of the Hawaiian magazine *Paradise of the Pacific*. It had taken three months to reach Southport. Perhaps it had come around the Horn and all the way to England by sea instead of crossing the American continent by train.

263

But it was here now and Kaiulani reveled in the images of home. Besides woodcuts of Diamond Head and the ships moored before Lahaina and the lava pool at Hale Mau-mau, there were delicate drawings of orchids and curved beaked birds called honeycreepers. There were articles on the expansion of the pineapple plantations and newly planted macadamia nut groves.

When she flipped to the very center of the periodical, Kaiulani's gaze fell on something that made her gasp: there was also a section dedicated to Kaiulani herself.

"Did you see this?" Kaiulani asked, waving a page folded back to an engraved likeness of Kaiulani beneath the title HAWAII's HOPE, and the byline: BY ANDREW ADAMS.

Hannah grinned broadly. "I've been waiting for you to discover it. It's all nonsense: says you have a sweet disposition and lovable manners. Must be about some other princess."

Kaiulani chucked a shoe at her friend, then her eyes lit up with hope. "The queen must have given her permission for this article to appear. Do you think...could it mean?"

"That we get to go home soon?" Hannah ventured. She stared pointedly at the panes of glass darkened by layers of frozen soot. "How soon is soon?"

There was a diffident knock at the door. At Hannah's call Theo Davies entered.

"Papa Theo," Kaiulani gushed, brandishing the magazine. "Did you know about this? Were you keeping it as a surprise?"

When Theo did not reply, both young women looked up with alarm. Her guardian's features were pinched, as if he had an unrelenting headache, Kaiulani thought.

"What has happened?" she asked, rising to her feet.

Theo extended three telegrams clutched in one hand.

This was no joyous celebration about being summoned back to Hawaii. The last time Theo brought news that affected him so badly it had been the death of the king.

Not the queen! Surely Liliuokani could not have died?

Or worse! Not Papa!

Hannah moved to stand shoulder-to-shoulder with her friend.

Kaiulani extended her hand in a silent request for the messages.

The first flimsy sheet of paper read simply: *Queen deposed.*

The second added only: *Monarchy abrogated.*

The third gave the instructions: *Break news to princess.*

Kaiulani swayed slightly and Hannah steadied her. The princess bit her lower lip as she struggled to make sense of the news.

"Do you need to sit down?" Theo Davies asked. "Perhaps a glass of sherry, or a compress for your eyes?"

"No, thank you," Kaiulani replied. "I need to think about what is to be done, and I need information. Please, Mister Davies, about this news. I need details: how this happened and when; where the queen is and if she is safe; if America is involved or not. Please find out all you can."

Papa Theo looked surprised at the degree of control Kaiulani exercised over her emotions. Perhaps he had expected a schoolgirl's emotional outburst.

What revealed itself instead was the dignified resolve of a royal princess.

"I'll see to it at once," he said.

* * * *

265

1973

Sandi's cup of coffee and half-eaten scrambled eggs grew cold. She broke off a handful of breadcrumbs and tossed them onto the *lanai*, where two impatient blackbirds scolded her.

"I've spoiled you," she addressed the brazen creatures. They blinked at her with golden eyes. "Go back to Auntie Hannah. She'll feed you. Let me work."

Sandi turned off the overhead fan, which threatened a stack of loose papers. She chronologically shuffled a sheaf of personal letters written to Kaiulani from Andrew and from Annie. Layered together, the correspondence gave two different perspectives of the same events.

Andrew's report of the arrest of Queen Liliuokalani and the takeover of Honolulu by American soldiers was written from a newsman's perspective. Hard lead facts: Who, What, When, Where, Why, and How. The news was interwoven with his sorrow at the betrayal of the monarchy and his genuine concern for the physical safety of Kaiulani.

His masculine hand etched fearful thoughts to her.

> *Even though you are far from home, you must take care.*
> *The men who have forced Liliuokalani to step aside will stop*
> *at nothing to prevent you from taking your rightful place as*
> *Princess Royal.*

Sandi wondered if the princess might have survived to live a long and happy life if she had not returned to Hawaii.

As for Annie, the same events unfolded far away from her day-to-day existence on the north shore of Maui. Political intrigue in Honolulu was to her only a sad irritation. Tyrannical soldiers in Honolulu came second to the news about Annie's husband and her baby. So much had happened in the two years since she had returned to the Islands, including a whirlwind courtship with a long-time admirer and a wedding under the big banyan tree. Not long after, she had felt precious life growing within. Then her son was born, and her life had wrapped around his life. Colic from teething. First step. First word. Annie's ordinary life continued, even while the soul of Hawaii was being raped by greedy men.

Sandi read each letter as though it was newly written and the information fresh.

There were nights when she awakened from a sound sleep and for a moment could not remember what century she was living in. This morning the scratchy music from Auntie Hannah's Victrola set the stage. Sandi expected to scan the busy harbor and see Andrew Adams perched on the seawall as he wrote his weekly missive to his beloved Kaiulani.

Sandi felt a vague irritation at the stiff formality of Andrew's letters. Why didn't he tell her how much he loved her? "You wasted so much time, Andrew," Sandi scolded. She folded Andrew's letter and replaced it in the stack. "What were you afraid of?"

Sandi stepped onto the *lanai* to watch as the *Royal Flush* returned from the morning whale watch. Archie maneuvered the boat through the narrow channel and into the slip as if he were parallel-parking a VW Bug along a curb. He glanced up, spotting her. The hook touched his brow in a sort of pirate salute.

She heard herself say, "What are you waiting for? What are you afraid of?"

She blinked with surprise into the opalescent blue of the sea. Was she talking to Andrew Adams—or to Archie? Or were her words meant for her own heart?

Shaking her head, Sandi turned away. "What century am I living in?"

* * * *

Victorian England

The expression on Theo's ruddy face was as patronizing as his tone to Kaiulani. "Your cousin Koa has been sent to Washington as an emissary for the queen."

Kaiulani arched an eyebrow in surprise. "Koa? But I am next in line to the throne."

"Of course you must release a public statement. Don't worry your little head about it, my dear. I'll compose it, and you may sign it."

Kaiulani lifted her chin defiantly. "We are speaking of my queen. My people. My throne. My nation. If I can't speak myself for these things, then how can I defend what is mine? How can I justify my right to the throne?"

Theo's thin mouth curved slightly. He bowed his head in acknowledgment. "No disrespect, Your Royal Highness."

"Thank you. I'll go to work now. If you would be so kind as to read and offer your opinion when I've finished my draft…"

She prayed as she left Theo's presence, "Wisdom. Only wisdom, Lord."

Kaiulani labored for hours, crafting her statement into final form.

Sent to *The Times,* the communique was nevertheless intended for American consumption:

> *For all these years I have waited patiently and striven to fit myself for my return to my native country. I am now told that Mr. Thurston is in Washington, seeking to take away my flag and my throne. I am going to Washington to plead for my throne, my nation, and my flag. Will not the great American people hear me?*

After supper, Theo scanned the powerful, emotionally charged message, then gazed at her over his reading glasses. "You...you are going to Washington?"

"Should I allow Koa to speak for me? No one can speak to the president in my place."

"Kaiulani, you are just a girl," Theo argued. "Who will listen?"

"Perhaps someday the Hawaiians will say that Kaiulani could have saved us, but she didn't even try. I *will* go."

"Is there no reasoning with you about this?"

"I'm of age. It seems my nation and my throne will be stolen from me by America if I stay here and do nothing. Tell me what I have to lose?"

It was as if her guardian saw the woman she had become for the first time. "I suppose I believed you would forever be a child. Now I see. You are determined."

She did not back down. "With or without your help."

"It seems I am the one who has no choice." He wrote instructions on monogrammed stationery and called for his secretary. "Taylor!"

Obsequious and overly deferential, the tall, cadaverous man entered the room at his master's call. A stack of correspondence was in his hand. "Mr. Davies?"

"I need you to arrange immediate passage to the States for myself and for Mrs. Davies. For Princess Kaiulani and her companion, Hannah."

"Immediate, sir?"

Kaiulani's fierce countenance bored into the red-rimmed eyes of Davies' servant. "I have written out our travel needs and schedule. As you can see, Hannah and I also require passage booked by rail to San Francisco and then a ship all the way to Honolulu."

"Sir?" the astonished Taylor asked.

Theo replied, "Her Royal Highness is of age. I can neither keep her from leaving England, nor dictate where she travels."

Kaiulani gave a sharp downward thrust of her chin. "And this is my statement about the political events taking place in my kingdom. Please see to it that copies are released to the press both in England and cabled to the United States."

Kaiulani's passionate appeal would cross the Atlantic ahead of her. It would speak for Kaiulani until she arrived in New York, while providing no opportunity for newsmen to interview her and twist her responses.

After all, the only journalist she completely trusted was now a missionary in Hawaii.

Kaiulani missed his counsel and wondered what Andrew thought about the changes to *Hawaii Nei*.

Chapter Nineteen

....

Four days after receiving the grim news from home, Kaiulani and her small entourage stepped aboard the White Star ship in Liverpool. The resounding boom of the ship's horn was like a war cry, stirring her heart.

"I've been in exile far too long," she said to Hannah.

Sea birds cried and circled overhead. A wave of exultation swept through Kaiulani as the great propellers churned and the shores of England receded into the mist.

Long after Theo and his wife retreated to their stateroom, Kaiulani and Hannah stood together at the rail.

After a long silence Hannah spoke. "The good hand of the Lord is with you now."

Kaiulani inhaled deeply, taking in the fresh sea air. "I'm certain of it." The wind and rush of water seemed like a song. "Hannah, we've been together a long time. No one ever had a friend like you."

"My life is yours. You know that." Hannah smiled gently. "We were little girls together. Who could imagine…we've traveled so far from the banyan tree at Ainahau."

"I wonder what we'll find when we come home?"

Behind them the steward rang the dinner bell. The movement of the great ship took Kaiulani back to the first time she met Andrew, so many years before.

The many-decks-tall SS *Teutonic* was nothing like the old *Umatilla*. There was nothing remotely resembling a cargo ship about this opulent liner. Theo had taken his charges down to the shipyard at Liverpool to watch her launch just a few years before. Hannah and Kaiulani's first-class cabin was distinctively appointed in bird's-eye maple.

Shipboard entertainment featured paid musicians and actors. There was no place for amateur theatricals now. The recollection made Kaiulani smile. Despite the antagonism between the "three little maids from school" and the egotistical Scotsman, it had been a simpler, gentler time to be alive.

Back then all Kaiulani's future had been bright and hopeful.

Now she wondered who she would be if her mission to America was not successful. What use had the world for a woman who had been trained to be a queen, if her throne no longer existed?

* * * *

Even before *Teutonic* docked in New York, Kaiulani prepared herself to be bombarded at the gangway by questions from the press.

"You look pale," Hannah said.

Kaiulani's fingers trembled, but her voice was steady. "Speaking for our people is my duty—my reason to live. God help me remember how angry I am at what they are trying to do to *Hawaii Nei,* and I'll forget my fear."

The princess dressed the part of a dignified royal heir: gray traveling gown over which she wore a dark jacket. Her hair was swept up and knotted at the back of her head, on top of which she wore a restrained formal hat. Hannah followed immediately behind her, then Theo Davies and servants.

The journalists began shouting their queries even before the princess reached the dock:

"How do you feel about the loss of your kingdom?"

"Do the Hawaiian people support the new government?"

"What do you hope to accomplish by going to Washington?"

"Is it true the Provisional Government wants the U.S. to annex Hawaii?"

"Won't that make you an American citizen?"

Kaiulani focused her clear brown eyes on the tallest member of the press corps. Leveling her gaze midway between the ridiculous, too small bowler hat he wore, and the cigar clamped between his teeth, the princess delivered her prepared statement:

> *"Unbidden I stand on your shores today where I thought to receive a royal welcome. I hear that commissioners from my land are asking this great nation to take away my little vineyard...they would leave me without a home or a name or a nation..."*

Prince Koa met her at the dock. He gathered her into a carriage with Hannah, while leaving Theo and the others to follow in another conveyance.

Koa looked nervous. "You know the queen sent me to Washington."

"I know," Kaiulani replied. "I'm just here to help any way I can."

"Yes, well," Koa continued, "are you sure...that is, some people think—"

"Just say it, Koa. What are you fumbling about?"

"There's a rumor you will cut a deal with Thurston to make yourself queen, with him to run the government."

Hannah almost leapt across the carriage at Koa's throat. "How dare you? How can you even think such a thing?"

Holding up protesting and defensive hands, Koa said quickly: "Not me! I don't think it. It's just, you know, reports."

"Rumors!" Hannah shot scornfully.

"Probably planted by Thurston's men to drive a wedge between us—between me and the queen," Kaiulani ventured.

Koa wiped his forehead with a white handkerchief. "Glad that's settled."

Passing east across Manhattan, they heard a newsboy shouting: "Read all about it: Hawaiian princess says grandsons of missionaries trying to steal her kingdom. Says missionaries sent faith and freedom to Hawaii, but now their descendents seek to undo their fathers' work. Read all about it."

"That was brilliant planning by Mister Davies—cabling your speech ahead so it could be printed the same day you arrived," Koa complimented.

"That was Kaiulani's doing," Hannah corrected. "She thought of it herself."

At the Brevoort House Kaiulani was treated as visiting royalty. The hotel manager personally escorted her entourage to the suite of rooms, already overflowing with bouquets of flowers from well-wishers. "And may I congratulate you on a wonderful speech, Your Highness," offered the manager. In his cutaway coat and tails he looked like an official dignitary himself. "Particularly when you said"—the manager consulted a newspaper account—"'Who will stand up for the rights of my people? But I am strong in the faith of God and in the knowledge that seventy million Americans in this free land will hear my cry and not let their flag be used to dishonor mine.' Splendid! Well said, Your Highness."

As he bowed his way out of her rooms, the hotel official remarked, "Beside the cards, there is a telegram that was delivered with that bouquet of red roses. It's just there, beneath the vase."

Hannah seized the yellow envelope and opened it, then passed it to Kaiulani. *Be very careful,* it read. *You are courageous, but there are those who will stop at nothing to prevent your success.*

It was signed, *Andrew.*

Chapter Twenty

....

Rotund, jolly, and forthright, President Grover Cleveland projected an image of good fellowship. There was heartiness and trustworthiness with his stout frame, broad face, and long, rumpled frock coat. He reminded Kaiulani of two people she had known: the London preacher, Gipsy Smith, and an elderly *kahuna* who lived in Lahaina on the island of Maui. The princess did not mention either comparison to the president.

Cleveland's elegant and stylish wife, nearly three decades his junior, went out of her way to make Kaiulani and Hannah feel welcome. Seating them in the Blue Room in high-backed chairs upholstered in blue and gold roses, Mrs. Cleveland poured their tea herself.

"My dears," she said, "I want you to be perfectly comfortable. I confess I was so intimidated when I first came here to this mansion, but now I feel quite at home and we want our guests to feel the same, don't we, Big Jumbo?"

"Yes, my dear," Cleveland replied. His voice was much higher in pitch than Kaiulani expected from a man whose weight exceeded a quarter of a ton.

The invitation to visit the Executive Mansion was extended as a social courtesy because Kaiulani's status was not official. Nevertheless, she took heart just to be meeting the American president and dressed accordingly. From the purple ostrich plumes atop her brand-new hat to the long-sleeved, fitted bodice and pleated skirt of her flowing day dress, Kaiulani looked every inch a princess. "Thurston's minions want to convince the Americans we are not fit to govern ourselves," she had told Hannah. "I want to convince Mister Cleveland otherwise."

The Blue Room's oval ceiling was plastered with a pattern of interlocking blue and lavender circles. From its center hung an enormous gas-lit chandelier with scores of globes. Above the fireplace was a massive gilt-and-blue framed mirror, and the doors were outlined in hangings of heavy navy fabric. In sum, it was the most elegant chamber Kaiulani had ever seen and she told Mrs. Cleveland so.

"Thank you, Your Highness," Frances Cleveland replied. "You know, Grover and I were married in this very room."

Kaiulani felt her heart lift at the First Lady's words. By using Kaiulani's title, was Mrs. Cleveland signaling it was not yet official policy to acknowledge the end of the monarchy? She glanced at Hannah, whose triumphant look could only mean she'd sensed the same hopeful sign.

In a far corner of the room was a gilt birdcage suspended from a tall stand. In it was a mockingbird that whistled and called in a dozen bird languages. "Your family enjoys pets?" Hannah inquired politely.

Mrs. Cleveland smiled. "Our baby, Ruth, likes to pull our poodle's ears, so we don't let her near the bird!"

"If you would permit," Kaiulani offered, "when I reach home, I would love to send you a myna bird. They are very cunning creatures and also can mimic sounds they hear."

"Splendid," the president agreed. "Capital idea." Then he added, "My dear, I read with great interest your statements in the papers. I especially liked your appeal to the American people. We have many things in common, you and I. There are many in this Congress who disapprove of me and my ideals, but I rely on the good sense and fair play of the people to vindicate me.

"While I cannot officially give you any assurance today, I thought you might like to know privately that I am withdrawing the treaty of annexation from consideration. What's more, I shall be sending a commission of inquiry to your homeland to investigate the circumstances surrounding the change of government. I wish I could do more." Lines of sorrow creased the brow of this jovial giant.

Kaiulani's hopes, so lifted by her reception by the President, plummeted again. Presidents, the same as monarchs, could not always accomplish what they knew to be right.

* * * *

The next morning, back in their hotel room, Theo Davies brought Kaiulani a copy of a Washington paper. Through his Secretary of State, President Cleveland had issued a statement regarding the Hawaiian situation:

> *I am utterly opposed to the annexation of Hawaii. It would pervert the mission of America. It would lower our national standard to endorse a selfish and dishonorable scheme to acquire the Islands by force and violence.*

"Well done, Princess," Theo Davies praised.

Kaiulani shrugged in self-deprecation. "I didn't really speak with him about politics. He came to his own conclusions."

"You showed him what a liar Thurston is," Hannah corrected.

"You served your people as only you could have done," Theo said. "And they will not forget."

"But the president made no promises," Kaiulani reminded them. "It's a statement of his personal support; nothing more."

* * * *

1973

Sandi's shopping cart blocked the aisle as she stared, too long, at a rack filled with potato chips. A young, brown-skinned woman with a toddler in her cart cleared her throat to pull Sandi back to reality.

"Excuse me?" the woman said, maneuvering around Sandi.

"Oh, sorry! Sorry." Sandi grabbed a jumbo bag of Fritos and tossed them into her cart.

She stared at the huge, expensive sack of greasy corn chips that could serve fifty beer-drinking football fans at a tailgate party. Why Fritos? She really wanted locally made Maui Chips, like the kind Archie served to his tourists on the *Royal Flush*.

"What am I doing here?" Sandi shook her head.

Behind her, Archie's amused voice interrupted her reverie. "Okay. So now I'm curious. What *are* you doing here?"

She looked up, startled to see him. His cart was filled with sodas and carrot sticks, ranch dressing, and a dozen bags of Maui Chips.

At the sight of his face, it hit her like a ton of bricks. She was falling in love with Archie.

"I was looking for those," she replied moodily.

"I got them all." He tossed a sack into her cart. "Want more?"

"No, thanks." She replaced the Fritos in the rack and did not look at Archie.

"I was going to say, if you want more, you'll have to sail away with me."

"Oh, I…no. Can't."

He threw another cellophane bag into her cart. "A bribe."

She shook her head. She imagined his lips close to hers. A moonlight sail and swimming in the warm sea. "I've got a bunch of work to do."

He cocked his head slightly, as though he saw through her excuse. "I might be able to fill in some details. Family history and all that."

Sandi twisted her wedding ring on her finger. "Andrew—I mean, Archie!— I'm…I'm married, remember?"

Her words were like a slap. "Whoa."

"This is really difficult for me, but…my husband…five years is a long time, but I still can't—"

Archie scowled at her. "I'm talkin' a couple bags of Maui Chips here, not—"

"It isn't you. I know it's not you. It's just that I really, really like you. I haven't let myself like any man, see? Not for many years. I forgot what it felt like to—"

An old man reaching for bean dip stepped between them.

Archie waited until the shopper rounded the corner. He swallowed hard. "I get it," he said somberly. "And if I'm really being honest with myself, and with you, I guess I'm feeling the same way. Beautiful."

"Dangerous."

"Sandi."

"Please, Archie. Not now."

"Safeway is a weird place for this, but here we are. I want you to know—I have thought about you a lot."

"Oh, you mustn't!"

"But I have. And I do. And I probably will. So, I'll just tell you: I'll stand down. No confusion. You need to be sure. He deserves that."

"Thanks." She did not look into his face. "My love lives in the past. To survive, I've got to stay focused on the present. I have no future to offer anyone."

All verbs being conjugated, Sandi pushed on, paid for two bags of Maui Chips, then drove to Airport Beach, where she had a good cry.

Chapter Twenty-one
....

Republic of Hawaii, 1897

Kaiulani slipped out, and the cabin door clicked shut behind her. Hannah's sleepy voice called after her. The thrumming of the ship's engines was like a great heartbeat in the night, or the distant rhythm of Hawaiian drums.

Wrapped in a blanket, Hannah padded after Kaiulani. The deck was empty beneath the starswept skies. Kaiulani braced herself in the railing at the bow, like the figurehead of an old whaling ship. Salt spray stung her cheeks, awakening memories of home, true home, and beloved faces almost forgotten. Kaiulani inhaled deeply. Familiar aromas of her homeland filled her senses. The triangle of islands, Lanai and Molokai and Maui, loomed up from the sea as the ship steamed through the channel on its way to port in Oahu.

"Do you smell it?" Kaiulani asked as Hannah joined her.

"Wood smoke?" Hannah's voice was almost inaudible. "Look. Signal fires on the beach."

Distinct light beamed from the Lahaina lighthouse, sending letters and words in dots and dashes as the ship passed. Was Andrew standing on the beach watching for her return? Did he see the glimmer of the passing ship and know she thought of him? A rush of longing swept over her. *"Aloha nui loa,* dearest Andrew," she whispered.

New bonfires sprang to life on the hilltops of other islands.

Had the captain signaled the return of Hawaii's Hope? Was the name of Princess Kaiulani a beacon awakening her people from their long sleep?

The two women did not speak for a long time as the vessel cut through placid seas.

At last Kaiulani said, "You know me so well, Hannah. I have no friend like you."

"And you know my heart maybe better than I know myself," Hannah answered.

"You were God's gift to me after Mama died. You kept my soul from flying away with grief."

"You are my friend. My sister."

"I was thinking tonight, as I smelled the fragrance of our islands so close, about when I saw your face, your smile, through the branches of the banyan tree."

Hannah hummed. "As little girls, our loss was so much alike I couldn't tell your sorrow from mine. Our mothers, both gone to heaven. We were left together to taste delicious secrets with our tea."

Kaiulani held her hand. "We consoled one another with laughter."

"Always."

"And with truth, Hannah. When I need truth, you have always given it to me."

"I have tried."

"I need the truth now."

"Well?"

"Do you think the Lord will let my life make a difference for good? For my people?"

Hannah leaned her head against Kaiulani's shoulder. "That's why you were born, Kaiulani. For the sake of God's truth and for His Kingdom."

"Thurston and the rest—they are so strong. I feel so young. Still like such a child. Mama said before she died that I would never be queen."

Hannah took Kaiulani by the shoulders. "Remember the words of Jeremiah. The prophecy! 'Say not, I am a child: for thou shalt go to all that I shall send thee, and whatsoever I command thee thou shalt speak. Be not afraid of their faces: for I am with thee to deliver thee, saith the LORD.'" [23]

"I'm only afraid that I will fail my people."

Hannah shook her head, refuting Kaiulani's fears. "The Lord has made you a wall of bronze against those sons of missionaries who, like the sons of Eli, have turned away from God. Your story will be told for generations. How a girl was chosen by God to stand firm and speak truth against the thieves and hypocrites who have come to steal the land that is not their own. Remember? The Lord has declared, 'I will utter my judgments against them touching all their wickedness, who have forsaken me…. Thou therefore…arise, and speak unto them all that I command thee: be not dismayed at their faces…. For, behold, I have made thee this day a defenced city, and an iron pillar.'" [24]

Kaiulani turned her face to the broad swath of the Milky Way. A shooting star flamed across the sky above their heads. She cried, "*Ke Akua Mana E!* How mighty You are, O Lord!"

The two women, arm-in-arm, stood silent before the majesty of their God. The steamer emerged from the channel, and signal fires receded in the distance.

At last Hannah said quietly, "A big day ahead. Go to sleep now. I'll wake you at dawn."

* * * *

"Kaiulani?" Hannah's gentle voice was accompanied by the aroma of freshly brewed coffee. She drew Kaiulani back from a dream of her mother. "The sun is almost up. Almost home."

Kaiulani, still drowsy after a short few hours' sleep, raised up and sipped the hot brew before she uttered a word. "I was dreaming about Mama," she croaked.

Hannah placed the breakfast tray on the side table and sat on the edge of the bed. "Oh?"

"Funny thing. I have not dreamed of her before, but she was with her brother."

"With the king?" Hannah seemed impressed and interested. "Did they have any good advice for you?"

"Nothing at all. Not a word. Just sitting together smiling, like when I was a little girl. Laughing and talking between themselves. I came in, and they both looked up and smiled at me." Another sip of black coffee. She held it on her tongue, savoring its strength. "Can we see Oahu, you think?" Swinging her legs out from the covers, she was barefoot but still dressed in a rumpled skirt and blouse.

"Diamond Head. Makapuu Point."

"I want to see Oahu before I change. Come on." She and Hannah dashed from the cabin and hung on the rail.

The island reared up from the ocean floor, scraping the belly of the clouds. Color seeped through the predawn mist. Daybreak, like a flame on the wick of a candle, danced on a jagged peak. Light flowed like water down the verdant green folds of the *pali*. Foamy breakers, churning in shadow at the base of rocky cliffs, glowed with rose and gold and violet reflections of the sky.

Kaiulani lifted her head and stretched slender arms as if to embrace her homeland, like a long absent lover. Her lips moved as she sang the Hawaiian translation of Psalm 150: "*E halelu aku oukou ia Iehova:* Praise the Lord, Jehovah!"

Hannah joined Kaiulani. "*E halelu aku i ke Akua, ma kona wahi hoano; E halelu aku ia ia, ma ke aouli o kona hanohano!*"

They harmonized the ancient Polynesian melody to which the words of King David had been set. It seemed as though each note spoke new colors into existence. "*E halelu aku ia ia, no kana mau hana mana; E halelu aku ia ia, e like me ka manomano o kona nui.*"

"Hannah, we are home at last," Kaiulani said.

A moment more the women feasted on the old familiar sights. Then Kaiulani returned to the cabin to wash and dress and prepare for what lay ahead.

Chapter Twenty-two
....

Dressed in the eye-catching brilliance of royal Hawaiian yellow, Kaiulani was the very embodiment of Hawaii's Hope as the steamer pulled into harbor. Hannah stood at her elbow on the deck. "Remember who you are. *Alii* of Hawaii. And Daughter of the King of Heaven. For such a time as this."

Kaiulani squeezed Hannah's hand, then waved to the cheering crowds. She held her tears in check at homecoming. Her smile returned the love she felt overflowing from their hearts.

She and Hannah had left Honolulu as schoolgirls. Kaiulani was returning home as a woman who had loved, sorrowed, and matured. She had known triumph as she won the respect of British society and the ear of the American president. The awakening of Kaiulani's soul called her home in defiance of Thurston and the evil men who usurped the government. Queen Liliuokalani was under house arrest. Would the tyrants of the new Provisional Government also arrest Kaiulani? Her simple prayer was that Grover Cleveland could halt the inexorable march of greed and deception that gripped her kingdom by the throat.

What would this homecoming mean, both for the princess and for her people?

Queen Liliuokalani no longer lived in the palace but under guard in her private residence.

The *haoles* of the Provisional Government lorded it over the Islands. Called the PGs, they closed opposition newspapers and arrested political enemies. Kaiulani knew they also lived in fear of the American president.

President Cleveland wanted to be fair. Still, as America drew closer and closer to war with Spain over Cuba, he found few supporters committed to maintaining Hawaiian sovereignty. After all, America still needed sugar and a naval base in the Pacific. The Provisional Government was distasteful, but the preservation of order was preferable to chaos.

All these things were in Kaiulani's mind as she and Hannah arrived at the Oceanic Wharf from which they had sailed many years—a lifetime—ago.

Now, as then, the docks thronged with her people. Now, as then, they sang to her and carried a burden of *Aloha* along with the masses of flowers. Now, as then, they saw in Kaiulani their ray of sunshine. But Kaiulani saw clearly in their weary faces and ragged clothes that the happy, pleasant people she had left behind were indeed oppressed and broken.

She looked to her right at Hannah's shaken countenance. "You see it too?" she asked.

Hannah swallowed hard and nodded. "'They break in pieces thy people, O LORD, and afflict thine heritage.'" [25]

Kaiulani felt hot tears brim at Hannah's words. The terrible dream returned to her mind. The old woman standing in the sea because there was no land left in Hawaii upon which she could stand.

Suddenly the monarchy and the kingdom were driven from Kaiulani's thoughts. She spotted her father standing on the dock.

"Oh, Hannah, it's Papa. There's Papa!" And then the tears spilled over.

Hannah took her arm. The two women hurried down the gangplank. Crowds pressed around her, singing the song written for her in her childhood.

> *"O ua mau pua lehua…*
> *Bring forth the wreath of lehua*
> *The wreath for our beloved Princess*
> *Loving hands with maile didst weave*
> *A beautiful crown for Kaiulani."*

Their voices and the scent of flowers filled the air as she moved among them. Then, with the Polynesians' exquisite sense of *ohana*, family, they cleared a path between her and her father. They lifted over her an arch of flowers to form a tunnel of fragrant remembrance as they sang.

> *"And upon thy head we will place it,*
> *How lovely and charming to behold there."* [26]

> *"Aloha!"*
> *"Aloha!"*

Kaiulani returned their welcoming cry, then said breathlessly to Hannah, "We must never leave home again."

Papa Archie, gray and careworn from the months of chaos, reached out to enfold her in his arms. *"Aloha nui loa,* Kaiulani. You are the first ray of light in my life many months." Then he embraced Hannah as well. "And Hannah, my dear, look at you! You two have grown side-by-side, like twin trees."

Unable to speak, Kaiulani's throat ached from emotion. Locked in the arms of her father, Kaiulani heard a diffident cough at Papa's elbow.

Kaiulani's heart leapt. Andrew Adams waited patiently to offer his welcome. "*Aloha.* Heard you were landing today," he said.

She fell into Andrew's arms. "I didn't expect you here. Last night we sailed through the channel. I saw the lights of Lahaina and… Andrew! I'm so glad! You are here! Waiting!"

"Even in Lahaina we got news you were coming. I'm not the most welcome person to the PGs. They've shut down my newspaper and forbidden me to write. But I couldn't miss today. Welcome home." He paused a moment, then emphasized her title. "Princess."

"Andrew, will you stay with us? At Ainahau?"

Andrew and Archie exchanged somber looks as the rough vigilante guard of the PG pushed at the back of the crowd. "Thank you. No, I have a room. Kaiulani, you'll want to go home now," he said, stepping aside. "I'll call again soon, if I may."

"Do, please do," Kaiulani urged. "We have so much to talk about."

Suddenly there was the sound of a scuffle at the back of the crowd. She looked up. Two dozen armed soldiers of Thurston's PGs ordered the crowd to disperse as they made their way toward her. When she looked back, Andrew had vanished. The Hawaiians began to melt away from the threat. Flowers lay trampled on the ground.

Hannah grabbed Kaiulani's arm, pulling her back from her father. Raising her chin defiantly, Hannah stepped between Kaiulani and the troops. "Stay quiet," Hannah hissed to Kaiulani. "No matter what happens, stay quiet."

Archie nodded. He put his arm around Hannah.

The leader of the vigilantes scowled at Archie, blocking their route to the waiting carriage. "Do you know it is against the law for Hawaiians to gather? We could arrest you all."

"I'm here to welcome my daughter home." Archie hugged Hannah. Kaiulani stared at the red-faced *haoles* over Hannah's shoulder.

"Your daughter." The leader snorted as he glared at Hannah. "Get her out of here before there's trouble. Understand?"

"Come along, my dear." Archie helped Hannah into the carriage first and then Kaiulani followed. The driver tapped the reins on the back of the team the instant they were seated.

"Well done, Hannah." Archie breathed a sigh of relief. "With the queen under arrest, I was concerned these savages might also arrest Kaiulani. A royal princess in prison. A show of their strength."

"Would they do that, Papa?" Kaiulani asked. "Is it so dangerous?"

"Worse." Archie stared out at the knots of destitute people gathered to see her pass by. "There was a reason you were not called home. Now you're home, I'm glad you are here, but Kaiulani, there is danger everywhere. You are a threat to Thurston and the others. The people love you so."

She closed her eyes. The aromas and the sound of the spinning carriage wheels on the gravel drive to Ainahau seemed so familiar, yet everything had changed. Kaiulani wished she and Hannah had never gone away at all. The sign on the gate still read *KAPU*, forbidden, but armed soldiers of the Provisional Government watched the driveway to the house from across the road.

Kaiulani heard the cry of her peacocks, as if they knew she had come home. But home would not be the same. The house would be altogether new, she realized. Papa had written that he had torn down the old dwelling to build one suitable for the heir apparent and future queen of Hawaii.

Did any of that matter now? Would it ever?

* * * *

Only when the gates of Ainahau closed behind them did Kaiulani feel as though she could breathe. The carriage road curved toward the house, but Ainahau indeed was no longer the home she had known.

The great old banyan tree still stood, but everything else had changed. Papa's letter of warning had not prepared her for the beautiful new frame house that stood in the place of her childhood home. A broad, covered porch stretched the entire width of the structure. The grand entry was festooned with floral arrangements to welcome her.

She felt her smile waver as it came to her that Papa had built the place expecting a princess and then a queen to occupy it. Perhaps the dying prophecy of Kaiulani's mother was coming true: "*You will never be queen.*"

"Welcome home, Kaiulani." Papa helped her from the carriage.

Hannah followed as father and daughter walked arm-in-arm into the tiled foyer. Exhausted by the journey, Hannah's familiar cough began again. She could hardly breathe as she turned aside and sat on the *lanai* to wait alone.

To Kaiulani's right was an elegant drawing room, two-score paces in length and half that in width, meant to be a gathering place for state receptions. Floors and paneled walls were clothed in precious wood from the island forests. Royal symbols of the coronet and *kahili* were entwined on the woodwork. Tall windows looked out over the sloping lawns where her flock of peacocks strutted. Up the grand staircase was a suite of private rooms for her personal use. A library filled with books was just off her bedchamber.

At last they climbed a flight of steep steps to the sunny roof garden. The view of Oahu and the sea spread out before her.

Most of the Crown lands were in the hands of the PGs. Even the crown jewels of Queen Liliuokalani had been auctioned off by Thurston's cronies. Revenues that had always helped the destitute native population now paid the anti-royalist troops who guarded the prisoner-queen and patrolled the city streets.

Kaiulani looked toward the banyan, where she had spent such carefree hours. Beyond that was the sea, where the ragged old woman of her dreams had warned her of all that had come upon her people. For a moment, Kaiulani wished she had not returned. The reality was much harsher than her nightmares.

She pictured her mother, laughing in the sun, as Kaiulani had played at her feet. She remembered the large sensitive eyes of Robert Louis Stevenson as he looked at her as the Hope of Hawaii. *"Child of a double race..."*

For the first time in her life, Kaiulani was ashamed of the Anglo half of her heritage.

Where was the home of her heart?

"Papa," she said, breathless at the sight, "there is only one thing more I must do before I really feel home."

"What is that?"

"I want to ride up to Nuuanu. To visit Mama's grave. And Papa Moi's."

* * * *

Kaiulani's footsteps traced the inlaid koa-wood floor of the grand reception hall. The day that had begun with such promising sunshine and iridescent blue skies had turned dark and threatening. Fat raindrops hammered the birds into silence and knocked the *pikake* blossoms from the bushes. Rumbles of thunder rolled down from the *pali*.

Bare of any furnishings, the extravagant size of the room made it feel more like an auditorium or gymnasium than a queen's audience chamber. Forty steps along one wall she and Hannah paced, then across beneath the crossed *kahili* standards that now seemed to suggest mockery rather than honor.

"It will clear this afternoon," Hannah ventured. "We can still get out and go riding."

Kaiulani regarded her friend. Hannah had awakened with a chill that morning and still had a slight tremor in her voice. "When it warms up, and the trails dry out some," Kaiulani said.

Gravel crunching beneath iron-bound wheels drew their attention to the expansive views beside the entry. In the distance were the waters off Waikiki, today more gray than azure.

In the foreground Clive Davies alighted from a shiny black carriage. "Wait here," Kaiulani heard Clive's booming voice order. The driver, a Hawaiian, turned up the collar of his coat and leaned back into the scant shelter provided by the vehicle's folding roof.

Clive, holding aloft his umbrella, strode briskly up the walk. He had filled out since returning to Hawaii. The vest of his suit strained against his watch chain. His fleshy face had lost the definition of chin and cheekbones.

Under the portico, Clive wiped mud from his feet, set aside the umbrella, and removed his hat. He approached the door, which Kaiulani opened before he knocked.

"Clive," Kaiulani said in greeting, "it's good to see you."

"Yes," Hannah added in a strained voice. "It's been some time. You look…prosperous." The way she voiced the adjective made it sound less than complimentary.

"Very busy," Clive returned. "Very."

Kaiulani waved her hand around the empty hall. "Would you like to come into the north wing? We can sit down."

A peal of thunder cracked like a rifle shot overhead.

"No, no, thank you," Clive replied. "Can't stay. But I have something to say to you, Kaiulani."

He stared pointedly at Hannah, who coughed as she said, "You'll excuse me, won't you, Clive? I have some mending to attend to."

Clive waited until Hannah had left the room before taking Kaiulani's hand. "I haven't wanted to stay away," he said. "You must not think that. It's just—the Provisional Government thinks you are the focus of rebellion."

"How can I have anything to do with rebellion?" Kaiulani challenged. "It's they who are the rebels. I am the lawful heir apparent."

Clive's face twisted. "Yes, of course. But you must understand my position. You and anyone who associates with you are under suspicion."

"Well, then," the princess returned, "I will miss you, but I wouldn't want you to jeopardize your *position*."

Clive fumbled with his gold chain, drawing the watch before suddenly jamming it back into the waistcoat pocket. "I'm doing this very badly," he admitted.

"Clive," Kaiulani said, not unkindly, "we've been friends a long time. Why don't you simply tell me what's on your mind?"

Inhaling and apparently gathering his thoughts, Clive said, "You know I'm on your side. First, last, and always."

"Yes," Kaiulani returned. "You and your family have always been kind to me."

Clive frowned, then continued. "You once said to me that as HRH Victoria Kaiulani you could not love me."

"Please, don't," Kaiulani cautioned. "Clive, don't—"

He rushed on, undeterred by the fingers she placed across his lips. "But you said as Kaiulani Cleghorn you did care for me. You did say that, didn't you? Didn't you?"

Kaiulani stared at him. How could he care for her and not see how much pain this subject caused her? Or did it not matter to him?

"Now that you're a private citizen, free to love where you will, can't you see yourself loving me?" He was pleading now, perhaps reacting to the stiffening Kaiulani felt in her frame and features.

"Clive," she said sternly, "I can only care for my people. For *Hawaii Nei*. If I allow myself to think, even for an instant, that I may fail, then I am *pau*—finished—and of no use to anyone. Can't you understand that?"

"I understand that this is not a fairy tale with a fairy-tale ending," Clive said, mimicking Kaiulani's gesture at the empty room. "I know money is tight. I know your father's business is in difficulty. Kaiulani, think! I care for you! I can rescue you from this...this hollow shell. Married to me, you won't be in danger anymore. Life can be good for us."

The thunderstorm moved off toward Diamond Head, growling and grumbling as it went.

"Clive," Kaiulani said, "thank you. I mean that; truly I do. But you do not know me. Not at all. I will go to my grave as a princess—a champion of my people. To do anything else would be to sell them out and abandon them to their fate. Your friends have raped our islands. Stolen what is not theirs. I can't be part of that."

"I see," Clive said stiffly, jamming his hat firmly on his head. "Well, I can't be responsible for what happens to you. If you refuse me, you are on your own."

"I am never on my own. The good hand of the Lord is upon me."

"You may find heaven too far away to protect you now. Goodbye, Kaiulani." He turned on his heel and stormed out of the house without looking back.

Kaiulani stared at the restless sea. What had happened to the boy they had known in England? It was as if Clive Davies had died inside. Certainly his love for her had turned bitter when she refused him.

She felt Hannah beside her but did not turn. "Out there," she said, "beyond the reef. That's where I saw the old woman in the surf. Nothing solid under her feet. No land left on which to stand. Is that where we are? Is Clive right? Am I foolish to continue hoping?"

Hannah's voice rasped a bit when she replied. "I saw a dark shadow cross his face when he looked at you. A shadow. Very dark! Kaiulani, listen. It's dangerous for you to remain here. There was danger in Clive's voice when he spoke to you. He isn't safe anymore. Not the boy we knew. He's no friend of Hawaii. You don't love him in the way he wants your love. You must leave Ainahau, Kaiulani, or I'm afraid he will take your love—steal what you will not give him freely."

Chapter Twenty-three

....

Kaiulani had promised herself she would make this journey up the Nuuanu Valley at her first opportunity after arriving home. Ever since leaving England to return to Hawaii, she had thought about visiting her mother's grave. Now, heedless of the swollen clouds threatening to unleash a torrent of rain, she and Hannah were in the red carriage with boughs of jasmine blossoms and baskets of plumeria *leis* with which to deck the monument.

Kaiulani had been warned against attending any public gathering that could be viewed as rebellious by the ultra-sensitive Provisional Government. Without actually forbidding her to go outside her home, the message was clear: any action that might enflame the Hawaiian populace would not be tolerated.

Kaiulani ignored the threat. "I am going to visit my mother's grave. Let them make of that what they will."

Mauna ala, the "Fragrant Hills," existed as a volcanic ridge half-way between *mauka* and *makai,* the mountains and the sea. The royal mausoleum also marked the final resting place for Uncle David and the spot where Kaiulani herself expected to be buried someday.

Almost as soon as the carriage left Ainahau's gate, word about Kaiulani's destination circulated among the Hawaiian population. First in twos and threes, then in larger numbers, friendly, sympathetic faces collected to trudge alongside Kaiulani and Hannah. They murmured expressions of sympathy. Many carried palm branches to offer in loving remembrance of the royal family.

It had only been one hundred years since King Kamehameha the Great followed this same route to his final battle for supremacy over the island kingdom. One hundred years from savagery to civilization; from idol worship to Christianity; from being almost unknown by the rest of the world to being coveted by powerful nations.

From self-rule to having no voice in their own affairs?

From the start of the dynasty to its end?

Kaiulani would not dwell on politics today. Her purpose and her thoughts concentrated on remembering and honoring her mother.

The crowd around the carriage numbered only about a hundred when they encountered a pair of soldiers of the Provisional Government on horseback. These two guardsmen did not challenge Kaiulani's progress, but they did dig in with their spurs and gallop off toward Honolulu.

The progress up the highway rapidly took on the air of a solemn procession. Columns of Hawaiians flanked the carriage, carrying their palm branches like *kahilis*.

"Or like spears," Hannah said to Kaiulani. "Thurston would not permit any such"—Hannah had to pause to catch her breath—"any such honor guard at the docks. But he can't stop this one."

Ten minutes later, as the number of impromptu attendants reached five hundred and the head of the throng reached the foot of the ridge, Kaiulani was not so sure Hannah was right. Posted across the lava flow, blocking further progress toward the cemetery, were thirty PG troopers, armed with rifles and bayonets.

Their captain, a scruffy-haired, scruffy-bearded young man of no more than twenty-five, ordered the crowd to turn around and go home. "Disperse!"

"His voice squeaked," Hannah whispered. "Do you think he's frightened?"

"Perhaps," Kaiulani returned. "And frightened men can be dangerous."

"Disperse at once!" the officer repeated. "Gatherings of Hawaiians are forbidden by order of the Provisional Government. Anyone participating in an illegal assembly may be arrested."

Angry growls came from some of Kaiulani's attendants. Some dropped their palm fronds to pick up stones.

There was palpable tension in the air.

Kaiulani stood up and waved for silence. "This is neither a gathering nor an assembly," she said. "I am going to visit my mother's grave at Mauna ala. Won't you let me pass?"

The captain hesitated. Kaiulani saw his fingers pluck at the sword by his side. "My orders—"

"Do your orders involve shooting women and children?" called a familiar voice. Andrew Adams stood on a small knoll of black rock beside the road. "Or bayoneting innocent people going to a cemetery? Because, if so, the whole world will know about it. I'm a newspaperman and a correspondent for several American papers."

"My orders," the PG captain stated again.

"Do you want to be known as the man who ordered the Mauna ala massacre?" Andrew demanded. "Do you think your chiefs will approve? What's your name, so I get it spelled right?"

"I have a solution, Captain," Hannah called. "Let the carriage pass. We will go pray at the grave and then come back here. The people will disperse after we return."

"Andrew," Kaiulani called, "please ride with us."

"My honor, Your Highness," he answered.

"Thank you," Kaiulani said to Andrew and Hannah as the line of guards parted and the carriage rolled through. "Both of you."

"You know your people would have charged bayonets and bullets," Hannah said.

"Waving palm branches," Andrew added.

"I know. I'm glad that was not required."

"This time," Andrew said, helping the two women down from the carriage beside the mausoleum. "Just remember: Thurston won't forget about your people's loyalty either. As for me, please forgive me if I don't stay, but I think I should leave by another route. I don't fancy my chances of escaping arrest this time. Good-bye, Princess, Hannah. Stay safe."

"God bless you, Andrew," they cried in unison.

* * * *

1973

Sandi stopped to pick up her picnic lunch from the kitchen.

Joe read off the contents of the basket. "Ham and cheese on wheat. For One. Hold mayo. Small bag Maui Chips. For One. Fresh fruit bowl with strawberry yogurt. For One. Pineapple upside-down cake. For One. Oh, look. Four Cokes. Gonna find somebody thirsty on the way?" He lowered the list and eyed Sandi with disapproval. "How can anybody so pretty as you order a picnic to go, and everything you order to go is For One?"

"I can't eat more than one sandwich."

"So you don't like Archie? I know plenty of handsome guys who could teach you to surf. Teach you to scuba."

She shook her head. "Oh, Joe, you know." She tapped her wedding ring as she passed him a twenty-dollar bill.

Joe counted out change. "Your husband is one lucky fella. When he comes back, he can ask me! I'll say, Sandi won't even eat a ham-and-cheese sandwich with another man. Drove all the way to Hana alone!"

"I'm never alone. John's right here, Joe." She patted her heart.

He shifted his weight uncomfortably. "I know. I know. You're a good lady, Sandi. Lots of *Aloha.*" He slid the cash drawer closed. "Where you gonna stay tonight?"

"Hotel Hana."

"Oh, yeah. There ain't any other hotels in Hana. Room for One. No phones. No TV. Nothing to do."

She held up her camera. "I have plans. Any suggestions where a girl can have a picnic—for One—on the road to Hana?"

"Wailua Falls, maybe. Waterfalls and pools everywhere. You'll see. Like paradise. Road to Hana's pretty crazy. We all know you don't really know how to shift gears. You drive safe, huh? *Aloha.*"

With a wave, Sandi tossed the basket into the Toyota. Still smiling, she concentrated on a smooth exit from the parking lot. Joe and his cadre of relatives gathered on the *lanai* to smoke cigarettes and bet whether she could clear the lot without popping the clutch.

Miraculously the little car glided smoothly away from the Pioneer Inn. With a glance in the rearview mirror she saw the Hawaiians applauding and cheering her.

For an hour and a half, Sandi followed a pineapple truck across the island. At Paia the dirt-caked vehicle turned onto a farm road, and Sandi turned onto the twisting road to paradise.

Not one for statistics, Sandi reviewed what she had heard of the road: fifty-two miles from the airport to Hana; fifty-nine bridges in that same span.

With a pounding heart, she gave up the notion of counting them after a dozen.

As soon as the little car was pointed south along Maui's east coast, the jungle closed in around the road. Sheer rock walls made Sandi hunch over her steering wheel, only to gasp when a canyon's gash opened unexpectedly. Ravines choked with bright green leaves and florescent yellow blossoms framed picture postcard waterfalls.

Slowing to a crawl, Sandi jumped when a pickup behind her bellowed its impatience. "Sorry, sorry." She waved out the window. The road itself was barely big enough for two lanes; the turnouts were practically nonexistent.

What was the count of the curves? Six hundred? Sandi no longer believed anything about Hana was exaggerated. At least second gear worked for this entire trip. Anything above thirty miles an hour felt dangerously fast.

Somewhere along the way she passed the famous ninety-foot-high Wailua Falls. She did not notice. When at last the road sign identified the turnoff for Hotel Hana, Sandi's picnic lunch "for One" remained uneaten in the basket. Because she had to steer with one hand and shift with the other, she could not hold a Coke can. "Ah, well." She sighed as she checked in and carried her provisions to the cottage. "I'll have a ham sandwich 'for One' for my supper."

It was dusk when Sandi lay down for a nap. Hawaiian music drifted across the grounds. Steel guitars and ukuleles accompanied a female vocalist singing "Little Grass Shack."

Through the window of her dim room, Sandi heard the laughter of lovers strolling across the broad lawns of the resort.

The pangs of loneliness overrode the hunger pangs she felt.

"Oh, Jesus," Sandi whispered. And then, "Oh, John!"

A heavy sleep washed over her like the waves against the rocky shore.

What was that song? "Blackbird...broken wings...learn to fly..."

The last chords died away. A voice called to her, "Sandi?"

She heard herself answer. "John? Is that you, honey?"

All human sounds fell silent, replaced by the rush of wind in the trees and the hiss of waves across sand. It was late. Midnight?

"Sandi?" It was John's voice.

Directly overhead, the full moon was bright enough to cast shadows. Sandi, suddenly aware of the stillness, opened her eyes.

John stood framed in the doorway. The moon shone behind him. It was too bright for her to see his face.

"It's you, John."

"Hi." There was a smile in his voice, like when he walked in and asked her what was for dinner.

"Ham and cheese. Pineapple upside-down cake," she answered, although he had not asked.

"For one." He sounded sad.

"You can have mine, honey." She tried to sit up but couldn't move.

"You can't do this anymore, sweetie," John said. "Life's gotta be for two."

"I miss you," she cried. "When are you coming home?"

His words were like wind chimes. "You were always beautiful, Sandi. The moonlight on your skin."

"Oh, John! It's been so long. So long! Please." Desire for his touch uncoiled in her. "Will you stay awhile? Touch me?"

"Will you remember me?"

"I will. I do!" she cried.

"Don't let life pass you by, Sandi."

"Come home, John!"

He said softly, "Sandi, I am home. Safe. Don't worry anymore."

She began to sob. "Oh! I'm dreaming."

"Yes."

"I don't ever want to wake up."

"But you must. Five years. Sandi, time for you to wake up."

The light behind him dimmed until she could see his features plainly. Ruggedly handsome, he smiled at her with his sideways grin.

"I will always love you, John."

"I love you," he replied.

"Can I come with you?"

"Not yet. Too much life for you to live. For me. Live it."

"Not without you! I can't do it without you."

"It's okay, Sandi. Remember? Remember the blackbird? Time for you to fly again."

So bright. So bright! She could not keep her eyes open against the glare. Calling John's name, she sat up and reached for him.

He was gone.

The plaintive song of a night bird summoned its mate.

Chapter Twenty-four

....

Republic of Hawaii

The north wing of the new house at Ainahau was completely sheltered from the afternoon sun. Though it was not a tall chamber, the floor-to-ceiling windows admitted plenty of light. Louvered screens allowed the sweetly scented winds free passage. Depending on the direction of the breeze, the air was either tinged with *pikake* or the sharp tang of a screen of eucalyptus trees.

Papa Archie had commissioned the room as Kaiulani's retreat from the cares of state—a place where the princess could gather with her closest friends for pleasant conversation. Though Kaiulani had no official duties, it still served that purpose, even if only shared by Kaiulani and Hannah.

The noon delivery of the post arrived. From the handful of letters, Hannah snatched up a letter from Annie. She scanned it briefly, then shared the contents with her friend. "Annie says the north shore of Maui is a wonderful place to raise a family," Hannah reported. "The Provisional Government doesn't even try to run things there."

Flipping over a page, Hannah continued, "She also wants to know why no one warned her that an eighteen-month-old boy could be such a handful!"

Hannah paused to dab her lips with a handkerchief before resuming. "She also says she and Kawika take the baby and go into

Lahaina once a week for shopping. They often see Andrew there." Frustrated by the lack of response, she asked, "Do you hear me, Kaiulani? She says they see Andrew Adams."

Kaiulani lifted her eyes from the pale blue stationery she was studying. "Sorry. I was reading a letter from the queen."

"Bad news?"

Kaiulani bit her lip. "Worrisome. She wants me to agree to marry Prince Koa."

"Koa? Not really?"

"She says it's for the good of the monarchy—to preserve the bloodlines of the *Alii*—and that the people would support such a match. She says I may have to choose between him or a Japanese Imperial prince."

"Koa, or a Japanese prince?" Hannah repeated. A spasm of coughing made her shoulders shake.

Kaiulani looked up with concern, but Hannah waved her off. "I'm all right," Hannah said, taking a sip of water. "It was the shock. You won't agree to either, will you?"

Kaiulani spread her hands helplessly. "She is grasping at straws. Keeping a royal line, even if there isn't a throne. She wants to keep hope alive."

Hannah grimaced. "So the queen and Thurston actually agree on something. Your own people love you so much, Kaiulani, they would die for you. If you had said one word or raised one finger, they would have charged the bayonets of the soldiers so you could carry flowers to your mother's tomb. While you're alive, you are a threat to the PGs."

Kaiulani requested. "The *haole* soldiers and Thurston's men would fill every empty grave with freshly dead Hawaiians—and for the slightest reason. That's what haunts me, as it must Queen Lili-uokalani. She surrendered her authority to save lives. I wouldn't have anyone, not one life, lost for my sake."

Hannah said quietly, "I saw it in Andrew's face: he would willingly die for you. He is a changed man. Love has turned him around."

Hannah and Kaiulani raised their heads at the coarse laughter of men from outside. Kaiulani's eyes widened. Had the soldiers come to arrest her?

Abruptly there came rough pounding on Ainahau's main entrance. Without a pause the hammering continued, growing more insistent and harsher.

Kaiulani exchanged a glance with Hannah, then stood.

Hannah leaped to her feet. "I'll go. What if you're wrong? What if the PGs have come to arrest you?"

Waving Kaiulani to keep back out of sight, Hannah padded down the corridor, past the grand reception hall, to the front door. The booming of fists echoed in the house.

"What do you want?" Hannah demanded.

"U.S. Marines," was the shouted reply. "Open the door."

"Yeah, and be quick about it," another said.

Judging from the powerful voices, the impatient callers could kick in the door if they chose.

Hannah opened it a crack. "Yes? What is it?"

A half dozen uniformed *haoles* ringed the front step. One of them had a tripod topped by a large wooden box. "This is where Kaiulani Cleghorn lives?" another demanded. "Well, we want to get our picture taken with the ex-princess. Something to show the folks back home, see?"

"Yes, I see," Hannah said, gesturing behind her back to Kaiulani, warning her to stay back. Hannah smiled at the men. "Yes, I am Kaiulani. I'll be happy to oblige. Shall we take the picture here on the front step?"

Kaiulani felt sick with fear for Hannah's safety. She had just said she would not have one life lost for her sake, and yet Hannah was standing in her place!

She leaned heavily against the wall and prayed as male voices and laughter intruded on the peace of Ainahau. "Well, you're a pretty thing." The American accent was clear. The marine's tone was as suggestive as if Hannah were a girl in a saloon.

Kaiulani's heart pounded. "Oh, Lord! My rock and my fortress! Spread Your wings over my Hannah! Give Your angels charge over her to defend her. Please, Heavenly Father, I don't know how to pray!"

Suddenly a gruff male voice barked, "What are you up to? Who gave you permission? Clear out, or I'll have you in irons!"

Silence.

Hannah's gentle reply. "They came to the door. Said they wanted a photograph with the princess...with me..."

"Trespassing. My apologies, miss. I'll do my best to see it don't happen again. Not with my men, anyway. But you'd best stay out of sight. Lock the gates, see?"

The words *Aloha* and *mahalo* seemed blasphemous on the tongues of the departing soldiers.

Silence.

The door swung open slowly. Hannah, pale and weary, entered the house. Her breath came in wheezing gasps. She groped for a chair. Kaiulani helped her to the sitting room as her shoulders convulsed with coughing.

Minutes passed before Hannah could speak. "You heard?"

Kaiulani, shaken, nodded. "What can we do? The KAPU sign didn't stop them."

"It won't stop them. They'll come again. I saw it in their expressions. Oh, Kaiulani! These are not men with human hearts!" Hannah began to cough again. Covering her mouth with a handkerchief, she fought to breathe, tried to catch her breath. The white linen was stained with drops of blood.

Kaiulani had seen this sign of sickness before. "Hannah, my dearest, come on. Come on. Let me help you to bed."

* * * *

The western sky still glowed long after the sun had set. The grandfather clock in the foyer of Ainahau struck ten times as the cool evening breeze from the ocean ruffled the curtains. Peacocks plaintively called to one another as they flew up to roost in the branches of the banyan for the night.

An Oriental servant Kaiulani did not recognize cleared away the dishes.

Papa said, "The house servants are all Chinese now. I know enough of their language to make my wishes known. And they don't know enough English to spy on my conversations."

"Papa, can it be so bad?" Kaiulani asked.

Archie stroked his beard. "They'll all be approached by Thurston's men now that you're home. I hope I'm right, and there are none among the staff who understand what we're saying. We must speak Hawaiian when we talk over important matters. I've sent word to Andrew. He'll be here soon."

At that a knock sounded at the door. Papa rose and went to answer it.

Sobered by the warning, Kaiulani looked across the table at Hannah's darkly somber expression. "What is it, Hannah?"

Hannah glanced up quickly. "*Aloha au iā 'oe.*"

"And I love you." Left hand on her heart, Kaiulani clasped Hannah's hand and kissed her fingertips. "*Kaikaina,* my sister."

Andrew's voice preceded him as he returned with Papa Archie.

Andrew was dressed in a rumpled white linen jacket and trousers. His striped cotton shirt was open at the neck. Kaiulani's heart leapt as he entered the room. Sweeping off his broad-brimmed straw hat, he bowed slightly. "Princess Kaiulani and the lovely Hannah."

Kaiulani smiled at him and touched the empty chair beside her. "Andrew, dear friend."

He hesitated and tucked his chin as if the title *friend* had struck him. "I'm glad to see you. Grateful to God that you are alive and unharmed."

"So far," Kaiulani replied, grasping both his hands.

Andrew, Kaiulani, Hannah, and Papa moved onto the *lanai.*

For a moment, just a moment, all the worries that had loomed at Kaiulani's homecoming vanished.

The Chinese servant followed, carrying their coffee and pineapple-upside-down cake onto the *lanai.* Stars lit the sky.

As they settled into their cane-backed chairs to savor the evening, Kaiulani exchanged a knowing glance with Hannah. "Papa," she said, "Andrew is always welcome. But I don't believe you invited him for a late evening social call. If Andrew came here when he could arrive unobserved, there must be a reason."

Papa Archie looked embarrassed, but Andrew leaned forward with a serious expression. "I told your father that I don't think it's safe for you to stay on Oahu at present. There are rumblings about you among the PGs. You're too popular."

"And what do you suggest?" Kaiulani asked crossly. "Should I go back to England?"

Hannah put one hand on her chest as a spasm of coughing overtook her, but with the other she touched Kaiulani's shoulder. "Sorry," she said when the rasping stopped. "Kaiulani, don't be so hasty. Hear Andrew out. You're no use to your people if you're dead. Or under house arrest like the queen."

"I am under self-imposed confinement. I can't stick my nose out of the gate. Andrew, if you have any ideas…"

Andrew stared up at the constellation of Orion striding majestically across the heavens. "You have friends on the Big Island, don't you?"

Papa Archie said, "Yes. Parker Ranch. Kaiulani has a cousin there too."

"Parker Ranch?" The thought of horseback riding and the freedom to go out was appealing. "Is that what you suggest?"

Kaiulani was surprised at Andrew's reply. "No," he said. "But that is the story I will send as a dispatch to the papers. We'll leak the news that you're on the Big Island. Enjoying your stay with friends."

Papa Archie leaned forward. "Yes. But where?"

Andrew hesitated as the servant emerged and poured another cup of coffee. The journalist waited until the attendant left, then lowered his voice. "Where I will escort you—with your agreement and your father's permission—is to Ulupalakua, in up-country, Maui."

Suddenly the image came clearly to Kaiulani's mind: a pristine, white clapboard ranch house, high up on the flank of Haleakela. Surrounded by big trees and hidden sometimes in the clouds hanging about the mountain, it was a pleasant, secluded place. "I was there once with the king…with Papa Moi," she recalled. "Mister Stevenson was there as well."

Papa Archie's face brightened at the suggestion. "The king's old house. Closed up. I know the ranch foreman. It can be arranged easily."

Andrew fixed his gaze on Kaiulani. "Listen. You'll be safe there. Free."

Hannah cried, "Oh, Kaiulani! We can ride every day."

Archie sat back, satisfied. "Your mother loved that house. Ulupalakua!"

Kaiulani clapped her hands. "On the slope of Haleakula, overlooking the sea. I remember! We saw the whales breach when the sun was silver on the water."

Hannah laughed. "We learned to milk goats. Remember? The *paniolos* let us ride the ponies of their children."

Kaiulani's eyes filled with tears at the prospect of living in obscurity and freedom. "There was no place in the islands where we had such joy."

"I'll come up from Lahaina once a week with supplies," Andrew promised. "I'll bring letters and carry out any messages you need to send. Then, when things quiet down in Honolulu, or we get rid of Thurston and his crowd, I'll bring you home."

Papa Archie steepled his fingers and studied the faces of Kaiulani and Hannah. "The happiest I have seen your faces since you returned." He turned to Andrew. "I am depending on you, Andrew. You can sail to Maui from Ainahau."

* * * *

The women, bundled in travel capes, waited on the beach beneath Ainahau. Beside them, one coal-oil bull's-eye lantern was nailed to a palm tree's trunk. Standing atop a low post a few yards farther toward the waves was a second gleaming beacon.

Andrew, who had gone to locate the rowboat hidden earlier for tonight's purpose, returned to Hannah and Kaiulani. "The channel through the reef is narrow but passable," he said by way of explanation. "When the captain sees these two lights as one directly atop the other, he knows to come straight ahead to anchor."

Even as Andrew spoke, a dark shape knifed across the face of a distant phosphorescent swell. "He's right on time," Andrew said.

He assisted Hannah into the dinghy, then returned for Kaiulani. His hands felt warm on her arms and his breath warm on her cheek.

Once they were seated, he launched the boat, Andrew's boots squelching in the wet sand.

The princess sat in the stern of the craft; Hannah in the bow. "You see the light on the ship?" he asked. "Keep your eye on it, and give me corrections if I'm headed wrong."

Kaiulani watched Andrew's sure, strong strokes on the oars. There was no wasted motion. Each pull powered them nearer to their escape with a minimum of noise. Kaiulani wanted to tell Andrew how much she admired him: his plan, his strength, his courage, his commitment to her cause. But now was not the time, and this was not the place.

He caught her looking at him. "Not exactly rowing in Regent's Park, is it?" he joked.

"How do you know we can trust this captain?" she asked.

"Old friend," he replied. "Hawaiian captain who worked in the sandalwood trade with my father. He'd sooner die than betray you."

"He knows who we are?" Hannah asked.

"Yes, but not the crew," Andrew cautioned. "Keep your hoods up and your voices soft. You'll be fine."

The freeboard on the schooner was low. Two steps up a rope ladder, and they were aboard. The captain murmured a greeting, then bustled them aft to the deck behind the cockpit before setting his crew of three to hoisting anchor and making sail.

"What's her name?" Hannah asked. "The ship's?"

"*Ho'ololi*," Andrew replied.

"Good," Hannah approved. "'Transformed.' May this night transform all our lives for good."

An off-shore breeze wafted *Ho'ololi* beyond the black gap where white breakers surged over the coral on either side. With the wind from the port quarter astern, the skipper ordered the sails set for the crossing between Oahu and the island of Lanai. Soon the water sang along the lee rail as *Ho'ololi* set her keel into the waves like an eager horse attacks the track.

The stars were radiant overhead. "Is it true the ancient Polynesians could navigate across thousands of miles by the stars alone?" Andrew asked.

"So my grandmother taught me," Kaiulani said. "The channel between Kaho'olawe and Lanai is called *Kealaikahiki,* the road to Tahiti. Our people came from there, I think."

"How brave they must have been," Andrew said. "Not just the sailing, I mean, but giving up all they knew—their life back there— to go to a new, unknown land."

Impulsively Kaiulani reached out and grasped Andrew's hands. "But they took their families with them. It's not about houses and land. If you have those you love around you, you are home."

Hannah coughed softly. It was not a sound of disapproval, but still it caused Kaiulani to stiffen and draw back from Andrew's touch.

"I'll ask how long the captain thinks we'll be," he said.

Just ahead a whale announced his presence with a puff of air that rang like a kettledrum and an iridescent spout of vapor that hung in the air like a magic mist. *"Aloha, kohola,"* Hannah greeted the animal. "Are you going to Maui? Will you show us the way?"

Halfway across, Kaiulani and Hannah huddled in their cloaks to sit close together on the deck. Kaiulani leaned back against Andrew as he sheltered them from the cold, and she slept with the greatest contentment since returning to Hawaii.

Almost before she knew it, the West Maui Mountains were blocking a swath of the eastern heavens and the lights of Lahaina loomed ahead. "We could have landed on the south shore and taken the old wagon road to King David's place," Andrew said. "But this way even if someone talks about two women coming ashore off a ship, they won't know where we went from there."

Chapter Twenty-five
....

Three saddle mounts and a packhorse already loaded with supplies waited at a stable on the outskirts of Lahaina.

Hannah and Kaiulani kept their features obscured within the depths of their hooded cloaks. Long before the sun climbed above Haleakela, the party of riders, with Andrew leading the pack animal, was well clear of the town.

Kaiulani heard Andrew ask directions to Kahana, a village north of Lahaina. Their destination was really far to the southeast.

They rode at a slow but steady pace. Showing too much haste would arouse suspicion. Circling the cape called Olawalu, they crossed barren, dry land, inhabited only by workers in the cane fields.

Their travel kept them near sea level. A pod of whales paced them for a time, breaching and splashing as if to encourage the land-bound travelers. "Do you suppose...one of them...is the same whale we saw...last night?"

Hannah's halting words caused Kaiulani concern.

Hannah saw and shook off her worry. "I'll be better...soon as you...are safe."

Crossing Maui's central valley, the trio began the steep ascent of Haleakela's flank. Ten thousand feet high at its summit, the dormant volcano called the House of the Sun dominated the skyline like the side of an ocean liner seen from its waterline.

The heavy cloaks, discarded in the heat of the valley and tied behind the saddles, were soon pressed into service again. They climbed from cane fields and red earth into the regions of pastureland and black lava-rock. The temperature rapidly cooled. Purple cascades of jacaranda trees gave way to red-blossomed acacia and soon after to cleanly scented groves of pine.

And still they ascended. The journey from Lahaina to Ulupalakua, though begun before sunrise, would take all day. They pressed ahead with few pauses.

Hannah nodded in the saddle. Fearful her friend would fall, Kaiulani called to Andrew, "We need to stop. We need rest."

Hannah roused from her doze. "Not on my account."

Kaiulani insisted, "We're stopping here."

"It's time," Andrew agreed.

The princess uncorked the canteen looped over the horn of her saddle and took a long drink, then offered the container to Hannah. "No," Hannah replied, "don't need it yet. Let's go on now."

They set out again, single file, up the narrow trail. Kaiulani led the way, and Andrew brought up the rear, with Hannah in the middle of the string. Kaiulani glanced back to check and saw Hannah take a drink from her own canteen.

All of Maui's central valley lay spread below them. Checkerboard squares of cane fields made the distant landscape appear to be a well-groomed English lawn. From this elevation Kaiulani saw both shores of the island and beyond. Not even halfway in their ascent, the lowlands of Maui seemed as if a single large wave could rush across the island from north shore to south.

Whales breaching in the channel beside the submerged volcanic cone of Molokini were no more than stray white threads on a blue quilt. Kaiulani sighed with the remoteness of the place. This was so far removed from Honolulu and politics and danger. Apart from concern for Hannah, Kaiulani felt her spirits lift the way the translucent clouds forming on the sea floated upward toward the House of the Sun.

If only Andrew could stay at Ulupalakua with them, Kaiulani thought.

Where had that notion come from? Kaiulani reprimanded herself. This was an escape from real evil—not the plot of a romantic story. Andrew was helping her deal with real wickedness. He was not the hero of a novel, like Dick Shelton in *The Black Arrow* or Rudolf Rassendyll in *The Prisoner of Zenda*. Besides, he was their link to the outside world, to news, to supplies and to Papa. He couldn't remain with them, even if such a thing were proper.

Kaiulani shoved the thought away but, unbidden, it continued to plague her all the rest of the ride to Ulupalakua.

Hannah, despite her protests, was completely exhausted by the time they reached the white-painted frame house amid the towering trees. She was pale and shaking.

Andrew lifted her off the horse. She could not stand, so he carried her into the house. Kaiulani swept aside a sheet covering a sofa so Andrew could lay Hannah there. "Princess," he addressed her formally, "if you'll build a fire, I'll bring in the supplies and see to the horses. Then I'll come help you open up the house."

Wrapped in a blanket, Hannah shivered as Kaiulani put a match to the kindling already prepared on the hearth. Who had made this provision for their need? Was this fire laid when her uncle, the king, was still living? When Kaiulani and Hannah and Andrew had all still been in England?

When the monarchy was yet sound and the future all soirees and ball gowns?

Andrew came in carrying a canvas-wrapped bundle of provisions. "There's enough here for two weeks, but I'll be back in one."

"You won't—" Kaiulani glanced at Hannah to see her friend was sleeping, then resumed. "You won't try to ride down tonight, will you? The trail is so treacherous in places."

"I thought I'd sleep in the barn," Andrew admitted.

"You will not," Kaiulani corrected forcefully. "We'll move Hannah to bed, and you shall sleep on the sofa."

Andrew grinned. "As Your Majesty commands, but I smell like horse. Which, by the way, I still have to unsaddle and turn into the pasture."

Kaiulani caught him before his booted steps left the porch. The crescent of a two-day-old moon hung above the waves to the west. Throwing her arms around Andrew's neck, she kissed him, soundly, vigorously.

And he returned the kiss with fervor.

"The horses," he said in a husky voice. "They...I..."

"Go on," Kaiulani said, giving him a playful shove. "I know you won't believe it, but I know how to cook. I'll have supper started by the time you get back."

* * * *

The frame house creaked in the wind swirling down from Haleake-la's summit like a sailing ship running headlong into a crashing sea. Her timbers groaned and sighed. The coals on the hearth glowed with new life when a downdraft in the chimney touched them.

The same way something in Kaiulani was sparked by Andrew's touch.

Kaiulani was unable to sleep. Settled in the king's bedroom, her thoughts ranged from what was happening back in Honolulu to Hannah resting in the adjacent chamber.

Always, her musings came back to Andrew on the sofa. It was impossible to believe they had ever been enemies. Ever since the night Andrew met the Lord, he had been Kaiulani's truest, most devoted friend. Far more important than Clive's grand declarations, Andrew offered practical help and guidance.

Tonight's kiss had awakened desire within her. Once released, it was impossible to call back. She could still taste his lips, feel his arms.

In the same strong-minded, direct way she made all decisions, she wanted him to stay near...always.

But the strength of her desire frightened her. Could she abandon her people, her duty, to run away with Andrew? What if she wrote a letter of farewell to the queen? Could a princess abdicate? Could Kaiulani stop being royal and just live?

She wanted to put herself before Andrew and ask him to help her choose. For once in her life, she actually wanted the choice to be made for her. She wanted him to fold her in his arms and declare he would never, ever let her go.

A mourning dove cooed softly in the folds of the Chinese jasmine outside the window. She should go check on Hannah, Kaiulani told herself. She should see that her friend was covered up properly.

Of course, if she walked a few steps farther, out into the reception room, she would be beside Andrew. It would not be proper to do such a thing, but hadn't he wrapped her up and kept her warm on the schooner crossing from Oahu?

Should convention and propriety keep her from doing the same for him?

Hannah was sound asleep, perfectly cocooned in blankets.

Kaiulani knew she should go immediately back to her bed; knew she was traveling a dangerous road.

She felt herself being drawn to the sofa as a magnet draws iron. Her breathing quickened as she drew nearer and nearer to where he lay.

Only...he wasn't there. Blankets neatly folded on the sofa and boots missing from beside the front door, Andrew had risen in the night and left.

Andrew left without even saying good-bye? After tonight's kiss?

Clearly he did not have the same feelings for her that she had mistakenly had for him.

Kaiulani dashed back to her bed and crawled beneath the covers. Closing her eyes, she prayed that every thought of him would vanish before morning.

* * * *

1973

From the veranda of her room, Sandi enjoyed the ocean view and a cool afternoon breeze. Auntie Hannah was napping after her lunch, serenaded by some forgotten crooner on her gramophone. After the record was over, the gentle, rhythmic hissing from the machine's idle spin continued, wafting to Sandi's ears. She raised the last sheet from a neatly compiled stack of letters from Andrew to Kaiulani and began to read.

> *Dearest Princess,*
>
> *Even as I write this letter, I am preparing for another journey on your behalf. Knowing I will soon be in your presence again, and how I feel whenever I am, I cannot contain the truth of those feelings any longer.*
>
> *Kaiulani, I love you. I believe I have since I first met you, but for propriety's sake, for the sake of our friendship and your office, I hoped I might have the strength to love you from a distance. But the darkening of my days in your absence has forced me to admit that this will never be enough. I must be with you for all time.*
>
> *I cannot deny the imprudence of this feeling, and for that I am ashamed. Neither do I know how such a love might survive, were you to bless me with requital. You are, after all, ordained in your station by our Sovereign King and I, your humble subject.*
>
> *Yet, it must be. For without you, I am not merely alone. Without you, I am not.*

I tremble at the idea of my clumsy declaration falling under your gaze. Can you see how my hand shakes? For if you are wise, and I know you are, you must spurn such passion as irrational and impossible.

But if I am loved at all by God, then your love will surely follow. For He cannot have put in me such sacred devotion to you, without He also…

"Well, way to go, Andrew!" Sandi applauded. "You finally got around to telling her, buddy."

A knock sounded from the interior of the hotel, but Sandi realized it was on Auntie Hannah's door. She laid the letter aside and listened as the old woman rose slowly from her bed and shuffled toward it. The latch popped and the hinges squeaked as she pulled the door open for some unseen guest.

Sandi heard voices but couldn't make out what they said. The conversation was brief, and Hannah's door closed again within seconds. Before Sandi could resume her reading, though, the rapping fell on her own door.

She gathered the precious papers and brought them inside the room, laying the stack on the bed. Glancing quickly at her reflection in the bathroom, she pressed a few strands of windblown hair back into place and padded to the door.

Before she could reach the knob, the knock repeated. "Coming," she called sweetly, sure it was Joe or his wife, Emma, bringing her some afternoon snack.

The reality waiting outside her room made her vision swim and her knees weak. Two men, both in army dress uniforms, stood in front of her door, their caps tucked under their arms. Auntie Hannah stood just behind them.

"Are you Missus Sandi Smith of Westwood, California?" one asked. "Wife of Private John Smith?" His uniform identified him as a captain.

No, she wanted to scream, *no, I'm not!* She'd had such a visit before, when they first told her John was missing in action. It was terrible then, but missing was preferable to... She gulped and nodded.

"Missus Smith, I am Captain Aaron Roberts from A Company, Second Battalion, Twenty-Fifth Infantry, Schofield Barracks, Hawaii. The Secretary of the Army has asked me to express his deep regret that your husband is believed to have been killed in action in March of 1970 while escaping from a prisoner-of-war camp."

"Believed?" Sandi asked, clinging desperately to the thinnest hope of a mistake implied in the word.

The captain cleared his throat. "Another soldier who was in the camp with John positively identified his photo this week. He says he's buried near where they were held."

"Oh, God." Sandi stumbled backward into her room. Bumping into the bed, she slid to the floor, clutching her face in her hands. The men and Auntie Hannah all followed her in. "Is there something we can get you, ma'am?" Roberts asked, echoed by the other man. "Do you need a glass of water?"

Sandi just shook her head as Auntie Hannah patted her shoulder. "My poor dear," offered the old woman.

Roberts spoke again. "The Secretary extends his deepest sympathy to you and your family in your tragic loss."

There were so many questions that lingered in her mind. She never imagined that it would end this way. If ever she'd allowed herself to contemplate his death, she always thought he'd be returned to her, for a proper burial. "What"—she tried to ask—"will he...come home?"

"Unfortunately, I don't have that information. Now that we know where you're staying, you'll receive more information as soon as it becomes available."

"Missus Smith." The other man spoke up. "Is there anyone else you'd like us to be in touch with on your behalf? Any calls I can make?"

Sandi's parents flashed through her mind. It was so hard hearing the news herself, she certainly didn't want to think about having to inflict it on anyone else. But she couldn't pass that off on these men.

Distantly, as if detached from her own anguished tears, she briefly considered the difficult job these men had to do. She wondered how often they were called upon to make such tragic visits and if they felt each family's grief compounding, day after day.

"Thank you," she croaked meekly, "for coming."

The response was unexpected, and the men glanced at each other, as if trying to decide how to answer. Roberts spoke first. "I am truly sorry for your loss, Missus Smith."

They turned in silence and left, closing the door behind them.

Auntie Hannah knelt wearily next to Sandi and hugged her, rocking her gently.

Sandi whispered, "I dreamed about him. He came to me. Oh! I think I knew when I saw him. He told me he was home. I didn't know what he meant. I should have known!" She began to sob quietly.

Auntie Hannah held her close and stroked her hair. "There is a saying among my people: *Aloha me ka paumake.* It means, 'My love is with the one who is done with dying.'"

Chapter Twenty-six

....

U.S. Territory of Hawaii, 1898

Along the eastern border of Ulupalakua was a mountain stream. Bursting out of the heart of Haleakela, high up the volcano's mossy, green hide, the creek bubbled to the sea.

Just now the stream's passage was disrupted by Kaiulani's feet dangling in the current. She and Hannah sat atop a lava stone wall.

"I'm running away by being here," Kaiulani said.

Hannah turned her face toward the sun, as if to absorb strength with its warming rays. "If you hadn't come, you would be arrested, or dead."

Kaiulani studied their reflections in the water. They were so alike, in body and heart. "Sometimes, when I let myself think about what is happening, my heart is so heavy. Thurston and his men. They have stolen the joy, the soul of our people."

Hannah raised her eyes heavenward. "What they have stolen, they took from the Lord. They have no fear of Him, Kaiulani. And so God Himself will personally deal with them."

"They aren't content to take our land and destroy our constitution. They take pleasure in destroying lives. In tearing down the work of our hands. There are times it has made my faith falter. I pray and ask, 'Where are You, Lord?'"

Hannah tossed a pebble into the pool. "The ripples of our faith, in spite of evil men who hate us, will touch eternity. We mustn't give up, Kaiulani. We must continue to trust, no matter what. The devil really hates it that we, whose ancestors worshipped idols, are now Christians. The devil hates it that we cling to God, even though we are betrayed by the sons of missionaries."

"It's little comfort for me sometimes. I pray and wait for God to answer."

"The answer is already written. Your prayers and faith in spite of cruel men will be God's eternal answer to Thurston when he tries to enter heaven."

"What good am I here?"

Hannah put her arm around Kaiulani. "This is the word of the Lord to you. I read it this morning: 'Strengthen ye the weak hands, and confirm the feeble knees. Say to them that are of a fearful heart, Be strong, fear not: behold, your God will come with vengeance; he will come and save you.'" [27]

Kaiulani shook her head in admiration. "You remember everything you read." She tapped her heart. "You remember it here."

"Only true things."

Neither woman spoke for a long time. At last Kaiulani said, "What would my life have been like without you? You are the mirror of my soul."

Hannah searched Kaiulani's face. "Sometimes I can't tell where your thoughts end and mine begin."

"I'm coming to like it here. Maybe I don't want to leave here, ever. You?"

Hannah hesitated for a long moment. "The truth?"

"Only the truth."

"I'm homesick."

"Home? This is home for now. Where's a better place?"

Hannah turned her face skyward. "I've been dreaming of my mother lately. I recognize her from the photographs. But I think I'd know her anyway. "

"Does she say anything?"

"Nothing. She just stands quietly smiling beside my bed. Gentle, kind eyes. Like she's waiting for me. When I see her, I know I'm dreaming, and I don't want to wake up. That's what I mean when I say sometimes I just want to go home. *Aloha me ka paumake.* My love is with the one who is done with dying."

Kaiulani replied, "Oh, but you can't leave me, Hannah. I will not permit it! What would I do? How would I manage? I'd have no one to talk to."

Hannah laughed. "Andrew comes once a week."

"Not enough. Besides, he's a man. Men are good for some things, but not all."

"Well then, I promise I won't go anywhere without your permission."

* * * *

Fleecy clouds sailed past so close overhead they seemed touchable. Hannah and Kaiulani relaxed in wooden chairs on the lawn beside the king's house, staring at the procession of vapors. As if the sky mimicked the sea, the clouds resembled a mass migration of whales. The illusion was palpable: Kaiulani felt she was swimming with the *kohola* of the clouds. Earth was no longer firm beneath her, but spun and twirled.

Dizzy, Kaiulani ducked her head. Though the day was pleasant, Hannah was bundled in sweater, cloak, and two blankets against a chill she could not seem to evade. A book, untouched, lay shut on her lap.

"Too cold here," Kaiulani announced.

"Shall we go in?"

"No, I mean, here on the mountain. We need to get you back to a warmer part of the island."

"Nonsense," Hannah argued. "I'm much better. The air is so clean. I don't want to leave."

Hannah was improved since coming to Ulupalakua. She coughed less and slept better. But she simply was not regaining her strength fast enough.

Kaiulani studied the road leading down the mountain, then chided herself. Today was Andrew's day to bring supplies. Her breath quickened at the thought. Ever since daybreak Kaiulani had watched for his arrival, though it would be at least noon before he came.

The certainty of that conclusion did not stop her from checking every few minutes to see if he was in sight.

Kaiulani scanned the hillside. Walls of coarse lava rock, built in bygone ages by unknown hands, snaked across the hillside to the west. They not only bordered fields but appeared to divide the mountain. Below were dry slopes covered in gorse and prickly pear thickets. Above were brilliant green grasslands, shading upward into gauzy mist.

Kaiulani couldn't stop herself. Once again she studied the trail for Andrew. She felt her heart leap: two riders were silhouetted against the slope. With a certainty born of many rehearsed greetings,

Kaiulani recognized Andrew by his straw hat and the way he sat the horse.

The other rider looked familiar too. "Hannah," Kaiulani said with excitement. "Papa's here. Papa came with Andrew!"

* * * *

Teakettle whistling on the stove, Papa Archie and Andrew gathered around the kitchen table with the two women. "I'm so glad to see you," Kaiulani said to her father for the fifth time. "You're not very good at letters, Papa," she scolded.

When he did not react to her teasing, Kaiulani waited for the bad news she knew was coming.

"The U.S. has done it," he said with a mournful shake of his head. "Annexation. President McKinley did what your friend Mister Cleveland prevented as long as he could. The Kingdom is no more. Even the so-called republic is gone. Hawaii is now American territory."

There was stunned, grieving silence, broken at last by the scream of the teakettle. Hannah rose from her chair.

"I'll go," Andrew insisted, jumping to his feet. "You always make it too strong."

Kaiulani's eyes darted about the room. This day, this moment so long dreaded, had actually, finally arrived. Now visiting marines would be right to take a picture of the ex-princess. "How...how is the queen taking it?"

Archie's face twisted into a grimace. "Still feisty as ever, I'll say. The PG is trying to steal Crown property before the territorial commission makes final its decision about land. The queen has gone to Washington to fight them."

"Good for her!" Kaiulani said staunchly. "As soon as Hannah's better, I'll go help her, if she wants me. After all, I'm in no danger now. I'm merely a private citizen. An *American* citizen," she added with an expression of distaste.

To Kaiulani's surprise, her papa shook his head.

Andrew, returning with the tea tray, took up the explanation. "There was an armed rebellion. Hawaiians, and *haoles* too—those opposed to the high-handed treatment of the queen—gathered near Diamond Head. They had weapons and anger, but no plan."

"They were defeated?"

Archie nodded somberly. "Some killed. The rest rounded up and imprisoned. They may be hanged."

"No! Oh, no, Papa!" Then Kaiulani said, "But I don't understand. I wasn't there, and I'm no longer the heir apparent. What threat can I be to Thurston now?"

Andrew said forcefully, "Remember the crowd who would have charged bare-handed into bayonets for your sake? Well, they still feel that way, Kaiulani, and Thurston knows it. With the queen away, you are, or could be, the main rallying cry for rebellion. Arrest would be the least you could expect if you returned to Ainahau now. You must stay here longer."

Kaiulani peered with pleading eyes into her father's face.

This time he did not melt to her wishes. "Andrew's right," he said. "Here where it's safe."

* * * *

The four played bridge, but without enthusiasm. It was a way to pass the time, to avoid speaking about annexation. That was all. It grew late. Papa and Hannah went to bed. Andrew went to check on the horses.

In her long white nightgown, feet bare, Kaiulani wandered among the trees dotting the Ulupalakua estate. Many had been brought by visitors to be planted here as gifts to the king—living mementos of other places, other worlds. Kaiulani sheltered herself from the breeze churning up from the sea in the lee of a cherry tree donated by the Mikado, the emperor of Japan. A few paces farther she rested her hand on the rough bark of a plane tree, twin to many she had seen in London. The sapling was given to Kalakaua by Robert Louis Stevenson.

Her thoughts churned like the wind. Who was she, now that the monarchy was no more? She could not live here and be a recluse, of no use to herself nor anyone else. Moonlight revealed an antler-like clump of ferns growing in a crook of the plane tree's branches. The tree, very English. The fern, very Hawaiian. They lived together amicably, it seemed, but one did not become part of the other. They still had recognizable, separate lives.

Was that how Kaiulani would always exist? Would she never be able to reconcile the Scots and the Hawaiian portions of her soul? One bit of her cried out for an ordinary, peaceful life. The other clung to a powerful sense of duty.

She turned at a footfall behind her.

Andrew stood beside the tall pine. "Saw you moving out here." He stepped close. Close enough for Kaiulani to sense his nearness, his maleness. "You look like an angel. You *are* an angel." He draped a shawl around her shoulders, adjusting it close around her neck. His hand caressed her face. "Kaiulani."

She laid her index finger across his lips. "When can I go home? What is my life if I am only here? A moon shadow with no substance?"

When Andrew pulled her into his embrace, she did not resist. "It may be...a long time," he admitted. "Until it's safe."

"But how can it ever be safe, unless I'm already dead? Buried here on the mountain, or truly buried in Mauna ala, next to Mama—what's the difference?"

It was Andrew's turn to hush her, which he did with a kiss. "There are things we don't know yet. But what's important in my life, in *our* lives, I'm now completely certain of."

The moon sailed, untroubled, across the sky. Shadows of tree and fern blended into one.

Chapter Twenty-seven

....

Kaiulani could not endure waiting around the ranch house any longer. It had been almost a week since Andrew's last visit. During all those days, it had rained. There had not even been a chance to go outside except to dash to the barn to feed the horses.

Andrew's next arrival still lay another day ahead. Every facet of life, of duty and of probable futures, had been discussed with Hannah. Both women were weary of discussions that never had conclusions.

"We are in God's hands," Hannah urged. "We must be content in that."

"I'm going riding," Kaiulani declared. "Not far. I won't be gone long. But I have to get out and clear my head."

Hannah cast an anxious look at the sky. The incessant rain had stopped, finally, at dawn. Swollen dark clouds obscured the sky in every direction. "This is just a break in the storm," she said. "Don't go."

Kaiulani frowned and ducked her chin. Taking her friend's hands in hers, she said again, "I won't go far. Please don't worry. But I must get out or go crazy."

"Then I'll come too."

Kaiulani shook her head. Both women knew Hannah was too weak to ride. "Stay here and get the stew cooking," she urged. "I'm sure to be cold and famished when I'm done with my foolishness. Then you can say 'I told you so' over a hot meal."

The strawberry roan Kaiulani selected for the day was a stocky gelding named Lono. He was sure-footed over the rocky ledges and eagerly attentive to his rider. His ears pricked up at her approach, as if agreeing with the need to stretch and move.

The trail Kaiulani selected was a curving path circling Haleakula. It was not even a trail, much less a road. Lono picked his way carefully, but stones loosened by the torrents clattered beneath his hooves.

Kaiulani's destination was a cinder cone, a volcanic outcropping that stood out against the mist-shrouded horizon like a black fang. According to legend, the rocky tooth marked the beginning of a trail leading over Haleakula's summit. Centuries before, it had been the means of escape from attacking foes.

"Get up, Lono," Kaiulani urged. "Escape. That's what we want."

No more than halfway to the cinder cone the skies opened, and the rain began again, heavier than before. The downpour was like a solid gray wall of water. The trail disappeared from sight no more than three paces before and behind.

Kaiulani pulled the slicker around her shoulders and retied the cord securing her hat. Horse and rider bent their heads into the storm.

No jumping of rock walls today, Kaiulani reminded herself. This was no canter in the English countryside.

Lono walked delicately over rock ledges. Places where the trail descended, he placed his feet carefully and slowed his pace without Kaiulani's urging.

Once he refused to move forward. Kaiulani peered into the sheets of rain. "Nothing there," she said, studying a grassy mound. "What's got you scared? Let's get home."

She tucked her heels into his flanks. Lono moved sideways but would not advance. "Get on with you," Kaiulani said, kicking him in the ribs. "Get!"

The horse, trembling, took three strides forward.

And then the thin dome of weedy soil over the collapsed lava tube gave way, dropping horse and rider into a muddy pit.

Lono kicked as he floundered. Kaiulani leapt from the saddle to get away from the flailing hooves.

As she slipped and sprawled in the mire, Lono got to his feet first. Scrambling out of the pit, he took off down the trail toward home…alone.

* * * *

The rain hammered on the tin roof of the ranch house. Hannah's view of the world beyond the *lanai* was like peering through a waterfall. The deluge fell without ceasing for half an hour, then got heavier and more violent.

"I know she turned around as soon as the rain started," Hannah said to herself. "She'll be back soon."

The waiting stretched into an hour. The princess had been gone far too long already.

Hannah sniffed the air. In the inattention of her anxiety she had let the stew burn.

While she was salvaging supper, she heard a horse whinny that was answered by a chorus of neighs from the stable. "Good," she remarked aloud. Heaving a great sigh, she threw a cloak over her head and went to the door.

Outside, pawing nervously at the lawn, was Lono…riderless. His flanks and belly were covered with dark red streaks. Hannah felt her head swim. She put a hand to the railing to steady herself, then called into the torrent, "Kaiulani! Are you there? Kaiulani, answer me!"

Pausing only to slide her feet into boots, Hannah dashed out to seize Lono's trailing reins. Touching the animal's flank, Hannah's palm came away red. "Mud," she muttered to herself. "It's just lava mud."

Heedless of the rain that poured down the collar of her cloak, drenching her to the skin, Hannah mounted Lono and cantered out of the yard. "Show me," she urged the horse. "Take me to her."

The double set of fresh hoofprints were overflowing puddles of rainwater. There was no doubt about the right trail. But how far had Kaiulani gone? Was she injured? Was she knocked unconscious?

Every few yards Hannah cried, "Kaiulani! Where are you?" All too soon her voice was reduced to a quavering croak. "Oh, please, God. Help me find her!"

Heaps of lava rock took the form of goblins looming up in the downpour. The arms of a clump of prickly pear cactus ordered her to halt.

Shivering uncontrollably, Hannah pressed on up the mountain. Her clothing clung to her body, offering no further protection against wind or water.

Another ghostly shape appeared out of a solid wall of water. It gestured at Hannah with red-streaked arms and shook its mud-curdled hair. "Hannah," she heard Kaiulani call, "I'm here. Here."

Hannah could not speak. With lips tightly clamped against a pain that seemed to be crushing her chest, she agreed to stay in the saddle and let Kaiulani lead the horse toward home.

* * * *

How could Andrew get up the mountain? Hannah needed a doctor soon!

Rain pelted the roof of the house. Hannah, eyes glassy and clenched teeth chattering, stared into the roaring blaze of the fireplace.

Kaiulani tossed another log on the fire. The room was stifling, yet Hannah could not get warm. She laid yet another quilt over Hannah. "Better?"

Hannah shook her head. "I—am—freezing—to—death." She convulsed with coughing.

Kaiulani knelt beside her. "Oh! Oh my sweet girl. My darling girl." She put her cheek against Hannah's. It was clammy, cold like death. "Please, Jesus! Jesus!"

Hannah turned her face to Kaiulani and put her arm around her shoulder in an embrace. "Don't—cry." Her complexion was a sickly yellow. There was no color in her lips.

"Look what I've done to you! Oh!"

Hannah croaked, "No. Kai—don't—"

"I'll make tea. Can you drink some, do you think?"

Hannah attempted a smile, but the hacking seized her again. Kaiulani held her until the convulsion released. She kissed her forehead and hurried to make a steaming cup of tea with three sugars. Carrying it back to the bedside, Kaiulani propped her up and held the cup to her lips. "Please, Hannah! You've got to try."

It seemed to sap all Hannah's strength to take the first sip.

She swallowed hard. For an instant her eyes cleared with a look of thanks.

"Yes. Good girl! More? Please try! Oh! *Iesu!*"

At the name of Jesus, again Hannah sipped the brew, then closed her eyes and sank back. *"Baibala Hemolele."* She sighed. "Read—please."

Kaiulani rushed to the bookshelf and searched for an original copy of the first Hawaiian Bible from among the volumes. As she touched the well-worn volume, the fleeting thought came to her that this Bible had been translated into Hawaiian in part by missionary Asa Thurston—Asa, grandfather of Lorrin Thurston, architect of the betrayal of the Hawaiian people. How far the children of the righteous had fallen in their worship of wealth and power!

Kaiulani closed her eyes a moment and prayed that her heart would not be bitter against God because of what evil men had accomplished. "Speak your love into our broken hearts on this dark night of our souls, O *Iesu!*"

Hannah turned her head toward Kaiulani's whispered prayer. "Please, read—*Ke Akua Mana E!*"

The Bible fell open in Kaiulani's hands to Psalm 91. Her eyes fell on verse 2, and she began to sing the words as she read, *"'E olelo aku au ia Iehova'* (I will say to the Lord), *'Kuu puuhonua, kuu puukaua hoi'* (my refuge and my fortress). *'Kuu Akua, e paulele aku au ia ia'* (my God in whom I trust)."

Kaiulani paused. Hannah sighed with relief. "My heart is warmed. You—must—trust."

Kaiulani sank down. Her lips near Hannah's ear, she sang, *" 'Aole oe e makau i ka mea hooweliweli i ka po'* (you will not fear the terror of night). *'No ka mea, e kauoha mai no ia i kona poe anela nou'* (He will command his angels concerning you). *'E malama ia oe ma kou mau aoao a pau'* (to guard you in all your ways)."

Hannah whispered, "This is—His promise—to you, Kaiulani."

"For you too, sister of my heart."

Hannah answered firmly. "Verse 12 for me soon." She recited from memory, *"'E kaikai lakou ia oe, ma ko lakou mau lima'* (on their hands they will bear me up). Soon!"

"Oh, Hannah, please! Your love is to me more faithful than that of men. Don't speak of leaving me! I can't bear it. I can't!"

Hannah said, "In place of Kaiulani, Hannah must sleep—beside your mother at Mauna ala."

"I won't permit it!"

"'E hoonui aku au i kona mau la' (with long life will I satisfy him). *'A e hoike aku no hoi au ia ia, i kou hoola'* (and show him my salvation)."

Kaiulani clasped Hannah's hands. "Yes, Hannah, you must live! You will live a long life!"

"No, Kaiulani. I want to go home. Don't you see? You must live—live long—safe, happy...in my place."

"Oh, *Iesu!* I can't let her go! Please! Please!"

Rain drummed upon the roof and sluiced off the eaves.

Kaiulani wept and prayed for help to come.

* * * *

The storm had broken. Morning sun shone brightly through the windows. Kaiulani had slept through the night beside Hannah, warming her, keeping her soul from flying away. Clammy cold had become a burning fever, yet Hannah had lived through the night. Was that not reason to hope?

"Oh, Hannah." Kaiulani kissed her cheek. "You're still here."

But Hannah did not reply. She only caressed Kaiulani with her eyes. Her breath was labored, coming in shallow gasps. Her heart beat fast like a little bird's.

The approach of horses' hooves sounded on the gravel. Kaiulani leapt up and ran to the window. "Oh, Jesus! Thank You! Thank You, Jesus! Hannah! It's Andrew! And Papa! They're here! They can take you to a doctor! You're going to get well! You'll see!"

Barefoot, Kaiulani rushed from the house and threw herself into Andrew's arms. The details spilled from her as he and Papa Archie followed her into the house and to Hannah's bedside. "And then my horse fell. She came looking for me in the rain. Pneumonia, I think. I couldn't leave her to go for help. I couldn't help her! Oh, I prayed all night you'd come back for us. To take us back to civilization. She must have a doctor's care!"

After one look at Hannah struggling for breath, the men flew into action. Andrew said, "There's a buckboard in the shed. I'll harness the team."

Archie instructed Kaiulani, "We'll get her to Honolulu."

"I must go with her." Kaiulani's eyes filled with tears. "I won't leave her."

"You can't come. More dangerous for you now than ever. Kaiulani, you must stay behind. We'll take care of her. Good as new. You can't come."

Hannah opened her eyes and focused on Archie. "Papa—Archie?" Each word was a breath.

"Sweet Hannah, what's this? What's all this?" he asked. "My sweet girl."

Hannah reached for him, clasping his sleeve. "I—am—your—daughter."

"Of course. Of course, Hannah."

Her other hand, trembling from the fever, groped for Kaiulani's right hand. Hannah cried, "Listen. You must listen! I dreamed, and from this moment, behold—I live and die—as Princess Kaiulani Cleghorn."

Kaiulani dropped to her knees. "Please, Hannah! Don't say this. Please, promise me!"

Hannah tried to raise up on her elbow but failed, falling back on the pillow. Andrew burst in. "All ready to go."

Hannah's voice was fierce. "I—am—Kaiulani Cleghorn!"

Deep brown eyes sought Kaiulani's soul. "I dreamed—Mama was here last night—Kaiulani, please, I want to go home."

"No!" Kaiulani cried.

Andrew, panting, stood back as Kaiulani threw herself across her friend. His knowing gaze locked on Archie's.

Archie said gently, "Kaiulani, we must hurry if we are to get her down the mountain."

Hannah rasped, "You must stay behind—live in my place."

Kaiulani kissed Hannah's fingers. "I won't let you go!"

"I'll be there—to meet you—when you come home."

"Hannah! How will I live? Who will I talk to?"

Hannah's voice was gentle, tenderly pleading, "I am asking—your permission—to go home."

Kaiulani could hardly speak. She sobbed against Hannah's neck. "Oh, Hannah! My beloved sister. My dearest friend."

Hannah captured one of Kaiulani's tears on her fingertip and held it to her lips. "Your tears are mine. It is written, someday—Jesus will dry every tear. Kaiulani, for this cause I came into the world. I have no choice now—from the beginning my steps were ordered by the Lord. My sister—your permission to let me play the role of the princess one last time. Please—let me—go." She held Kaiulani's hand to her heart.

Kaiulani nodded, sobbing.

Hannah smiled. "You live now as Hannah—in my place. Promise me—you will live a long and happy life."

Kaiulani replied, "I promise. Anything. You promise to be there, waiting, when I come."

"I will. And watching with those who love you. You live for us both. You must live out our days with joy." Hannah looked toward Andrew. "This one—my beloved—she is Hannah now. She will marry you. You will love her well—for all her life?"

Andrew answered, "I will."

Hannah sighed. "Then I am ready. Ready. Kaiulani? *Mahalo. Aloha,* my beloved sister—my friend. *Aloha nui loa.*"

"*Aloha,* sweet Hannah. *Aloha nui loa. Aloha me ka paumake.*"

* * * *

1973

The old woman's warm brown eyes brimmed as she studied Sandi's face. She caught a single teardrop on her index finger and held it to her lips in a gesture spanning quiet decades of unforgotten love and friendship

"*Aloha me ka paumake,*" Sandi whispered.

"My heart is with the one…"

"…who is done with dying," Sandi finished.

"Yes. So now you know the truth." Kaiulani reached out to Sandi, enfolding her in an embrace as if she was a small child in need of comforting.

Sandi laid her head against Kaiulani's chest. "You've kept the secret." Sandi's voice caught in her throat. She could not finish her thought. The old woman's heart was strong after a lifetime of beating for two lives.

"For almost seventy-five years I have lived on, since we said *Aloha*. No day has dawned, no sun has set, without my heart remembering her great love. She died in my place. She is home, waiting. I am certain of it. Hawaii's legend has become history. It is written that Princess Kaiulani died, and thousands mourned the day she was buried in Mauna ala, the 'Fragrant Hills.'"

"Near your mother and the last king of Hawaii."

The Princess Victoria Kaiulani did not reply to this statement of fact. She stroked Sandi's hair. "Someday the true King of Heaven and Earth will return, and we will all cast our crowns at His feet. He will judge and set all things right. It is written then that our Lord will dry every tear, and there will be no more sorrow. No more sorrow." She released Sandi and smiled into her face. "Do you understand?"

"Yes." Sandi sat back on her heels.

"Do you believe?"

"The evidence is irrefutable." Sandi glanced at a file containing decades of personal letters signed, *Hannah Adams,* which were unmistakably written in the handwriting of Princess Kaiulani. "What about your life? You and Andrew?"

"We were married that same month in a small ceremony in The Mission House. God blessed us with three beautiful daughters and a son. One of my daughters, Hannah is her name, is Archie's grandmother. I was always partial to her, as you can guess."

The faded photographs and ancient tintypes on the walls and dressing table took on new meaning for Sandi. As never before she understood what the Bible meant about the "great cloud of witnesses." [28]

"Do they know?" Sandi asked.

"A handful know the secret. There were 144 of us at our family's Christmas picnic. Impossible to keep a secret with so many."

"Archie?" Sandi's eyes widened.

Kaiulani laughed. "Archie is named for my father."

As if summoned by Sandi's thoughts, Archie knocked on the half-open door. *"Aloha!* Gramma?"

"And here he is." Kaiulani extended her arms to her greatgrandson. "Look at him. Handsome. Just like my Andrew. My heart skips for joy every time I lay my eyes on him." Kaiulani leveled her gaze on Sandi. "He tells me you would make a fine first mate for the *Royal Flush.*"

Suddenly the name of the sailboat took on new significance. Sandi felt herself blush at Kaiulani's frank declaration. "I—I...he never told me that."

Archie crossed his arms and towered over Kaiulani. "If Her Royal Highness says it, you can believe it."

A blackbird perched on the railing of the lanai and cocked his head at her. *Broken wings...learn to fly....* Sandi gazed at Archie's face and knew why she had come—why Kaiulani had chosen to reveal the secret to her. She had not come to Lahaina looking for love. In spite of everything, love had found her in Lahaina. Her heart filled with an overwhelming sense of joy. It was time to live again.

The old woman clasped their hands. *"Aloha.* It is a sacred word. Life is too short to wait, my children. I have asked the Lord if I might live to see my great-great grandchildren before I go home."

Archie touched Sandi's cheek and pulled her close. He kissed her gently. "What do you say, Sandi? You and me on the *Royal Flush*?"

Sandi sighed with contentment in his embrace. "Yes. Yes! Sounds like a winning hand to me."

About the Author

....

BODIE THOENE (pronounced *Tay-nee*) has written over fifty works of historical fiction. That these best sellers have sold more than twenty million copies and won eight ECPA Gold Medallion Awards affirms what millions of readers have already discovered—that Bodie is not only a master stylist but an expert at capturing readers' minds and hearts.

In the timeless classic series (coauthored with husband, Brock) about Israel (The Zion Chronicles, The Zion Covenant, and The Zion Legacy), the Thoenes' love for both story and research shines. With The Shiloh Legacy and *Shiloh Autumn* (poignant portrayals of the American Depression), The Galway Chronicles (dramatic stories of the 1840s famine in Ireland), and the Legends of the West (gripping tales of adventure and danger in a land without law), the Thoenes have made their mark in modern history. In the A.D. Chronicles they step seamlessly into the world of Jerusalem and Rome, in the days when Yeshua walked the earth. New novels from Bodie include the political thriller *ICON*, *The First Stone*, and The Zion Diaries series.

Bodie, who has degrees in Journalism and Communications, began her writing career as a teen journalist for her local newspaper. Eventually her byline appeared in prestigious periodicals such as *U.S. News and World Report, The American West,* and *The Saturday Evening Post.* She also worked for John Wayne's Batjac Productions and ABC Circle Films as a writer and researcher. John Wayne described her as "a writer with talent that captures the people and the times!"

Bodie has long been intrigued with the personal accounts of history. The romantic and often mysterious stories based in Hawaii have held a special enchantment for her. "There, the past and the present overlap through the lives of elders sharing their memories," Bodie says. "When I met that old Hawaiian woman, who was making *leis* in the shade of Lahaina's banyan tree, I was entranced by her photos—and her personal remembrances of Princess Kaiulani. The rumors she shared shed new light on the old story, as if Romeo and Juliet had a happy ending. As she told me the legends and the romance, I knew I must write it one day."

Bodie and her husband, Brock, have four grown children—Rachel, Jake, Luke, and Ellie—and seven grandchildren. Their children are carrying on the Thoene family talent as the next generation of writers, and Luke produces the Thoene audiobooks. Bodie and Brock divide their time between Hawaii, London, and Nevada.

www.thoenebooks.com
www.familyaudiolibrary

Notes
....

1   "To Princess Kaiulani," Songs of Travel and Other Verses, Robert Louis Stevenson, http://www.online-literature.com/stevenson/songs-of-travel/29, 2/15/2010.

2   Psalm 19:1–3

3   Psalm 19:4

4   "A Wand'ring Minstrel I," *The Mikado*, by W.S. Gilbert and Arthur Sullivan, http://www.leoslyrics.com/listlyrics.php?hid=aEeHmYrPois%3D, 2/15/2010.

5   "Braid the Raven Hair," *The Mikado*, by W.S. Gilbert and Arthur Sullivan, http://www.leoslyrics.com/listlyrics.php?hid=bYCuLwLBptI%3D, 2/15/2010.

6   "Libretto," *The Mikado*, by W.S. Gilbert and Arthur Sullivan, http://www.jumbojimbo.com/lyrics.php?songid=5864, 2/15/2010.

7   "Three Little Maids from School," *The Mikado*, by W.S. Gilbert and Arthur Sullivan, http://www.guntheranderson.com/v/data/threelit.htm, 2/15/2010.

8   "Braid the Raven Hair," *The Mikado*, by W.S. Gilbert and Arthur Sullivan, http://www.leoslyrics.com/listlyrics.php?hid=bYCuLwLBptI%3D, 2/15/2010.

9   "A Long Time Ago," by Jim Croce, 1972, http://www.lyricsfreak.com/j/jim+croce/a+long+time+ago_20241120.html, 2/16/2010.

10 "Sorry Her Lot Who Loves Too Well," *The Mikado*, by W.S. Gilbert and Arthur Sullivan, *HMS Pinafore*, 1878, http://www.allthelyrics.com/lyrics/gilbert_and_sullivan/sorry_her_lot_who_loves_too_well-lyrics-1148335.html, 2/16/2010.

11 "In the Bleak Midwinter," Christina G. Rossetti, http://www.hymnsite.com/lyrics/umh221.sht, 2/16/2010.

[12] "In the Bleak Midwinter," Christina G. Rossetti, http://www.hymnsite.com/lyrics/umh221.sht, 2/16/2010.

[13] *The Gondoliers*, Act I, by W.S. Gilbert and Arthur Sullivan, http://download.franklin.com/cgi-bin/franklin/ebookman_free_preview?cpogs10, 2/16/2010.

[14] "Regular Royal Queen," *The Gondoliers*, by W.S. Gilbert and Arthur Sullivan, http://math.boisestate.edu/gas/gondoliers/html/royal.html, 2/16/2010.

[15] Romans 10:14–15

[16] 1 Kings 3:5, 7, 9

[17] 1 Kings 3:10–13

[18] "Where He Leads Me," Ernest W. Blandy, http://www.cyberhymnal.org/htm/w/h/e/wherehlm.htm, 2/16/2010.

[19] Proverbs 18:24

[20] "There Is a Fountain Filled with Blood," William Cowper, 1772, http://www.cyberhymnal.org/htm/t/f/tfountfb.htm, 2/16/2010.

[21] Jeremiah 1:5, 7, 9–10

[22] Psalm 94:5, 7

[23] Jeremiah 1:7–8

[24] Jeremiah 1:16–18

[25] Psalm 94:5

[26] "Lei No Kaiulani," by Charles King, 1898, in *Kaiulani, Crown Princess of Hawaii*, by Nancy Webb and Jean Francis Webb (Honolulu, HI: Mutual Publishing, LLC), 1962, 1998.

[27] Isaiah 35:3–4

[28] Hebrews 12:1

POST CARD
CARTE POSTALE
Love Finds You

**Want a peek into local American life—past and present?
The *Love Finds You*™ series published by Summerside Press
features real towns and combines travel, romance,
and faith in one irresistible package!**

The novels in the series—uniquely titled after American towns with unusual but
intriguing names—inspire romance and fun. Each fictional story draws on the
compelling history or the unique character of a real place. Stories center on romances
kindled in small towns, old loves lost and found again on the high plains, and new
loves discovered at exciting vacation getaways. Summerside Press plans to publish at
least one novel set in each of the 50 states. Be sure to catch them all!

Love Finds You in Revenge, Ohio by Lisa Harris
ISBN: 978-1-934770-81-8

Love Finds You in Poetry, Texas by Janice Hanna
ISBN: 978-1-935416-16-6

Love Finds You in Sisters, Oregon by Melody Carlson
ISBN: 978-1-935416-18-0

Love Finds You in Charm, Ohio by Annalisa Daughety
ISBN: 978-1-935416-17-3

Love Finds You in Bethlehem, New Hampshire by Lauralee Bliss
ISBN: 978-1-935416-20-3

Love Finds You in North Pole, Alaska by Loree Lough
ISBN: 978-1-935416-19-7

Love Finds You in Holiday, Florida by Sandra D. Bricker
ISBN: 978-1-935416-25-8

Love Finds You in Lonesome Prairie, Montana by Tricia Goyer and
Ocieanna Fleiss
ISBN: 978-1-935416-29-6

Love Finds You in Hershey, Pennsylvania by Cerella D. Sechrist
ISBN: 978-1-935416-64-7

Love Finds You in Bridal Veil, Oregon by Miralee Ferrell
ISBN: 978-1-935416-63-0

Love Finds You in Pendleton, Oregon by Melody Carlson
ISBN: 978-1-935416-84-5

Love Finds You in Homestead, Iowa by Melanie Dobson
ISBN 978-1-935416-66-1

Love Finds You in Golden, New Mexico by Lena Nelson Dooley
ISBN: 978-1-935416-74-6

COMING SOON

Love Finds You in Victory Heights, Washington by Tricia Goyer and
Ocieanna Fleiss
ISBN: 978-1-60936-000-9

Love Finds You in Calico, California by Elizabeth Ludwig
ISBN: 978-1-60936-001-6

Love Finds You in Sugarcreek, Ohio by Serena Miller
ISBN: 978-1-60936-002-3

Love Finds You in Deadwood, South Dakota by Tracey Cross
ISBN: 978-1-60936-003-0

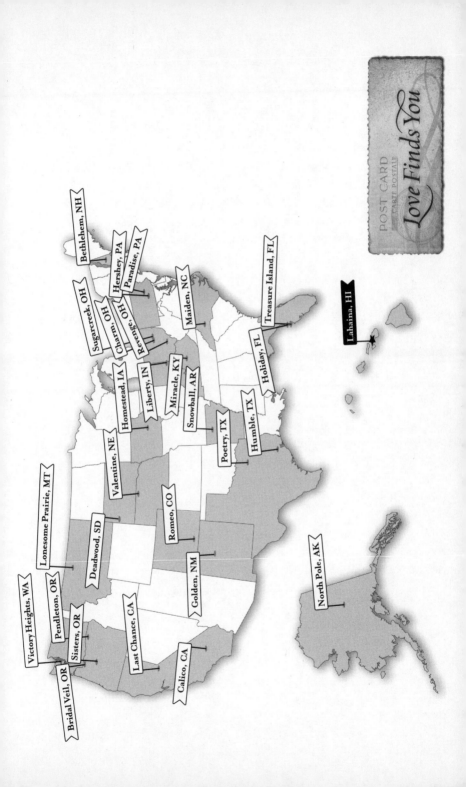